LOST

Dear Carla,
Here ya go!
I hope you love Lost.
Luv,
Sarah xo

"Author's Copy"
14/15

SARAH ANN WALKER

Sarah Ann Walker

Copyright © 2014 1101 Sarah Ann Walker

Cover Design: James Freeburg

All rights reserved.

ISBN: 0991723139
ISBN-13: 978-0991723133

This book is a work of fiction. Any reference to real people, or real locales are used fictitiously. Other names, characters, places, and incidents are the product of the author's imagination, and any resemblance to actual events or locales or persons, living or dead, is entirely coincidental.

LOST

DEDICATION

To Jakkob

Loving you has been the greatest gift of my life.
You are my son and my reason to be better.
I love you more than anything in this world, never forget that-
Not that I'll ever let you forget.
xoxo
Mommy

To S. M.

I never had the chance to tell you how I felt about you before you were lost.
And I still miss you.

LOST

LOST

CONTENTS

Acknowledgments i

Introduction

Loved

... and LOST

LOST

LOST

ACKNOWLEDGMENTS

I want to thank my husband once again for the beautiful book cover.
I want to thank my parents for giving me their support.
I want to thank my sister Brennah and her children Zakkary, Piper-Ireland, and Teaghan for thinking their YaYa is pretty cool.
I want to thank Paola for still being my best friend for a quarter of a century, and then some.
Thank you Silvana for being my partner in crime.
Thank you Brenda Belanger, my Boston Bruins Beauty.
Thank you Chris Carmilia, for being the very first Blogger to read me.

Thank you Deniro, Amy, Christina, Paula, Randi, Christina, Ann, Megan, Diane, Wendy, Joan, Sleepy, Jen, Stephanie, Diana, Darcy, Sandy, Katica, Crysti, Gladys, Michelle, Sam, Cori, Glenda, Diane, Dena, Lisa, Rosanna, Mark, Coach & Christine, Ashley, Doug, April, Laura, Suzy, Carla, Alanna, Michelle, Tracy, Melannie, Lou, Suzanne, Glenda, Michelle, Leisa, Retta, Lustful Literature, Triple M Books, Chris' Book Blog Emporium, Mommy's Naughty Playground, Twisted Sisters,
& A Pair of Okies, to name a few...

I want to thank all the readers and bloggers who supported me this last year. I wish I could name you all.

Thank you Cheryl Shockley-Dent for being a constant, kind, patient friend to me this past year.
And thank you Kim Rinaldi for being tough when I need it, for feeling bad afterward, and for *always* having my back when I'm neurotic.

Sarah
xo

LOST

INTRODUCTION

"Why are you in here, Sophie?"
"Will you listen to me?"
"Of course."
"Because you have to listen. You have to be patient and you have to wait for the whole story so you know why I'm here. I'm different than I used to be and you have to listen to what changed me. Can you do that?"
"Of course I can."
"I hope so..."

Breathing in deeply, I release the pain and I speak our story.
"I saw him yesterday- The man I will always love.
I saw him yesterday, and today I want my end.

I saw him, and he looks as dead outside as I feel inside.
I saw the man I love and he broke the final piece of my heart; the only piece that kept beating when everything else had died away with the absence of him.
I saw him yesterday, and I too am now as dead outside as I am inside.

But you have to know the quick and the slow that was our beginning to fully understand the agony of our end.
There is no other way to show the depths of the end than to love the intense beauty of our beginning.

We are both gone from this world, by choice and by circumstance.
We are both dead, among the living...

Oh, *god*. I can't take this pain anymore."

LOST

LOST

LOVED

Sarah Ann Walker

CHAPTER 1

I come from a very nice, ordinary family, with one twin brother and two loving parents. We are normal, from a good part of town, with just enough money to not struggle, but not enough money to be frivolous or carefree.

As a foursome we are totally average, and yet my parents' love is not average in the least. My parents have always loved each other wholeheartedly, and my brother and I have looked at our parents beautiful relationship with a kind of awe. They are amazing together, and because of their love we have always known what real love looks like.

My brother and I have known love at its finest, and we even learned from our parents that you can argue or fight with each other but that you always loved each other regardless. We saw love when our parents kissed in the living room to end a fight before they rose to go to bed together. And we knew love when they simply smiled at each other among the chaos of 2 children around them.

We knew my father's words verbatim; "Never say anything bad to the person you love when you fight. Never call them a bad name in the heat of the moment, and never make them feel badly about themselves because those words stay forever. Even after the fight is over, your words will stay to hurt and haunt them forever."

So it was not uncommon for our parents to abandon us for a weekend once we were teenagers for what they liked to call, "Rejuvenating Us Time." They would leave us with smiles and giggles, which of course made me and my brother gag when we realized they were actually going to get laid. They weren't exhibitionists though, nor did they imply they still had a sex life, it was just my brother and I couldn't help but see the look between them, or the head nod *get upstairs now* with a sly grin, or even the whisper before they both claimed to be very tired on a Friday night as they went to 'sleep' together early. Our parents tried for privacy, and my brother and I desperately tried to ignore what they may or may not be doing in their bedroom together.

Over the years, as I watched the relationship between my mom and dad, I likened them to Tarzan and Jane, Barbie and Ken, or Cinderella and Prince Charming. I thought of them as normal in life but totally abnormal in love, which was something I truly admired growing up.

My parents just had this thing- almost a tangible love that filled a room when they walked in. They didn't necessarily have overt displays of affection, but it didn't matter. When they were in a room, you could feel the love that tethered them together. You could see the tie between them, and you could feel the life of love they shared with each other.

My parents have always been amazing to me and my brother, and to each other. They are the ideal, and Steven and I have always looked for that ideal as we grew up.

On a personal note, it should be said I have no monsters or demons in my past. There are no tragic secrets or hidden horrors in my young life. I was never abused or hurt, and nothing bad ever happened to me as I grew up. I was always just as I was; a good girl in a loving home with a nice life.

I was always just straight-forward Sophie. I didn't lie or manipulate my surroundings, and I told my parents the truth about everything as they listened, advised, and guided me into adulthood.

I don't remember my parents ever yelling or belittling me or acting disappointed in me, whether I disappointed them or not. If I made a mistake, they simply explained how I could do something differently, or they explained what they would have done differently, without me feeling chastised or punished. They spoke to me clearly, almost as an adult among them, until I learned to listen to their advice as an adult would, instead of behaving as a highly dramatic child being scolded would have behaved.

My parents also gave me a certain amount of freedom growing up because I had earned it and kept it. When my curfew was finally lifted at 17 for example, I didn't push it. I stayed within an hour of my previous curfew so they knew I was being responsible with my new freedom. And when I was given a car, I made sure I never drank and drove, drove like a teenage lunatic, or crashed my car being stupid. I didn't screw up, which allowed me to continue earning the trust of freedom they gave me.

I was allowed the freedom to grow, within undefined guidelines, and I was thrilled for this room to grow. Steven was given the same freedoms as me, but as soon as he screwed up they were taken away from him, until a set amount of time passed and he seemed responsible enough to be given his quasi-adult freedom again.

Essentially, Steven and I learned and lived to grow and mature responsibly because of our wonderful parents. They gave but expected maturity and growth in return, and Steven and I loved to be all that they believed we could be *because* they gave us the freedom to live and learn.

My mom and dad gave to us until we screwed up, and I loved this way of living because it made me always want to be better. I didn't fear what might be taken away from me, instead I strived for what I might gain by trying harder. It made me want to always be better, and live better, and try harder. It made me want more from my comfortable life.

Sadly, Steven was a little slower understanding this, but then again he was a boy, and everyone knows girls are much more mature than boys at that age. Eventually Steven caught on though, and he strived to be more as well.

Of course I had some issues, just not the typical teenage kind. I didn't act like an idiot over boys, begging and crying, or fawning over them for attention. I never acted like a drunken tart, crying and dramatizing nothing moments into cataclysmic events. I never acted like an insecure moron with boys as a teenager, or with men as an adult. I loved but I didn't settle because I decided early on whether consciously or not that I would *never* settle for less than the love I wanted.

I had known and watched true love my whole life with my parents, so I always knew what I wanted, and I lived my life with an understanding of the kind of love I desired. Therefore, no drama was necessary.

I loved until I would wake up and realize that I needed or wanted more from my boyfriend, though I did try to make it work for a while before I left. In my relationships I put forth the effort needed, and I was a good girlfriend until I knew it wasn't enough. I loved them for as long as I could, but I moved on when the reality of the need or the desire for more surfaced, and then I left.

I'm not talking about needs, like the need for things or stuff though because I didn't need things from men. I mean a deeper need for more within the love we shared, because realistically I've always been very self-sufficient, so if there was something I wanted I worked hard for it. If I wanted to own something, I worked until I could buy it. These physical objects of desire didn't make me run from my boyfriends, I left when my *internal* needs surfaced.

When there was something missing, or a need or want within the relationship *as* the relationship, that's when I moved on. I left when I knew I wasn't completely in love with them, or when the relationship lacked something for me. Over time, I studied the relationship in its entirety and acted accordingly, so if I was unsettled I didn't settle. If I felt the need to flee, I fled, and I was *always* good at this. My leaving a relationship was like a gift I had- an ability to leave any relationship well.

Every single relationship I've ever had, from the easy dating to the intense couplings were ended by me, and ended in a way that my boyfriends always wanted to stay friends with me. I knew how to make a man feel special, which in turn made him want to make me feel special.
I didn't necessarily manipulate them, and I wasn't conniving, I just knew what they wanted to feel, so I made them feel it. Some wanted to seem strong, so I played up my small stature for them, and some wanted to be cared for, so I was more nurturing toward them. And because I have always been able to read men, I also knew when it was the right time to leave them. I had 3 serious relationships before I was 24 and they all ended the same, with friendship and respect.

When I was a teenager Darren was the first 'love of my life'. He was everything I wanted from a boyfriend; actually he was everything every girl I knew wanted as a teenage boyfriend. Darren was athletic and handsome and caring, and the first love of my life until I matured and realized he wasn't my forever kind of man.

My second long term relationship in University with Derek was pretty much the same for me emotionally as my relationship with Darren. I was invested on the surface, but I think I always knew we would end.
Derek and I loved each other as we grew together into adulthood. We even ended up living together off campus, until I left him after a year and a half later when I again realized he wasn't going to be what I wanted in a partner long term.

And finally, my third major relationship was with Joseph, who was a nice and loving man though he had a few hang ups and lots of baggage. He was significantly older than me, so he had already had an adult life before me. He already had an ex-wife, 3 teenage children, and a career, to my nothing yet.
He was nice and loving and he treated me very well, but after one innocent conversation between us about the future, I realized he was done with his future, whereas, I was just starting mine.

LOST

I was 24 to his 44 and I wasn't done with life yet because I still wanted a future the way I imagined it. I wanted a husband, and a home, and a child of my own. I wanted things, but Joseph wanted us as we were, static in our relationship. Joseph was content with where he was, but I was discontent with were I wasn't. So I ended our relationship with his friendship, support and understanding.

As I said before, I have ended all my relationships but I was never mean or bitchy, and I never demanded things or held grudges. I just knew when it was time to end it, and I always ended my relationships while they still loved me enough to let me go when I asked. There was never any resentment or hostility from my boyfriends when we broke up, though there were sometimes tears and promises for more, but I didn't give in, so they accepted the end for what it was- I needed more, and I needed to move on.

When we were together I gave them what *they* needed always. I was loving and innocent with Darren, fun and friendly with Derek, and mature and worldly with Joseph. I became whatever role it was they needed from me, but I never played the role of a woman with needs, until I left them.

When I hit the wall that told me I was done trying for them, I would finally wake up and stop playing. It was when I saw my future again clearly, that I walked out of their lives for a life for myself. It was then that I left them for myself, because I needed to. But I gave them everything to make them happy when we were together, and that's why they always let me leave as friends. I had never hurt them until I left, so they couldn't be mad at me *when* I left.

Inevitably, I would wake up to my needs and to the life I wanted, see their complete absence from my future life, and I would leave once and for all. And that was the pattern of my life until I was 24 years old.

CHAPTER 2

After I broke up with Joseph, I moved into a cute little apartment not far from downtown, but on the safer side. It was a walk-up and I was on the ground floor with a view of the side garden from all my windows on the left and a view of the open driveway on my kitchen side. It had hardwood floors and built in wall shelves and bookcases. It even had wide window ledges for plants and a beautiful original marble fireplace and mantle, converted to an electric fireplace for safety, which lost very little of its charm due to the modernization.

I loved my apartment immediately, and on any given night you could see yuppies pushing a baby buggy, or drunk University brats walking around the baby buggies on their way to the bars and clubs. You heard music and saw lights everywhere but never loudly or obnoxiously, it was more like a constant hum and lightness in the air.

I could walk out my front door to the most amazing cafes or find the best super market hidden behind rustic looking doors. There was absolutely nothing garish in my neighborhood, from the art galleries, cafes, pubs, vintage stores, and bars, to the people who lived within in. There were rich professionals and poor students, old Volkswagens parked in front of brand new Jaguars, and everything in between.

Once I was settled in walking around the neighborhood to investigate, I felt like I fit within the village. I was single among many singles and there was very little to be afraid of because the area was always active, so I felt single among many.

I did see a homeless man leaning against a wall moaning, covered in dirt once, but otherwise, there was nothing overtly bad around my new neighborhood.

I was a 24 year old, finished her schooling, looking for the perfect career opportunity in her new home. I had travelled some with Joseph while I worked as a waitress looking for my career, and I was finished with my partying twenties, looking forward to my future among new IKEA furniture and herbs in my kitchen window.

I reacquainted myself with a few friends in my new singlehood because like most people in a relationship I couldn't help but be less visible to my girlfriends. But once single again, I quickly reacquainted and re-engaged in their lives, becoming close again to my friends as we picked up where we all left off effortlessly.

I still waitressed, went for job interviews and waited for the career I could sink my teeth into forever, but I had enough savings to furnish my new home, albeit cheaply, while I lived off my tips for the day to day stuff like food and coffee.

Honestly, I was very happy, and I felt good in my new place in the village when I started over again after my break up with Joseph.

So that was my life from July 1st until the beginning of October. That was the temporary life that made me happy. I continued to look for a career, and I continued my shifts at the restaurant, earning just enough money to sustain my calm, single life.

I loved my life at that time, but by the middle of October when I was becoming bored again I took on a second job at a health food store half a block away from my apartment for a change.

Before the job came along, I had always been aware of alternative medicine, reading up on it and even studying it casually. I wasn't super health conscious by any means, but I did take vitamins and I did read up on cool herbs and their uses medicinally. I even learned a little about herbs from an older neighbor, Marcy, while I planted my garden at the apartment.

So when I saw the 'Hiring Part-Time' sign in the store down the street, I immediately applied. And within the 4 days between dropping off my application at Sunshine and Life and receiving a call for an interview, I crammed as much knowledge into my brain as possible.

I had found the vitamin and herb 'Bible' according to the book retailer and I studied it from start to finish. Even after I received the call, I continued cramming, because that was my way. I wanted the job, so I made sure I was as ready and as knowledgeable as possible before going in, which I think landed me the job within minutes.

The owner and manager, Terry, was a total hippy- a *corporate trial lawyer* hippy, and I liked him immediately. He was the funny cliché- short, thin, balding with a small ponytail, dressed like a slob, but driving a brand new Lexus.

Terry was down to earth but with a weird sense of humor I had to figure out quickly because he seemed to use humor often to get his point across. Terry was so cliché I even laughed to his grin when his dress pants rose at the ankle and I saw Berkenstock sandals with no socks in cool October.

   I liked him as soon as we met though and he seemed taken with me, especially when I explained Herbology was relatively new to me, but I was studying it hard and fast. I told him I was planning to keep the herb 'Bible' under the counter to use as a reference, and thankfully, Terry knew the book I was reading and studying, and he approved of it, so I was hired that Thursday and started work the following Monday.

   And from the moment I began, I loved the store, the feeling at work, and the people I met who were as awesome and as diverse as Terry.

   I met long haired hippy-types, totally gorgeous yuppies, and average University kids. The customers were young and old, and through them I learned the herbs needed to heal everything from insomnia to cancer, and the vitamins, minerals and herbs used to heal everything from tendinitis to depression. I was told which herb combinations the students used before exams to increase brain power, and I learned about the amino acids they used to help curb their hangovers when the exams were completed.

   I even met an older woman who had been dying of cancer- *terminal* cancer with less than 6 months to live who had been fighting it for 8 years. She told me her story which made me choke up at the counter, but she and her husband just smiled as she asked me, "Do I look dead yet," which made me laugh through my nearly falling tears.

   I love the Sunshine and Life, and if there was one thing I experienced universally, it was kindness. Every single person from young, poor, old and wealthy came into the store kindly. I was given homemade baked goods with all natural ingredients, to soaps and scents made from people's home remedies. I was treated to delicious breads, and gross cookies, which truly needed a little sugar to help the flavor in my opinion. But I took it all in with an excitement I hadn't felt since after the first few months I spent with Joseph.

   At the store, I tried different herbal teas, and I tasted a few sugar free foods. I even tried a Tofurkey sandwich given to me by Terry after his huge Thanksgiving party which did actually taste like turkey, just without the texture of it.

LOST

When I took my second job I worked 5 day shifts at the store and 4 evening shifts at the restaurant a week, with my days off rarely coinciding with both jobs, but I didn't care. They were each so different that if I left the store for the restaurant, it was such a change of pace I didn't feel overwhelmed or exhausted by my 14 hour days because I enjoyed the people in the store, and I enjoyed putting on my Sophie professional face in the upscale restaurant I waitressed at afterward.

But when the days hit that I had to neither work at the store or restaurant, I did enjoy my full day off. Those were my special days when I crammed everything in I possibly could. From driving to a huge supermarket for groceries, shoe shopping or lunch with a girlfriend, to maybe getting my nails done, a haircut, or the oil changed in my car, I did everything I could. Those rare days off were crammed with the average person's weeks' worth of errands, and after I had my errand day, I always felt completely settled and back in charge of my life.

I enjoyed both my jobs but Terry knew I wasn't going to stay forever, as did my restaurant manager, Denise. They both knew these were my temporary jobs while I searched for my forever career because I had a degree in Office Management, and a certificate in Human Resources. I was not a waitress, nor a health food guru, but I was excellent at my jobs, so both Terry and Denise liked me enough to want more of a future for me, though they did wish I would stay with them long term.

However, 7 weeks after I began at the store I received a call for an interview for a forever career. I received the call to meet for an interview on a Friday afternoon which I thought was weird, but I was excited about it regardless.

I told Terry I needed Friday afternoon off, and I called Denise to let her know I would be a little late for my evening shift. I told them about my interview and each wished me good luck, but Terry did throw in a funny, 'I wish you... *tank* the interview', with a chuckle.

After the interview was scheduled, I researched the company and the position in question and I knew it was my forever career. It was everything I wanted in a career, with room to advance and grow. And though the starting pay was equal to both my jobs, minus the tips, I figured if I got the job, I would ask Denise to keep me on weekends so I could continue making my tips for spending money and extras.

So on Friday, November 26th, I went for my interview prepared and professional. I arrived 20 minutes early but was left waiting for close to an hour, which being totally honest pissed me off at the time. I've never been late a single day in my life for anything, so to be left waiting until 3:35 for a 3:00 interview drove me nuts inside, though amazingly, I didn't let my irritation show.

While waiting, I eventually started talking to another woman in the waiting room to kill time, and she and I seemed to hit it off quickly. She and I talked about nothing and everything, from our families, where we grew up, our education, to even our dating/marital status.

At one point we even joked about her skirt being shorter than mine so she probably had a better chance at the job if a man interviewed us, which made us both laugh. When we exchanged names, she introduced herself as Deborah, and joked, 'Which is a lot classier than Debbie- as in *Debbie does Dallas*, thank god.'

But eventually, the doors down the hall opened and a man stepped out to walk toward us. He introduced himself as Eric, shook my hand and asked me to follow him in, while apologizing for the delay. When Deborah stood behind me at the same time I remember looking at her with a mix of *oh shit* and confusion regarding whether the interview was to be for both of us, but she just smiled at my confusion and followed me and Eric down the hall.

Once seated, Deborah again introduced herself with a grin and said she was actually the head of HR. She then promptly explained, "Though completely unethical, I enjoy meeting applicants in a comfortable setting away from the closed doors, and personality-less confines of an actual interview. It's kind of a mini interview to best see a person's true demeanor and personality."

Before I could reply though, Eric then proceeded to interview me in the 'personality-less' way I was accustomed to which was actually a relief. I knew how to answer those questions during an interview, nearly scripted, and that's what I was prepared for.

All throughout, I was good, too. I never stumbled over my words, nor needed a moment to answer any given question. I could tell I rocked the interview by the way Eric seemed to relax the longer we sat and spoke. So when Eric was finished asking questions and the end, *is there anything you want us to know about yourself* was asked, I exhaled and answered truthfully.

"I work hard. Period. Both my current employers will be sad to see me go, but both like and respect me enough to let me go. I always look for more, and I enjoy the challenge of learning more. I never disappoint anyone, and I honestly believe I am the right fit for this job because I'm excited about it and I'm prepared to work hard for it. Basically, I will not disappoint you if I'm hired." And then I smiled.

After we three shook hands, Deborah pulled me aside a little and asked, "Do you know you were the first person I talked to out there who just spoke to me plainly? You didn't eye me up, looking for an advantage over me, and you didn't feel the need to make yourself feel better or more qualified by bragging about yourself to me. You just spoke to me as a person, not as a competitor for the position, and that has set you apart in my eyes, Sophie." Smiling at Deborah after she spoke, I practically ran for my car I was so excited.

Replaying Deborah and my interaction in my car, I realized I had inadvertently aced my interview with her, as well. And she was right. I have never had to bring anyone down to raise myself up because I'm just myself, and I had always been very comfortable with myself. I didn't ever play emotional games because I had no tolerance for them from others.

I did see Deborah as an attractive woman, but I spoke to her as an equal, though she had age and experience working for her. I knew at the time she was way more qualified than me, but I didn't brag or boast to feel better about myself, because there really was no point. I knew she was better than me, so why bother acting like a fool in front of her by bragging about myself.

So the very next day on Saturday afternoon Deborah called to offer me the job, which I gladly accepted. Actually, I was a little embarrassed as I gushed to her how much I had wanted the job. I even called Deborah completely unethical in her interviewing practices, but said I was willing to overlook them because it got me the job, which made her laugh at me.

Deborah said I was to start the following Monday, December 6th, which she believed would give me a few days off before I started my new job- not that I wouldn't finish up working until the following Sunday, but if she believed I would take a few days for myself, I let her.

God, I remember how excited I was that weekend. I called everyone I knew to tell them about my new career. My brother was excited for me, and my parents were proud of me. My friends thought it was cool that I was going to be an office manager and HR Rep. And though I enjoyed all the praise and excitement from everyone, I was just thrilled I was finally starting my life.

After speaking with Denise, she agreed to a Saturday or Sunday shift each weekend after I finished up my full week at the restaurant. And Terry was awesome and sad to see me go after so little time at the health food store, but he told me not to worry about any uncovered shifts, only if I promised to stop by for some Christmas Tofurkey in a few weeks, which made me gag and laugh as I agreed.

Thinking back on that weekend, I remember after all my phone calls, I felt ready for anything. I had one week left at Sunshine and Life and at the restaurant, but I had my entire future ahead of me.

CHAPTER 3

I met Peter in Sunshine and Life.
I met Peter, and I saw the life I wanted. I saw the man I wanted and the life I dreamed of. I couldn't understand why, but I looked at a total stranger and everything stopped for me in that one moment of time.

It was Wednesday of my last week at Sunshine and Life, and I met the man who would change my life indefinitely. Though at the time I couldn't possibly know to what extent, I did know I would be changed by him.
Much later, when I would question our first meeting Peter would say it was his aura and our connection that changed me. Sometimes he said fate or kismet had played a hand in our lives crossing paths. He had endless answers as to why I felt the initial strangeness inside me when we met, but I've never known if any of his explanations were true. I just know I felt strange when I met Peter, and it wasn't necessarily a welcomed feeling for me at the time.

Standing behind the counter reading, I looked up as Peter walked in asking where the organic soap was. He asked such a basic question; a question without hidden agendas or alternate meanings, but I found myself still as he spoke. He asked me where the soap was moved to and I felt unsure of myself for the first time in my life as he stood there waiting for me to answer him.
Thinking back, I would love to remember something meaningful happening or something dramatic occurring in those first moments I saw him, but there really wasn't. He was just a guy in a store looking for something specific to buy, waiting on the silent girl to answer him.
Returning to the counter minutes later he had 2 bars of soap with him; Calming Chamomile, and Terrific TeaTree, and nothing else.
Standing at the counter with his soap you would have thought from my asinine reaction to him though, that he held a gun to my head. When Peter stood in front of me, I simply paused at the counter and couldn't speak. I didn't know what was wrong with me, and I didn't understand

what was happening to me as he stood there waiting for me to surface.

I had never known the insta-love crap some people talk or write about, and I sure as hell didn't believe in love at first sight. And honestly, that isn't what happened.
I didn't look at Peter and love him- I looked at Peter and felt unsure of myself and confused. I felt off center, and actually, fairly immobile as we stood there silently. But I couldn't explain it then and I still can't. There was just something about him that threw me off.
Looking at Peter standing at the counter felt like a trippy déjà vu to me. I felt like there was more to him and more I should understand about him, but as I tried to quickly figure it out I was also sure I didn't know him at all.

"Hi. How long have you worked here?" He asked me with a friendly smile.
"Um..." But I didn't know the answer. I was suddenly very confused thinking of my new job and the job at Sunshine and Life, and I was just *confused*. I was an absolute blushing, stuttering idiot actually.
"How. Long. Have. You. Worked. Here?" He asked again slowly with a smirky grin.
"Do you live around here?" I questioned instead of trying to figure out what the hell was going on with me.
"Yeah, not far down the street off Elm. You?"
"Yes. And I've worked here for 7 weeks but this is my second last day," I spoke, finally breathing right while pulling my head out of my ass.
Looking at me a little too seriously, he asked, "You don't like it here?"
"Actually, I love it here but I just landed a good position in a huge company so I'm leaving. It's what I went to school for." And with a little excitement seeping through, I added, "I'm starting my career this Monday."
Nodding his head with a smile, he responded, "Good for you. You don't really belong here anyway, I can tell."
Feeling weird and surprised by his comment, I blurted out, "Why don't I belong here?" And while I waited for his answer, I slowly came back and grew my spine again, feeling more like myself.

Smiling again at me after a minute to ponder his answer first, he tilted his head slightly and said what I didn't expect to hear in my wildest dreams.

"You lighten your hair, and I doubt its organic dye. You have fake nails, and you're wearing leather shoes and I think that's your leather purse on the counter behind you. You're wearing Obsession perfume, which I love by the way, and you have diamond earrings. You probably dabble in holistic medicine and maybe use some herbs for sleep issues, or aches and pains, but I don't think you're a true believer. You don't seem like a real convert, more like a quasi-herbalist who probably knows her stuff, but only from a textbook."

"Um..." I remember feeling totally offended even though his freaky observations were pretty damn accurate, but he continued past my shocked silence anyway.

"Not one single thing I just said was meant as a judgment, I swear. Honestly, I love your hair and nails. Your shoes and purse are awesome, and well, who doesn't like diamonds?" He grinned, but I was pissed.

I suddenly felt like an idiot, and like the poser he just called me. I was angry that some asshole walked into the store and talked to me like I was some high maintenance woman who didn't belong among the hippies and yuppies I loved. I felt like I was playing a role suddenly among the people in the village, which I wasn't. So I took the soap from the counter, rang them in, and told him the price which he could read from the other side of the register anyway.

Slowly pulling out his money while staring at me like he wanted to say something else, he gave me a twenty as I made change without speaking, and bagged his soap quickly.

But when I handed him the bag he tried again. "I really wasn't trying to offend you, I just know people really well. I can usually tell what kind of person someone is by observing them, but I wasn't trying to insult you. I just knew this wasn't really your scene."

"It's fine. I'm not offended."

"I'm Peter," he said as he offered me his hand.

Looking at Peter, I felt insecurity for the first time in my life. In mere minutes, he made me question my life and he made me question myself.

Looking at him in that moment I also thought of all the 'burning bridges' conversations my parents had with Steven and I. I pictured telling him to piss off and low and behold he was my new boss's son, or something equally as screwed up. But I knew how to speak to people, so I swallowed my anger and insecurity and leaned forward to shake his hand calmly.

"No name?" He smirked again until I gave in.

"Sophie."

"Well, I'm sorry I didn't meet you sooner, Sophie. Best of luck at your new job. And again, I'm sorry for sounding like an asshole. I'm really not, though sometimes it comes across that way when I'm honest."

Nodding his head, Peter then turned and left the store as quickly as he entered. He came in, disrupted my life, and then walked back out smiling like I wasn't totally annoyed with him.

And after he left I realized I didn't like the way he made me feel. It was like I was covered in insecurity suddenly, and I was never insecure in my life. I had always belonged wherever I was at because I made myself belong. So shaking myself coherent and thinking about what he said after he left, I decided all the physical observations he made were stupid.

My own boss Terry, was a total hippy, herbalist, tree hugger, Who. Drove. A. Lexus. So what if I put a lighter rinse through my hair in the winter months or had fake nails? It was only because I always had ONE broken nail among my other 9 perfect ones and it drove me nuts, until I finally gave in 2 years earlier and just made them all fake for convenience sake. And diamond earrings? Had he seen the rich yuppies in this artsy neighborhood? Why did they fit in but I didn't?

Exhaling again, I put him out of my mind almost as quickly as he barged in. I didn't have time for obnoxious men, and I didn't enjoy or like acknowledging men who weren't in my forever plans anyway.

*****

The following day during my last shift on Thursday, Terry and 2 other employees who *did* fit the hipster, vegan model of a health food store employee showed up with a Good Luck cake made with real sugar, chemicals, and fattening chocolate deliciousness.

Terry hugged me and told me I was always welcome back if my corporate career didn't work out, and though I knew he was joking I appreciated the sentiment anyway. Happily, like me and my former relationships, I ended everything at Sunshine and Life, and with Terry and my fellow employees well.

But shortly after the cake was sliced, Peter came into the store and to my surprise he knew everyone working. Terry gave him a hug and Margaret kissed his cheek and welcomed him back with a hug as well. Listening to them talk, I didn't know where he'd been, but I didn't really care. He was an irritant to me the day before and a nothing to me that day.

As I pretended to ignore them, Peter walked directly to me after his quick hellos, and smiled as he handed me a black and white notebook. Handing over a notebook with a grin, Peter seemed to be waiting for something from me but I didn't know what he wanted other than the little thank you I muttered. So looking at the book, I attempted to open it silently, but he stopped me by placing his hand on my own while asking me to wait until I left for home.

And after our little exchange I looked around awkwardly as Peter stood silent before me, until I noticed a strange look from Terry aimed at us. Looking at Terry, I tried to figure out what he was thinking, but I really didn't know Terry well enough to read what the look meant.

Finally after a minute of uncomfortable silence between us, Peter asked, "What company are you going to work for?"

"Halton Facilities on Paramount. I'll be training to take over the office manager position and eventually I'll be working as a HR Rep as well."

"Wow. Good for you. That's really great, Sophie," he replied sounding truly excited for me.

"Thank you." And that was all we said.

After a final smile and a little pat on my hand which was still resting anxiously on the notebook, Peter left the store with a quick goodbye to Terry. As soon as Peter left however, Terry approached me to ask how I knew Peter, which seemed strange considering Peter was clearly a customer in the store. I wasn't sure of Terry's angle, or whether he was being friendly, or slightly possessive, so I answered honestly while hiding the notebook away in my purse.

"I don't know him. I just met him yesterday. Why?"

"Just curious," Terry said as he casually walked away to greet a customer walking in, and nothing more was said to me about Peter.

2 hours later after another piece of cake with Terry, I was officially done at 4:00. Grabbing my winter coat and boots, I bought a few teas, a book,

and 2 bags of yummy veggie chips that I loved before I hugged Terry and Margaret goodbye and headed home.

As I left, curiosity about the notebook was killing me, but I forced myself not to act on it in the store. I didn't want anyone asking what was inside the book, so I patiently waited until I finally returned home at 4:50 to toss my bags on the coffee table before jumping on my couch just dying to know what was inside the dollar store looking notebook.

Opening the first page, my name was spelled out in beautiful calligraphy with detailing and little designs all around the page, but turning the first page I was shocked to find an even more beautiful charcoal picture of myself.

Actually, I was stunned when I lifted away the waxy paper in between the first and second pages to see the drawing. The portrait was very good, and Peter was obviously very talented, which completely surprised me.

Looking at the picture I felt that weird déjà vu again, but more I just kind of freaked out inside. I can't even explain it, but I think it's the feeling you get when someone new acknowledges you. Or like the feeling someone gets in a new relationship at the beginning. Everything was exciting in that moment. *I* was excited in that moment. I was warm and shaky with the tingles, and the freaky butterfly stomach-thing. I was unconsciously smiling, staring at the beautiful portrait of myself that Peter had drawn.

It was amazing really. The lines were so crisp and clear and the shading blended so well that even though it was charcoal, you could almost see my eye color and my lighter hair through the dark charcoal. Even my face was an exact likeness, so much so, that it seemed more like a black and white photograph of me instead of a drawing.

Staring at the drawing, I really couldn't believe Peter remembered so much detail of my face when we had only spoke for those 10 minutes the day before. I couldn't believe anyone could remember so much of someone and draw them so perfectly.

With a big smile plastered on my face, staring at the drawing forever, I finally turned the next page to a hand written note from Peter.

I think you're awesome, Sophie, and I wanted you to know that in case I made you feel badly yesterday because that was NOT my intention.

I was hoping you might use this book to write down your thoughts sometimes like I do. Then maybe one day we could trade books and read what we're really thinking. I would like to know the beautiful Sophie who worked at my favorite health food store but who I never had the pleasure of knowing before she was gone.

Take care,
Peter

That's what Peter's note said with a phone number at the bottom. And I'm not going to lie, *what the hell* bounced around my head instantly. Share a journal together? *Seriously?*

After reading the weird note, sadly, the beautiful picture was forgotten, and the calligraphy turned into scribble before my eyes. I was totally out of my element with the strange man known only as Peter.

All I wanted to do in that moment was call Terry and ask why he gave me the strange look when Peter handed me the notebook. I wanted to know if Peter had done this before with another employee, and I wanted to know what the hell he was up to. I really didn't understand Peter's intentions, so I needed help from Terry understanding Peter because I was totally confused and that was a feeling that made me very uncomfortable.

At one point though I almost started laughing when I grabbed a pen from my purse, flipped the page, entered the time and date and wrote: Peter- You are a freak show!!!

I remember thinking Peter was acting like those creepy guys in a few novels I had read. Stalkers and possessive assholes, and strangely about the women who find it sweet and amazing when they are loved so hard.

In real life when a man acts like a possessive asshole, or like a stalker, we run- and maybe even get a restraining order while we're at it. Those men scared the hell out of me because they were not normal, nor easily understood. They were not men I understood how to love so I could easily leave when I realized they were not in my plans. And that was how I felt about Peter.

From the giddy, butterfly feeling I had looking at my name and the beautiful charcoal drawing he had made of me, to an absolute inability to understand his intentions moments later from his weird note; I was shocked and weirded out.

The notebook suddenly held all the fascination of a game of Russian roulette for me. So I decided after that intense moment to put Peter out of my mind, and I decided to focus on the coming days and on the new forever career that was waiting for me.

CHAPTER 4

On Monday morning I arrived at my new job early, and though I was excited to be there, I kept it together. I showed total restraint and professionalism, though admittedly I was nervous as hell and feeling a little overwhelmed. However, once I was lead to my new office by the receptionist, I calmed down significantly.
Sitting in my new chair, placing a photo of me and Steven taken at my college graduation on my desk felt right as my only possession. There was nothing else of my personal belongings or personal life that I intended to share with my new co-workers until I was settled in, because as far as anyone at work would be concerned I had no personal life, and that's the way I wanted it.
After brief introductions by the main receptionist to the rest of the office staff I was lead to an impromptu meeting with the current office manager, Carole, who was leaving for our sister store out of town. I was briefed on what she did, which was way more than I anticipated, and I was given a slight overview of my job description. Signing authority and essentially office carte blanche was decided after a 3 month probation period, which made perfect sense to me. Plus, until I fully understood my role within the company I didn't want the added responsibility of signing authority.

My day began smoothly, but by mid-morning I was completely overwhelmed and understandably scared to death of my new job. It seemed like Carole could just knock out everything asked of her, make decisions on the fly, and calmly make decisions yes or no to our fellow employees. It was daunting to watch, but I kept my notes handy, scribbling any explanation given with my own side notes for later investigating.
Finally, after perhaps the longest morning of my life, Carole asked me at 11:55 what I was doing for lunch, to which I calmly replied, "A liquid lunch, for sure," which made her laugh at me.
When we parted for lunch, I sank into my own office chair with an

exhale. I remember sitting there thinking anyone who starts a new career within a new company who says they took to it immediately was a liar. No one could possibly grasp all there was to know within the 2 weeks I had to spend with Carole shadow training.

After lunch Carole and I went over payroll together which was good because the following Monday was the day payroll was submitted, so I was able to watch, study, and learn the payroll system that was used by Halton Facilities with her as practise. I was glad to see this before I was totally overwhelmed with information because other than a generic handbook there was no other program like it on the Internet to study.

Finally, at 4:30 I was told I could leave if I wanted to. Carole explained the office hours were 8:30 to 5, but with the option to take only a half hour lunch each day, or on any specific day if we wanted or needed so we could leave a half hour early.

Carole explained it was a company policy which most used in the summer when children were out of school, or playing sports, so the parents could leave early. It was a cool policy which was popular by everyone, even the childless employees. I was then told I had to monitor it however because it was based on an honor system and a few employees liked to 'forget' they took their full hour lunch when they tried to slip out at 4:30.

At the very end of my first day Carole gave me a little pep talk, and explained I was handling all the information well, and she believed I would be fine. She reminded me that she was only a phone call away if I needed her once she left and I thanked her endlessly for everything.

Parting for the day, I finally walked from her office to my own as she yelled down the hall, "Enjoy your liquid *dinner*," to my embarrassment and humor.

When Carole and I were through as I walked back to my temporary office, the receptionist stopped me suddenly by yelling, "These are for you, but I don't know who they're from," as she handed me a beautiful vase and bouquet of my favorite roses.

I was surprised and assumed Steven or my parents sent them as a good luck gesture, yet as soon as I looked at the card's envelope I knew why the receptionist, whose name I couldn't remember at that moment, added the second statement. Clearly, the envelope had been opened multiple times, which pissed me right off. Looking at her, I realized she was going to be a shit-disturber so I had to work my magic on her quickly to get her in line before she rolled over me when Carole left.

Taking my flowers from her without acknowledging her in the slightest, I entered my office, dumped my notes on my desk, plopped into my chair and took a deep breath of my beautiful blue roses- my favorites.
Smiling, I tore open the envelope but was again surprised by Peter.

Dear Sophie,
I hope you have a wonderful first day.
You've been on my mind since I met you.
Peter
545-3188

Rereading the note, I had those weird butterflies in my stomach again and a stupid smile on my face as I passed through mental exhaustion straight into excitement. Peter and his roses became an instant distraction from the monumental hill I had to climb in my new position.
So after exhaling all my tension, I left 5 minutes later with my notes, purse and huge bouquet of blue roses, saying a generic goodbye to my co-workers without making eye contact with what's her name, the private note reader.

Once I arrived home, I kicked off my snow covered heels on the mat, collapsed onto my couch and finally exhaled. I was exhausted but exhilarated. I loved all the responsibility my job required, but it was daunting to think in 2 weeks I would be alone with it all.
I also thought about Peter and knew I had to thank him for the beautiful flowers, but I was nervous. Peter had shown entirely too much interest in me from just a quick 10 minute meeting in a store. I was a little turned off by his attention, yet admittedly, also intrigued by it.
Actually, if I was being totally honest, I couldn't stop thinking about him at the time, because the flowers seemed to have cemented his place in my mind. Even when I tried to think about everything I had learned earlier at work, my mind would frequently wander back to thoughts of Peter.
Eventually, I even found myself trying to remember exactly what Peter looked like. I tried to piece him together before I made the call because I wanted to be totally prepared when we spoke so I maintained the upper

hand.

I remembered he had blue eyes and brown hair, and he was tall, but not overly so. He had an average body, but that was questionable because of the heavy winter coat he wore. I thought he had clear skin, and nice full lips, and though he seemed totally generic in his looks, I remember he was somewhat compelling nonetheless. I remember he was someone you would never say was hot, but he was someone you felt very attracted to regardless.

I thought he could even be my type, if I had a type, which I didn't. Many conversations with girlfriends revolved around this very topic of my 'type', because there was no pattern to it. I had loved the athletic gorgeous high school fantasy for all girls, the slacker grungy attractive University guy, and the established slightly heavy older man.

I liked heavy so I was dainty, and I liked smaller so we were similar. However different they may have seemed on the surface, I had loved them all equally though. Actually, I think I just loved the man I loved, not his physical attributes, and I'm fairly sure that's an honest assessment, not just the politically correct one most woman would say whether true or not. If I loved them I loved them, no matter what they looked like, until it was time to move on.

So after my dinner and shower, I finally settled in beside my blue roses and dialed Peter's number.

Waiting, I prepared for a grateful but aloof thank you, mixed with a warning to avoid more from him. I didn't want anything to happen, whatever that could possibly be because I had a new life and a new career starting, and my career needed to be my focus in life at the time.

"Hello?"

"Hi, Peter. This is-"

"Sophie..." He breathed heavily leaving my name just hanging there between us.

"Um, thank you for the beautiful roses, they were a very kind gesture for my first day at work. I really appreciate it. Thank you."

"Are you hanging up already?" He asked to my confusion.

"Yes, I have a big day tomorrow, and I need to read my notes from today. But I wanted to thank you first before it became too late. So thank you," I spoke quickly trying to hang up, but he continued anyway.

"Did you like the color?"

"Yes, actually. Blue roses are my favorite, though a little difficult to

find."
"Not when you know where to look. They're my favorite, too. Have you been to Bedouins on Cedar? They always have blue roses. And obviously they deliver."
"Um, no I haven't, but I'll make sure to check it out. Thank you again, but I really have to go now and get back to my work."
"You have to go? Or you want to go?" He asked simply.
Exhaling into the phone, I was annoyed by his straightforwardness, but decided on honesty.
"Well, both actually. I *do* have to look over my notes because this job is important to me, and I don't know you so I would like to go now. But again, thank you."
"Maybe one day I'll be important to you," he said so calmly I was immediately confused by him. Thinking quick about a kind response, I tried to appease him as best as I could.
"Yes, maybe you will be. I should go though. Good bye Peter."
But again he spoke like he was oblivious to the fact that I was trying to be nice while hanging up quickly. "Have dinner with me on Friday night to tell me all about your first week."
"I can't. I have plans," I lied.
"Then Saturday."
"I have to work."
"Really? Where?"
"I waitress one day on the weekend."
"When do you relax?" He asked with a serious tone I was unused to.
"I don't know. Whenever I'm not working, I guess."
"When do you have fun?"
"When I do," I stated a little more than annoyed.
"Where do you live?" He asked changing the subject quickly.
"I'm sorry?"
"We're do you live? I think you said you were close to the health food store. Didn't you?"
"No, I didn't."
"Oh, well... *do* you live close to the store?"
"No," I lied again.
"Okay. Well, I'll see you on Sunday at noon. Are you working then?"
"Yes," I lied again as I realized dealing with Peter was suddenly making me a pathological liar.

"Well, you just told me you work *one* day on the weekend, which is Saturday, so Sunday you're free. I'll meet you at noon on Sunday at Murphy's in the village. Have a great week, Sophie," he said cheerfully as he hung up on me.

And I remember *what the fuck*-ing my way to the kitchen for some chips. Staring at the cordless phone in my hand waiting to call him back when I cooled down, I thought he was insane and annoying and pushy and just totally *what the hell?* I also didn't think he would listen to me if I called back to tell him I couldn't meet him on Sunday, so I decided to ignore him completely instead. I decided to ignore him *and* stand him up on Sunday because honestly I didn't feel attracted to his behavior, but rather irritated and annoyed by it.

Men didn't order me around and men didn't demand things from me. I always led my own life, and I had never let a man bully me or force me into doing anything I didn't want to do, so I wasn't starting with him.

Remembering that Monday in December, it's almost funny now how I had no idea that that was the first day of my new career, and it was also the last day of my life.

CHAPTER 5

The following days were just as mentally challenging as the first had been, and really, just a total blur for me. I had so much information to retain that I felt like I was back in University cramming for some horrible exam I believed I wasn't ready for.

I spent every day watching and listening to Carole closely, and I tried to anticipate her answers before she gave them, with honestly only about 50% accuracy. I was overwhelmed still but feeling a little more like myself as I slowly took hold of my surroundings and relaxed a little within them.

I was also starting to speak casually with the 14 employees in the office, and I learned through asking the sneaky, untrustworthy, private note reading receptionist Madeline to do multiple tasks for me as an 'on the down low', she felt included and much more helpful to me. I understood that by creating a situation where she felt trusted by me, she was actually becoming a little trustworthy *for* me.

During my first week in my new career I also received a beautiful vase of blue roses every single day at 11:00 in the morning with a note.

Sophie
I'm looking forward to Sunday.
Have a great day,
Peter
P.S. 5 days to go... 4 days to go... 3 days to go... etc. as each day passed with the beautiful delivery.

I received my flowers everyday like clockwork until Friday when my roses didn't arrive on time. And I'll admit it, I was bummed.

Originally, I was embarrassed by the deliveries because they were a little much and I didn't like the attention I was getting as a new employee. I knew all the office staff were looking at my flowers, and maybe even reading the notes before I was, which made me nervous of their judgments so soon after I started. I also knew they were all waiting to see if my flowers arrived at 11:00 each day because even Carole asked on Friday if my delivery had arrived, which it hadn't.

Strangely, on Friday I was rose-less and confused. I thought over lunch maybe Peter had stopped sending them because I rudely hadn't called him again to thank him after each delivery. Or maybe because he was bored with the game already he stopped. I didn't know why, but admittedly, I thought about my lack of roses for the better part of Friday afternoon with a bit of disappointment I couldn't help.

I was definitely intrigued by Peter and his tenacity, and I was also a woman, so obviously that kind of attention was exciting, regardless of the poor timing for me professionally.

However, by 4:00 Friday afternoon Madeline came barging into Carole's office with my flowers to my surprise. Practically bouncing, she was dying to hear what the card said, so I threw her a bone. Opening up the envelope beside Carole as Madeline watched on, I burst out laughing as I read.

Scared ya, huh?
Just kidding.
I'm still looking forward to Sunday.
Have a great day,
Peter
P.S. 2 days to go...

Reading the note again out loud I watched Madeline swoon and Carole grin at me. But I quickly put it away and continued working beside Carole for another 20 minutes until 4:30 when we could both leave early after our shortened lunch break.

Grabbing my purse and flowers when I left, I felt proud of myself for doing well, and for loving the challenge of my new job. I was happy that Carole had every confidence in me even though I had no previous experience to speak of. And I was also proud that I kept my shit together even though a few times during my first week I was so overwhelmed I could've had a mini-meltdown in my office over lunch.

*****

Friday night, when I finally returned home from my long week, Steven was waiting for me outside my door with a bottle of tequila and Chinese takeout, my favorite. Smiling as I walked closer, Steven dropped the food and hugged me so tightly I was nearly bruised until I laughed and shoved him off me.

"*Sooo*... were you a rock star this week?" He asked while I unlocked my door.

"More like the background singer, but I feel like I'm going to rock it soon," I grinned.

"Trying to show me up again? You know, good twin versus bad twin? Girl versus boy? Dad's favorite versus Mom's?"

"Nope. I'm both their favorite and you know it. So you'll just have to stay the pathetic, loser twin," I said sternly.

"Ha! You wish," Steven laughed walking to my kitchen with the food, but I could see he was honestly interested and excited for me, so I spilled.

"Seriously, it was amazing and scary and totally what I want, but really intense, too. I watched Carole who's leaving, balance getting the office staff to do what she needs done with a firm tone, but without an ego or bitchiness. It's almost an art form the way you have to lead people to work without making them feel like they're being pushed into it."

"Kind of like you and your men?" Steven smirked as he spilled half the chicken fried rice on a plate for me.

"No... Maybe. I don't know if that applies though. I don't lead *my men* as you call them, I just don't let them push me around. But I did stay with them until I knew without a doubt that they weren't the one for me, that's all. Like mom and dad knew, and still know. So why make the relationship something it isn't? You know this, we've gone over this a hundred times. I try to be with a man in a relationship until I know it isn't right and then I leave. And you try out every girl you've ever met hoping to find one that's right. By the way, there's only been 3 serious relationships, but you make me sound like a serial monogamist or something. I'm 24 and I've loved 3 men my whole life, which really isn't many," I said justifying my love life though I clearly didn't have to for anyone, even Steven.

"It's all good, Soph. I'm just teasing, and I think you're too awesome to settle, too."

"Thank you," I whispered as Steven leaned in for a side hug.

I loved my brother, nearly to death, especially in those moments-moments where we just talked, open and honestly with no filters or masks. Steven was my brother, but an absolute joy in my life as well, and I've always known if I didn't have to love him because he's family, I would have loved him anyway.

When we walked back to the living room with our plates piled high, he and I settled in as I described my entire week, minus the Peter thing. I told him about the people at work and about the actual job requirements. I told him everything and he listened to me with rapt attention, until he suddenly hopped up and told me we were going to a pub down the street for too much alcohol to celebrate, which I agreed to.

After his announcement I changed quickly, and Steven and I walked down the block to one of the first pubs available in my awesome neighborhood for a night of drunken fun together.

4 hours later, at only 11:30, Steven and I slurring and shameless after horrible singing, endless shots, and one quick table dance later by *him*, held each other steady as we swayed ourselves back to my apartment to crash. I was such a lightweight drinking, it was always embarrassing but fun to drink, especially with Steven.

After fighting with the lock while laughing my ass off, Steven fell into my apartment, crawled to the living room, and proceeded to pass out on my couch mumbling, 'Love you, Soph," while I stumbled for my bathroom before passing out sideways fully clothed on my own bed.

The following morning at 11:00 while I nursed a brutal tequila hangover quietly and Steven continued to sleep, I answered a sudden knock on my door to another vase filled with my blue roses.

Smiling at the delivery woman, it took only seconds in my hung over half brain to realize something was wrong though. With a shiver down my spine I wondered how Peter knew my address. I knew I didn't tell him where I lived, and I really didn't think Terry would've, but I had to be sure. So diving for the cordless I called the store and waited.

With a shaking deep inside me, I asked Terry what I think I already knew, and I was right. No he didn't tell Peter where I lived, and he hadn't seen Peter since my last day at the store the week before.

When I hung up with Terry, I found myself almost panicking as I walked around my home. Walking, I tried to breathe but all I really saw were the

5 vases filled with roses in varying stages of life and decay all over the place. There was a vase in my bedroom, one on each end table in the living room, one on the kitchen table, and even one in the bathroom window. Holding the sixth vase, I suddenly felt overcome with a feeling of discomfort I wasn't used to.

   I felt very unsettled, and weird things didn't happen to me because they had no place in my life. I wasn't a control freak about my life to the extreme, but I was definitely the driver. I didn't allow for others to influence me, and I didn't allow others to hurt me. I was Sophie, and my gut told me something was wrong with Peter.

   After the flowers arrived I waited another 15 minutes until I couldn't take it anymore and I finally woke Steven from his drunken slumber to tell him everything about Peter.

   Listening to me, Steven slowly woke more and more before I was finished the story of the strange guy I met the week before. After my story while I had Steven's complete attention I went and grabbed the notebook with the drawing and showed him. I held out the strange black and white notebook as Steven looked on silently.

   "Um, the picture is amazing, but I see how the note seems fucked up. Share a journal with each other? What a freak."

   "I know, right? Then the roses every day."

   "Well, that's just a guy trying to get in your pants, Soph. I've done it myself. Well, not with roses, but like bought a girl a coffee every day at her work until she finally gave in, went out with me and we screwed around. It's kind of the same thing, except an expensive way of bedding you."

   "What about the look from Terry?" I begged.

   "Maybe he was jealous. You are-"

   "I doubt it. I wasn't hippy enough for Terry. He just liked me as an employee," I said sure of my take on Terry.

   "Sophie, no offense, and though it grosses me out to admit it, guys think you're pretty hot and I'm sure Terry wouldn't have minded sleeping with you, just like I'm sure this Peter wants to."

   "It's not about being good looking. Terry knew I wasn't like that, *or* his type. I think he knows something about Peter that made him look at us weird. And fine, maybe Peter just wants to screw me, but how does he know where I live?"

"He followed you?"

"What? That's creepy!" I gasped. "Men aren't supposed to follow women home. Would you?" I asked knowing the answer.

"Um, I have. Sure..." That was not the answer I expected to hear from my brother. "I once followed a girl from the bank who was super hot smiling at me inside the bank, so I made a game of it. Every time she turned around on the street, I smiled at her until she finally stopped beside her car and we started talking. I got her number and even went out with her a few times."

"So you're a total freak, too," I accused feeling a little better.

"I think all guys can be when they're trying to get laid. Seriously, I've followed women, and I've bought them things. God, I've even serenaded them at karaoke bars. I once begged a girl on my knees in front of her friends for her number, making them all laugh at me. But I got her number, and I got laid, too. Actually, I have about a 90% success rate with my wild attempts to score chicks," he grinned, making me groan.

"Ew... *Visuals,* Steven," I moaned as he laughed.

"Sorry. I say meet him tomorrow for lunch and see what he's like. It's just lunch in a crowded pub so you'll be safe, and I'll meet you there to make sure you're safe. I'll sit across the room and we can have a secret hand signal if you want so I'll know when to interrupt to get you out of there if he seems too creepy," he said smiling at his stupid secret hand signal idea. "Meet him for lunch and see if he's a freak, or just some guy who was taken with you and wanted to impress you with roses. Maybe he's awesome. You never know."

"Okay, but this isn't the way I usually do things," I admitted in my defeat.

"I know, but you're too rigid with your 'forever plans' Soph," he quoted. "I think you know before anything has even started with a guy if you're gonna leave him. Look, I knew you were going to leave Joseph the first week you started dating, though he was totally in love with you right from the beginning. Even Dad knew you were going to love Joseph, but not love him as your 'forever'," he quoted again. "You don't seem to even give a guy a chance."

Plopping down on the couch beside Steven, I felt totally offended. "I do give them a chance. I was with Darren all through my teen years, and Derek for a year and a half. I was even with Joseph for 11 and a half months, so I'd say that's giving them a chance. But why stay? If I know there's something I'm missing, why would I stay?"

"I agree you shouldn't settle, but I also think you always find something wrong with them and you can't let it go. You're not perfect Sophie, and neither is anyone else."

"Wow... I know I'm not *perfect,* Steven. What a shitty thing to say."

"You're really not, Soph," Steven cut me off. "You have all these shitty things about you that we have to put up with," he said seriously.

"Like what?" I asked shocked.

"You always tap your foot when you're pissed, letting everyone know we did something wrong. Like now," he said as I stopped moving my foot.

"I can't help that! It's like a nervous twitch or something," I whined.

"And you always have to pee. Like *always.* Every single road trip, or vacation, or even short drive to the mall we ever took had to be mapped out by mom and dad for the closest bathroom."

"Oh my god, because I have a small bladder I'm not perfect?" I asked laughing.

"And you're really bitchy when you have PMS. Mom used to warn me to stay away from you when you were PMSing, which incidentally I didn't want to know because then I had to think about you on your period which was gross for me. But at least with the heads up, I knew not to bug you too much that week."

"Piss off, Steven. I don't have PMS, and I'm never a bitch."

"Are you PMSing right now? Because you just told your twin brother to piss off, and you've hurt my feelings," he said pouting.

Laughing at his fake pout, I caved. "Okay... I get it. But honestly, I know I'm not perfect. I do know that. But I try to be, so I'm not disappointed in myself."

"But you don't have to be. Ever. You're pretty great, Sophie, so just relax. Meet this guy for lunch, talk to him and see what he's like before you walk away. If you're still weirded out by him, then you'll know. But just give him a chance to be weird, okay?"

"Okay," I relented. I figured if Steven could be a stalker when trying to get laid, then maybe Peter could be, too.

A half hour later, Steven showered quickly and left my apartment for his own. He loved my nice apartment and hated his crappy one a few blocks away in a different part of town. So before he left, we talked about him moving into this part of town when his lease was up in 2 months. I even promised to keep an eye out for a vacancy in my building, though the

chances were pretty slim.
   The people who lived in my cool walk-up were lifers. The only reason my unit even became available was because the older woman who lived there for 18 years met an older man and they moved in together. Otherwise, most people in our cool 8 unit building had been there for years because everyone knew what a gem the building was.

CHAPTER 6

   Saturday night I worked my shift at the restaurant, and returned home by 2:45 after staying to have drinks with Denise and a few of my friends after work. I stayed late and we broke every rule; from drinking after hours, to pouring from the bottles unmeasured. Drinking together, Denise wanted to know all about my new job, and she was a doll about me leaving her for only one shift a weekend.
   In my tipsy state, I told Denise and the girls about my new job, then I spilled about the Peter thing. I told them what he had done, and why I thought he was a freak, but just like Steven they didn't agree with me.
   Arguments were made about why I should chill the hell out, and why I should just screw Peter for his efforts. Denise whined about her fiancé Martin never buying her flowers again after their engagement and Cori whined about never once receiving flowers from her own boyfriend, ever, which I found sad.
   Basically, I was told to meet Peter with Steven secretly watching, enjoy the attention, see what he was really like and maybe even get laid for the first time in months after leaving Joseph. When they were through lecturing me on what I should wear for my date, we had one final shot as I laughed at my horny friends, and I finally took a taxi home.
   Crashing by 3:15am, I was absolutely exhausted from my weekend. I rarely got drunk, because I found drunk women to be fairly obnoxious, and I rarely drank to excess, but I had twice in one weekend. So I had pretty much met my partying quota for the coming 6 months.
   Finally, when I crawled into bed still drunk I couldn't help but think of Peter. Slowly, through all the conversations with the girls and with Steven earlier, I allowed myself to open up to the possibility of Peter. I stopped the decision of *never going to happen,* instead deciding on a *we'll see what happens* mentality. I figured the worst that could happen was I didn't like him at lunch and I left with a friendly acceptance that he wasn't for me.

*****

When I was ready just before I left, I called Steven to cancel his secret chaperoning since I felt fairly safe at the pub in the daytime. Plus, I didn't think I could keep a straight face if I knew my brother was watching us. And I *really* didn't think Steven would behave during the lunch, which would probably make me laugh throughout like I was insane.

So walking to Murphy's at 11:45 alone, I was freezing cold but excited. I found myself almost anxious to get the lunch over with so I could put it behind me once and for all. I wanted to know one way or the other how it was going to go, because I had thought about it to death.

Opening the pub doors, my slightly hung over brain was quickly assaulted with sound as I tried to adjust to the sudden darkness inside which replaced the snow covered brightness from outside. Taking in the room, I spotted Peter immediately when he stood up from a corner booth to greet me with a warm smile.

"Sophie... You look beautiful," he said immediately as I approached.

"Thank you," I smiled as I removed my black leather coat and red mittens and scarf.

Hanging everything on the hook to the side of the booth, I knew Peter got an awesome ass shot which I was okay with because I had dressed casually, but to impress. I wore my knee high black leather boots, skin tight dark jeans and a loose, low neck red sweater. I knew I looked good, without looking like I was trying too hard to look good.

Taking him in when I sat down, neither of us spoke immediately which was awkward, but not overly so. It was like we each knew we were checking the other out casually, but blatantly.

Looking at Peter, I realized he was better looking than I had originally thought. He was a little plain looking, but taking him in as he looked back at me silently, I found myself strangely attracted to his plain features. He had lovely blue eyes, brown hair, full lips and pale skin. He looked very average, but he hand an aura around him that seemed anything but.

Wearing a black pageboy cap, and a green bomber type jacket, Peter didn't look like he was trying too hard to impress me either, which strangely relaxed me further.

"Thank you for all the roses this week, but you really shouldn't have. It was a little much, though I appreciated it," I said to break the silence between us.

"It was my pleasure. I just wish I could've seen your face when you received them, especially on Friday when they were late," he grinned.

"Did you think I had forgotten to send them, or that I had given up already?"

Smiling, I nodded. "Yes, I figured you'd given up the chase quickly, and yes I was thrilled when they finally arrived at 4:00. How did you get my home address to send the flowers yesterday?" I asked figuring it was best to get the creepy question out of the way before continuing.

"I saw you leaving Drinks Friday night with someone, so I made sure you were safe when I saw you and him stumbling down the street together. I didn't know which apartment was yours though until I walked in after you and saw S. Morley on the 2nd unit nameplate. I guessed you were S. Morley but that's why I wrote Sophie on the envelope, in case I was wrong so one of your neighbors would pass along the flowers to you."

"How do you know I wasn't walking to my boyfriend's place?" I asked testing him.

"I didn't. But you didn't call me again all week to tell me to stop because you had a boyfriend, so I assumed it was safe," he said smiling.

"How did you see me at Drinks? We're you following me?" I asked a little aggressively with my elbows on the table trying to read his face.

"Nope. I was across the street at O'Sheys with my sister who was having a smoke outside when I spotted you. It was a complete coincidence, I promise. Plus, I'm not really a stalker," he said leaning back against the booth casually while motioning for the waitress.

Looking at Peter casually moving on from my questions made me realize I believed him. His answers made sense because O'Sheys *was* right across the street, and it was always packed on Friday nights, but I still needed more.

"Okay, so why am I here?"

When Peter paused for a moment and looked at me kind of sadly after my question, I was truly uncomfortable with the way I felt. I didn't like the sad look aimed at me and I certainly didn't like the feeling of being inspected by Peter.

"So we can talk, eat lunch, and maybe get to know each other better." Again he was answering so casually he put me at ease *and* he made me feel a little bitchy.

"Why me?"

"Why not you?" He countered, and I was stumped.

I wanted to say a variety of answers that sounded a little pathetic, which I wasn't. I wanted to remind him he thought I was a poser at the health food store, and I wanted to say because we had met twice, and he was acting weird with all the flowers and the notebook. I didn't know what I wanted to say, but his straightforwardness was causing me to lose my edge around him.

"I don't know why not. You just seem a little forward or something."
Exhaling, Peter almost took my hand but stopped just short to awkwardly hold a napkin on the table instead.
"Well, I knew I had unintentionally offended you the first time we spoke. And if you hadn't been leaving Sunshine and Life I would've had time to stop back in to show you I wasn't an asshole until I could ask you out to lunch. But since you were leaving I thought I'd send you flowers instead, which obviously worked because you're here," Peter answered without sounding arrogant at all.
Seconds later, the waitress arrived and I ordered a coffee before Peter ordered a BLT. After pushing me to have something to eat, he finally stopped when I insisted on just coffee, adding I wasn't hungry which was another lie. I was starving after my night drinking, but I didn't want to commit to a set amount of time with Peter. I felt like I needed the easy escape of just coffee between us.
Smiling, as he waited for the waitress to leave, Peter totally surprised me by asking, "How was work?"
"Awesome," I replied honestly. "I have a lot to learn, but I think I'm going to love it. And it's exactly what I want and what I went to school for, so I feel good about it," I answered quickly.
"And the people?"
"They were great, why?"
"Just curious. I want to know about you," he answered calmly again.
"Well, I'm fairly private, so why don't you tell me about you," I countered as my coffee was placed in front of me.
"Okay..." He grinned at my deflection. "I'm 31. I have 2 parents still together, and I have 2 sisters, both older and married with families of their own. I work for a steel company sending out reusable metals to smaller companies to utilize and recycle. And I'm single. I've never been married, though I came close once. Well, close in that we were engaged, not close in terms of an actual wedding date. I draw in my spare time and I have a huge herb garden in my backyard which I use to make my own herbal soaps, detergents, hand lotions and hand cleansers, but I turn my backyard into a closed greenhouse all winter. I own my own home which I struggled to pay for each month when I bought it at 23,

but I don't struggle with the mortgage any longer. And I drive a pink car," and when I suddenly smiled he continued. "Yes, pink. I got it for a bargain from my sister, and couldn't refuse it even though the color is a bit much. I tend to walk everywhere however, so I rarely drive it."

Then after a moment of pause, Peter finished with, "And I'm fairly relaxed overall. Good?" He asked smiling while leaning back against the booth waiting for me to digest his information.

Staring at Peter in silence, I was starting to really like him the longer he spoke.

"Why did your engagement end? Who ended it?" I practically whispered.

"*That's* what you question?" He smirked. "Okay. Patricia and I were together for a few years, 20 to 23, and we were engaged by 22. We were just so awesome together that we didn't realize we were no longer a young couple in love. Somehow we had become best friends who finished each other's sentences but there was no spark between us. We held hands out of habit *not* because we wanted to hold each other. So Patricia brought up our fading relationship first before I had the balls to do it, and I agreed with her totally. After our talk we tried harder, almost forcing intimacy that wasn't really there. We tried with sex, and little gestures, and overall communication, but 6 months later sitting at the dinner table of her parents' house we started talking about it again and realized nothing had changed or felt better. We were a cliché. We loved each other but weren't in love anymore," he smiled sadly.

"So that night, right at the kitchen table, we figured out how we could break up without freaking anyone out. And we were okay, though admittedly I cried once and she cried a few times, but overall we were okay with breaking up. When we told our families, her parents understood, and my parents were sad but understood. After that night we just ended everything until the phone calls slowly stopped and we stopped seeing each other over time completely. But we really were fine somehow."

Nodding my head silently, I waited so he would continue past my silence, desperately wanting to hear the rest of his story.

"A few months later Patricia saw me with another woman and she was jealous, so she called me and we had a good long talk. But it turned out she was more insecure than jealous. She was still single and hated that I might have moved on quicker than she did, which made her think she must have lacked something I had needed, hence her insecurity. So we talked, I reaffirmed how amazing she was and we moved on again. And that's what we did for 3 years. We called each other every few months, checked in, made sure everything was okay, then we hung up for another few months. And 2 years ago Patricia called me and told me she was getting married and I was invited to her wedding which I went to with a date and we were good again," he smiled.

"Her husband is a terrific guy and he shook my hand, invited me over for dinner, which I went to, and we all had a great time. I've spoken to her a few times this year as friends, with her husband in the background yelling she's a pain in the ass and for me to come over and take her back, joking of course. So that's it. That's how Patricia and I were engaged, but never close to marriage, and how we ended up as friends," he smiled a little and stopped.

Looking at his sandwich which had been placed in front of him while he spoke to me, Peter seemed to be in a different place for a moment, so I let him be. I knew that place well- the one where you say what's expected of you but you feel like there's something else inside you that you wish you could say as well.

After a bite of his sandwich, Peter's focus turned back to me, and he asked me if I wanted a bite of his sandwich, which I did. Unbelievably, I leaned over the table as Peter brought the sandwich up for me to bite.

Laughing at myself, I was embarrassed as I chewed. "I have *no* idea what prompted that. Other than my brother, I don't think I've ever taken a bite of someone's sandwich before. I'm sorry," I mumbled while chewing with my hand hiding my mouth.

"No problem. It was kind of sexy, though I would have preferred strawberries or something equally as juicy to lick off your chin. But it was sexy nonetheless," he grinned, making me laugh again.

Standing up, he walked to the bar and came back with another coffee for me and a glass of water for himself. Once back, he laid a napkin down and put the uneaten half sandwich in front of me, telling me to please eat with a gentle tone.

"Your turn. Tell me about you," he smirked at my groan.

"I'm 24, with only one brother, a twin brother actually. My parents are alive and well and disgustingly in love with each other which is pretty awe-inspiring, but gross for Steven and I to watch. I lived in the same house since birth until I moved out. And I'm the better twin," I said with a wink. "I have friends, a nice apartment, and now my career is starting, so I feel pretty happy right now."

Nodding, Peter asked, "Have you felt pretty unhappy *not* now?"
"What...? No, I've been fine. Why?"
"It was just the way you said you feel pretty happy *right now*, it sounded like you've felt unhappy before."
"No, I've always been very happy and secure in life. I know exactly who I am and what I want. So, no, I've never been unhappy."
"Really? Wow. You're amazing then," he looked up as the waitress placed another BLT in front of us, which Peter again split, placing half on his own plate while pushing the new plate toward me.
"I don't know what you mean," I said a little shaken again by his candor.
Staring right into my eyes, Peter said softly, "You are very beautiful Sophie." What? My head was spinning. "You're like the perfect package- intelligent, highly motivated, blonde, great body, green eyes-"
"Blue eyes," I corrected. It was such a surreal moment for me I couldn't believe I interrupted him.
"Your blue irises have amber in them making them appear green in this lighting. So to me they'll always be green. I really want to hold your face in my palm," he whispered. Pausing again after he spoke, all I thought as he stared at me was *what the hell?*
Confused, we looked at each other until he finally did just that. Lifting and moving his hand to my face he gently cupped my cheek, and I actually found myself looking at him as my head tilted for a better fit in his palm. Who the hell I was in that moment I didn't know.
"You're so warm," he whispered.
"I know. I'm always like a furnace." I actually said furnace like an idiot which almost made me laugh at myself again.
"Tell me what you love," he asked suddenly as he moved his hand back to his glass of water.
"What I love? Um, my family and friends, my job, my brother, I don't know. What do you mean?"
"I mean what do you love? Coffee? Flowers? Puppies? Moonlit walks? Music? Poetry? What do you love?"
As I stared at Peter, honest to god, part of me wanted to say him in that exact moment. But obviously I wouldn't dare, and I didn't really. There was just something so unreal about him, he acted like no other man I had ever known. He *was* like no other man I had ever known. There was something so intriguing about Peter that I found myself feeling an internal pull toward him. My body was actually humming with the

excitement I felt for him.

"I love many things. I don't know. My brother mostly, I guess," I looked at Peter as he prompted me to go on with a head nod. "I love music, sure, but not country. I only like a few poets, but I love Leonard Cohen for some strange reason, especially his novel Beautiful Losers though I don't like his music as much. I love candles and candle holders, a little too much actually. You should see my place," I grinned. "And I love watching life and participating in it whenever I can." I said, thinking at the time what a weird thing to say.

"You're so beautiful, Sophie," he said again and I suddenly felt annoyed.

"So you've said. I know, my perfect fake nails and my highlighted hair are beautiful. I get it."

"Um, no, though you look very nice, that isn't what I meant at all. When you said you enjoyed watching life and participating whenever you could, I thought you sounded beautiful. You sound like an old soul wrapped in a gorgeous package. I wasn't trying to offend you; the opposite actually. I wanted you to know I found your *words* beautiful."

Exhaling again, I knew I sounded like an idiot, so I tried to fix it.

"You didn't offend me, I'm sorry. My looks are just annoying to me. I've found myself over the years trying to overcompensate my looks with anything and everything I could intellectually, so people didn't assume I was a moron. My looks are a hang up for me, which sounds stupid I know, but they just are. My parents made Steven and I work for everything we had, no shortcuts ever. So when people assume I had it easy, or maybe used my looks to get ahead, I feel insulted and almost defensive. I can honestly say I don't care about looks at all. I've never been attracted to a man who was simply good looking, because I feel like looks don't count or something in a relationship. Um, I can't explain it."

"You just did, quite eloquently. If it helps, I find you butt ugly," he said so seriously I couldn't help but gasp and start laughing.

"Butt ugly, huh? So these killer jeans and sexy red sweater, which I look fabulous in by the way, doesn't do anything for you?" I asked grinning.

"Nope. Would you like anything else to eat?" He asked changing the subject while I found myself almost fishing for a compliment from him.

"No, I'm good."

"Who were you with Friday night?" He asked making my head spin again from another subject change.

"Oh, my brother, Steven. We were celebrating my first week of work."

"Really? Do you always drink so much when you're with your brother?" He again asked way too seriously.

"If I feel like it, yes. Why? It's really none of your business how much I do or don't drink, is it?" I felt totally defensive of Steven as I tried to stare down Peter.

"No, it's not. I'm sorry. I just thought it was weird seeing you stumble down the street the way you were with him. It seemed so out of character for someone as self-possessed as you come across. I didn't take you for a get hammered on a Friday night kind of woman."

"I'm not. But again, we were celebrating and we had fun, and I'll drink when I want to. How much did *you* drink with your sister that night?" Jesus, Peter made me feel like I was PMSing with my mood swings.

"I don't drink. So, none."

"*Never?*"

"No... I don't like to feel out of control. Plus I was a sloppy drunk when I was younger. I wasn't able to stop before passing out or throwing up, which was a drag for my friends who had to carry me around or drop me off on my parent's front steps. Once, I had this close call when my friends didn't know I had left a bar without them, until I walked home and tried to break into my neighbor's house to go to sleep. Incidentally, I was only 20, so I stopped drinking young enough to never be one of those 20-something idiots who always makes an ass of themselves when drinking with their buddies."

"Do you have a drinking problem?"

"I don't think so. I'm just a sloppy drunk, so I don't drink, which doesn't really seem like a drinking problem. Does it?"

"I guess not. But does it bother you when other people drink?" I felt like I should understand this alcohol issue clearly before we continued.

"Not at all. I'm usually the designated driver, so I'm quite popular with my friends and sisters on the weekends," he said smiling.

And for some reason I felt like I needed to justify my drinking to him. I wasn't sure why, but I just blurted out, "I don't drink often, Peter. I only did this weekend for fun. I had a lot going on and I said hello *and* goodbye to many people this week, so I needed to let loose a little. But really, I don't drink often," I said almost begging him to understand.

"It wouldn't matter if you did, I'd take care of you anyway." Oh my god, he stunned me with that one sentence.

"Um... I don't need anyone to take care of me. But thanks."

"Well, I would anyway. Do you want to go for a walk?"

"Okay..." I heard myself say through my muddled brain.

Once bundled up, we went for a walk together. I was lucky the sidewalks were nice and clear because though my leather boots were awesome to look at, they very much lacked any traction. But Peter seemed to sense I may land on my ass at any moment anyway, so he took my hand and pulled it through the crook of his arm, which was very sweet, and somewhat otherworldly for sure.

We walked down the main strip of the village with Peter explaining many of the pubs and restaurants beginnings and pasts. He had lived around the corner since he bought his house at 23, so he'd seen a few changes in the last 8 years.

Peter pointed out the flower shop with my blue roses, and he showed me a little dive, junk store which outside looked like a dumpster but inside had thousands of knick-knacks, collectible antiques, and trendy little pieces that I loved.

And within seconds of entering Pandora's I found an awesome set of candle holders I had to have. They were awesome blown glass male and female Art Deco-like candle holders with dark colors throughout. Peter even joked he wished he had seen them first so he could've snatched them up before I did.

After Pandora's we walked past the shops and landed at a little chocolatier as I died- absolutely *died*. Everything I could have ever imagined as chocolate they had. *Everything...*

Reserved, mature, professional Sophie left the building the second we walked in as I smiled. I was like a PMS to the extreme, hormonal basket case. Looking at every single shelf, opened and closed, I almost chose a hundred things to buy.

After the woman behind the counter offered me a piece of chocolate, I moaned out loud as I nodded I'd take it. Even when Peter looked at me with a funny grin, I didn't care what he thought because I was surrounded by chocolate. Special, beautiful, handmade *chocolate*.

When I finally came back down from my high I realized I had been staring at everything for so long, Peter was leaning against the wall near the door. Feeling totally embarrassed when he grinned at me, I finally just asked what the best was, and I was lead to the expensive section under the glass counter, where I found my ultimate- dark chocolate with sea salt, my absolute favorite.

Dark chocolate I loved, but with sea salt I was in heaven. Looking at the different weights, I finally just pointed out a friggin' slab. Like the whole slab. An awesome slab which totaled $80.00 dollars but I didn't care.

After the slab, I finally picked a box of hot chocolate packets and asked for 2 hot chocolates to go as Peter finally joined me at the counter offering to pay, which I vehemently declined. I lied and told him half the slab was a Christmas gift for my mother, and though I think he knew I was full of shit he didn't press me further, he just smirked at me.

Eventually walking out of the Chocolatier, I handed him his hot chocolate as he smiled at me like I was scary.

"Was I really that bad?" I couldn't help but ask giggling.

"Um, you were a little scary for sure. I thought it best to stay out of your way beside the door with easy access to the street should you start snarling or growling," he said way too seriously as I laughed.

"I don't think I would have hurt you much, I promise. But you have no idea how delicious and awesome it feels savoring a piece of dark chocolate only to have a little salt granule crunch between your teeth. It is the best, most delicious experience ever," I teased right back, leaning my head against his shoulder feeling so happy in that moment.

I was happy with my chocolate, of course. But I just felt happy. I felt like we had the best first date ever. Well, I hoped first date, because after my performance over the chocolate I may have scared him away forever.

But he smiled and wrapped one arm around my back, holding my chocolate slab and candle holder bags in the hand with his hot chocolate so he could hold me to his side.

When we made it back to Murphy's, Peter asked if he could walk me home, and I agreed. It was close to 4:00, my feet were killing me, I had laundry to do, and it was the best Sunday I had had in years.

We made small talk on the walk home, and I learned more and more about Peter. He told me about his job, and his family, where he went to school, and what he liked to do in his spare time, which was draw or prepare his herbal soaps and lotions.

I found out he went to art school but dropped out because he couldn't draw on command like the teachers required, so instead of continuing to struggle, he went to a trade school and his drawings became his passion instead of his career.

I found out so much in one day I felt like I was talking to a man I had known for years, as opposed to a man I had only spoken to for 4 hours.

When we eventually arrived at my place it was awkward though. I didn't want the day to end, but I didn't want to jump in bed with him either. I wasn't ready for him to leave me yet, but I didn't know how to ask him to stay. I was happy and excited to know more about Peter. So when he nervously asked if he could call me, I said yes.

Turning toward him I was going to give him my phone number but he said he already had it. But when I questioned how, he said simply, Caller ID.

"Then why didn't you call me all week?" I asked confused.

"You didn't give me your number on purpose, and you didn't say I could call," he replied easily.

"Okay, well, you can call me," I whispered finding myself standing closer to him than absolutely necessary.

Practically standing against him, Peter surprised me when he said quietly, "I'm going to kiss you tomorrow, Sophie, after we've had a chance to come down a little from this high. I really want to remember our first kiss, so I want to wait, okay?"

"Okay..." I whispered again.

Standing at my door I was becoming a total Barbie tart with Peter and I knew it. I wasn't sure how to change it as it happened though, but I *was* aware of my breathy, moany behavior and I really wanted to be embarrassed by my behavior. I wanted to pull myself together and act like the Sophie I knew, but I just couldn't. I was smitten and enthralled by the feeling of being with him.

Unbelievably, when Peter turned to leave me with a smile I wanted to beg him to come into my apartment anyway. I wanted to cook him dinner and share my favorite chocolate with him. I wanted to kiss him, and talk to him, and make him fall in love with me.

Jolting in the hallway, I remember stunning myself back to reality with that quick thought. Hiding my surprise at myself I smiled at Peter while opening my door as he walked away telling me he'd call me later.

Turning to lock my door behind me, I remember leaning against my closet thinking *wow*.

I was stunned by my behavior and thought processes, or lack thereof. I had spent 4 hours with some stranger and I was thinking about wanting him to fall in love with me. I was actually thinking like an idiot, destined for heart break.

LOST

Moving from the little doorway, I sat down on my couch and tried to think clearly. I knew I didn't *make* men fall in love with me. I never made anyone fall in love with me, nor did I give it a thought as it happened. If it happened and they weren't my forever I tried to stay and work at the relationship until it wasn't working and then I moved on. I knew I didn't force anything, but I felt like I kind of wanted to with Peter.

CHAPTER 7

I spoke to Peter later Sunday evening when he eventually called me. I waited for him to call, even though I was dying to call him. I waited because *he* said he would call, and I didn't want to look desperate if I called him first.
  Settled in on my couch, Peter and I spoke for an hour and a half, learning more and more about each other. Actually, I learned more about him, only answering a few questions when they were posed to me because I was still nervous about giving away too much information about myself.
  I wanted my privacy. Well, truthfully, I wanted to seem a little mysterious because I found myself wanting to play this relationship right. I wanted to be everything Peter wanted from a woman though we hadn't actually had *that* conversation yet.
  Peter and I spoke on the phone until he had absolutely had to leave for work he said with regret. I learned that his job was nightshift work, so he worked at night during the week, and slept in the days. But when I asked if he would be tired because he had spent the day with me instead of sleeping, he said no. Actually, what he said was, 'I'm so happy that I spent the day with you, I'll be riding this high all night. So don't worry about me,' and I smiled at his charming confession.

  We eventually hung up at 9:00, and I was sad to end our amazing conversation. There was something about Peter that drew me to him. There was something so wonderful and calm about Peter that I felt excitement for the start of a potential relationship between us.
  I was anxiously excited to speak to him again the next day while I finished my laundry, tidied my apartment and laid out my clothes for work.
  I was excited when I showered and dressed for bed. And I was excited about Peter as I lay in my bed with a smile I couldn't seem to get rid of, no matter how many times I called myself a loser.

*****

The following morning at 8:00am there was a knock on my door before I left for work. Unbelievably there was a knock, and I was both shocked and happy when it was Peter standing in the hallway.

Opening my door, I took him in with a huge smile. Waiting, Peter didn't speak and I couldn't move. We experienced one of those weird moments of complete solitude in our thoughts, together.

"I wanted to see you before you went to work. And I brought you a coffee," he grinned.

"Thank you."

"And it's tomorrow," he whispered as he leaned in close to me.

Suddenly kissing me, I remember thinking thank god I had already brushed my teeth and was already dressed for work, until I stopped thinking entirely. I didn't care that he was messing up my lipstick and I didn't care that I had to leave for work in 20 minutes. I just wanted Peter's kiss in that moment.

Kissing, I was swept up in him and his beautiful kiss. Peter had that slow, sexy kiss thing going for him. The kind that starts its own rhythm and ends with a moan for more. He held my head with one hand and my back with the other. He practically bent me while he opened me up for him until I was taken.

Peter kissed me for what felt like a lifetime. He kissed me and I was shocked to realize I wanted a forever with him in that moment.

When he finally pulled away, his thumb wiped the moisture from my lips and he actually sucked it off his thumb. Watching him, I felt something deep inside me, almost like a craving so intense, I wanted to push him against the wall and kiss him harder. I wanted more, but I didn't take it. I let Peter lead our first kiss because it was his to lead.

"I should let you get to work," he smiled again so sweetly I actually felt it in my heart.

"Thank you for the coffee," I said without acknowledging the awesome kiss between us.

"I'll call you later, Sophie. Around 7:00. Will you be home?"

"Yes..." I moaned, thinking I'd make sure I was home at 7:00 just for his call.

"Have a good day, Soph," he smiled again as he turned to walk away.

Watching him leave I looked at him realizing I desperately didn't want him to go. I actually felt such a strange pull toward him I wanted him to stay with me. I wanted to stay home with him all day. I wanted Peter in that moment more than I wanted my forever career. I wanted him so badly, I felt nearly insane for him as he slowly exited my building.

Running back into my place after he left I honestly felt like I must look different. I felt so different inside I couldn't believe as I stared in my bathroom mirror there weren't physical changes to my appearance. I was surprised that I still looked like Sophie Morley, just with slightly smeared lipstick around her mouth, and a huge stupid smile.

Leaving for work 10 minutes later, I ran for my car, nearly slid on the ice, laughed at myself, and hopped in for the 20 minute drive to work. I drove to work with a stupid smile, and with a giddiness I didn't know I even possessed as I danced in my seat and sang along with the radio, badly.

When I arrived at work, I was still thinking about Peter and his kiss and I had to concentrate very hard on learning my new job from Carole all day. I was distracted way too often and it bothered me, even though I couldn't seem to help the distraction I was suffering.

I wasn't the kind of woman who let a man distract her, and I wasn't the kind of woman who acted love struck and stupid. I never acted weak or simple, and I never acted giddy in a relationship- not that we were in one at that point, but probably. And that reality of a relationship, after only one day of knowing Peter scared the hell out of me.

Over lunch I analyzed the shit out of myself and realized I was acting like a psycho. Peter and I had had one date, one *day* together and I was thinking about our 'relationship'. I was obsessed with defining us, and I was desperate to have some kind of hold on him which was crazy. So I made myself chill out.

I decided after my half hour lunch I would stop the bullshit obsessing, and I would focus on my job. I knew relationships always ended but my career had the potential to be forever, but only if I pulled my head out of my ass, which I eventually did.

The rest of the afternoon blurred into notes, multiple guesses about Carole's next move, and questions here and there. I stayed focused and alert about my job only, forcing Peter out of my mind all afternoon.

And by 4:30 I was spent again. Intellectually, I was totally drained which made me question whether this draining was going to always happen, or if it was merely because I was learning everything from scratch. I watched Carole seem to handle everything well, and I didn't feel inferior to her, just ignorant of the position and demands; therefore I convinced myself that I wouldn't always feel so tired at the end of the day once I was settled into a routine of my own.

  When I returned home, changed into my grubby clothes and made myself pasta for dinner, I suddenly realized I hadn't received any roses all day. Not that I expected them, and not that the roses could continue indefinitely, but I did feel a little disappointed that the blue roses thing was over. I had enjoyed the attention a little because it let me know Peter was thinking about me throughout the day like I was thinking about him.
  After dinner, I looked over my notes on the couch and admittedly, looked at the clock way too often. I was suffering that insane the clock has stopped moving phenomena all people experience when they're desperate for something to happen at a specific time. The hour between 6 and 7 absolutely crawled by as I anxiously waited to talk to Peter again. But he didn't call.
  7:30 came and went, and so did 8:00. By 9:00, I was actually angry, and by 10:00 I felt sad. I knew I was feeling mental over Peter, and I didn't like it, so I went to sleep shortly after 10 instead of waiting any longer.
  Picturing Peter's kiss in bed, and reliving the amazing feelings I felt inside me during the kiss were completely eclipsed by the sadness pulling at me because he hadn't called. I felt stupid and embarrassed that I had put so much potential into a man I had just met. But my feelings were what they were, and I couldn't help the stupid disappointment I felt.
  All I knew as I settled in for sleep was I wasn't going to give Peter anymore power over me emotionally. I would cut him off before I became more invested in any potential of Peter in my life.

*****

  When I woke at 6:30 I started my day as I always had before Peter. I showered and shaved, washed and dried my hair, dressed in a black wool knee length dress with a navy jacket over top. I even wore black tights and knee high boots to give me height and confidence to carry me through my day.
  I was down to 4 days of training left, and I needed to get my shit

together so I didn't fail my job or myself once Carole left me to fend for myself.

At 8:15 however, there was a knock on my door, and I was pissed.

Feeling annoyed and totally over him, I walked to the door, opened it without any drama and said, "Hello," in my I'm not putting up with any shit from you tone.

"Wow. You look lovely, Sophie. Sorry I'm late, but I brought you coffee," Peter smiled, which annoyed me even more.

"Thank you. I appreciate it, but I really don't have time to talk. I have to leave for work soon," I spoke calmly taking the offered coffee from his hand while attempting to close the door.

With a bit of a frown, Peter asked, "What's wrong?"

"Nothing at all," I replied slightly clipped because I wasn't doing this with him. "I have to go Peter."

"I'm sorry I didn't call you last night. Did you get my message?"

"What message?" I asked stunned.

"I left you a message on your machine at 2:45. Did you get it?"

"No. Just a minute please," I said closing the door in his face. A *message* I thought while mouthing *shit* in the hallway. Stalking to my dining room, to the poorly placed practically hidden answering machine, I lifted the goddamn book off the machine and there was the blinking light! *Shit,* I breathed again. I didn't look, or think to look, or even think the night before about a friggin message. I was just too obsessed with waiting for his call to think about anything else.

Hitting play, a message from Steven came in about my parents' house for dinner on Sunday as usual, but I skipped over it until the next message came through.

'Hi Sophie, I'm going into work early today by 3:30 for a friend who needs the evening off. I'll be working straight from 3:30 until 7:30 in the morning but I wanted to let you know so you didn't think I wasn't calling you, or that I was blowing you off. You should also know I thought of you all day. Oh, and kissing you was like a little piece of heaven for me- almost as good as your dark chocolate with sea salt. Well, for me anyway. I'll hopefully see you soon.'

Exhaling, as the warm and fuzzies settled in my stomach I had a moment of total humiliation. I didn't know how to fix my behavior without looking like the insecure idiot I already did to him. I was embarrassed and out of time. It was 8:25 and I had to leave for work.

So grabbing my purse, keys, and coat, I walked to my door with all the confidence of a moron and opened my door calmly. But Peter was grinning at me like he knew what an idiot I was.

"Did you finally get my message?"

"I did. I'm sorry, I didn't see I had messages. I'm not usually so..." but I couldn't think of the right word. Saying I'm not usually such a chick was derogatory to women everywhere, but that's what I felt like. I felt like I had totally chicked out with the drama and insecurity.

"Did you think about me yesterday?" Peter suddenly asked.

"Yes..."

"Did you think about me this morning?"

"Yes..."

"Okay. So we're all good. I told you I would call and I did. I'm sorry if you thought I wouldn't. And I'd like to spend Friday and Saturday with you if you're not busy?"

"I'm not busy I don't think," I whispered lying. I was calling Denise later to cancel my Saturday night shift. Period. "I'm sorry for acting like an ass."

"It's okay. We're new, so emotions are always heightened, I know that. Can we talk about it tonight at 7:00? I *promise* to call," he grinned.

"Okay. But I really have to go. I can't be late my second week. I hope you understand?"

"I do. Have a great day," he said stepping away from the door as I turned to lock it.

Gently pulling my coat from my arm, he slipped my coat on me and even started doing up the buttons very close to my face. He was way inside my personal space, and I felt very uneasy with our closeness, but he just focused on the buttons and not my flaming face, or my residual embarrassment.

Walking me to my car, Peter opened the door, and lifted my face for a little peck on the lips before he stood back on the sidewalk and waved me away.

After smiling at him once more, I started my car and drove like a speed demon to work. I sped to work and made it with 5 minutes to spare which was actually 10 minutes later than usual, but still early enough to not be pissed at myself one time for being almost late.

Entering my office, I grabbed my notes and charged down to Carole's office to start my fourth last day of training. I entered Carole's office, smiled hello, and made a serious effort to put all the Peter stuff out of my head. And though it was hard to focus on my job, I did it. Eventually.

*****

   Peter called me that night at 7:00 sharp, but he didn't bring up my earlier behavior or the misunderstanding between us. Peter acted the same with me and I was grateful.
   We spoke on the phone about nothing and everything for 2 hours while he made his lunch, walked into his greenhouse to water his herbs, and washed some dishes from his dinner/breakfast when he arrived home by 8:45 that morning.
   We spoke until 9:00 when I sadly let him go to take a shower and get ready for his night shift. I let him hang up, but I wanted to stay on the line for another 2 hours.
   I just couldn't get enough of Peter and our conversations, which were common, and lovely, and prolific, and real.
   After we hung up, I thought about the beginning of our relationship and realized we were real people. We weren't the sexy, rich people in novels, and Peter would never buy me a new Mercedes or whisk me away on a last minute European vacation. We were real, and we acted real.
   We had bills and jobs, and we were people who wanted to make time for each other. We were real, and I found that refreshing in the novel filled world of 'you're not good enough', or 'you don't treat me like the men in the books treat their women.' We were so real that little kisses, and 'have a good day', and thoughtful coffees in the morning meant something to me.
   After we hung up I realized I didn't need a fantasy with Peter- I wanted a reality. I wanted a life, and a beginning to something real and tangible, not made-up and destined to fail. I realized I wanted Peter completely.

   And that was our first official week together.
   Peter stopped by every morning with a coffee made just how I liked it, and I left for work with excitement for both work and Peter. I was exhausted every night by the time I left work, but quickly rejuvenated when I spoke to Peter at 7:00 on the phone.
   I was happily finding my way through the 2 new life-altering events that were consuming my days. I was also happily waiting for more time spent than a simple hello and a quick kiss each morning with Peter.

CHAPTER 8

    Friday night, I arrived home by 4:55 to Peter at my door. Waiting for me, I couldn't help the huge smile on my face, or the butterflies in my stomach when I looked at his handsome face. I had secretly been looking so forward to Friday and Saturday with Peter, that seeing him felt like a huge present waiting for me at my door.
"Hi..." I grinned.
"Hi back," he smiled before he kissed me.
    Right against my door he kissed me and I was grateful I had chewed gum on the way home. I was also thrilled I had freshened up my makeup, and spritzed my body in the car with perfume. I hadn't expected him to be at my door, but I wanted to be ready for him just in case.
    Pulling away, I couldn't wipe the smile or blush from my face, even as I hunted for my keys in my huge purse. And when I finally opened the door I was again taken by surprise when Peter turned me and dropped to his knees in front of me. He dropped to his knees and a whoosh left my chest at the intensity of the situation. I was stunned, and in that intense moment when he held my calf in his hand I felt everything else melt away.
    Looking up at me for a second, Peter proceeded to untie my lace-up ankle boots until they were dropped on the mat behind him. When they were removed in silence, I couldn't move until Peter stood towering over me again. Standing still, it was such an amazingly intense act, one which no man had ever done to me before, I felt petite and cared for in that moment by him. Again, I felt a little messed in the head by his actions toward me.
    When he slowly unbuttoned my coat and hung it on the rack I waited for his next move in silence. I barely knew how to breathe, never mind speak but I was aware of feeling too much for him too soon. I was nearly winded by the intensity of Peter all around me.
    "Come sit with me," he said taking my hand as I let him lead me into my home.
    Walking into my apartment for the first time, he didn't acknowledge my

place one way or the other. He didn't look around, or scope the place out. He simply walked to the couch, sat me down, and then sat on the opposite end, taking my feet with him, as he began massaging my admittedly aching feet. He massaged my feet gently while I panicked about potentially smelly, boot wearing feet, but he didn't seem to notice or care. Whether my feet smelled or not, Peter just told me to relax at the beginning until he massaged me into physical silence and calm.

As he massaged me, I remember thinking this shit doesn't happen to real people in real life, and no one finds this kind of man. He seemed and looked so normal on the outside, yet he had this weird, passionate, almost romantically sensual side to him that I had never known before him.

I thought briefly about Peter and my past relationships and realized Darren was too young to ever be like him, while Derek was too immature to act like him. And Joseph was too old to put forth as much effort as Peter did. Peter, however, was like a dream come true for me. He was a man I knew I could love, maybe even forever.

After a half hour massage in silence, Peter finally spoke.
"I love your home, Sophie. It's exactly what I expected. It's neat and tidy, but whimsical with all the candles everywhere. You really do have a candle holder fetish, huh?" Smiling, I nodded at him. "I love your Christmas tree, too. It's adorable."
Shaking myself back to my surroundings, I finally spoke. "You should see it lit up. It took me years, but I finally found real purple lights. Like dark purple, not the bright, pinkish-purple kind."
"I think I will," he said standing to walk to my tree.
Finding the cord behind, he lit my tree and everything changed in the room instantly. It was no longer darkened with only the hallway lighting us from behind, but it suddenly had a soothing, festive purple feel all through my apartment.

And yes, purple had a feel. It could be both sexy, but also pretty and calming. Purple lights sparkled over every surface in my living room, even reflecting off the hardwood floors. I felt warm and surrounded by Peter in that moment between us. It was almost an ethereal moment that I wished would never end.

Eventually, after maybe 20 minutes of quiet between us, Peter asked, "Do you want to go out for dinner, or would you like to order in?"
"Um... Order in. Do you like Chinese?"

"Love it. Do you have a menu?"
"Yes, one sec," I replied walking to my kitchen.

Opening the drawer, I was still smiling. I felt so happy with Peter in my home, I felt giddy and completely unlike myself, so much so, I actually had to shake my head to clear it.

Thinking of Peter in my home was making me want to be ready for him sexually, too. I actually wanted him sexually, which was rare for me because sex was always just sex- almost an afterthought. I liked it okay, but not enough to crave it or demand it from my partners. Sex was just a necessary part of any relationship, I knew, so I had it with my boyfriends when they wanted it.

Thinking about sex with Peter, I remembered my parents had always lectured us about the importance of sex in any relationship, and how without it there could be no lasting love or intimacy to be found. They would make Steven and I cringe when they spoke of sex, but in that moment, contemplating sleeping with Peter, I suddenly felt there may have been more to my parents' gross lectures than I had previously understood. Thinking of sex with Peter caused a flutter deep inside me that made me want to be with him in every way I could.

Amazingly, after we placed our order together, when I rose to leave him for a quick shower I didn't feel uncomfortable leaving him in my home unattended. I don't know why I was comfortable; maybe it was just his gentle tones or even his frequent smiles, but there was something about Peter that just instilled trust from me.

So I showed him my hidden stereo and CD rack and handed him the TV flicker to use if he wanted as I left the room. Walking behind him on the couch to head for my bathroom Peter suddenly raised his hand for my own and kissed my hand as I passed. He actually kissed my hand and turned to smile at me, and I was done.

Peter was just so sweet I realized I wanted him badly. I wanted to jump him right there, or I wanted him to jump me in the shower. I wanted to jump on the couch and kiss him passionately, and I wanted him to grab me and kiss me hard. But I quickly grabbed a towel and clothes from my bedroom and jumped in the shower instead.

After the world's fastest, most productive shower ever, I dressed in my sexy jeans, paired with a baggy, sloppy, short black sweater so it didn't look like I was trying too hard to impress, and I rejoined Peter in the living room with my hair still tied up on my head.
I saw the food had arrived, and was placed all over the coffee table with plates and cutlery, and 2 lit candles- thankfully not 2 important candles I would have had a stroke over being lit, but 2 good candles nonetheless.

"Wow. That came fast. How much was it?" I asked, even as Peter shook his head no to me paying for dinner.
"My treat Sophie. I haven't had Chinese in a while, and you've had a long week, so just enjoy," he said as I sat down beside him.
Scooping all of my favorite's sky high, I knew my ability to scarf down endless amounts of Chinese food before feeling bloated and overdone was shocking, but I figured Peter might as well know that about me from the beginning.
Smiling at my plate, Peter laughed. "I'm impressed you aren't doing the second date, 'oh, I'll just have a salad' thing, which drives me crazy by the way. I hate eating dinner with a woman knowing she isn't satisfied but willing to suffer so I won't think she looks like a pig or all bloated or something while eating."
"Not me. I typically eat when I'm hungry, and suffer the bloated belly consequences later," I grinned.
"Good to know," he smiled in return as we ate in silence while older Coldplay played quietly in the background, which I loved.

"Christmas is almost here. Are you busy over the holidays?" Peter asked while biting into an egg roll.
"Horribly. My parents always have a huge Christmas Eve party for tons of family and friends, then Steven and I either crash there, or have to drive back by 8:00 Christmas morning before our mom freaks out. Then Christmas Day we go to my Aunt Carla's house for another huge feast with like 20 relatives. It's exhausting actually, and over the years I've come to realize I need Boxing Day just to recover from the 2 days before it. You?"
"Pretty much the same. Christmas Eve at my grandparents, Christmas morning at my parents, and for the last 4 years Christmas dinner at my sister's house once she took over for my mom."
"So we're both super busy," I said sounding kind of sad. Honest to god,

if I could've stabbed myself with my fork I would've after hearing myself.
  "What time do you finish work on Christmas Eve?"
  "We close at 3:00."
  "Maybe I can stop by at 3:30? What time do you go to your parents?"
  "5 or so..."
  "Okay then, I'll see you at 3:30 on Christmas Eve," he smiled and my heart sped up again.
  "Okay..." I grinned.

  After we finished eating, put the leftovers in the fridge and tidied up the dishes, Peter asked me if I wanted to go out, which I really didn't. I felt full, and happy, and just comfortable with him in my home.
  I wanted to talk more, and maybe kiss a little, which reminded me to go brush my teeth quickly. So excusing myself again, I walked to the bathroom as he followed me to the living room couch.
  And when I returned to the couch minutes later, Peter had put on Matthew Good's Avalanche album, which I loved. I loved Matthew Good, so I explained to Peter that I enjoyed tuning out the actual music, while just listening to Matthew's words, which prompted a long conversation about the merit of good song writers versus the merit of good music sellers.
  We talked about the sellouts, and about the true success stories. We discussed bands we had previously loved but who changed with fame and notoriety. We talked openly and honestly, even arguing over bands I hated that he loved, and vice versa. Yet even as we argued, it was lightly, and with a true attempt to understand the other's point of view.
  Somehow, before I knew it Peter was lying on my couch with his head propped against the end with my head on his shoulder and arm. I laid beside him in a semi-spoon position, as he held my left hand entwined with his own. When he spoke, he would raise our hands in the air to make his point, or I would raise my head off his shoulder and arm to look at him as I made my own point.
  It was so natural and beautiful between us as we spoke, the hours seemed to fade away. I actually found it kind of soul-consuming the ease and comfort I gained from Peter's calm when we were together.

"I want to sleep with you," Peter suddenly whispered while kissing my hand.

"Okay..." I answered a little too breathy as I unconsciously moved my butt suggestively against him.

"Um, just to sleep, Sophie. I want to sleep beside you and wake up beside you in the morning." And though he spoke softly, I was totally embarrassed by my assumption as I blushed and had to look away from him before he saw my humiliation.

Without a doubt, Peter threw me off. I didn't understand Peter like I did everyone else. It was unnerving and even frustrating not being able to figure him out easily. So when he pulled at my hand and said 'Hey...' I had a hard time looking back at him.

Something about my humiliation made me almost cry. I think if I had been alone, or talking to him over the phone, I would have cried. But I wasn't alone, and I wasn't going to further compound my stupidity and embarrassment by crying in front of him, as well.

"Sophie... I want to have sex with you, just not yet. I like where we're headed and I don't want to rush it with nervousness and the potential insecurity of first time sex."

"I don't want to sleep with you, either," I blurted out sounding ridiculously defensive.

"Sophie, please. *Trust me* I want to sleep with you, but I've done the have sex quickly thing, and the relationship always ended after the sex was used up. Once the infatuation was over, I realized I didn't really feel anything for my partners, or not enough to form a lasting relationship. And I don't want to do that with you."

Listening to Peter I realized how thoughtful and mature he was. He always said everything right, and I hated it. When Peter spoke I felt almost a step behind him emotionally. Everything he said was true, I knew that. But I hated that it was him who said it because I looked like a horny teenager, while he looked like a mature adult. I hated feeling like an ass around him, which I felt like I did frequently.

"It's fine Peter. Everything you said makes perfect sense. Can we just drop it? I'm fine," I said again sounding defensive.

"Sophie, how many men have you slept with? And how many of them meant something to you?"

"How many woman have *you* slept with?" I countered.

"16, I believe. And when you take out Patricia and the one before her, that's only 14 woman in the last 8 years. A fairly conservative number- slightly less than 2 women a year, approximately," I could see him grin as he pulled me back down and leaned over me.

"And how many of them meant something to you?" I asked dying to know.

"Maybe 6 or 7, but to varying degrees of course. There were women I thought I cared for, and there were woman I *wanted* to care for but didn't. I was never an asshole though, and I've only had 2 one night stands, so really my number is more like 14 overall and 12 without Patricia and Mandy before her. So now my number seems more like 12 in 8 years which really equals 1.5 women a year. Not bad, huh?" He teased.

"No, not bad by guy standards, I guess. I know my brother sleeps with dozens of women each year, so yes, your number seems fairly conservative," I admitted on an exhale.

Why I felt so tense about our conversation, I couldn't explain, other than I was feeling a type of jealous nervousness or something. I don't know exactly what I felt though because I had never felt jealousy before in my life.

"So...? What about you? How many men do I have to compete with?" Peter grinned.

But for some reason I didn't want to answer Peter's question. Not that I had anything to be ashamed of, far from it actually. I just knew he would have follow up questions, and I didn't really feel like getting into my past relationships with him in case he learned more about me than I was ready to give.

"Wow. *That* many?" He teased.

"No. Only 3 and a half," I admitted.

"Please explain the *half* first," he grinned again.

"Um, he was between 2 and 3, and we knew each other, but we weren't together, so it was kind of a one night stand, but not really, because he tried to date me before and afterward."

"But the 'half'?"

"Well, I'd been drinking a little, so I was sober enough to know what I was doing, yet tipsy enough to not care at the time. Afterward, I left right away instead of suffering the walk of shame the next morning. And as I said, he wanted more but I didn't. So yes, I slept with him, but it's more like a half because it was so different from my other relationships and not like me at all," I exhaled knowing even justified it still sounded ridiculously one night standish.

"And the 3 who mattered?"

"I'm not sure what you want me to say. Like details? A relationship synopsis? The whole story? The short version?" I sat up away from his arms, leaning against his thighs in the middle of the couch.

I couldn't explain why the conversation bothered me. Actually, I had NO idea why it bothered me. I knew I had absolutely nothing to be ashamed of, but retelling of my relationships scared me with Peter. I think I was a little afraid he wouldn't like me anymore if he knew I had had a life before him. Or maybe he'd judge me, or I don't know... something. I just felt closed off and less comfortable with him suddenly.

"Why do you seem so tense right now? I won't judge you Sophie, if that's what you're thinking. Are you in a relationship right now that you're hiding from me?"

"No. Of course not."

"I didn't think so. So why should your past matter to me?"

"Exactly. Why does it matter to you?" I questioned defensively again.

"It doesn't *matter*. But I would like to know about you, and that includes the people you've been in relationships with. I want to know what turns you on, and what makes you run away. I certainly don't want, or even need sexual details, but I'd love an overview of what made you happy with them."

Exhaling, I decided to confess. "Um... Well, I left them all, which either says something good or bad about me... usually, I think good. First there was Darren my high school sweetheart, but I broke up with him when I eventually realized he wasn't strong enough for me. Then there was Derek, my boyfriend in University who didn't feel motivated enough in life, so also not motivated enough for me. And then there was Joseph who was much older and-"

"How much older?" He interrupted.

"20 years exactly."

"Wow, good for him. A hot young blonde girlfriend," he smiled.

"No, Joseph wasn't like that. He was calm and cool, and not about appearances. He just loved me because we were companionable. I didn't require much looking after so we were both happy, until I realized he was too comfortable, and I would go without if I stayed any longer. But when we broke up as friends a few months ago, we stayed friends. He actually sent me that Christmas card," I said pointing to the mantel with cards. "So that's it. My 3 men in a nutshell."

"Do you realize I said I wanted to know what made you happy with them, and you could only tell me why you left them?"

"Well, I think that's the way it usually is, right? By the end of a relationship the bad always overshadows the good you may have had, otherwise you would stay together."

"You're right. But I would like to know how they made you happy. Maybe you'll tell me one day?"

"Maybe..." I said looking behind me at the clock.

I think I was suddenly suffering my fight or flight, which usually meant flee. I didn't like to talk about my past, and I rarely divulged personal information, both of which Peter had pulled out of me, however few details that was. So pausing to ground myself I suddenly felt drained.

"Are you tired, Sophie?"

"Yes..."

"May I spend the night with you?"

"Yes..."

"Good. I didn't sleep off my night shift last night so I'm fairly tired myself. Do you have a toothbrush I could use?"

"Sure. I buy my brother a new one almost monthly, so I think there's a packaged green one under the sink."

"Thanks. I'll meet you back here?" He smiled with his hand on my back.

"Okay," I agreed jumping up nearly running for my bedroom, which thankfully was perfectly tidy.

Undressing and dressing quickly, I found my 2 piece stars and moons pj bottoms with matching tank top. Throwing them on, I knew I looked comfy without trying for sexy, but the shelf bra in the tank made my boobs look great and kept them where they should be while sleeping, which was a relief.

After Peter exited the bathroom, he checked me out from head to toe then kissed my lips before I could use the washroom myself. Smiling at him as he pulled away, I left him for my own teeth brushing and anti-sex pep talk before walking into my room and calling him to follow me as I stood against the wall.

Standing in my room as Peter joined me was awkward, I remember that. It was awkward the moment Peter walked into my bedroom, looked around, then paused like he didn't know how to get into my bed.

"Where do you usually sleep?" He spoke softly.

"Right on this side, facing out, so I think I'll be able to see and prevent an intruder before he kills me," I said laughing at myself.

"Okay, then. I'll be against the wall so you can get the intruder for me," he replied pulling my comforter down and sliding into my bed against the far wall.

Looking at Peter as he lay down, I was suddenly struck with almost a pain in my chest. There was something about that moment with him, something so promising and hopeful, I found myself feeling emotional. I couldn't explain it, and I actually hated the feeling in my chest. But it was there anyway, nearly bringing me to tears.

"Come here, Sophie," Peter whispered on his side with his arms open, and I did.

Sliding in next to him, I let him pull me into his arms while he spooned me warm. Kissing my neck gently, Peter whispered in my ear, "What do you want, Sophie?"

And before I could stop myself, I whispered back, "To be adored..."

After my words, I was glad he didn't acknowledge what I said, and I was relieved he didn't throw out some meaningless words. We were too new to feel that intensely for each other, but my statement hung in the air around us, even as Peter wrapped his arms tighter around me, resting against my back in silence.

In our silence, I realized that was exactly what I wanted, and what I'd been missing in my life. I had been loved and cared for, and I had created situations filled with love and acceptance. I had people respect and love me since I could remember, even as a child. But I had never felt adored.

In our silence I realized that is what I had been looking for my whole life- the man who would adore me.

CHAPTER 9

When I woke up the next morning I was hot as hell. Actually, I was nearly suffocating with Peter wrapped all over me. His face was in my neck, and I was leaning on my side with one of his thighs under my back and the other leg thrown over me. I had his arm wrapped around my chest and I was so uncomfortable and overheated, I almost panicked.

Pushing Peter off me while trying to edge out from under his leg proved a challenge though. For an average sized man he held me in almost a death grip. Pushing again, I moved my head to look at his face and that's when I saw him smiling at me.

"Jesus! You're so friggin hot. Would you mind getting off me," I asked with a huff making Peter laugh at me as I continued to push at him. "If you ever sleep over again, remind me to open the window, even in the dead of winter, okay?"

"Yup, I'll remind you when I sleep over again. Even in a blizzard," he again laughed at me and my distress.

Sitting up, I remember having to wipe my brow of my matted down sweaty hair, while glaring at him. "*When* you sleep over again?"

"Yup. *When*. So what do you want to do this morning?" He asked looking at the clock.

"Well, I'm going to have a cold shower to lower my core body temperature to acceptable levels, then I think coffee to start."

"How about I rinse off quick then go get us coffee while you shower? Sound good?"

"That sounds excellent. But would you mind getting me a French vanilla with a shot of chocolate? I like to start my weekends off with a little chocolate," I said grinning.

"No problem. Just give me a minute," he replied while fighting his way out of the sheets and blankets he had nearly destroyed in the night.

Watching him walk out of my room to the bathroom, I was again taken by surprise by the complete comfort I felt with him in my home. He was in my home which wasn't typically something I did, and I was okay with it. Actually, the more I thought about it I realized I was usually the visitor in my relationships.

I had moved in with Derek and Joseph when they asked me to, and before we lived together I rarely had them sleep in my own place because I liked my space to remain mine. Thinking about Peter made me suddenly realize I think I always believed it was easier to leave them when *I* could do the leaving, rather than forcing them to leave me when I left.

After Peter's shower, he redressed in his cargo pants, awesome black sweater, and kissed me on the lips before leaving my room and heading out my front door for coffee, just before I jumped in the shower, shaved quickly and washed and conditioned my hair even quicker.
In the shower I found myself obsessing over all things Peter. From the way he slept practically on top of me, to his complete ease and security of speech when we debated, I couldn't stop thinking about him. I just couldn't get over how amazing he seemed.
Actually, I suddenly found myself wondering why he wasn't married already with 2 kids and a beautiful wife, which totally stressed me out. So I decided in the shower I had enough insecurity regarding Peter at that moment and I'd let that one go.

After my shower, when I practically ran for my bedroom in a towel to change, I dressed for comfort, but attractively. I didn't know what our day was going to be like, but I liked the thought of spending it with Peter.
Once dressed, with my hair dried I made my way to the living room and Peter. Sitting on my couch with his feet hanging over the edge of my coffee table, he was sipping his coffee looking way too good in my home.
"I'm never going to be able to hear this song again without thinking of you," he absently breathed into the room. So listening, I realized it was Green Eyes by Coldplay.
"I really do have blue eyes, Peter."
"You really don't, Sophie. Blue may be the dominant shade, but your eyes really do highlight as green, especially with all the amber within your irises. I'm going to take a picture of your eyes and show you just how green they look in certain lighting."
"Okay," I agreed sitting down beside him as he wrapped his arm around my shoulder.
"I bought you your French vanilla with **2** shots of chocolate to really put you in a good mood," he teased.
"Thank you, but I'm in a pretty good mood without the chocolate," I whispered.
"Me too... I enjoy being with you. I just wish you relaxed a little more

with me. You're so guarded sometimes, it's almost painful to watch," he said as he kissed my head.

"I..." But I faltered.

"It's okay. I'll show you I'm a good guy and then you can drop your guard a little. I have to keep reminding myself that we've really only known each other for the last 6 days. It's hard because I feel good when I'm with you, and I feel like I've known you for so long, our actual time together seems to surprise me."

"Me, too. I was thinking earlier that I liked having you in my home. Or more like I'm okay with it, and that's not usually the case. I kind of like having my space and solitude in my own apart-"

"Soph! Sophie, open up!" I jumped when I suddenly heard Steven at my door.

"Holy shit! It's my brother!" I yelled in a weird panic as Peter sat up straighter.

"Sophie... We're having coffee on a Saturday morning, totally clothed," he grinned.

Knowing I looked like an immature idiot by my behavior, I calmed down and smiled at my stupidity, even though it did feel like we were doing much more together. We were physically clothed and decent, but our closeness seemed to suggest a kind of intimacy I didn't want Steven to see yet.

"Just give me a second to get rid of him," I said as I hopped off the couch for the door.

Throwing it open, I looked at a hammered Steven. *Shit!* 9:30 and he was still piss drunk.

"Sophie... I met the girl I'm going to marry. Well, probably not *marry* because she slept with me like 10 minutes after meeting me, but she was awesome. So if I *was* going to get married it would be to someone like her, but not as easy. I need to crash before I drive home, 'cause I think my car's down the street. Why am I always in the village now since you moved in?" He babbled.

"Steven... I have company," I pleaded quietly.

"Really? Who? The creepy notebook guy?" Steven asked trying to look around me, but Peter beat him to it.

"Hi Steven, I'm Peter- the creepy notebook guy," he said with a smile though I could tell he was annoyed. I barely knew Peter, but I had heard that slightly clipped tone before, coincidentally, when he discussed seeing me drunk with my brother the previous Friday, which was a total *oh shit* moment if ever there was one.

"Hey, Peter, the picture you drew of Sophie was awesome. She looked beautiful," Steven stammered while leaning against the doorway.

Flinching, I could almost feel the heat coming off Peter at the mention of the drawing.

"Would you like to come in?" Peter asked.

"Nah... I better go. I'll just call a cab. I was drinking with Heather til like 6:30 this morning, I think."

"I'll give you a lift home, if you need?" Peter offered.

"Really?"

"No problem. Let me just grab my coat. I'll see you later, Sophie," Peter said while not looking at me at all, which made my chest ache in that moment.

"I'll go with you," I begged.

But a 'sure' was all I got as reply from Peter who followed Steven already walking out the main door. Panicking, I grabbed my coat and my untouched coffee, quickly following after Peter and Steven as I locked my front door.

Once we all sat in the car, no one spoke. Actually, I think Steven had passed out immediately because he was breathing a little too loudly in the silence of Peter's pink car. And if the situation hadn't seemed so bad between me and Peter, I might have teased him a little about his car because it was really pink- like fuchsia pink.

Luckily, or maybe unluckily Steven didn't live that far from me so about 10 minutes later we were pulling into his front lot, as I tried to wake him. Pushing on him and calling his name, Steven finally stirred and looked around with a big smile for me.

"Thanks for the ride, Pete. You're a good guy," Steven smiled and shook Peter's hand as he practically fell out of the car at which point he yelled, "HOLY *SHIT!* This is a really fucking pink car, my man," while laughing his ass off.

Practically groaning over my idiot brother I was so scared to look at Peter in that moment but to my relief I heard him laugh as we watched Steven stumble to the front doors of his high rise apartment.

So turning to Peter, I whispered, "I'm sorry."

"It's all good. It IS a really fucking pink car," he smirked.

"Yes it is, but you know that's not why I'm apologizing."

"Well, why are you sorry then?" I could see he wanted me to say it.

"I'm sorry about the creepy notebook guy comment."

Pausing for a moment after my words, Peter exhaled before asking, "Is that what I am to you? *Creepy*?"

"No. Not at all," I pleaded. "I think you're amazing, I just didn't know what to think then. You freaked me out a little, so I asked Steven's opinion. And it was Steven who told me to meet you last Sunday. He thought I was being too... I don't know. But he told me to chill out and meet you for lunch and just see what you were really like before I gave up."

"That notebook was private, Sophie. Just between you and I."

"I know but it was weird to me; it still is a little. I mean share our private thoughts with each other? I didn't *know* you."

"And you do now?"

"I'm trying to. I want to. I like you, Peter. And I want to like you more."

"Okay, but will we have secrets between just us, or will I always have to question what you tell your brother, or even others?"

"No, of course not. I don't gossip, and I don't tell my girlfriends everything about my life. I was just creeped out by how persistent you seemed."

"I was perusing you. And I didn't think drawing you a portrait and asking to know your thoughts was all that creepy," he defended.

"Okay, well I did. I don't share my thoughts, Peter. I don't write them in a journal, and I sure as hell wouldn't let anyone read them if I did. But now that I know you a little better I can see why you would've liked that idea. I understand a little better the kind of man you are," I said desperately to relieve the tension in the car.

"And what kind of man do you think I am, Sophie?" He asked looking honestly curious.

"Um, a thinker. Artistic. Warm. Caring. Intense... I don't know. Not my usual kind of man, so I was a little scared."

"And now?" He asked turning his whole body in his seat to look directly at me.

"I'm not that scared anymore," I said plainly. I wasn't going to give any more of myself to him when we had this tension between us. I just couldn't, especially since I was the one struggling.

"Do you still want to spend the day with me?"

"Yes. Do you?" I countered nervously.

"Yes, but please no more surprises. If I freak you out or seem too intense let *me* know. Maybe I can scale it back until you're comfortable, or maybe I can explain it until you're more comfortable with me. I don't want you to ever be afraid of me, Sophie."

"Okay," I replied relieved. I knew I was going to absolutely *kill* Steven later but in that moment I was just happy that everything was out in the open with Peter.

"Do you need to stop by your place before we go out?"

"Yes, please," I whispered as Peter took my hand in his as he turned in Steven's long driveway for my apartment.

*****

After we arrived back at my place, there was still a heavy tension that I think both of us wished wasn't there. I felt sad and slightly hurt by the tension because it was too soon to already be ending as far as I was concerned.

"What's wrong, Sophie?" Peter asked as he stopped me in the hallway.

"Nothing," I lied because everything suddenly felt very wrong between us. But he just looked at me and waited for more, so I gave it. "It's too soon to feel this tension between us," I admitted on a whisper.

"Come here," he said pulling me back to my bedroom. Sitting on the bed, he pulled me beside him and then he took my face into his hands and he kissed me.

Peter kissed me in that way that was all his. It was sexy as hell and mind-consuming. He wasn't fast or demanding, but he made me feel explored. He kissed me until I was leaned back on the bed and pushed further into it. I was kissed by Peter who would pull away when I least expected it to be looked at, smiled at, studied, then kissed again.

Peter kissed me, then slowly began touching me as well. He touched my hips and moved across my stomach. He moved under my sweater and traced his fingers along my bra and under until he touched my nipples with his fingertips. Just a touch, but enough to make me try to speed up the kiss.

I tried to drag him into a deeper kiss with my hands in his hair, but he never sped up. He continued kissing me with his full lips creating a strange, suspended feeling of being worshipped, but not taken.

He never thrust his tongue in deep, but would slide his tongue into my mouth, catch my own, suck it deep into him and release me. He worshipped my mouth in a way I had never been kissed before.

When he was under my sweater I decided to help. Lifting my arms I reached for my own sweater and drew it overhead, even as I said, "Just a second," and leaned over and up to the window above my bed. Pulling the dark blinds quickly closed I settled back down on my bed with him.

"Why did you do that?" He questioned against my lips.

"Because it was too bright in here," I whispered back.

"I don't need darkness to be with you, Sophie," he kissed me again.

"Well, I need it. I don't like..." But I couldn't finish. I felt insecure and nervous with him this first time.

Peter seemed like the type of guy who would be fine with nudity, even daylight nudity, but I wasn't. I never had been. I was okay with my body, even with some of the obvious imperfections, but I sure as hell wasn't ready to be naked in daylight with him.

"Sophie..." He seemed to moan into my mouth, but then he began seriously touching me instead of talking further.

Within minutes, my bra was removed and my jeans had been unzipped and pulled from my legs, even as he crawled back up my body after removing his own sweater. Settled in between my raised knees, Peter kissed me, and held my face with his hands. He kissed me even as his weight held me down, and I was dying.

I was so aroused, and turned on, and just ready for him. I had that strange oogly feeling in my stomach and my hands were desperate to feel him. I trailed my fingers down his back and tickled his sides briefly as he kissed me and moaned into me.

Eventually, our bodies started moving against each other- him in his cargo pants and me in my panties. We continued kissing but I needed more from him.

When Peter eventually moved to my side, he slowly slipped his hand into my panties, and I nearly jacked off the bed by the feel of total stimulation. I actually felt my body hot and wet against his fingers. I felt so aroused I knew I was ready to be taken by him.

"You're so wet, Sophie... I want to taste you," Peter suddenly whispered against my mouth embarrassing me.

Unbelievably, I remember feeling turned off in that split second from his words, not turned on. I seemed to freeze all my movements on my bed. My arousal lessened, and my body froze beside him.

I didn't know what was wrong, but I was uncomfortable. Peter's words weren't explicit, or even filthy, but they kind of felt like it to me. I couldn't explain what I felt, but the atmosphere seemed to change around us and it was completely my fault.

"What's wrong?" Peter asked sliding his hand away from me.

"I don't know," I answered truthfully. I just wasn't comfortable with him anymore.

"Tell me exactly what you're thinking right now. Please?"

"Darren was too young to be good in bed. He lasted for like 2 minutes. And Derek was fast and hard because he thought speed and grinding against me was good sex. And Joseph wouldn't have acknowledged my body one way or the other. He just kissed me and then he entered me. But they all thought I was something to be loved and... But not spoken dirty to," I admitted trying to look away from him, but he held my face to him so he could look at me.

"And...?" He pushed.

"I don't know. You made me uncomfortable when you talked about me and my body like that."

"Saying you were wet?" I nodded. "That's not a bad thing, Sophie."

"I know. It just embarrassed me for some reason. I'm not used to dirty talk I guess. I'm sorry," I moaned embarrassed while trying to pull my face away again.

"That wasn't dirty talk; that was a sexy observation," he tried to soothe.

"I know, but it was different than I know. But I'm not a freak, or a prude, or anything. I'm not at all. I just felt weird when you said that to me, and then I felt..." But I had no more words. The longer I explained myself the more ridiculous and embarrassed I became.

"Baby... Remember I told you about the first time sex nervousness and insecurity? Well, that's this. That's *all* this is. You're going to feel insecure about your body, and I'm going to feel insecure about my penis size," he smirked. "You're going to want to move like a pornstar, though it does nothing for you, because you're going to want me to think you're awesome in bed like a pornstar. And I'm going to hold onto my orgasm for as long as humanly possible, so you think I'm an amazing lover who doesn't get off until you do, even though I'll be thinking about anything other than you so I don't go off quickly," he smiled again and kissed my lips. "That's all this is. So talk to me instead, and maybe we can avoid the typical mind fucking all couples suffer with during new sex."

"I feel like such a child right now," I whined sounding exactly like a child.

"Don't. You're insecure about being with me, and I'm nervous, too. I could lie here with you for the next 6 hours and tell you everything I find amazing, and beautiful, and sexy about you-"

"Would you?" I huffed a little nervous laugh.

"I can if you want," he smiled. "Or I could just kiss the shit out of you until you don't feel insecure with me anymore," he said leaning back down to my lips. "You're amazing, Sophie. I promise."

"Thank you. You seem amazing, too."

"Do you want me here with you?"

"Yes..." I whispered because I really did.

"Then be here with me, and let me be here with you."

When I nodded, Peter started another one of his long, drugging kisses that sipped at my lips and stole the thoughts right out of my head.

However long later, Peter was back in my panties, slipping them from my body as he stopped kissing me and moved down me as well.

Naturally, I was insecure again. I thought of my scent, and I feared my taste for him. I know women are always nervous of that, and I was no different. So I tried hard to stop my nervousness until I realized Peter was looking right at my body but doing nothing to me.

"Your scent is amazing, Sophie, if you're worried, and I can't wait to taste you," he said staring at my eyes as he slowly licked me with a moan.

When I moaned in return, Peter began. With his fingers he impaled me and with his tongue he consumed me. He spent forever between my thighs, and though I writhed and moaned I couldn't quite get over. I was stuck, as usual, at that plateau between arousal and pain. I hit the edge where I had to stop, because I just couldn't take the intensity anymore. Begging him to stop, I pulled his face away from my body.

"Have you ever had an orgasm before?" Peter asked gently crawling up my body to rest his head on my chest.

Stroking his hair from his face, I admitted, "Yes, but not with a partner. My body's weird. I hit a plateau I can't get over, then again it happens, until usually the third time I can get off. But I've only been able to do that with a toy or in the shower," I admitted totally embarrassed.

"Why not with a partner who knew the issue you had?"

"I don't know. They never tried three times? Once I learned I *could* get off if I stopped twice and went back until usually the third time I succeeded, it just seemed like too much work with my last boyfriend. I don't know why. I just can't orgasm with the first or second round of stimulation. It's not you, I swear," I spoke again feeling mortified but not wanting Peter to feel inadequate in any way.

"Please don't be embarrassed with me, Sophie. I want to know everything about you, and these are the things I want to know. Knowing what you need is what I want. Knowing what will bring you closer to me, is what I crave. I *need* to know you, Sophie."

Oh, *shit!* He was saying those things in an environment of insecurity, and he was making me all screwed up again. I wanted to cry at his sweetness. I wanted to kiss him and love him, and make him mine forever. I actually wanted him as a forever.

6 days after our first afternoon together, and 5 days after our first kiss, I was thinking of forever with Peter. I was thinking of forever in a way that mapped out my entire future. I was thinking of the forever where I looked at this man and knew I was secure and happy and fulfilled for the rest of my life with him.

There was no rhyme or reason to it, and there was no stopping the feelings in my chest. I just felt them and I hated them. Actually, I feared them mostly, I think.

I thought of every insta-love book I had ever read and rolled my eyes. I thought of my parents telling Steven and I since birth that they knew the very millisecond they met that they were meant to live for each other. I thought of all the cheesy romantic films I didn't understand and all the clichéd saying of love at first sight that made me laugh.

I thought about everything, until I realized tears were slowly falling down my temples into my hair and onto my pillow.

All I knew for sure as I lay on my bed with Peter against my chest was I wanted to love this man forever.

When Peter eventually lifted his head and saw my tears, I smiled and shook my head 'don't ask', so he didn't. Crawling back up my body, he cradled me into his chest and began talking about everything and nothing again to ease the upset in the room.

I learned that he loved his sisters, but that they had tortured their younger brother growing up. He even joked that I better not ever try to put makeup on him because he had deep physiological scars from it, making me laugh at his seriousness of tone.

I learned Peter was bullied in Grade 7 when he transferred to a new school. Then one day in November, after 2 months of daily bullying, one of the asshole bullies took his notebook away from him and saw Peter's cartoon drawings. The bully started making fun of Peter's drawings until he slowly stopped and said they were really good.

  Peter told me while grinning that he was a wimp and scared to death of the grade 7 and 8's at his new school, but after the notebook incident, Peter was slowly welcomed into the fold, and even praised for his cool superhero drawings by the other kids.

  Peter was always a decent student, but he never tried hard in school, and he admitted to coasting through school on his charming, quiet personality.

  Peter told me he was just average in life, except with drawing. After high school he received his scholarship to the only art College he ever wanted to attend but he was shocked by how hard he found direction, and his inability to produce anything worthwhile when he attended. Inevitably, after much thought he chose to quit art school instead of suffering to the point of hating drawing.

  He told me about his parents who were a teacher and a nurse, and very average people. He loved his sister's and one of their husbands but didn't like the fake persona the other brother-in-law exuded. But he loved his 4 nieces and nephews, so he played nice with said pretentious brother-in-law to keep the peace in the family.

  Peter spoke and I took in each and every little piece of information I could. I loved hearing him speak, and I loved learning everything I could about him.

  However long later he did try to engage me as well. He asked questions I answered and many I didn't. I gave him the bare minimum to appease him, but nothing too soul defining or telling.

  And if I had to explain my aloofness at that time with Peter, it would be this; I was afraid to give him more of myself when I was too insecure about the future for us.

  I wanted a forever with this man, but I feared the ending. I felt nervous about giving more of myself that he could hurt me with later, because that was what I felt with Peter. I felt the absolute reality of being hurt by him. I knew the depth of my feelings were insane, and I knew I hadn't ever felt this way about anyone else in my life.

  Therefore, Peter became the one man who could leave *me*- making me hurt forever when he left.

*****

By 2:00 in the afternoon after deciding to go for a walk through the village, I eventually asked Peter to close his eyes, which made him laugh at me and my ridiculousness as I ran from my bed in just my underwear for a quick shower.
While I showered, re-shaved, and cleaned the arousal from my body, I smiled like a loser the whole time. Even when I told myself I was smiling like a loser, a little giggled bubbled up at my continuous smiling. I was a complete moron for Peter, and I didn't seem able to shut off the feelings or the giddiness he provoked in me.

So an hour later we walked to the village again, and eventually stopped for dinner at Murphy's. We ordered greasy food, even as I mentioned I was going to get fat, and we drank coffee to warm us from the winter weather outside.
We were calm and relaxed, and smiley, and totally about each other, even in our silences.
However, once we started eating Peter told me quite abruptly before I had finished my cheeseburger that he had to go. He stood, looked around the pub from our booth, and said he had to leave.
In my shock, I quickly wondered what I had done wrong, but he leaned in and kissed my lips, and stopped looking around to just stare at me intensely. I was so confused by the whole situation, I desperately wanted to know what was wrong.
"I'll meet you back at your apartment by 7:00, okay?" He begged me.
"Okay, but what happened? Why do you have to go?" I begged back.
"Nothing. I just forgot I had something to do, but I want to see you soon. I'll be back by 7:00. Just trust me, okay?"
"Okay," I relented.
Even though Peter was smiling at me I could still see distress or something on his face. He looked around the pub again, and then reached for his wallet but I stopped him. I could pay for our burgers and fries, and I didn't want him to think I was taking advantage of him so I insisted on paying.
"I'll see you soon, Sophie," he smiled, but again he looked around the pub like he was afraid of something.
His behavior was so weird, I suddenly felt uncomfortable with him. I was uncomfortable and honestly didn't want him to stay with me any longer, at least not then. He was acting strange and almost paranoid,

which was making me feel a little paranoid as well. But just as quickly as his mood changed, he left with the promise to see me in 2 hours.

After he left, I finished my burger quickly and paid, leaving the pub to walk home alone. I couldn't stop thinking about Peter's strange behavior when he left me, but eventually I decided to forget it. Yes, it was weird, but I didn't know him well enough to know if he was always that way, so I let it go.

Walking home I stopped in Pandora's again, and decided to look for a Christmas gift for Peter. I knew we were new, and I knew gifts were a little too soon, but Christmas was on Friday and I didn't want to not get him something, so I looked around until I found the perfect gift.
Browsing around I found another set of candle holders just like the ones I had bought the weekend before which Peter had loved as well. They were the same, but slightly different and the person on each candle holder looked very similar to me and Peter. They were similar, but the one difference from my own set which I knew he would love was the female had green eyes and blond hair. They were beautiful blown glass candle holders with the image of a brown haired man and a blond woman inside, and they were lovely.
Choosing silver, vanilla scented taper candles to match was a perfect choice. I loved them, and I truly thought they were the perfect gift for him because Peter would know I was thinking about him over Christmas.
He would know I was thinking about him, he just wouldn't know I was thinking about him like the obsessive, falling in love with him way too quickly psycho I was actually becoming.

*****

When I returned home with my gifts, I immediately called Steven, the little shit. And after only one ring he answered as I knew he would which made me smile.
"I'm sorry, Soph! Fuck! I really didn't mean to cock-block-"
"Ewwww..."
"I didn't even think for a second that he might be there. Sorry. Honestly, I was just so hammered I needed to crash on your couch so I

didn't think. Actually, I was too drunk to think. Was he mad?"

"Not really about you stopping by PISSED OUT OF YOUR HEAD. But the *creepy notebook guy* comment sucked."

"*Fuck.* Sorry. I didn't mean it bad-"

"No, 'cause that would ever sound like a good thing to say," I argued.

"I know. Should I talk to him?" Steven offered.

"God, no! We're fine. We actually kissed and made up," I grinned. "And we spent the day together, and he's coming back in a half hour, so it's all good. Just please don't do that again, okay?"

"What? Come over hammered to crash at my sister's? Or call my sister's boyfriend creepy?"

"Both. Seriously, Steven, I really like Peter and I don't want anything to screw it up, okay?"

"Okay. Sorry, Soph. Are you going to mom and dad's tomorrow?"

"Could I get out of it if I tried?"

"No. Why don't you bring Peter?"

"Nope. Way too soon. I don't want him to think I'm that into him yet. I want to play this one cool because he's kind of awesome."

"But you shouldn't play games then, Soph. Not if you really like him."

"I'm not playing games, I'm just not going to be the first to ask for things. I don't want to scare him away, and he makes me want to ask for things which is weird for me. I-" But I couldn't really explain what I was thinking or feeling, even to Steven. I couldn't even understand it myself.

"It's different when you feel something, isn't it? I know how you are with men, kind of standoffish, which usually draws them in, but then you're not happy and you end it. So maybe do this one different. Maybe be honest and not so, like ice-queenish, or something."

"Ice Queenish?" I laughed.

"I'm not lecturing or criticizing. I just know you, so I'm trying to help," he defended, and I knew he was.

"I'll try. But it's just not something I'm used to. I don't like putting myself out there."

"Nobody does. And he's probably feeling the same way, right? So maybe give in a little this time and see what happens. And yes, I totally sound like the smarter, more mature twin right now, but don't freak out about it, kay?"

Laughing, that was exactly what I had been thinking. Steven never gave the good advice, I did, and Steven never guided me either, I guided him. So this was also new for me. My head was so full of sudden changes, and I didn't know if I liked any of them, even though I felt happy, too.

"I gotta go. I'll see you tomorrow."

"Have a good night, Soph. And ah... is his car really as pink as I remember?" He questioned with a grin I could actually hear.

"Yup. Like Barbie pink," I laughed.

"Wow. He is very, *very* secure in his manhood. Good for him," he laughed before hanging up.

CHAPTER 10

Thinking about Peter while I waited for his arrival, I decided I was going to be better with him. I would try to share my thoughts, and I would try to open up to him a little more. Peter was a sensual, intellectual man, and I figured he was probably used to women who knew their bodies, and knew their emotions, and I wanted to be like that with him. Actually, *he* made me want to be like that for him. So I decided I would try to be.

20 minutes after hanging up with Steven, Peter arrived 5 minutes late but I didn't let his lateness affect my mood. Opening up the door, I was immediately assaulted by Peter and a kiss. Pushing me against the little doorway nook, he kicked the door closed with his foot even as he held my face to him and kissed the impatience right out of me.
I was then lead to my bedroom by my hand, until he pushed me into the middle of my bed on my stomach and proceeded to empty a little sack beside me.
"I'm going to massage your back with some essential oils that are sensual and exotic. I have real jasmine oil blended into a balm I made that costs a fortune but is so worth it. I also added a little rose and bergamot to heighten your senses," he said as he pulled my sweater from my body and removed my bra.
Everything had just moved so quickly from sitting on my couch waiting for him, to being half naked on my bed with Peter sitting on my ass, I felt like I was spinning.
Then he began massaging me and 10 minutes later I felt everything fade from my body and my thoughts. I moaned when I could no longer hold it in, and I squirmed when he touched me in a way that required me to move. I was mindless except for the one thought repeating itself over and over in my brain, *God, I want you.*
After another few minutes, Peter slipped his hands under my waist and unzipped my jeans. Pulling, he took my panties with him, and I was grateful that it was winter and the night had already darkened my room. But Peter went back into his bag again and pulled out a wide pillar candle to light on my bedside table.
Naturally, the candle gave off enough light to make me insecure of my

nudity, but before I could react, Peter whispered, "You're stunning by candlelight, Sophie," and I stopped panicking.

Peter began massaging my butt and thighs, slowly working his way down my body. He massaged me in silence until I was so relaxed I couldn't move anymore by choice.

"Close your eyes, baby," he spoke softly, and I did. "I want you to only focus your thoughts on what I'm saying and where I'm touching. Picture your calves right now. Feel my hands on them, and imagine me soothing all your muscles."

So I did as he told me, and unbelievably I could almost envision my own calves loosing up as they began to feel lighter in my skin.

"Feel me massaging your thighs. Feel their heaviness fading away," he whispered again, and I did feel it. He massaged in long strokes from the back of my knees up to the top of my thighs, never moving higher, and never stopping except to quickly add more delicious balm to his hands.

"Open your legs for me, Sophie," he spoke gently. And without thought I again did as he told me.

Pushing my left thigh out sideways, I opened myself to him totally. But he didn't move higher, he just massaged the inside of my thighs to my relief *and* disappointment.

When he snaked his arm between my legs with his hand on my stomach, Peter slowly flipped me to my back. Surprised by the movement but too relaxed to fight, I allowed my body to be manipulated by him, even as he moved his arm from between my legs.

And then he massaged my arms down to my palms. Again, with the same message; I was told to feel my arms growing lighter, which they did, and amazingly, I soon felt limp and boneless. I felt like I was floating around my room, no longer actually lying on my bed.

After a few minutes and adding more cream, Peter made a long sweeping motion from my shoulders, down my breasts, which made me gasp, until he reached my lower stomach. Over and over he swept down my torso, never stopping on my nipples which had pebbled, nor lower than my stomach which I wanted.

He was slow and methodical, and I eventually experienced the same sinking away sensation the rest of my body felt. I was with him I knew, but I felt far away and utterly removed from my body.

"Feel me touch you, Sophie," he whispered as his mouth closed over my left nipple.

Drawing my nipple in slowly, he continued to sweep his right hand down my torso, moving slightly lower than each time before. He suckled me, and blew air across the dampness on my nipple, while gently touching the top of my vagina with rhythmic movements meant to relax.

Opening me up slowly with his fingers, I felt him touch me as he changed to my right side. Pulling my nipple into his mouth, I felt the soft sucking sensation from my breast move lower to my abdomen as I found myself breathing heavier than I had ever before in my life.

"Do you feel your body, Sophie?"

"Yes..." I whispered.

"What do you feel?" He asked quietly while continuing to touch my body softly.

"I feel a pull inside me. I feel heaviness and weightlessness too. I feel aroused and comfortable, and I don't know- I feel something inside me," I moaned with my eyes closed as he slipped a finger inside me.

"Breathe, Sophie. Feel your body craving this intimacy. Feel your body giving you the moisture needed for me to enter you. Feel your clit throbbing, and your vaginal walls clenching around me as I enter you with my fingers," he whispered against my lips before he kissed me again.

I remember feeling everything in that moment. Every word he spoke felt like everything happening to me at once. He was playing my body and describing it to me perfectly.

I was so aroused, my body starting moving against him. I kissed him harder and I raised my numb arms around his shoulders to draw him deeper into me. When I moaned unconsciously, I knew I had never wanted anyone so badly in my life, until he abruptly stopped.

Peter whispered, "Keep your eyes closed, and feel your body's needs," even as he stopped touching me, until moments later he was back touching me again.

He must have removed his clothing while I was envisioning my body because he was suddenly back, lying between my legs, as he kissed me and slowly entered my body with his own.

Entering me slowly, Peter moved in a carefree motion without speaking. He just kissed me and rocked inside my body for hours it seemed.

Pulling out of me some time later, Peter crawled down my body and again took me with his mouth and fingers, with more power and urgency then before. He touched me and impaled me until I felt everything inside me change.

"Feel your body, Sophie," he spoke inside me.

With his soft words all around me I felt my dampness, and my swollen insides and my need clawing at me. I felt his fingers moving inside me, and I felt his tongue teasing me. I felt everything he did to me with such awareness, my arousal quickly climbed.

"Please..." I heard myself beg even as he quickened his movements for me.

Peter continued pleasuring me and I knew I was speaking and I knew I was begging. I knew I was moving, and I knew I was trying. I knew everything but I could make no sense of any of it. All I knew was I was being destroyed from the inside out and I needed Peter to save me.

When he again entered me slowly, while continuing the assault on my clit, I finally found myself edge into and past my release. With a guttural moan, and a twist of my spine, I tried to throw him off me. I tried to move him away from the intensity of my body. I tried to get away from everything he did to me, but he wouldn't let me go.

Still deep inside me, Peter grabbed me up by my shoulders and crushed me to his chest as he flipped us to his back. He moved us and I found myself crying.

I was suddenly crying hard, and I hated the confusion and desperation I felt in that moment. I hated everything in that moment.

"I don't know what's wrong..." I finally choked in the silence around us.

"It's okay, Sophie. I think this is just a post-orgasm release. You're over sensitized and emotional from coming and from the intensity of the physical events proceeding it. I had you very emotionally engaged in the moment you released, so you're just dropping. It'll pass soon though if you don't fight it."

"I've never felt like this before," I admitted on a rush.

"Good..." He smiled as he kissed my forehead. "I make some pretty good herbal creams and blended oils, huh?"

"I don't think it was the cream. I think it was you," I admitted sounding sad.

Thankfully, Peter didn't reply to my words, though he did hold me a little tighter and he did kiss my forehead once again as we lay in silence.

After a few minutes though I found the silence was bothering me. My tears had stopped and I was overcome with the sudden need to flee from him. So I told him I needed a shower, and before he could reply I simply pulled myself from his arms and raced for my bathroom.

Once inside the warm shower I really cried. I don't know why, maybe exactly as he said. Maybe that reaction was common with some women, and maybe it was even normal. But it wasn't for me.
I felt weak, and almost damaged after being with him like that. I felt like the person I was just 2 weeks ago was fading away and I hated the feeling in my chest. It was sadness and fear, I knew. But I couldn't stop the feelings from taking me over, even as I cried in the shower so Peter wouldn't see me so weak and lost because of him.

When the shower curtain was opened and I was still sitting on the tub floor crying, my humiliation felt so complete I immediately went into defensive mode.
Standing quickly, I put my face under the water to hide my tears and I turned to Peter with a fake smile.
"Want to join me?" I asked with a confidence I wasn't feeling at all.
"Sophie, please don't run from me. Talk to me," he said looking sad himself.
"I'm not running, I just wanted to freshen up," I lied again as I reached for his semi-erect penis. Pulling him by his body, he stepped into the shower with me as I took him into a deep kiss.
Peter moaned into my mouth, as I gave him the best hand-job I could manage in the close space of the shower. Turning him, I pushed him against the wall, and fell to my knees for a little payback, which was exactly how I felt.
I wanted to make him feel as out of control as he had made me feel. I didn't want all that romantic, loving shit. I wanted normal sex without all the emotional trappings. That's what I tried to do, but Peter stopped my attempt by lifting me back up by my arms.
"I don't need a blow job, Sophie. I need to be inside you, *with* you," he said while turning me to lean against the wall.
"I don't have any condoms," I realized suddenly.
"I'll pull out,"
"But what if-"
"Do you trust me?" He asked staring at me hard.
"I guess. But I can't have an accident," I pleaded.

"Neither can I," he replied.

So I threw caution to the wind, and chose to forget who I was. I was irresponsible for the first time in my 24 years. I knew this had the potential to be tragically life-altering, and yet I relented for some reason I couldn't understand.

I had never had sex without a condom. Not with my 3 1/2 men before Peter, and never in my wildest dreams. I just didn't live on the edge like that. However, I suddenly found myself willing to risk everything with this man, and that made me fear him even more.

After another kiss, I allowed him to wrap my left leg around his hip, and then I allowed him to raise my right leg around him. I let him raise my arms to circle his neck, and I allowed him to slowly enter me. I allowed him to move inside me slowly with no emotion showing on my face, because I felt nothing but fear and unhappiness all around me.

When Peter tried to touch my body, I pulled his hand away and whispered, "I'm too sensitive," which was true and not. But when he looked at me like he knew I had emotionally run away and he tried to pull my legs from his waist so he could stop, I stopped his retreat.

I needed to have sex and I needed to be screwed. I needed what I had always known so I could feel more like myself again.

Clenching and grinding, arching and moaning, I suddenly moved hard and fast against Peter. Pulling at him until I forced him to speed up his own movements I looked away from him as he got closer to his release.

And eventually when he forced my legs from his hips to stand, he came on my stomach like he promised. He came on me instead of in me and the fear faded slightly. After he came on my stomach a kind of relief took over, and I could finally breathe again.

"I'm going to go," Peter said sadly and my breath left me on a gasp.
"Why?" I asked too loudly.
"I think we need a little break from each other, that's all."
"I don't need a break from you," I heard myself practically beg.
"I think you do, Sophie. You're not even looking at me the same as you did earlier. You have this look on your face like I'm some kind of monster who's going to hurt you. I just can't tell if your fear is physical or emotional-"

"It's emotional," I said shocking us both.
"Why? Talk to me," he asked pushing my wet hair from my cheek.
"You scare me."
"Why?"
"I'm used to men falling in love with me, but with you I think it'll be the other way around and I don't like that. I feel like you'll use it to hurt me later or something. I'm just not used to feeling something for a man that I couldn't control, and you make me feel very out of control, which I hate."
"So we'll talk when you feel this way, and I'll assure you again and again that I'm not looking to hurt you. When you feel out of control talk to me, and I'll try to help. But you have to talk to me, Sophie. Because that closed off, fucking me without emotion thing you just did to me won't work. I'll walk away if I feel like you dislike me and this relationship enough to close down like that."
"I wasn't-" But he cut me off and continued.
"Fucking because you wanted to be fucked, while you looked at me like I was a monster, when I've done nothing to deserve it, hurt me, Sophie. I had just spent an emotionally charged, sexy as hell evening with you, bringing you to orgasm after only 2 attempts- not 3- in case you didn't realize, which made me feel very close to you, and then you did this thing- this angry fucking thing, and I feel let down by you. Remembering our first time together like that is going to haunt me."
"I'm sorry, I just freaked out."
"I know you did. We experienced a form of intimacy not many couples experience, but you shut down instead of opening up to me. I would have held you all night and spoke to you until you found yourself secure again, but you didn't let me," he moaned.
Feeling Peter's upset, I was stunned by my reality in that moment. Looking at him, I suddenly found myself burst out laughing.
"Do you even realize what you sound like? You're not real! Peter, you're good looking, normal-ish, with a job, and a mortgage, and a degree, and a small business, but you speak like some character out of a romance novel. You're just too much for someone like me. You don't even sound real, and I keep waiting for you to be a serial killer or something," I said still laughing.
"Well, I'm no serial killer, and I'm definitely real. Yes, I may seem more emotionally in-tuned to women than most men, but I grew up with 2 sisters I love, who I watched get their hearts broken over and over, so I listened to them tell me everything the men did to them, and I slowly

grew into a man who was more aware of women and their needs than other men. Plus, my dad cheated on my mom once and I know how low her self-esteem plummeted after the affair, well after they got back together. So I decided I wasn't going to be an asshole like that. But that's the only thing weird about me, Sophie. I don't want to be an asshole, and I won't change or apologize for it because you have hang-ups, or feel more secure with a typical guy."

"I'm sorry. I don't want that. But I will freak out sometimes, and you'll have to be patient with me."

"I can be patient. But only if you let me know what's going on so I'm not left wondering what the hell is going on between us. Because honestly Sophie, I feel this crazy pull for you, too. It's heavy, and intense, and all-consuming for me as well. I really like you, and I want to get to the place where I can adore you, just like you want to be."

"Oh... *See!* That's what I'm talking about," I laughed. "Jesus *Christ*, Peter. No guy talks like that. Can't you just be normal so I can chill out and stop wanting you so much?"

"Sure I can," he grinned. "Hey, Bitch. Get in the kitchen and make me a snack. I'm fucking starving," he burst out laughing as I smacked his arm.

"Close. Just leave out the bitch next time," I grinned.

"Okay. Can we get out of here so you can make me that snack? I'm starving."

"Okay..." I said with a gentle kiss and relief coursing through me.

A half hour later Peter and I were snuggled on the couch, me in my pj's and him in just his jeans eating grilled cheese sandwiches with tomato soup, which was his favorite he told me, of course. Because we couldn't even disagree about soup.

Sitting with Peter, I knew that night he was everything I had ever wanted from a man. I knew it and he proved it to me by sleeping beside me, talking all night, but never again attempting sex with me. He wanted to hold me only, he said, because he was worried I was a little too *emotionally fragile* for more sex after the night's earlier events. Instead, he slept beside me and warmed me all night in his arms.

The following morning when he returned after running to the cafe down the street for our coffee, we talked a little more and planned out our week. He had to work until Wednesday and I had to work until Friday at 3:00 on Christmas Eve, so he insisted he would see me right after work on Friday before the crazy holiday stuff started.

Then he left me at 11:00 Sunday morning. After 40 hours together, give or take, he actually left me to return to the real world.

He kissed me good bye at the door and told me he'd miss me. He said he'd try to stop by in the mornings because he didn't think he could go until Friday without seeing me. And when he admitted he couldn't go that long without seeing me I was instantly calmed because I had a bad feeling I was going to be in knots if I didn't see him for 5 days myself.

Later that day I drove to my parents' house with a perma-smile and explained Peter over dinner. I told them everything, shy of exact sexual details, but I did explain how amazing he was for me sexually, how I freaked out and acted like a psycho, and how he talked me back off the ledge.

My parents were supportive and understanding, and even described a little about their early days and the intensity they had for each other in their beginning as a couple.

Throughout our conversation Steven stayed somewhat quiet, but not overly so, until he told me when I was finished talking about me and Peter that he was a little jealous. He said his tramp from 2 nights before hadn't called him and he felt totally used which cracked me and my mom up.

Steven had been heard to say, 'love em and leave em' in the past, so he received no sympathy from my parents and I when he was loved and left.

After dinner while I waited for my one load of laundry to dry- the tradeoff for giving up my Sunday late afternoon for my mom- I explained my new job in detail. I told them everything I felt; my fears and my excitement over my new career. I even admitted to being scared shitless for the next few days that I was alone without Carole to guide and train me. However, I felt better when my dad pointed out that the last 2 weeks of the holidays were typically quiet and festive in an office setting, so I was starting as office manager at a good time to get my feet wet without being too overwhelmed.

When I finally left at 8:00, I felt remarkably better about everything. I was still thinking about Peter way too often in my opinion, but I listened when my parents said it was normal to be obsessed at the beginning of a new relationship until the infatuation wore off and you could settle into just loving your partner.

I was told to enjoy myself and not to let one of my 2 huge new events eclipse the other, but rather to try to balance them equally.

When I eventually walked into my apartment, I could still smell Peter's scents and lotion in my bedroom making me quickly realize I loved the smell of Jasmine. I had never really known it before him, but I couldn't imagine the rest of my life without the smell of it reminding me of Peter.

I also realized I had a message on my machine and I dove for it with the hope that I would hear his voice again before I went to bed.

"Hi Sophie. I'm going into work, but I wanted you to know I had a beautiful time with you- freak outs and all. I think you are amazing, and I look forward to knowing all of you. Sleep well... I'll see you soon."

And that was my night. Bouncing around my home, happily cleaning and tidying up everything to start my week off perfectly, thinking about Peter nonstop, while picturing the next time we would be together again.

CHAPTER 11

After making it through my first week as Office Manager with only 3 *what the hell do I do* desperate phone calls to Carole, I was done. Mentally, I was a vegetable, and physically, I was exhausted.
At the end of the day the staff invited me for a round of drinks to celebrate, but I declined with the excuse of last minute *oh shit* gifts I still needed to buy quickly.
I couldn't wait to see Peter, and I couldn't wait to get home. He and I had managed to speak at least once every day, and he had brought me coffee on Tuesday and Wednesday morning, but it wasn't the same.
The physical craving I had for him was like a slow torture. Every time I got my craving and need for him in check, we would speak on the phone or see each other briefly, and the yearning for him increased again.
I was messed up over him and I knew it. But we both were going to be off the following week, and Peter told me he was going to monopolize *all* my time over Christmas, which I desperately wanted.

When I finally made it home, fighting a ridiculous amount of traffic for a Christmas Eve, I walked into my building to a waiting Peter. Leaning against my door, he looked so good and I wanted to be hugged so badly I nearly wept with the need I had for him.
"What's wrong, Sophie?" He asked stepping toward me.
"Nothing at all," I smiled. "I just really need a Peter hug right now," I breathed even as he pulled me into his arms.
So dropping my purse and my satchel filled with notes, I absorbed Peter into my skin. From his scent to his warmth, I took everything I could from him in that moment.
"You feel so good, Peter," I whispered into his neck.
"What's wrong, baby?"
"Just a long week, and I missed you."
"I missed you, too. Let's go inside."
"Okay..." I whispered as I lifted my purse and searched for my keys.
Once inside, Peter stooped again to unzip my knee high boots, pulling them from me before removing my coat as well. Exhaling, I watched him care for me in his way, and silently, I loved everything about that

moment with him. He was like a sort of homecoming for me from my long week of career firsts.

Pulling me to the couch, he again massaged my feet like the most caring man I had ever known. Sinking further into the couch I watched him watching me until I couldn't handle the stupid grinning anymore.

"I have something for you, but I'm too tired to get it."

"Oh, yeah? I have something for you that I'd love to give you. Do you want it now?"

"Yes, please," I grinned as I sat up higher on the couch.

But when he tried to hand me my gift from his coat pocket, I panicked. "No! I want you to go first in case yours is better than mine!" I yelled as I jumped off the couch and ran for my bedroom closet.

Laughing at me, Peter asked, "Is this a competition?"

"Of course," I yelled back from my room. "It's the first real event gift, so I have to win."

"What about 'it's better to give than to receive...'"

"Oh, *please*. Nobody thinks like that. It's always better to receive an awesome gift," I smirked again as I entered my living room. "Here. Open it," I said handing him my gift.

Laughing at my seriousness, Peter slowly opened my gift for him. "But you loved these," he said looking at my mantel. "Oh! You found another set?"

"Yes, but they're a little different. Look at her."

"Ah, green eyes... I love them, Sophie. And the candles smell delicious. Thank you..." he said leaning in for a quick kiss while handing me my gift.

Tearing it open, I could tell it was a book, but, "Oh my god!" I was stunned. Opening the cover, I couldn't believe it was signed. "Where did you get this?" I asked still stunned by the signed copy of Leonard Cohen's novel Beautiful Losers.

"eBay," he smirked.

"When?"

"Um, right after we had lunch the first time. You told me you loved that book of his, so I looked and I actually found a signed copy. It's in really good condition, and they promised I'd have it by Christmas. It only arrived yesterday though, so I was a little panicked I wouldn't have it in time. But it's here now, so there you go," he smiled proudly.

Looking at the book, my heart was pounding. I wasn't going to lie and say I'm all into poetry, because I'm not. But there was always something about Beautiful Losers that I loved. I had a generic copy of the book, but holding a signed 1st edition was so amazing, I couldn't stop staring at it.

"Peter... It's just... I love it and I can't believe you would do something so thoughtful for me. This is the best present- the most thoughtful gift I've ever received. Honestly, I'm just... I love it," I choked. Not that I would cry over a book, but if anything could make me cry it would be Peter and his thoughtful ways.

"I'm glad you like it."

"I can't *wait* to show Steven. He's gonna freak out."

"He likes it, too?" Peter asked with a very satisfied smile.

"A little, but it's just such an awesome gift, he's going to be totally jealous," I grinned as I began crawling to him.

Straddling his legs, I took Peter's face in my hands, and I kissed him. I kissed him for the gift, and I kissed him because he kind of *was* a gift to me.

"I wish we had more time together," I whispered against his lips.

"Me, too. But we have all next week," he kissed me back.

"I just want to lay with you right now and breathe you in..." I heard myself say a little surprised by my own sentimentality. I was never sappy, but that's how I felt around Peter- sappy.

"I'll see you first thing Sunday morning. I'll come over early with coffee with a chocolate shot of course," he grinned.

"Ha! You do love me..." I smiled, and then jolted.

What the hell?! It was just an expression! But the look on his face, and the way my stomach dropped said more than anything I did by mistake.

I knew I had totally screwed up. But I meant it innocently. I was just like ha ha, you love me for the chocolate *only* and it didn't matter. But I didn't know how to get out of it, and Peter looked scared of me or something for the first time.

"It was just an expression Peter, I swear. I know you don't love me. I mean how could you? We barely know each other, and love takes time, and I know you don't love me. I was just saying because of the coffee." But I couldn't stop babbling. "I know you don't love me, I just meant it like funny you love me 'cause of the chocolate shot. I know, and I don't love you either," which made me back-peddle even more. "*Not* that I couldn't love you because I might, like one day. But..."

Holy shit! I was horribly aware that if silence could actually strangle someone, I would've had a garrote wrapped around my throat at that very moment. Jesus, there was no air, and no way to get out of the mess I had accidentally created. And I was miserable.

"I know what you meant, Sophie. Relax. It's all good," Peter said moving me from his lap while kissing my lips quickly to ease the burn of his rejection, I think. "What time do you have to be at your parents?" He asked like we were fine, which we clearly weren't.

"5:30."

"Well, I should let you get ready. It's already nearly 4:30, and I'm sure you want to freshen up," he said moving toward my front door.

"Peter..."

"We're fine, Sophie. I'll call you later to wish you a Merry Christmas, okay?"

Obviously we weren't fine though, and I was scared of him leaving, but annoyed, too. I felt like he was being a totally oversensitive idiot. I mean, of course I didn't mean LOVE. We hadn't even been dating, or whatever, for 2 weeks at that point.

"Yup. I'll talk to you later," I heard myself close down. I actually heard it as I spoke. I was sad and pissed off, and I couldn't hide my upset or disappointment in his behavior.

"Merry Christmas. Have a great night, Sophie."

"You, too," I said while standing to lock the door behind him.

I had the best gift ever followed by the saddest departure ever. I was a little shell-shocked by the turn of events; completely numb but shaky at the same time. So I decided, screw it.

Getting ready, I wore a beautiful red dress with matching black jacket, and a sexy pair of plaid high heels. I put my hair up in a cute bun, and darkened my make-up slightly. I made myself look better than I felt. I made myself look like the Sophie of only a few weeks ago, even though I felt anything but.

Making sure all my gifts were ready at the front door in large travel bags, I took one last look around, ignoring the amazing book screaming at me from the coffee table, then I left for the comforting feel of my parents and their huge Christmas Eve party.

*****

When I arrived at the party there were already a dozen people there and the Christmas music was playing and my mom was running around laughing with her apron on, and my dad was pouring drinks and Steven was even there before I was helping pour drinks with my dad.

A car had pulled up behind me, and as I turned while removing my own coat, the door opened to my parent's friends, Bill and Carey with loud calls of Merry Christmas, as my mom ran for the door.

Hugging me quickly, I was nearly pushed out of the way by my mom as she grabbed for the tray of deviled eggs Carey held in her hands. And then it seemed like the rest of the onslaught began as more and more people arrived within minutes.

There was a kind of awesome chaos all around me and I was distracted by everything everywhere. It seemed like within only 10 minutes, people stood everywhere and voices could be heard from every corner of the house.

I made my way to my dad and brother and was pulled into a big hug by my dad, lasting much longer than my mom's grab and toss hug. And when he finally let me go, he kissed my head and told me I looked as beautiful as always. He poured me my favorite drink- a tequila sunrise, and then he began the 'Sophie is the greatest' speech to all aunts, uncles, and family friends within hearing distance.

Subsequently, I was asked endless questions about my new job, and I answered them all with a kind of excitement I hadn't felt the past week. I even admitted to feeling overwhelmed which was quickly blown off by everyone as normal.

The whole conversation around the bar revolved around me for a good 20 minutes, until Steven finally saved me. Faking a request from my mom, Steven and I walked away, but not before he quickly made me another drink.

When we finally snuck upstairs to breathe in my room, Steven opened my window, sat on the window seat hanging half outside, and lit a smoke.

"What's wrong, Soph?"

"Nothing... Why?"

"That's your power dress," he said carefully.

"No. It's a red Christmas dress," I said confused.

"No, it isn't. You have worn that dress only a few times that I've ever seen and it's always because of something intense, like when we went to the summer family party right after you broke up with Joseph, or that time you went to that interview you knew you were too unqualified to get."

"Honestly, I have NO idea what you're talking about." And I really didn't. I knew myself, and I knew I didn't have weird hang-ups like that.

"Okay. Well, you do. I know it as your twin," he grinned. "That's like a lucky dress, or a power dress or something."

"I don't think so, but I'll certainly watch when I want to wear it next time." I really would watch too, because Steven made me feel totally self-conscious suddenly.

"How's the job?" He asked blowing more smoke out the window.

"Good."

"How's Peter?"

"Good," I replied easily.

"Ha! Another tell. You looked right in my eyes when you said good about Peter."

"We're talking, so of course I looked at you," I argued.

"Nope, you don't. Usually when you go to answer a question, you think for a split second, looking away from the person, then you look at them to give the answer. You always think before you speak, which is probably why you never put your foot in your mouth like I do. But you just stared right at me and said Peter's good, which means he isn't. So tell me what's wrong," he smiled knowing he totally had me. The bastard.

"I freaked him out... I said 'you do love me'," I quoted, "about chocolate in my coffee, which was a totally innocent thing to say, but from the look on his face and the way I felt afterward it didn't go over as totally innocent, even after I explained it was. So that's it. I freaked him out which is usually the other way around for me, and though he said he'd see me soon I felt like I damaged something, and I don't want to. Can I be honest?" I looked at my brother looking at me with so much love, I wanted to hug him.

"Always," he smiled.

"I feel like I'm falling in love with him, which is crazy and way too soon, but it's true. He is by far the only man I have *ever* felt like this about, and of course it scares me, but I don't like it either. I'm happy when I'm with him, but I feel miserable when I'm not, and I'm not that kind of girl. Well, *you* know. I'm not flighty and romantic, or sappy, but I am with him. Or I am in my head, and once in a while with him out loud, which he wants.

He says he wants to know everything I think, and everything I am, but when I kind of get sappy, or tell him something personal it makes me feel like shit, or scared, or even pissed off at him sometimes. And it's weird," I finally exhaled.

"So what's-"

But cutting him off I went for broke. "Guess what he bought me for Christmas?"

"I don't know," he shook his head.

"Guess! Never mind. He bought me a 1st edition, *signed* Leonard Cohen Beautiful Losers novel."

"Fuck off."

"I'm not kidding. It was such an amazing gift, and he bought it on eBay, like right after we met for lunch that very first Sunday- not even 2 weeks ago, and see? What the hell am I supposed to do with that?"

"Thank him with a blow-"

"*Ewww*... Don't go there, Steven! You're my brother! Gross." I said as he laughed at me. "Anyway, do you see how I could fall in love with him? Who does that? And he talks so weird, not like any guy I've ever met before. And he's super romantic, and like sensual, and sexy and like a beautiful lover kind of guy, and I hate it, but not really..."

"You really need to chill out, Soph. If he's as romantic and 'sensual,'" he said with quotes, "as you think, then he probably wants to hear how you feel about him. So what if you have feelings for him unlike what you've ever had before? You were never really happy with them anyway. Seriously. Just chill out. You thinking this much about your feelings is making you a psycho, and you're gonna scare him away with your thinking probably more than by how you actually feel. So just enjoy it," he said while sitting beside me on my bed.

Grabbing Steven in a tight side hug, I exhaled the tension of the 'you love me' slip.

"We should go back downstairs before mom kills us. Plus, I need a dozen or more drinks," I grinned.

"Me too... Being the voice of reason between us is fucking awful," he said as I burst out laughing.

So 3 hours later, and like 10+ drinks later, I was smashed. Totally, absolutely, completely polluted. And everyone knew it 'cause, well, I fell into the tree once, and I laughed like a fool when I spilled a drink down the front of my dress.

At one point Steven even brought me a plate filled with breads and crackers to absorb the alcohol, and my dad casually cut me off at the bar. Even my mom kept watching me from every single position in the living room she could see me from while she entertained all the other guests.

But by 10:00 I acted like a stupid, immature, 24 year old drunk moron, and sadly I drunk-dialed Peter.

"Hello?"
"Hi, Peter... I'm hammered just so you know, so nothing I say can be held against me right now or after this drunk-dial, okay?"
"Okay," he said sounding worried.
"I like you. A. Lot. You freak me out because you're awesome, but I. Don't. Love. You. Okay?"
"Okay. Where are you, Sophie?"
"At my parents'. In a party."
"Are you safe, baby?"
"Yes. Why?"
"I just want to make sure you're safe. Are you staying there tonight?"
"Problably." I knew I had to hang up. "I'm sorry. That's all I wanted to say. Merry Christmas, Peter. I'm sorry. I think I'll be embarrassed tomorrow, but I wanted you to know. I'm falling- ugh- but I don't love you. But you're awesome. Okay? And I love my present. And you totally win. Yours was way better than mine. Oh! When's your birthday?"
"July 4th," he laughed.
"Shit! Mine's February 28th, or March 1st, depending on the best night to have a party 'cause Steven and I were leap year babies. But you'll get to get me another present before I get you one, so you'll win again. IF we're still dating then. Crap! Sorry. *See?* I can't relax like Steven said about you, and I can't tell you stuff like you want me to because than I feel stupid. Sorry. Holy shit! I'm gonna die tomorrow. Remember, this doesn't count. I have to go."
"Why did you freak out when you said that to me earlier?" Peter asked seriously, and I panicked again.
"I didn't freak out. *You* did. You had a weird *oh no* face and you looked like I scared you or something. But I didn't mean it like that."
"No, I didn't have an *oh no* face about what you said. I was stunned that you would say something like that to me because you never speak

like that, and you never act so carefree as to slip up when you speak."

"'Cause I *don't* slip up when I speak. And sometimes it's hard to talk to you."

"Why?" Peter asked sounding intense again.

"I don't know…"

"Sophie, I wish you didn't have to be drunk to talk to me…"

"I don't have to be drunk to talk to you, but it's easier."

"Which means you have to be drunk to talk to me."

"No it doesn't. It means when I'm drunk I can talk to you easier." Ha! Oh… "Don't laugh at me, and please don't hate me. I'm supposed to give you a thank you blow job for the book," I giggled.

"*Really?*" Peter asked sounding all sexy.

"Yup. So think about that."

"Oh, I will…" he practically moaned in my ear.

"Okay. I'm going to lie down, so sleep well. Merry Christmas, and don't be mad at me, okay?"

"I'm not mad at you. Merry Christmas, Sophie. And by the way, I think you're pretty awesome, too," he said.

"Really?" I begged.

"Yes. Go to sleep, baby. I'll talk to you tomorrow, okay?"

"I miss you…" I whispered when I hung up, which was true. I missed him so much I felt it deep in my heart.

But I hung up before I said anything else. And rolling over, I threw the phone on the floor as I felt myself passing out, even though I still had a big stupid smile on my face.

CHAPTER 12

The following morning, Christmas morning was a nightmare for me.
My mom woke me up LOUDLY, and my dad and Steven had zero sympathy for me as they stood in my doorway laughing at my mom bouncing on my bed.
Begging to die, my mother handed me coffee and told me to get my ass downstairs in 2 minutes or I was out of her will, making Steven the sole heir to their non-fortune. So after a few attempts, I finally stood up, swayed, and made it to the bathroom for a quick gag and teeth brushing.
After using the washroom and washing my face of nasty makeup, I grabbed a pair of my old sweats and changed out of my tequila stained dress before I practically hobbled downstairs with each movement mirroring the throbbing in my head.
Incidentally, tequila sunrises, though delicious going down, are quite notoriously deadly the morning after, and I was suffering the proof.
Crashing on the couch, I grabbed a throw blanket, curled up, and wished to god everyone quieted down. The Christmas carols were making my head explode, and the smell of breakfast was turning my stomach, but nobody cared.
"Why don't you love me?" I whispered to my parents. "I'm the good twin..." I moaned making them laugh at me.
"If you're old enough to get drunk, then you're old enough to suffer, Soph," my dad grinned while handing me Tylenol and a glass of orange juice.
"Thanks, Daddy," I whined while popping 3 Tylenols.
"Okay! Enough whining... Who's first?!" My mom cheered as we began.

45 minutes later, one garbage bag filled with ripped paper, and stomachs growling, we were done. I was pretty happy with my loot, too. I even liked a sweater my mom bought me, which was a first.
Afterward, Steven was testing out his new digital camera, my dad was reading the instructions to his new GPS, my mom was reading one of the new cook books my dad bought her, and I was figuring out my new laptop, which was hard with my much slower, hung-over brain.
We eventually made it to the kitchen where my mom had cooked bacon

and eggs earlier, leaving them in a heated dish, while my dad quickly made toast and waffles for everyone. And I ate against my better judgment what I was craving- syrup covered bacon on top of waffles, which was delicious.

After breakfast my hangover lessened slightly, but I needed a nap in my own bed. So gratefully after begging, my parents allowed me to leave the Christmas nightmare of hung-over exhaustion I was in, to meet them at 4:00 for the next festive round at my aunt's house.

Kissing and hugging my parent's goodbye, I thanked them for everything and told them I loved them. I also thanked them for not lecturing me about my drunken behavior the night before, to which Steven informed me I had passed out before it got too interesting.

When I finally arrived home I was thrilled to see a blue rose taped to my door. A blue rose greeted me and I allowed myself to think about Peter for the first time all morning.

Finally, I thought about him and it was with sadness and happiness, which was warped. I was sad that we were struggling, but I was also happy that he cared enough to bring me a rose. The rose made me think that he still cared, even if I was screwing up our semi-relationship with all my bullshit insecurity.

Curious, I did want to know if the rose came before or after my stupid drunk-dial, which made me nervous. But then I decided he lived in my neighborhood somewhere close, so if he was pissed about my behavior he probably would've come over and removed the rose in the night. Or that's what I told myself, so I didn't have to think about us ending before we even started.

Once inside, I dropped my bags on the couch and made my way to bed. I wanted a shower, but I wanted sleep more. My hangover was taking way too long to lift, and I was pretty sure only a little sleep could cure it. But after crawling in bed with a sigh, I suddenly thought of my answering machine, as I jumped right back out of bed, jarring my brain against my skull, but I didn't care. I had to be sure. And when I saw the blinking light I knew he had called me. I just knew it.

4 messages from friends later and one from Joseph wishing me a Merry Christmas, finally, Peter was the sixth.

"Hi Sophie... Merry Christmas. I'm not sure if you remember but you called me last night, and it was the funniest, most pathetic drunk-dial I've ever received. You were *in a party* and you *prob-lably* were staying at your parents' house, which I hope was true. I want you to know I'm not mad at you, and I'm not freaked out by your call. I hope you had fun, and I'm looking forward to seeing you soon. Hopefully tonight, because I can't wait til tomorrow morning to see you. I can't stop thinking about you either, Sophie, which is freaking *me* out, too. I'll talk to you soon. Merry Christmas."

After I listened to the message twice, I couldn't even describe the relief I felt. I laughed when he mocked me, and I felt all warm and excited when he admitted to being freaked out. I was excited again, and I wanted to make this work without acting like a psycho anymore.

I knew I was acting like an immature, scared idiot with Peter, so I was going to stop. I wanted him to want me, so I was going to stop being so afraid of how awesome he was, and I was going to give him the reason to want me in his life, like I wanted to be in his.

I realized I felt totally insecure with Peter because I had never known or dated anyone like him before. I was insecure with him, but I was going to try to stop.

I was never insecure in my real life; I was always fairly confident, though I didn't act arrogant or entitled. But with Peter, I realized he was making me insecure just by being himself. He was different, alternative, semi-hippy- semi-not, sexy, caring, and a man I was quickly falling for.

Peter was who I wanted to love, so I was going to open up to him and give him the reason to want to fall in love with me, too.

Before I was picked up by Steven for my Aunt Carla's, after a nap, shower, and feeling remarkably better, I decided to call Peter. I called him with anxious knots in my stomach but he didn't answer.

"Hi Peter... Sorry again for the drunk-dial. But that was another first for me, so you should feel privileged. I'm on my way to Christmas dinner, but I'll probably be home around 9-ish. I'd love to see you tonight as well. I hope you had a wonderful Christmas. Talk to you later."

I almost said I miss you, and I almost said I can't stop thinking about you, too, but I decided to show him later how I was feeling about him.

*****

When I arrived home 5 1/2 hours later after Steven drove me back, I was greeted by Peter at my door again.

With a happy, relieved, excited whoosh of breath, I looked at him for a second before walking to him. Smiling, I realized Peter looked so good, and he smelled so sexy, and he just felt so right standing at my door. Giving him a huge hug, I released all the tension I had created for myself with him, and I enjoyed the quiet moment between us in the hallway.

"I hope you don't mind me stopping by," he grinned with my body plastered all over his. But instead of my usual smartass comment, I told him the truth. I wanted him with me which made him hug me a little tighter.

When we eventually pulled apart and entered my apartment, I realized I was exhausted. Plopping on the couch with Peter beside me, I snuggled up and just breathed him in.

"Did you have turkey for dinner?"

"Yes, and everything else you could possibly think of. My Aunt has a very eclectic dinner selection for every nationality of every relative or in-law who attends," I moaned.

"You seem to be suffering tryptophan overload," he smiled as I nodded. "Plus, it's been a long day. Would you like to sleep, Sophie?"

"I'm so sorry, but I just feel so tired now with you. Oh, because you relax me, not because you're boring," I grinned as he laughed at me.

"Come on... Go clean up and I'll meet you in bed. I'm fairly tired myself. And we have a whole week to be awake with each other," he prompted by pulling me off the couch.

"Okay..."

After a bathroom break, a super quick shower, and pulling on my comfy pajamas I met a very naked Peter in my bed. Totally naked, lifting the comforter for me, I was suddenly very, *very* awake looking at him.

"You're naked," I grinned with a slight blush.

"I have no clothes here," he grinned back. "Why don't you pretend you don't have any clothes here either?" He winked.

"Um..." He could be cute, too.

As usual, I was in a moment of physical insecurity, but deciding to screw it, I pulled off my pajama top and stood beside my bed topless. Not quite able to pull off my bottoms with all the light in my room, I decided to reach for the bedside light just as Peter decided to reach for me.

Moving himself into a sitting position on the edge of the bed with his feet on the floor, Peter took my breasts into his hands as he kissed each nipple. Cupping me, his thumbs caressed my nipples as he stared at my eyes. Doing that intense, watch my reactions thing again, I smiled down at him because I was unable to tell him I loved his touch.

When he leaned forward and pushed my breasts together to flick his tongue on each nipple in turn, I found my hands raise to hold his head closer to me.

"I missed you, Sophie."

"Oh god... I missed you, too," I moaned as he sucked a nipple deeply making my back arch closer to him.

"I love your breasts. They're much fuller than your small body deserves. That's not really fair, is it?" He teased.

"Nope, it's not fair at all. I got a good rack for sure," I laughed. "But I think they were compensated by the cellulite on my ass, so..." But Peter took that moment to suck harder while gripping my ass closer with his hand.

Moaning in my room, he was doing things to me. He was making me aroused and pulling me closer to him. Emotionally, I wanted to just jump him and have a piece of him deep inside me. But I knew Peter wasn't going to just screw me, so I relaxed into his arms and let him take me as he wanted.

"Can I shut off the light and just light a candle?" I asked with residual insecurity.

"If you need to," he looked up at me.

"I need to," I whispered, moving closer to my bedside table.

Lighting 2 tapers quickly, and shutting off the light, I moved back into position, hoping I hadn't killed the mood for him. But after only a second of delay, Peter pulled me closer into his arms onto the bed, so I was on my knees straddling his thighs.

Lowering his head, he again took a nipple into his mouth, as his hands started massaging my shoulders. Drawing his hands under my arms, he made long swept movements down my back as I arched and moved closer to his amazing touch.

"Stand up and take off your pajama bottoms," he told me. So I did.

Standing in the candlelight naked, my arms immediately crossed over my chest by habit until Peter pulled me back onto his thighs. Kneading my ass, he pulled me closer until I was seated right against his erection.

"What's wrong? You still seem nervous with me."

"I *am* still nervous with you. Plus, I have to suck in my stomach sitting like this," I grinned embarrassed.

"Really? This soft little stomach? You have to suck it in because I'm so perfect, with my washboard abs and my perfect love handles," he said before kissing me gently. "You're good, Sophie. *Very* good. And trust me, with you naked in my lap, your belly is the last body part I'm thinking about," he grinned.

Smiling at Peter, I whispered, "Perv..." against his lips as I kissed him but I actually thought *finally,* he sounded like a normal guy for once.

We kissed again while Peter continued kneading my ass as he moved me against him. And I felt his erection growing as I felt my own arousal building. Kissing Peter, I was enraptured- just short of completely mindless and loving the feel of him against me and his tongue inside me.

"Lie down, Sophie," he whispered against my mouth as he moved me to the bed. "How are you feeling?"

"Aroused," I said without thinking.

"Aroused is good," he said as he stroked down my body, stopping at my, "Open your legs wide for me," he said as I gasped at his touch.

He was so sexy and intense, and he truly turned me on. Looking at him, he waited until I opened my legs wide for him, bending my right knee up and out.

Looking at me, he continued touching me as he leaned in for another kiss. "I want to try something with you. I want you to tell me as your arousal climbs. I want you to give me a number from one to ten, so I know when you're going to reach your plateau, okay?" He asked as I nodded.

I didn't think I could actually vocalize a number while he touched me, but I would try for him. I would try because I knew I was becoming a woman who would try *anything* for him. There was just something about Peter that made me want to be everything he wanted me to be.

Peter continued touching me for a while as we kissed, and eventually I found myself climbing to maybe a 6 out of 10. I reached 6 when he asked my number and then he stopped touching me altogether.

Pulling me into his arms, Peter held me tight, and kissed my lips with a quiet, 'Good night, Sophie...' as I quickly slipped back out of my arousal into a comfortable exhaustion with Peter during the best Christmas I could ever remember.

CHAPTER 13

When I woke up Boxing Day morning it was to Peter gently moving against my back with his fingers slowly moving inside me. Gasping for a second as recognition set in, I groaned as he moved deeper inside me.

Arching into him, Peter moved his arm to rest at a better angle over my hip while he continued to penetrate me slowly with his fingers.

"Good morning," he whispered in my ear, but I couldn't respond. I had gone from dead asleep to highly aroused in seconds it seemed.

Turning my body slightly, I allowed for easier access to his hand. Turning my body, I *wanted* easier access for him to continue. Peter was pleasuring me and I felt it everywhere inside me suddenly and I didn't want him to stop.

"Peter..." I moaned as he touched on a spot deep inside me. I couldn't say for sure, but it had to be the elusive G-spot everyone raves about. Whatever it was, I was suddenly so aroused it became almost painful. So without thinking, I blurted out, "8. I'm an 8."

"Are you feeling the need to stop, yet?"

"Almost... It's getting there. It's almost too painful and I'm kind of stuck, I think," but I moaned again and even gasped when he rubbed against that spot again while his hand twisted between my thighs.

"Relax, Sophie," he said pulling his hand away, and I wanted to cry from the sudden absence of his touch.

When Peter slowly penetrated me from behind, I was wet enough that I didn't burn when he entered me fully. Moving slowly, Peter's hand fondled and tugged at my breast as I moved slowly against him. Almost immediately I felt my arousal slowly fade from the painful point I had reached minutes before while I relaxed into the soothing, comforting rocking motion between us.

"Give me a number, baby," he spoke quietly a few minutes later.

So thinking of where I was at but not wanting to insult him, I answered the truth. "Around a 4. I feel good with you inside me, but I'm not climbing high. I'm sorry..." I tried to soothe.

"Don't ever be sorry. And 4 is good. 4 means I get to build you back up," he said suddenly pulling his penis from me as I groaned again at the absence of him inside me.

Moving down my body, Peter lifted my right leg and placed his head on my inner left thigh. The position was almost obscene, but I couldn't fight it as his tongue slowly pleasured me. Placing my right foot on the bed, my leg was up and out of the way as he laid sideways on my left thigh with his face right against my body until he went further.

Impaling me with his fingers and using his tongue against me at the same time, I was assaulted by the quick pleasure. Feeling his tongue drag up my body to tangle with his fingers drove me crazy. My insides were instantly on fire, and my breathing mirrored my internal struggle.

I was lost, and moaning, and even crying out. Unconsciously, I grabbed his head and pulled him further into me as I writhed. He was killing me but I couldn't get over once again.

"I'm stuck! I can't... Ah..." I gasped, but Peter didn't stop.

With movements faster, and his left hand holding my right leg up and open, he continued his assault until finally, mercifully, unbelievably, I came in a quick, violent rush, as I screamed and my body writhed against his mouth.

"Peter!" I screamed when he continued to touch me with his mouth and fingers. "Please, stop! Oh, god..." I cried when he didn't stop but did slow down.

Moving suddenly along my body, Peter kept my right leg opened, fighting against my unconscious attempt to close them, and then he slowly entered me. Slowly, and with a tightness I hadn't known before him, he gently entered me until he was fully inside me and still.

"You're so tight and swollen after you come. You feel incredible, Sophie," he groaned as he started his own slow movement within me.

But I couldn't respond or even move. I was half dead watching him move inside me. I was a dead woman floating around my room, feeling his gentle movements deep inside me. I didn't move, and I could barely comprehend my surroundings.

All I knew in that moment was my heart was full of Peter.

"Sophie? Are you here, baby?" He asked me with a smile, so I nodded my head yes. "What number are you?"

With a hoarse voice I croaked, "I don't know..." while shaking my head to try to clear it.

"You're so beautiful when you're all post-orgasm relaxed. Do you know that?" But all I could do was shake my head, no. "I'm going to touch you and try to bring you back up," he said while still moving slowly inside me, even as I shook my head no again. "Yes I am," he grinned before leaning down to kiss me.

At that point Peter kissed me hard. Unlike his usually slow sexy kisses, this kiss was almost punishing. It was hard and demanding, and I found myself responding to it immediately. Wrapping my arms around his neck, I held him to my mouth as I kissed the breath out of him.

Waking quickly from my orgasm coma, I found myself moving against him as he sped up a little within me. Lifting my left leg all the way up to my chest, Peter moved deeper inside me. Pulling away from our kiss, he sucked on my nipples and even bit one gently with a tug as I jumped.

Sitting on his shins, Peter began rubbing my clit as he watched his body enter me. Licking his fingers and rubbing me harder, I felt my arousal climb almost immediately as he continued his deep penetrations inside my body.

When I moaned, he rubbed harder. When I arched, he penetrated faster. When I stopped moving altogether, he pushed my leg harder against my chest as he pounded inside me.

And then I felt the sudden release of another orgasm. Not as intense as the first one, nor as numbing, but it was an orgasm nonetheless. Watching him, I was slightly more coherent during my second release as he quickly pulled out of me and came on my stomach with a sexy shudder and groan.

Collapsing on my body, he turned us quickly so I was in his arms while I tried to catch my breath. Listening to Peter's heart pound against my ear, I smiled when he seemed just as out of breath and physically exhausted as I was.

While we slowly came down and leveled off I didn't say everything I had never felt before him but wanted to confess. Instead, I held him tighter to me, even as I felt lost within my surroundings.

I didn't speak, but there were all these loving words, and ridiculous declarations on the tip of my tongue. There were thoughts of insanity wanting to spill forth. There was an emotional, almost visceral need to claim him as mine forever, but I kept it inside. Barely.

We lay there as the exhaustion took me away from the words I wanted to say for the first time in my life. But I knew the truth.

I was in love.

I loved Peter, and I wanted him to love me, forever.

*****

Maybe a half hour later, I attempted to crawl out of bed, only to feel my skin almost stuck to his. Shocked by the grossness of us stuck together, I burst out laughing while I pulled away from him.

"Remind me to clean you up before I pass out like a caveman, okay?" Peter laughed.

"Um, yeah... That was gross," I laughed as I stood for the shower with a sheet covering me.

"Can we talk about earlier, Sophie? I'd really like to know how you felt."

"Can I have a shower and coffee first? I'm not half as intelligent pre-coffee," I grinned as I gave him a quick kiss on the lips and looked at the clock.

It was only 10:00am and I couldn't believe how much day we still had to explore each other. I couldn't believe how much I wanted a day to explore him completely.

After my shower and the tedious hair drying that followed, I found Peter still asleep in my bed. Looking at him as I stood in my towel, I couldn't believe how attractive he seemed to me then. I couldn't believe I originally thought he was average looking or plain. I couldn't believe I thought he was ever average because in reality he was anything but.

Looking at Peter sleeping on my dark wine colored comforter, he was absolutely beautiful to me. His hair was to his shoulders but a complete mess. His body was long and lean, toned, but not very muscular. His ass was nice, and his shoulders seemed wide. He had a long, dark scar on the back of his right thigh I wanted to ask him about, and he had a sexy Celtic cross tattoo on his upper arm with his initials P.C. underneath.

He really was nothing special, but everything amazing to me.

He looked like a fallen angel lying stretched out on my bed.

So on impulse, I climbed up the bed slowly and quietly, and laid my body against his back. Lying on him, I just listened to him breathe for a moment before lifting to leave him. Yet as I tried to move away his arm snaked out of the sheet and he pulled me back down on him.

"I didn't mean to wake you," I whispered.

"Stay... I love you lying on me. And I'm strong enough to hold you up when you need to be held, Sophie," he whispered back as I immediately choked up.

God, he was so good- like textbook good. He had every line imaginable, and yet they didn't feel like cheesy lines coming from him. They felt like the truth of Peter as he felt it.

"You're going to fall in love with me," I heard myself suddenly say as I froze against him.

"I know..." he whispered back to me.

And that was it. He said nothing further, and I couldn't speak. I could do nothing but fight back the feelings crushing my chest. I was beyond screwed for him, and though I knew it, acknowledging it to him seemed way worse. So I said nothing more in our silence.

Eventually, I slowly rose from his back and made my way to my closet. Grabbing another sweater and pair of jeans, I pulled a bra and panties from my dresser and shimmied them on under the towel. Pulling on my jeans next, I dropped my towel with my back to the bed and finished dressing.

"You're so amazing, Sophie," Peter spoke in the silence, and I smiled as I turned to him.

"I'm going to get us coffee down the street. Get up and get showered while I'm gone so we can figure out breakfast, or I guess lunch, when I get back, okay?"

"Yes, mam," he grinned trying to pull me back to the bed.

"Nope. I just got clean, but maybe I'll let you get me dirty later," I laughed at my sudden brazenness.

"Oh, I will..." he promised as I left my bedroom giggling.

*****

In the coffee shop, I looked around at all the Boxing Day specials before ordering our coffees. On a sale shelf, I saw a Bodum I had had my eye on forever but couldn't justify buying, but at 50% off I couldn't pass it up. Grabbing one, I decided on a second one for Peter as well.

Before I finished looking, I saw the liquor-looking bottles of coffee flavor on sale and happily found my chocolate shot, so naturally I snatched up 2 bottles as well. Then I grabbed croissants, bagels and cream cheese, a loaf of bread, and a few pastries for later. Leaving the coffee shop, I was much poorer, struggling with my mittens and bags, and the cardboard carrying tray of coffee but I managed.

Walking back home, I peaked in a little card store and everything was on sale, so I had to stop. My mom had taught me young the need to buy everything on sale to be kept for important events down the road, which was fairly cheap, but it left me with a box full of cool stuff ready in the hall closet for an impromptu party or a birthday I had otherwise forgotten to buy for.

20 minutes later, I bought a few cards, an adorable stuffed panda for someone else's future children, and a beautiful set of carved wooden candle stick holders I swore weren't for myself. I made a silent deal with myself that if I did end up keeping them then I had to dispose of a set I already owned, and since I couldn't think of a single pair of candle holders I could live without, I was fairly confident that the new set would stay in my future required gifts box.

Afterward shopping, I decided I wanted to go out window shopping and maybe slightly buying with Peter in the afternoon. Walking home, I was anxious to see him and I wanted my nearly cold coffee so bad, I tragically contemplated ruining it with a microwave warm up.

When I walked into my apartment courtyard, I laughed as I approached my bedroom window, knocked on it, and threatened, 'you better be out of bed' to Peter before entering the building. But opening the main door still smiling, I was shocked to see Peter standing outside my door pacing back and forth naked.

"What happened?!" He yelled at me as he grabbed my arms.

"What? I just knocked on the window," I gasped as the coffee carton twisted out of my hand and crashed to the floor when he grabbed me.

"Where the fuck were you?"

"What?!" I yelled shocked as I tried to pick up the spilling cups of coffee from the floor. "What's wrong?" I asked desperately when Peter pushed me to my ass grabbing for my arms again among the spilled coffee.

"Where were you?" He growled shaking me.

"I was getting coffee and breakfast for YOU!" I snapped when I found my spine again after my initial shock. "What the hell are you doing?" I screamed as I pulled away from Peter, picked myself off the floor and headed for my door.

"Sophie! Sophie, wait! I'm sorry, baby," he pleaded as he stood up behind me. "I was worried when you took so long, that's all," he begged, but I way too pissed to listen.

Walking to my kitchen I threw the bag of food on the kitchen counter, then stomped back to the table to put the bags of breakables down.

"Sophie... I'm sorry," Peter said trying to pull me into his arms again as I fought him. Actually turning my back on him, I was way too angry to even look at him at that moment, nevermind be touched.

"You better go, Peter. I'm really pissed, and I'm going to say something I shouldn't, so please go home. I'll call you later when I've calmed down."

"I'm not leaving until you let me explain."

"You *are* leaving because I told you to. So get out Peter! You have ruined an otherwise perfect goddamn morning, and I'm so pissed and hurt right now, I don't want to talk to you," I said with anger tears in my eyes.

"Please, Sophie, just listen for a minute," he said trying to remove my winter coat. "I was scared, that's all. You said you were getting coffee which takes like 10 minutes, but you were gone for over an hour," he said calmly. "I was scared something happened to you so I acted like an asshole, but I'm sorry. I was scared, and I took it out on you. Please, Sophie. You were gone for so long, I thought you were hurt or something..." he said so sincerely, I thawed a little.

Looking at the clock on my stove, I realized I had been gone for over an hour, but still... What the hell kind of reaction was that?

"Peter, if you ever put your hands on me again, or shove me to the ground, or yell at me like that, I will leave so goddamn quickly you won't even see it happening. I swear to god, Peter. I'm gone. Got it?!"

"I do... And I'm so sorry. I totally panicked at the thought of you being hurt. I will *never* put my hands on you again like that, I promise. Really, Sophie, I won't. I can't even explain why I felt so scared, other than I don't want anything bad to happen to you," he breathed against my back as he kissed my head.

"Peter, we're apart all the time, and I'm not going to allow you to act like a psycho every time I'm late coming home from work, or I stay out late with friends. So let me be really clear about this- if you *ever* act like that again I. Am. Gone." And I was.

I didn't care what I felt for this guy, I was not going to be pushed around or controlled by some fucking psycho with issues. Even if it was innocent concern for my wellbeing, the way he reacted was scary and he went way too far. I would leave him I decided in that moment if he ever acted like that again. *Ever.*

"I understand completely, and I'm so sorry, Sophie. I promise you it will never happen again. No excuses, but we're so new, and I'm crazy about you and I don't want anything bad to happen to you, but I completely overreacted, I know. Do you still want me to go?" He begged.

"Yes. I wouldn't mind going Boxing Day shopping with my girlfriend Kim for the afternoon. She asked me on Wednesday but I kind of blew her off for you. Maybe come over later or something," I said leaving the invite in the air between us unconfirmed.

"What time do you want me to come back?"

"I don't know. Later. I'll call you when I'm done shopping."

"Okay... I'm so sorry, Sophie," Peter whispered leaving the kitchen, still really friggin' naked, which almost made me laugh. But thankfully the anger was still simmering enough to keep my laughter in check.

5 minutes later, while I opened my new Bodum at the table Peter walked up to me. Kissing my head as I sat on a kitchen chair, he dropped to his knees beside me. Resting his head against my chest, and pulling me to him he again whispered he was sorry.

Exhaling all my anger, and feeling him so sad against me made me forgive him that ONE time. When I kissed his head, he relaxed further into me and squeezed a little tighter.

"I'll see you later, Sophie. Have fun shopping," he spoke quietly as he stood and walked slowly to my front door without me following him.

I didn't want to kiss him goodbye, or let him off the hook too easily. He needed to understand that I would never be tossed around like a goddamn doll again because he was scared. It wasn't going to happen, so I wanted him to really think about that once we were away from each other for the afternoon.

After he left and I stood to lock the door I called Kim's cell. Luckily, she still wanted me to shop with her, so we picked a place to meet for lunch before she started her second round of shopping, and I began my first.

Happily, I went out with my friend and I ended up having a fun day away from the intensity and confusion of Peter.

CHAPTER 14

When Kim and I returned to my place we were loaded down with bags of stuff. Laughing at all the fabulous buys, Kim even did a verbal tally of money spent versus actual costs and the savings we had made, which to her meant a free night out to dinner and drinks, which I agreed to, even as I laughed at her tragic attempt at math.

I was home, and my apartment felt like Peter as soon as I entered it. Whether Kim felt his presence I wasn't sure, but I did. Peter was all over every room, and he seemed to speak to me loudest from my bedroom when I entered to drop the bags of new clothes on my bed.

Once I was home I missed Peter horribly. I only spoke about him a little over lunch, but I gave Kim a kind of semi-description of our new relationship. I admitted the sex was hot, the intensity was new for me, and I was very happy... overall.

With the strictest of confidence I explained the earlier incident and asked her opinion of it, to which she shocked me. Kim actually swooned when I told her. To my horror, she thought Peter's overreaction was 'sweet'. Kim didn't necessarily approve of his behavior, and she didn't like him tossing me around, but she thought he sounded 'like a man in love navigating his way through the new relationship battlefield'- her words not mine.

Even after I told her she was mental, she just laughed and said she'd love a man who was so into her that he panicked if he thought she was hurt, which again I found insane.

After speaking with Kim I understood one absolute though, I had not changed so totally with Peter as to let that kind of behavior slide. I was stronger and smarter than that. I was still Sophie, just a slightly sappier Sophie, so I was going to watch for any more freak outs from Peter, and I would end things with him if they came.

I knew after talking to Kim who had had endless relationships and bed-buddies that I would never allow myself to be scared or hurt by Peter, no matter how much I cared for him. I knew I could be alone, and I would be. I had no problem being single and mentally well. I had been single and mentally well before him, and I would go right back there if he *ever*

treated me like that again.
 But I did miss him.
 Throughout the day I found myself looking for him in stores, and I even wanted his opinion on certain buys. I thought of him non-stop, and I almost ached for him all day. I had lots of fun with Kim all afternoon, but I wanted Peter.

 So after Kim and I had settled in and I poured us each a drink, we decided to have dinner down the street followed by drinks somewhere later. I wanted a girl's night of fun to remind myself that I was still fun without Peter.
 I didn't want Peter to think I was still punishing him though, so I grabbed my cordless and told Kim to help herself to anything as I left for the privacy of my bedroom.
 Dialing and preparing for Peter, I straightened my spine as I called.
 "Hi, Sophie... Please let me say it again. I'm very, *very* sorry about earlier. I'd love to have some perfect excuse for my behavior, but I don't. I was an idiot and I will *never* be like that again with you, I promise."
 "I hope not," I exhaled some tension.
 "I won't. I've had a long day without you thinking and analyzing my behavior, and I realized not only what an asshole I was, but how very unlike myself that behavior was. I've never touched a woman before, *ever*, so I scared myself a little as well by the intensity of my reaction. I'm crazy about you Sophie, and the thought of you hurt made me feel crazy. But even still, I overreacted and it won't happen again," he spoke sincerely.
 "Okay. I'll let it go this time, but I promise you Peter if it ever happens again-"
 "It won't ever happen again," he insisted.
 "Okay," I relented, because I really didn't want to talk about it anymore. Peter said it wouldn't happen again and I would just have to wait and see. There was nothing else I could say or do, so I gave up.
 "Can I come over to see you?"
 "I'm still with Kim and she and I are going out for dinner soon, then maybe a drink or two afterward. I'll call you later if you want?"
 "I want," he whispered. "Have fun Sophie, but be safe for me, okay?"
 "I'm always safe, Peter. Have a good night, and I'll talk to you later," I said but couldn't hang up.
 "Okay..." But he didn't hang up either. Suddenly we were playing the

you-hang-up-first game.
 "On the count of three?" I giggled as he laughed.
 "Okay. One, two, three..." I hung up.
 I didn't know if he stayed on the line, but I kind of felt like maybe he did. Whatever, I wasn't twelve, so I didn't feel too badly hanging up first. I did smile though at what total losers we were becoming.

After dinner at my new favorite dive Murphy's, Kim and I walked a few bars down the street to Drinks, which was surprisingly busy for a Sunday night. With the holidays it seemed like Drinks was the place to go in the village for most people who didn't have to work the following morning.
 Drinks was packed and loud, and filled with every variety of person you could imagine. Kim became Party Kim the second we entered, and though there was no place for us to sit, she ended up perched on a bar stool against some total stranger within seconds.
 After a quick round of drinks, and a shot of tequila later, I felt a man lean his arm across my back as he pushed me slightly into the bar.
 Looking behind me, he was without a doubt hot. He oozed sex appeal and charm, and when he whispered in my ear, 'what can I get you?' with a nod at the bar, I knew he was the kind of man most woman went home with. He was not a forever man, nor even a weekend man, but he was absolutely gorgeous, so definitely a *just tonight* man.
 But instead of telling him my drink choice, I mouthed 'no thanks', and pulled out my phone.
 Calling Peter, he answered on the second ring.
 "Sophie?" I think he asked, but the music was too loud, and the atmosphere was too crazy to really hear or understand anything, so I just spoke into my phone and hoped he could understand me.
 "I'm not drunk, just a little tipsy, and I miss you very much. Some gorgeous guy just offered to buy me a drink, but I turned him down immediately. Even looking at how hot he was, I could think of no one but you. I can't hear you at all, but I hope you can hear me. I'm at Drinks, and I'd like to go home with you in 30 minutes. I'm going to make sure Kim's okay, and then I'm going to stand out front and hope I see you. I miss you, Peter, even though you were a total asshole earlier. So that's it. I hope I see you in 30 minutes."
 There was no point trying to hear his reply, but I hoped he had agreed. Otherwise, in 31 minutes I was getting totally shitfaced with Kim.

After yelling in Kim's ear my plans, she pouted for a second, then got over it as the original shared barstool guy kissed her heavily between shots. I had one more shot of tequila, and nursed my tequila sunrise, but basically stood quietly, swaying to the music, trying not to get jostled by all the people in Drinks.

Finally, 25 minutes later, I couldn't take the wait anymore, so I kissed and hugged Kim goodbye to a round of catcalls at the bar. I made sure she was safe with cab money to get home, asked her new guy to watch out for her, which he said he would as he threw his arm around her shoulder, then I left the club for Peter, I hoped.

Fighting my way through way too many people, I opened the side patio doors where everyone smoked, and I saw Peter waiting against the patio fence for me with a smile.

Looking at him for a second, my pace sped up as I walked through more people to get to the front street exit and Peter.

"Hi!" I yelled accidentally from the residual hearing damage from the loud club as Peter laughed at me.

"Hi, back... Have fun?"

"Yup. Kim's hilarious, but the club is just too packed to even talk, so I needed to get out of there."

Taking me into his arms, Peter suddenly wrapped me up very tightly in the cold night. Feeling his warmth almost immediately, I couldn't even stop the sigh I released in his warmth.

"I missed you..."

"I missed you, too, Sophie," he said while squeezing me tighter to his side.

"Is your friend okay alone in there?"

"Yes. She's one of those women who can go out by herself, have a good time, maybe pick up a guy and do whatever, but she always makes it home safely. She's pretty ballsy, but not a total idiot."

"Are you sure she's okay in there alone?"

"Yeah. She's already picked up her man for the night, and he seems like he'll protect her from anyone else, so it's all good," I said starting to walk towards my home.

We had only 2 and a half blocks to walk, but it was absolutely freezing outside. It had also started to snow slightly when we were in Drinks, so my new shoes were slipping and sliding all over the sidewalk making me look way more drunk than the slightly tipsy I was in reality.

"Do you like my new not made for snow heels?" I laughed.

"Very much. Did you buy them today?"

"Yes, but with all the sale shopping I did, Kim convinced me they were pretty much free, so I have no guilt." I laughed. "I can't wait to show you the clothes I bought. Oh, and the set of candle holders..." I grinned.

"Of course. Because everyone needs a candle holder on every flat surface in their home," he replied with humor.

"Yup. In case of an emergency," I teased.

When Peter opened up his coat, he pulled me inside and held me tighter against the cold. It was such a simple gesture but it allowed me to rest my head on his chest as we walked home together. Feeling totally relaxed, I breathed him in and asked what he did all day.

"I worked in my greenhouse, had a thorough introspection, drank some herbal tea, and waited for you to call. I missed you very much today, and I find it a little overwhelming how strongly I feel about you."

"I know," I confessed. "We've only known each other really for 3 weeks today, but I feel it too. When that guy offered to buy me a drink, I didn't even think, I just turned him down. He wasn't you, and I only think of you now," I admitted a little sappy again.

"I'm glad..." Peter whispered as he held me tighter when we walked through my extra slippery courtyard for the main doors.

Once inside, I kicked off my new shoes, and leaned against the door staring at Peter. Breathing him in and inhaling his scent, I eventually moved to pull him down to my mouth to devour him with my kiss. I wanted to pull him into my body to make sure he never forgot me. I wanted to cement myself into his heart so he couldn't live without me. I wanted to be his entire world in that moment.

"Thank you for meeting me," I whispered across his lips. "I *really* wanted to be with you tonight."

"How much did you drink tonight?"

"2 shots, and one drink. I'm completely sober, Peter."

"Good, because I don't want to take advantage of you when-"

"You can take advantage of me anyway you want..." I moaned as I ground my body against his.

"Will you try something with me?"

"Yes..."

"Go change into comfortable clothes and settle in bed. I'll meet you there, okay?"

"Okay," I grinned, excited to meet him in my bed.

After using the washroom and cleaning myself thoroughly with a washcloth, I brushed my teeth and changed in my bedroom.
Sitting on my bed, I wore a little black nightie with spaghetti straps and a low bodice with matching panties. I felt sexy but almost shy as I waited for him to come to me.

A few minutes later, Peter entered my room carrying a tray with 2 mugs of something, candles, and massage oils.
"I don't need coffee, Peter. I swear I'm sober," I whined.
"It's not coffee. It's actually a uniquely blended herbal tea that heightens the senses and provokes a kind of mental clarity and physical arousal. It's powerful and almost drug-like, but with the right person it can be amazing. I wanted to drink it with you and experience it together," he said almost as a question.
"Okay... Do I get a massage too?" I begged.
"Definitely," he smiled placing the tray on my bedside table.
I was never a big herbal tea drinker, but this sounded so cool I wanted to try it with Peter. He seemed really excited and so sexy to me in that moment with his sweater removed, sitting on my bed in just his jeans, I would have tried anything with him. He *was* sexy, so I couldn't help but lean forward and kiss him again deeply.
Touching his chest, I trailed my fingers to his zipper and slowly pulled it down. "Take off your jeans," I begged.
Lifting to remove his jeans, Peter sat back down on the bed in front of me in just his boxers. Smiling, he sat in the middle of my bed and reached for a cup of tea to hand me.
"It tastes potent, but I added a little Stevia, a natural sweetener, so it should be drinkable," he smirked as I tried it.
"Um... Ew..." I managed after a swallow while Peter picked up his own mug.
"You look so edible in that lingerie, Soph. I want to rip it off and have my way with you," he grinned.
Smiling back, I dared, "Go for it," to his laughter.
"Just drink your tea first, ya tease."

Sitting closer to me as I drank the gross tea, Peter lit a Jasmine scented candle, and opened a bottle to pour some oil on his hands.
"This oil might stain your clothing."

"I don't care," I replied calmly.

Nodding, Peter started massaging my neck and shoulders as he faced me. He moved down each arm in turn until he did the soothing hand massage I loved. Moving back up my arms, he focused on my neck again and slowly moved to my upper chest. Under the bodice he massaged the top of my breasts like he actually was focusing on my muscles underneath and not on my breasts or nipples which was a little frustrating for me.

I found myself very aroused minutes later, especially when he told me to close my eyes as he gently raised my nightie overhead one arm at a time so I could continue holding my tea. Almost painfully teasing, Peter continued massaging my breasts, down my ribs to my waist and back up again.

When he stopped for a moment I opened my eyes to him drinking the last of his tea while staring at me with bright eyes.

"I love the scent of Jasmine now. I don't think I'll ever be able to not think of you and Jasmine together. I want it all over my home, Peter, because it's you to me," I whispered.

"Sophie..." He moaned as he leaned to put his mug down while taking my own nearly finished mug from my hands. Placing them on the table, he sat back in front of me and kissed me.

Slowly, and with a passion I had only ever known with him, Peter held my face to him and kissed me forever.

When Peter finally pulled away, I knew I was different. I could feel a difference in the atmosphere and within my body. I felt almost high, but still mentally aware of my surroundings. My body was buzzing, but I was very much aware of it.

Looking at Peter, I realized he and I were sitting in exactly the same cross-legged position, in just our underwear. We looked so lovely by candlelight I was almost heady with the need to be with him.

"Can you please touch me?" I asked desperately.

"What do you feel?"

"Aroused. Alert, but fuzzy in my body. Like I'm humming, I think."

"What else, baby?"

"I want to be touched, Peter. My body wants you, and I know I'm aroused. I can feel it," I blushed.

"Show me..." he whispered.

Lifting my knees together I pulled my panties down my legs and after placing them behind me on the bed, I actually sat back in a cross legged position, tilting my hips slightly, so he could look at my aroused body.

And amazingly, I didn't care about how dirty I seemed, or how intense my arousal was; I just wanted Peter to see how much I wanted him.

"I need to taste you," he groaned moving on the bed to lay at my body.

Pulling my hips up over his forearms, he essentially raised my body right to his mouth. Leaning backward on my hands, I nearly cried out when I felt his tongue enter me. Everything was just so intense and beautiful, and kind of fuzzy around the edges, but completely clear and focused between us at the same time. I was so in the moment, I felt every breath he took against my body and every movement he made deep inside me.

I swear I felt Peter in my soul.

Quickly, I reached the heights of my arousal. Moaning and rocking against his face and fingers, I was frantic with the need clawing at me.

"I'm going to... Ah..." I cried as he lapped at me quicker and pushed into me harder with his fingers.

When Peter suddenly moved and dropped me flat on the bed, and he moved to penetrate me abruptly, I didn't have time to acknowledge the change between us. He continued touching my body in a frantic rhythm with his fingers, but he moved with a slow, steady enter retreat motion with his body.

Minutes later, during the most amazing sexual experience of my life, I came. Loudly, painfully, and intensely, as the breath left my body on a groan, I came with Peter deep inside me. Feeling his slow movements inside as I came down, I realized how tight and full I felt.

"Please... You're too big now. You feel too much, or-" I struggled.

"Stop, Sophie. You're adjusting. Do you feel yourself loosening up?"

And I did but I was a little too sensitive and emotional to acknowledge the difference as he moved slowly inside me.

Watching each other, Peter slowly pushed himself into my body only a few more strokes, then pulled out to come on my stomach again.

Stopping all movement, Peter leaned up on his arms as he looked down at me with a beautiful smile.

"I feel like I'm still inside you. But you're the one deep inside me, Sophie," he whispered while leaning down to kiss my lips gently, which made me lose it again.

Crying, I pulled Peter down to me and held him against my chest. Running my fingers through his hair, I wept quietly as the events of the last hour played out over and over in my mind.

"Is it always going to be like this with you?" I begged.

"I hope so..."

"I've cried three times with you already, but like three times total in the last 2 years. I don't know what's wrong with me anymore."

"Maybe you just feel emotional by the connection between us, or maybe you're just finally allowing yourself to be emotional. I don't know why Sophie, but I'm okay with you open to me. It makes me feel close to you because I'm sure you're not like this with others."

Still threading my fingers in his hair as my tears slowly stopped, I answered the truth. "I'm never like this with others."

"Well, then, that makes me privileged to know you like this."

"Not scared?"

"Never scared," Peter said while lifting his head off my chest to look at me. "Let me care for you, baby," he said while slowly rising from my bed.

Pulling me toward him, he walked me to the washroom to start the shower. "Do you need your hair washed?"

"No," I said as he turned for my hair paraphernalia in the little wicker basket on my counter. Turning me from him in almost total darkness, Peter lifted my hair and wrapped it into a tight bun on my head with an elastic to secure it. Once satisfied my hair was good, he took my hand and led me into the steaming shower to care for me.

Washing my body from my neck down, Peter was gentle and loving. He would wash an area, then kiss it afterward. He raised my right leg onto the tub wall and proceeded to clean my arousal away with gentle sweeps of a cloth.

When he was finished with me, I offered to wash him, but he said he wanted to hurry and get into bed with me, which was exactly what I wanted as well.

After our shower, when I crawled back into my bed I was absolutely exhausted. The tea for all its sensual, mental clarity, also produced a calm, almost relaxed physical effect that was slowly wiping me out.

"I need to sleep, Peter," I whispered in my room as he joined me and blew out the candle beside us.

"Sleep, Sophie. I'm right here with you..." he whispered back. When he crawled into bed and spooned me warm again I felt that ridiculous emotion creeping back up to my eyes straight from my heart.

Peter held me tightly to him as I kissed the hand that rested against my chest before I quickly fell asleep in his arms.

But sleep didn't come peacefully that night. I had nightmare after nightmare, and endless bouts of terror destroying me.

Apparently, sometimes a reaction from the tea is night terrors because the brain is still way too active during sleep, which I wished he had mentioned beforehand. Though honestly, I wouldn't have changed our sexual, nearly prolific connection from earlier even if I had known what negative experience I might suffer while trying to sleep.

So all throughout my night of hell Peter held me tightly trying to calm me down when I woke from each nightmare. And after each attempt to fall back asleep, I felt like I was again gasping awake within minutes panicked and semi-delirious from the dreams. I was exhausted and unsettled, and truly afraid even though the dreams were unknown and indescribable once I was awake.

It was an awful night, but Peter never left my side, nor did he ever sleep through my nightmares.

And if I had been more philosophical, or even truly coherent at the time I may have looked at the dreams as an analogy for me and Peter. I would have understood then that we couldn't possibly have all the happiness we felt and experienced with each other without a nightmare creepy up to knock us back to reality.

But I wasn't that astute, and I didn't believe in fate or karma. Instead, I just tried to sleep again and again after each nightmare surfaced to knock me back on my ass that night, figuratively speaking.

CHAPTER 15

When I woke up Monday morning I felt like I had the worst hangover ever, which was saying something considering the hangover I had suffered just 2 days earlier on Christmas morning.

Groaning, I tried to move in my bed, but I felt weighed down and exhausted. My head was throbbing, and my mouth felt glued shut. I was a hot mess, and I knew it.

Eventually, I rolled to my side to look for Peter but he was gone. Looking at his pillow though, I saw a note that I quickly read.

Roses are red,
Violets are blue,
I love when I sleep,
With my hand on your boob.

I went to get you coffee.
We'll talk when you wake up... finally.
Peter
xo

Laughing at his funny poem, I questioned his 'finally' until I looked around at my clock and read 11:45. It was 11:45 and I was still exhausted from the worst nights sleep ever.

When I eventually made it out of bed, I quickly used the washroom, and hopped in the shower. I felt too gross to stand, but I needed my shower. Leaning against the tiles, I was surprised I was so exhausted from the little excursion required to shave. I had never been weak or sickly, but I suddenly felt like I was starting to get a bad cold with all the physical weakness and exhaustion in my bones.

Afterward, when I left the shower without washing my hair, I barely made it back to my bed before needing to rest again, feeling completely wiped out. Making it to bed without even stripping off my towel I closed my eyes for a minute while I waited for Peter and my coffee to come get me.

When I woke up again it was to Peter's arms and chest holding me. I could smell him and feel his warmth, so I snuggled in deeply as I inhaled his scent and relaxed.
"Sophie... You have to wake up baby. I'm getting a little worried," Peter said rubbing my back.
"I'm awake. I'm just tired."
"I know, but its 2:30."
"Really? Wow... I've never slept so long in my life," I said trying to shake the slumber from my head. I could feel I was sick, and I was still exhausted from it. "I think I'm getting sick," I mumbled.
"You are. You're fevered and you've been really out of it. Can you get out of bed, Sophie? I'd like to get you to the couch for some food?"
"Okay," I said trying to move but my arms were dead weight at my sides. "What day is it again?"
"Monday. You've only been asleep today."
As soon as he spoke I knew there was something about Monday. Oh, god, it was going to drive me crazy. Monday. There was something, and I was so agitated thinking about Monday suddenly, I almost lost my mind.
"Did I tell you anything about Monday? Did we say we were doing something?" I asked a little sleepily still, but shaky with my irritation.
"Not that I remember. We left the week open to each other with both our shut downs. We said-"
Jerking coherent the moment Peter mentioned work, I freaked out. "Oh my GOD! I have to get to work. Oh *shit!* I have to input payroll. It's mandatory. I knew I had to. I knew I had to go in. But I forgot!"
Gasping, I fought like hell to get out of my bed even as Peter reached for me. Pulling away from his hands, I overshot my wobbly legs and I hit the opposite wall with my shoulder as I landed on the floor. And crying out not from pain but pure frustration, I slapped Peter's hands off me when he tried to help again.
"I'm fine! I just need to get my shit together. If I don't get into work, 14 people plus all the department heads, my bosses, and myself included don't get paid on Friday. No one will get paid!" I yelled scrambling for

my closet on my knees.

Trying to stand up, Peter aided me by lifting me by my hips off the floor, as I fought to grab clothes. Fighting, I felt my strength fading even as I tried to stay strong.

"Sophie, you need to slow down. You need-"

"I need to get out of here. I only have until 4:59 to have all the numbers inputted. And it took Carole over an hour, and she knew what she was doing!" I screamed. "I'm sorry, but I can't screw this up. I just can't. What the hell did you make me drink last night?" I nearly cried.

"This isn't about the herbal tea. It's about-"

"My new job!" I was so screwed I couldn't even think straight.

"How can I help you?"

"Um, find me my black satchel with all my notes. I think it's beside the kitchen table. Find me- I don't know," I said sitting on my bed.

Struggling, I pulled a pair of slacks up my legs without even underwear in my confusion, then I grabbed a semi-professional looking burgundy sweater to wear. I was obviously braless but I wouldn't take off my coat in the office in case there were cameras, which I thought there probably were.

Stumbling to the bathroom, I slicked back my hair into another makeshift bun, and applied mascara and lipstick as fast as I could with shaking hands. Leaning against the counter for support, I saw just how pale and disheveled I looked.

Standing in the doorway, Peter asked to my growing frustration, "Do you really have to go in? Isn't there someone else you can call? You can barely stand up."

"No. There's no one else. I'm the new boss, remember?" I snapped.

"I'm driving you in then. Period," he snapped back to my relief. With Peter driving the 15 minutes to work I could read over my notes on inputting payroll as I struggled to wake up.

Running for my purse, and nearly falling off balance again, I took a deep breath and tried to calm myself. I couldn't screw this up, or I would be fired- plain and simple. When Carole and I discussed the Monday of shutdown she couldn't express enough that rain or shine, vacation or not, the office manager was responsible for coming in to input payroll. So naturally at the time I had agreed, said of course, and acted like it went without saying that I was up to the task.

Minutes later when I was ready to leave with Peter taking my arm in my bedroom gently, I knew I was acting crazy. I knew it, but I was so scared to make a mistake I couldn't really control the panic. I knew I could stop being such a bitch to Peter though. So stopping until he looked down at me I whispered I was sorry for snapping at him, and he nodded with a little smile as he continued to walk me to the door.

I realized outside we had to take my car because I had the security pass in the windshield that bypassed the security gates, so after settling in the passenger side, Peter began driving me to work with my clear directions.

When I woke up 10 minutes later, Peter was shaking my arm as we pulled into the parking lot.

"*Jesus.* I slept again? No! Those doors," I yelled pointing. "That's where security is so they'll let me in," I practically cried while searching for my name badge. "You can't come in because of security, but you can leave if you want. I'll call you when I'm done. I have to go!" I cried trying to open the door of my still moving car.

"Sophie! Stop it! Holy *shit*, you're scaring me. You need to calm down. You've got lots of time. It's only 3:10 so you'll be fine, but you have to calm down so you don't make a mistake."

Jumping in my seat and looking at Peter as he yelled at me, remarkably, I did calm down a little. He was yelling to help me not because he was an asshole, and I felt the difference clearly.

"I'm so sorry... but I just can't fail at this. I can't," I moaned desperately as I leaned in to kiss him quickly. "I'll call as soon as I'm done. Thank you for driving me, Peter. I'd be lost without you. I..."

But Peter stopped my babbling with a smile. "I'll see you soon. Please take it easy. You're really not well, Sophie," he said as he kissed me goodbye.

*****

Unbelievably, by 4:48 I had all the numbers inputted and sent. I had actually managed to do it with only one minor freak out and one quick set of tears when I couldn't balance one woman in accounting.

After everything was completed I wanted to lay my head on my desk so badly, but I was worried I'd fall asleep again, so I called Peter instead, then slowly, painfully, made my way down to the main floor through the conference room to the main reception area where a security guard sat. Looking out the window, I slumped in a chair to wait for Peter. When I called he told me he was around the corner, so I let myself finally relax in a chair as I watched for him.

Minutes later, a security guard touched my shoulder with an 'excuse me' as I jolted awake. Looking around I saw Peter in the window knocking on the glass motioning for me to come to him. Much calmer than before, I wanted Peter to care for me so badly in that moment I almost wept.

Looking at him as I stood up, I realized Peter looked like an angel to me. He was handsome, and wonderful, and he was holding blue roses in his hand and my heart melted at the sight of him surrounded by snow outside through the lightly tinted glass.

Standing and walking to him absolutely everything on my body hurt. Even as I reached for the door handle my head hurt, but all I wanted was to get to Peter.

Opening the door, I whispered, "Peter..." as he quickly pulled me into his arms.

Holding me he said, "Let me get you home, baby," to my relief.

"Thank you. Are those for me?"

"Of course," he smiled down at me, as he walked me to my car.

And struggling to walk, I moaned, "I'm really tired."

"I know. But I'll get you home, and I'll take care of you until you're well, Sophie."

"Thank you," I choked up suddenly as he helped me into my seat.

When Peter ran around to join me in the car, I couldn't hold myself up anymore. Bending my aching legs onto the seat and turning my body, I laid across the emergency brake to put my head in his lap. Lying there, he absently stroked my hair as I released all the tension I had felt for the last 2 1/2 hours.

"I did it. I inputted everyone, and I wasn't late, and everything's okay," I said wiping a tear that escaped my eyes as he smiled down at me while driving.

We arrived back at my apartment and I spent the next few hours sleeping on the couch beside Peter. He had undressed me and put me in loose pajamas, and he had even rubbed my neck before I fell asleep. He was calm and quiet and so sweet to me, I trusted him totally during that time between us.

Every time he asked me if I needed anything, or simply wrapped a blanket tighter around me I became more than sure he was my forever.

Later that night Peter finally convinced me to eat soup and a turkey sandwich, which was hard. I ate normally in general unless I was sick, then I wanted nothing to do with food. But Peter calmly persisted by lifting the bowl, or picking up the sandwich while not even looking at me, so I couldn't argue or refuse his attempts.

At 10:00, a CSI Las Vegas marathon was starting, and we stayed up until 1:00 watching 3 episodes together. I didn't really know the show, but I enjoyed it with Peter until I couldn't keep my eyes open again and he gently helped me to bed.

Peter was wonderful and loving during our time together. He acted like he was completely comfortable being my care giver while I battled either a really bad cold, or a weak flu. I was sick and wiped out, but he stayed the whole time with me to get me through it, and I was so grateful.

When I woke up the following morning at 10:30, I felt terrible, but better too. I had the physical symptoms of sickness, like a runny nose and eyes, and a very sore throat, but all the aches and pains were gone from my body. So I was better and worse, though I'm sure I looked much worse to Peter.

Cuddled up next to him, I again breathed him in and felt happy. I remembered him asking me a few times in the night when I'd wake briefly if I needed anything, but other than some fresh, cold water, I didn't need anything except Peter close to me.

"Good morning," he whispered softly in my ear.
"Good morning," I croaked with a flinch.
"I'm going to go buy you a few things to help you out. I would've yesterday, but I didn't want to leave you alone. How are you feeling?"
"Ugh..."
"This is usually the worst day, so you should feel better by tomorrow."
"Thank you for everything, Peter. But you can go if you'd like. I'll be fine. And if not I'll wuss out and call my mom or brother. I totally understand if you want to get out of here for a while. I wish I could," I grinned.

"I like taking care of you. It makes me feel good, and like, all manly or something," he laughed. "I was pretty sick 2 years ago and my sister took care of me until I was well enough to care for myself, and I remember how good it felt knowing I had someone in my corner."

"It's just a bad cold," I said trying to sound stronger than I felt.

"I know. But you do feel better with me here, right? So it's the same thing whether just a cold or a bad sickness. Everyone wants to feel like there's someone they can always turn to and count on when they need them," he spoke quietly.

"I have that with my brother. I would do anything for him, and I know he feels the same about me. We're very close, and I kind of wish you knew Steven, too, so you knew how amazing he is."

"I'll get to know him. But I don't really want to share you just yet," he said kissing my head.

"I know... When I was at work yesterday I missed you, and I wondered how awful it's going to feel next week when we're back to schedules and jobs, and real life, instead of this..." but I faltered. I couldn't think of the right word.

"Beautiful start for us," he finished for me.

"Yes..."

"Tell me something really bad about you," I asked squeezing his chest tighter.

"Um... I'm horrible at math."

"No, like bad about *you*. Like a personality trait. Give me something to work with," I grinned against his chest.

Pausing for a moment to think, Peter finally admitted, "I would suffer jealousy sometimes with my ex-girlfriends. Not too bad, and usually not enough to show. But it was there. And you?"

"I'm apparently- I have bad PMS. Like super moody PMS, at least according to my brother. But I don't know if it's true because I'm the one suffering it so everything I feel or say feels completely rational to me at the time. Then again, Steven might just be messing with me because he has to find something wrong with me, being as I'm the awesome twin," I laughed.

"I know a wonderful herbal tincture for PMS which my sister swears by now. Plus, there are these drops that help acute anxiety or irritability. I guess we'll just have to see how moody you get," he said pinching my butt.

"Uh huh. Thanks."

"When are you expecting your next period?" He asked casually.

Trying to answer just as casually through my discomfort, I admitted, "Around the 4th of January. I started on the 7th, during my second day of work. Why?" I asked a little embarrassed.

"So I know when to be extra careful with you, which was last week, actually."

"When I didn't see you. Do you want me to go on the pill? I can if you want?"

Shaking his head, Peter said, "I'm not a fan of hormone manipulation, but you do whatever you want Sophie. I just want to know your cycle so I can monitor our behavior during those 2 or 3 days," he said so nonchalantly, I felt even more uncomfortable.

"Have you done that often with women?"

"No. I was typically a condom AND pull out man, but I've slept with 2 women without condoms; one who was on birth control. So other than you I've only watched the cycle of one other partner. Does that bother you?"

"No. Well, yes, but it shouldn't," I said exhaling. "You are my first condom-less man, and I hate the thought of you with another woman like that, which is totally ridiculous, I know. But I can't help it. I don't like it," I confessed with a slow exhale.

"PMS?" He teased.

"Maybe," I groaned at my stupidity.

"If it helps, Sophie," he said looking at my eyes, "I've never felt this close to any woman as soon and as intensely as I do for you. You frequently take my breath away. And though I love this feeling, I'm scared of it, too. I'm often overwhelmed with the need I have for you," he said quietly while holding me tighter.

"'Cause you want to do dirty things to me?" I asked trying to ease the intensity.

"No, because I want to live in you as deeply as you're living in me," he whispered with a sigh.

Stunned silent by Peter's confession for a moment, I finally collected my thoughts enough to speak. "That was... Unlike anything I've ever heard before. I guess I dated non-romantics and men with little sweetness in them before. It's funny now because I didn't realize... Nothing. Sorry, I'm babbling," I said as I tried to get out of my verbal mess quickly.

"Please finish, baby. What didn't you realize?"

I was suddenly trapped between wanting him to know what I felt and not wanting him to know just *how* I felt. I knew he wanted me to tell him everything, but it was like jumping off a cliff I didn't even know I had been standing on with him. I found it hard to speak... until I just jumped and spoke.
"Please?" He begged again.
"Um, I dated men I think I knew wouldn't last... I think. I loved them each differently though. I did love them. But when I'm with you and you speak and act the way you do with me, I realize just how different they were from you. So I don't know if I dated them knowing it wouldn't last, or like, it wouldn't last because it wasn't you I was dating," I nearly groaned after my confession.
"That was one of the most honest, open things you've ever said to me-"
"And it sucked," I interrupted until he pinched my butt to shut me up as I giggled.
"You are so lovely to me right now. Always actually. I love hearing you try to be open with me. And I love these moments of yours which are candid and special. I love the Sophie you become with me in moments like this," he whispered holding me tightly to him.
"Well, I hate it," I groaned but then tried to ease up a little the more I thought about what I was saying. "Actually, I don't hate it. I just don't really know myself like this, even though I like feeling like this with you," I babbled again with my discomfort. Struggling, I tried to move away from him slightly but he held me tighter to him.
"Don't move away. Please stay right here with me," he begged with another kiss on my head.

After a few minutes of silence, Peter told me he had to leave me soon. To my shock, or maybe sadness, he actually had to go somewhere else and it bothered me though I tried not to show it.
"Sorry, Soph. I'll be back as soon as I can. I made plans with-"
"Peter, this week is your vacation, too, and so far you've been stuck with me for days being sick. It's no problem," I lied.
Shaking his head, Peter argued. "You've only been sick for a day and a half. We had a fantastic night together Sunday, and it's only noon on Tuesday. I have somewhere to be tonight, but I'm absolutely not leaving because I've been *stuck* with you," he exhaled. "I play the guitar with some friends in a funky little garage band we won't give up with age, so I

promised I'd see them later."

"I liked your funny poem yesterday," I suddenly said, thinking where the hell did that come from. Then I realized it came from my pathetic desperation to keep talking to him.

"Thanks," he laughed. "I didn't realize how sick you were when I wrote it, otherwise it might had been at least a little romantic," he smiled.

"When are you leaving?"

"Soon. Will you be okay? Would you like me to get you anything before I go?"

"No, I'm good. Thank you, anyway," I mumbled happily because I didn't want him to feel bad leaving me.

Speaking far more enthusiastically than required or that I even felt, I said, "I hope you have fun. Call me."

I desperately tried to sound casual without adding the later, or the soon, or the like five minutes after you leave me. I left it open like it didn't matter, but it did matter. It mattered to me if Peter called because I wanted him to call me.

"I'll call you later. We usually finish up around 10 when Cam's wife Emily starts getting pissed at us," he grinned pushing out from under me gently. "I'll just grab a quick shower before I make you some lunch and get out of your way," he smiled.

"You don't have to make me lunch, Peter. And you're not in my way," I tried to soothe myself when I felt the absence of his warmth around me.

While Peter showered I laid in my bed miserably. I realized I really had never gone first, nor had I loved first. I had never confessed my feelings, whether real or potential before the other person did. It wasn't in my nature to be weak or exposed with anyone, never mind with a man. And though I knew Peter didn't want me to be weak, I felt weak anyway. I couldn't help but think of all the ways I was becoming dependent on him; emotionally, sexually, and mentally.

I thought of how I felt during the brief moments we weren't together, and I loved my time with him when we were. I *was* dependent on him, already. So when I thought of the actual timeframe of our relationship, only 3 weeks, I was freaked out and overwhelmed by my dependency on him to make me feel.

But then I thought of all those people who say they just knew when they found the one they loved. They always say they knew instantly, and I kind of felt like I knew it too. Thinking, I tried to force myself to stop focusing on a timeframe that was acceptable to love so I could just decide *to* love.

In that moment, quiet in my room, with Peter here but absent from me I knew I loved him.

When I realized I loved Peter, the thought of him leaving me for the rest of the day and maybe the whole night created an awful pain in my chest. I was horrified to realize I was not only going to miss him, but I was going to be lonely without him. I was sad to realize I would be lonely for the first time in my life.

I knew I needed Peter in a way that though absolutely foreign to me, felt right somehow. Being with Peter made me happy and I wanted to live with that happiness for as long as I could.

*****

After he finished his shower Peter did make me a sandwich and some soup. He poured me a glass of orange juice, and he set me up on the couch before he left. He cared for me with little smiles, and with kisses on my forehead. Peter hugged me tightly before wrapping a blanket around me while kissing my lips deeply before he left.

So I let him leave with a smile and a 'have fun', but I ached deep inside my chest when he actually left me.

CHAPTER 16

During Peter's absence while I was sick, I called my girlfriends to pretend to be well. I called to pretend I was still connected to the world. I called to try to *feel* connected to the world.

I confirmed our New Years' plans, and I listened to Kim go on and on about her bar guy from Sunday night. I listened to an excited Kim who was quite smitten with the new guy, shocked even to hear she was inviting him to Amy's huge New Year's bash.

Afterward, I called and listened to my girlfriend Amy trash her boyfriend of 3 years for failing to propose again over Christmas, which she was sure was going to happen. But after 20 minutes I managed to convince her that there was still the potential for a New Years' proposal, or that he may even be waiting for the very romantic, albeit cheesy, Valentine's Day proposal.

I explained that he loved her obviously, so he was probably waiting for a very special moment to propose. I soothed her into remembering all the ways he had mattered to her over the last 3 years until she was calm and in love again. I talked Amy off the cliff of dumping Davis' ass for NOT giving her all she required, even as personally I was dying inside.

On Wednesday morning, I called and spoke to Denise about my shift that night at the restaurant. She could hear how sick I was, and said the restaurant would be slow, so not to worry about coming in, even before I told her I couldn't. But as we spoke briefly, I realized there was more to be said to Denise though.

I needed to end working part time because I didn't want the infrequent shifts over my head when I could be doing something, or *someone* else. After a few minutes learning about her Christmas, I finally explained I was sorry but I couldn't work part time anymore with 'everything going on'.

I didn't specify it was about Peter and not about my new job, but she assumed it was about my new job, and she understood the new demands I had to fulfill. Denise made me promise to pop in anytime, and to please keep in touch, which I promised I would.

After Denise, I called my brother to check up on him since we hadn't spoken for 3 days, but Steven heard my residual sickness instantly. He even offered to come over when he was finished work, but I turned him down quickly. I didn't want him to see me because he could read me and he'd know there was more going on with me than just our usual every day or every second day check-ins.

Keeping it together as we spoke, I chose to not deal with my sad reality without Peter, instead talking to Steven about his newest conquest- a hot little number he had seen two times since Sunday night, with plans again for later that night.

Steven was being almost low-key about his new Michelle which made me think there was more going on between them than Steven's usual bang and run. So naturally, I wanted to cry again when I heard about Steven and his new Michelle maybe being more than the little nothing special he was used to with all his other women.

I couldn't help feeling sad that Steven maybe had something special starting, while my something special wasn't with me, but I didn't let it show. I kept it together enough to encourage Steven to enjoy his new Michelle, and to not sleep with her too quickly, so the infatuation didn't have time to burn out before the relationship even started. I nearly quoted Peter verbatim to Steven, which of course only made me miss Peter more.

So that was my day without Peter. I reestablished myself among my friends and my brother, while ghosting around cleaning and tidying my clean and tidy apartment with a runny nose and a sore throat.

Essentially, I spent Tuesday and Wednesday morning miserable. And by Wednesday afternoon when I hadn't heard from Peter in 28 hours, I almost lost my mind.

I was alone and shaky, and scared and confused. I was so sad without him I couldn't stop crying. I couldn't handle the fact that he didn't want me anymore or that he hadn't called me to say goodbye.

In my sad desperation, I even poured a little of his jasmine scented massage oil on *his* pillow, as I thought of it, hugging the pillow tightly so Peter's jasmine could surround me. I lit his candle before I fell asleep in the afternoon, and I dreamed of his arms wrapped around me as I slept horribly.

By Wednesday evening I was officially a mess. I showered, shaved, and washed my hair knowing I was getting ready for him, unsure of how exactly he was getting to me. I didn't know how he was coming to me because I didn't know how to stop the absence of Peter from my life.

In the course of 33 hours without him, I missed Peter until it was a constant ache in my chest. I missed him until I simply couldn't take it anymore. I couldn't stop obsessing about all things Peter. And no matter how hard I tried, I couldn't stop myself from missing him.

Eventually, after I had decided I didn't care about being weak anymore, I grabbed the phone among all the cast-off tissues, sandwich plates, and drinking glasses all over my coffee table, and I called him.

I held my breath as I dialed, and I exhaled when he answered.
"Hi Sophie," he answered without pause.
"Hi..." But, well, I *was* me, so talking openly was still difficult.
Thankfully, Peter continued the conversation for me. "How are you feeling?"
"Terrible," I sighed.
"Still? That's not good, Soph. Your cold should've lessened by now. Have you been eating?"
"Of course," I answered quietly because I couldn't admit to everything I wanted to say.
"What's wrong, baby?"
"I don't feel well," I huffed again at my stupidity.
"Like how?" He asked clearly sounding concerned.
So bracing myself, I said all I could. "Um, it's not the cold..."
"Then what is it? Tell me what you need from me." And that was when I knew what he wanted.
In that very moment I knew he was testing me, and provoking me, and almost daring me. He wanted me to tell him what I needed from him, and he wanted to hear me give into our relationship. He wanted me to give into my needs, and he wanted me to give into *him*, completely.
So inhaling deeply, I went for it. "I miss you..." I moaned with a dramatic exhale.
"Why?" He asked like a complete asshole, which made me almost snap at him but thankfully I reeled in my temper before yelling as I tried to speak the truth he needed from me.
"Because you matter to me."
"Why?"
"Oh, *god*. Why are you doing this to me?" I cried. I was exhausted and

sad and I still felt like shit, and I just wanted him to stop. "Please stop. You *know* why."

"Why do you miss me?" He asked seriously, almost like he didn't actually know the answer. So I gave him the best answer I could.

"Because, Peter... I think you might be a forever for me. I think. And I want to try to be a forever with you instead of..." but again I couldn't find the words.

For all my ambition and drive, my good grades, and verbal talents. For all my kindness and security around others, I was totally screwed with Peter. I was so out of my comfort zone the words were just gone, like they didn't even exist. I didn't even know what they were supposed to be or what they should have sounded like coming out of my mouth.

"Peter... *please,*" I begged desperately.

In that moment I didn't care how pathetic I sounded because I was sad and depressed. Though I had never known the feeling of depression before in my life, it felt like others had described it so I was pretty sure it was depression I was suffering. And I was exhausted from it.

"I'll be over in half an hour," Peter finally said. "I've missed you, Sophie, so much. But I'll see you soon," he said as he disconnected.

Listening to the sudden dial tone, I exhaled all my nervous tension. Breathing finally, I fell back onto my couch from the crunched over the coffee table position I had held for the better part of our conversation, and I tried to relax my mind.

I tried to get excited for his arrival, and I tried to be happy. But the sadness hadn't lifted with our conversation, and the pain was still throbbing inside my chest. I missed him, and I knew being without him was too much for me to handle. Even with the potential for a recovery when he came to me, I still couldn't find any happiness in anything because he wasn't with me when I needed him.

So I walked to the front door to unlock it, followed by a bathroom break and a good teeth brushing before I pulled my hair into a proper ponytail, and I washed my nasty face.

In the bathroom I looked at myself thoroughly. I wore leggings and a huge sweater, and though my clothes were clean I was sloppy looking. I wore no makeup so my eyes didn't pop, and my lips looked smaller and less defined without lipstick. I stared at myself and realized I just didn't look like me at all anymore.

Walking back to my living room to lie on the couch while I waited for the sadness to lift, I realized I really wasn't the same anymore, because of Peter.

*****

A short while later I heard Peter knock on my door as I sat up. And in a quiet voice, so unlike my real voice, I said come in to my door slowly opening while I kept my back turned from him as he approached.

Seconds later when Peter finally stood before me I looked at him through my tears as he squatted down in front of me to gently rest his hands on my knees.

"What's wrong, Sophie?" He asked me in a whisper.

"I don't feel right anymore. Something's wrong with me, like I'm sad or something, and I hate this feeling..." I confessed quietly.

"Do you want me to leave?" Peter asked, which made me shake a little.

Looking at Peter after he spoke, he seemed so calm I felt like he was ready to leave me. He seemed so ready to leave this new us we had been trying to create, I hurt more inside. But after a moment of thought, I found myself shaking my head slightly, breathing a nearly silent 'no'.

There was a part of me though that truly wanted to say yes. I found myself blaming him for all the upset inside me which kind of made me want him to go. But then I thought about how much I loved being with him, and I wanted him to stay.

Instead of a coherent answer I heard myself ask, "Why isn't this easier?" As I hung my head in sadness.

Tilting and lowering his head so he could look into my lowered eyes, Peter whispered, "Because we care for each other deeply. If we didn't care so much, we could walk away. But we do care, so it makes the good amazing and the bad much harder," he spoke gently. "I missed you when we were apart, Sophie, and I know you missed me. So why didn't you call me sooner if you needed me? You could have stopped missing me and been with me. Why did you wait so long?"

"Because you didn't call. And I didn't want to be weak. I, um, I don't call men, they call me," I admitted embarrassed.

"I'll always call, but not because you won't. I'll call because I want to see you. But there can't be games between us, because I won't play them."

"I wasn't playing games, I just..." but again I stopped speaking as reality

set in. "I guess I was playing games, but I didn't mean to. You're different for me and I don't know how to do this."
Nodding, Peter continued. "I think I know that, but it still hurts me when you won't just be with me however feels natural to you. You fight whatever's going on between us and I don't know why. Why can't you just be with me, in every way you want and need without stopping and holding back? Why can't you just tell me when you need something, so I can give it?" He asked so seriously I felt something break deep inside me.
"Um... I don't know how to fail, Peter. I- *they* failed, I didn't," I said truthfully, which really was the truth as I saw it. Whether right or wrong, my 3 relationships failed because of a shortcoming of theirs, not mine.
"I was so good to them, providing everything they needed without getting my own needs met until the moment I decided I was done, and then I left them. But I might fail with you because we're very different."
"Why do we have to fail?" He asked sitting beside me on the couch while taking my hands into his own.
"I don't know... because I'm driven and intense and not as much fun as I used to be because I want to be a successful adult, and you're- *no offense,* but like interesting and passionate, and into alternative holistic medicine, and you cook with organic chicken, and you massage and stuff. I don't know how to explain what I mean. Not that you don't work, but you're not driven like I am and I'm scared you'll stop liking me later if I'm all professional, striving for more, and you're all relaxed and happy with where you're at," I paused afraid, but Peter nodded for me to continue.
"Um, I think I just picture me all intense in my thirties and you all relaxed and disgusted with me when I fight for more or something. I wish I could explain it, but I think we're going to fail and this time it won't be your fault, it'll be mine, and I don't want that."
After another moment of pause between us, Peter finally exhaled and said, "We've barely started and you've already ended us. Why do you need to do that?"
"I don't know. So I'm prepared for it?" I asked the question for us both.
"Why not prepare for being with me happily for as long as we can? And if in the future, next week or 30 years from now we end, at least you enjoyed me and loved our relationship while we were together. Why not live with me happily hoping nothing goes wrong, instead of being unhappy making everything go wrong? Because at this point Sophie, you're the only one hurting you with all your mental garbage and over-

thinking."

"I'm more of an expect the worst and everything else is cake, kind of girl," I replied with a sad grin.

"But I may surprise you."

"You do. Frequently. And that's part of the problem. I can't really figure you out."

"So ask me and I'll tell you. Or just stop trying to figure me out. What's the point? I could tell you everything you want to hear, and then life changes and I do the opposite of what you figured anyway. The minute you called me, I dropped everything to come to you because you needed me and wanted me. I dropped everything because you asked me to come to you, Sophie. Do you see that?" He asked as I nodded.

As I looked at him silently I realized trusting Peter was all I could do. Peter was an anomaly for me. He was intense and relaxed. He was beautiful and egoless. He was everything I wanted in a package I never even thought to want. Peter was just Peter, and it was him that I wanted.

"I want to just enjoy you, I really do. But I'm new to these feelings, and I'm new to this kind of life. I'm new to being *with* someone, so I try to change everything into something I know and understand. But I don't understand you, or this amazing thing between us. But starting today, I'm going to try. I promise I'll stop all the shit in my head, and I'll just try to be with you as we are. Like right now, I'll start trying, I promise."

"You don't need to make promises, Sophie, you just need to be with me. However you are, as long as you're with me openly, we'll be happy together, I promise," he said pulling me close to him. "I missed you, Sophie. Very much."

"I missed you, too." I exhaled. "I was a bit of a loser while you were gone," I confessed laughing at myself.

"How so?"

"No way. Too embarrassing," I giggled.

"I drew and painted you 9 times since I last saw you," he laughed. "I left Cam's house and started painting, and before I knew it, it was almost 4 in the morning. Seriously. There are 9 portraits and paintings of you in my living room. It's a little creepy and shrine-like, but I couldn't stop myself."

"That *is* creepy," I grinned. "I just poured your jasmine oil on a pillow and cuddled up to it. You're way sicker than I am," I laughed as he pinched me again while pulling me into his side.

Then we were silent. Maybe processing all the confessions, or just enjoying each other a little less sadly, I didn't know. But I felt okay within the silence until Peter finally spoke a few minutes later.

"You look terrible, baby. And I mean that in an endearing, concerned way."

"I know. This cold has been ridiculous, and I look a little Rudolph over here with the red, runny nose issue I've got."

"I brought a tincture to help, if you'd like?"

"Please," I said as he moved me a little to go in his jacket pocket before he walked to my kitchen.

When Peter returned, he handed me a shot of orange juice with some funky brown oily looking crap on top of the juice.

"Spin it in the glass quickly so they blend together, then shoot it back. The tincture tastes terrible but it clears up the sinuses and it also has wild cherry bark for your sore throat."

So holding the glass I swirled it as he said with a little mumbled thank you before I shot the drink down. Gulping it down was pretty gross, but I hoped it would help.

After placing the glass on the table, I said, "Friday is New Years'," almost as a question. "Do you have any plans?"

"I do. My sister Carrie begged me to watch my niece a month ago, before you, so I agreed. Do you have plans?"

"Um, yes. My girlfriend Amy is having a huge party and I said I'd go. She's had it for the last 3 years and it's awesome. It's huge, loud, and very immature and I love it..." But suddenly thinking of Amy's party I couldn't stand the thought of being away from Peter again.

"We could always meet up later? My sister promised they'd be back by 1:00 at the latest, which isn't too bad. I could meet you here later, or..." And now he left the plans open.

"Maybe I'll just stop by Amy's, then meet you at your sisters?"

"Whatever you want. But I *would* like to bring in the New Year with you," he smiled which made my heart melt because I wanted that too.

"Okay. So that's the plan. I'll go to Amy's, put in an appearance, then I'll meet you at your sisters shortly after midnight. Sound good?"

"Very. And if my niece is still up, I'd love for you to meet her. I'm totally in love with her and she knows it. Moira tends to get whatever she wants from her Uncle Peter," he smirked.

"I can't wait to meet her then. I'd love to see you wrapped around a little girl's finger."

"Then open your eyes, Sophie, and you'll see me wrapped around yours," he said so suddenly the very atmosphere in the living room changed.

"I don't want..." But that was another lie. I did want that. I wanted it totally so I felt like we were even in this relationship.

"Kiss me Sophie, like you mean it. Don't think, and don't talk. Be with me like we both need, and just kiss me," he breathed quietly.

And in that moment between us, after all the words and emotions, the stops and starts, the insecurities and fears, I knew our reality. I knew we were officially beginning the greatest love story of my life.

I looked at Peter asking me for a kiss and I knew I would give him everything. I was going to change, and I was going to be everything he needed me to be. I would learn to be open with him, and I would learn to ask for what I wanted and needed from him.

In that powerful, charged moment between us I knew without a doubt that I would love him forever.

So I kissed him.

As I climbed into Peter's lap, wrapping my arms around his neck, I looked at his beautiful face before slowly moving in to kiss him. When our lips touched I was so happy and relieved, everything inside me jolted with a kind of peaceful homecoming. The pain was gone and the fear instantly disappeared. I knew as soon as we kissed that I was where I needed to be.

Peter kissed me holding my head in his hands closer to him. He kissed me back as desperately as I kissed him. We kissed each other as other couples made love; desperately, passionately, thoroughly, and with a promise of love to carry us into our lives together.

When my sweater was removed, I raised onto my knees, so he could kiss my breasts, and when his hand slid down my tights, I moved my legs further apart for him. When he touched my body I moaned into his mouth as he took me into another deep kiss.

Moving, I was held by Peter as he kissed me to my bedroom. Moving, our kisses remained and our touches continued. I lifted off his sweater in the hallway, and snapped his jeans at my bedroom door. We undressed as we walked together to our final destination.

When the back of my legs touched my bed, Peter dropped to his knees, pulled my tights and panties with him, then paused breathing in my scent. He paused, as I held his head tighter to me. He paused and everything inside me became tight with my need.

Placing me on my bed, Peter crawled up my body for another kiss that wiped my mind clear of everything but us.

In that moment Peter was *everything* I knew. From his scent to his touch, to the look in his glistening eyes, I knew only him.

Looking at his beautiful blue eyes I shook with the love inside me. And when a tear slid down his cheek I looked at him with nothing less than the greatest love I could offer, until Peter whispered, "I don't want to face a single day without you, Sophie," then I wept in his arms from his confession.

We made love together after his confession, cemented as the couple I had always wanted to be. We made love slowly, passionately, and without reserve. We moved and moaned, and shook and cried together.

He kissed me and touched me and brought me to my plateau before sliding deep inside me. He kissed me down and built me back up. He touched me with his fingers and tongue until I was gasping and shaking, until Peter brought me to the end of my struggle as he finished me.

Sliding back inside me, he touched me until I came in his arms with a groan and a gasp as my mind blanked, and my body caved in on itself.

Peter made love to me, came inside me, and finished our beginning.

I could feel Peter and I were together finally. And I knew I would love him forever.

And that was the quick and the slow of me and Peter.

In mere weeks, filled with every insecurity and fear I possessed, we had come through our struggle into the beginning of the greatest love I would ever know.

That quiet, amazing night in late December, Peter and I began our beautiful life together.

*****

Days later, New Year's Eve came and passed for us. I went to the party at Amy's, and Peter met me at my place after babysitting. We met at 1:30 in the morning and we made love until we were nearly lifeless in each other's arms early the following morning.

We made love beautifully, and with an intense desperation for each other, as we rang in the New Year with love and promise. We were together and we promised to fight for each other. We promised our lives to each other, and I was awakened by his need for me in his future.

From that night on I never fought Peter or my feelings ever again. I didn't necessarily verbalize my love as much as he did, but I showed him each and every day how important he was to me, and he did the same as well.

I finally understood there was no understanding my feelings for Peter, so I let go. All I knew was I loved him instantly because he was mine to love.

I had unknowingly claimed Peter from the first day we met for lunch, but I hadn't realized it until I surrendered to loving him forever.

CHAPTER 17

Over our last few days together before real life returned I gave Peter a key to my home. Unbelievably, over our final dinner together without any work responsibilities, I was so sure of our future I handed Peter a key without thought or conditions. I made a key and handed it to Peter over dinner Sunday night.

I knew I was sure of my decision, and from his reaction, he was stunned I would commit so fully, but thrilled that I did. Peter jumped up and attached my key to his keychain and then he ran back to the table to kiss me because he knew what that single key meant, and he cherished it, I could see immediately.

*****

I went back to work the following Monday with Peter waiting for me in my apartment when I returned. After a horrible day back, filled with anxiety and upset, I couldn't wait to be back in his arms.

I had made a huge mistake when I entered the payroll the previous week. I had forgotten to include everyone's stat days on the payroll calculation so everyone came to me Monday morning angrily. I had made a huge mistake and there was nothing I could do to fix it. I knew I had been sick at the time, but I took in their anger and didn't give any excuses for my mistake.

My coworkers and even my boss were livid with me, so I explained the error as ignorance when I factored in the pay period my first time. And after hiding in the bathroom for 10 minutes to cry and collect myself, I eventually made it through the long day of upset.

When I walked in my front door that night defeated and beyond exhausted, Peter helped me. He held me as I cried at my mistake, and he offered support when I felt ungrounded. He stayed with me until he absolutely had to leave to collect his things for his own job. He stayed with me for as long as he could while I tried to forgive my error and move on. He stayed with me with the promise to again meet me right after work the following morning, which he did.

Peter became a man who was with me always and endlessly with support and love whenever he could be.

After the work nightmare, and Peter's sweet kiss hello the following morning with my coffee and chocolate shot, I braced myself for the coming day. I was sure I would be either fired or seriously reprimanded, but neither came because of Carole.

Amazingly, Carole had apparently come to my defense and told my immediate boss she hadn't reminded me about the unseen stat days, nor had she called in on my first solo payroll to check in or help should I need it. Carole saved my ass and I was beyond grateful when I called her to thank her for helping me.

After everything settled at work, I remember walking back to my office with a relief I couldn't hide so I could immediately call Peter to let him know what happened, and to beg him to meet me at home, as I now referred to it between us.

With relief and his calm reassurances, he said he'd meet me at home by 6:00 and I finally exhaled all my anxiety. After hanging up with Peter I realized I was happy I still had my job, but I was more excited to see and touch Peter again.

Returning home at almost 5 o'clock, Peter surprised me by already being inside though. Waiting for me, Peter opened the door quickly, pulled me to him and kissed the holy hell out of me right against the front door. Kissing me, my coat and boots were removed as I was moved to the bathroom in Peter's arms before I even processed what was happening.

Kissing me, Peter finally pulled away from my lips as he gently pushed the bathroom door open with his foot so I could look around at all he had done in my absence.

When he released me from his arms I saw every single surface of my bathroom held a blue rose in a single thin little vase. On every surface and against every wall there were at least 3 dozen single roses in a single little vase all over my bathroom and vanity. On the sink, the sides of the tub, the window ledge, and even on the back of the toilet. Everywhere I looked held a blue rose, and I was stunned.

Unable to speak, I just stood there like a moron. I looked all around, as he held me around my waist but I just couldn't speak. My bathroom looked beautiful, as much as any bathroom could.

I then noticed the 2 candles floating in a bowl in the bubble-filled bath, and I sighed. I wanted to sink in the water so badly, my body took me to the water as I pulled off my clothes quickly and slid in the water to Peter's bright eyes watching me.

Sinking into the water with a moan at the sudden warmth all around me, I opened my eyes to Peter leaning casually against the wall until I begged him to join me. My tub wasn't a giant old claw foot, but it was way bigger than an average apartment sized tub, and I desperately wanted Peter near me.

"Please, Peter?" I begged even as he removed his clothes quickly and slid in behind me.

Holding me, Peter asked about my day so I told him everything. From the good parts to the fear and insecurity, to me thinking of him way too often and missing him way too much. In Peter's arms, I confessed everything, and amazingly, it was getting easier. I felt less fear of his reactions to my confessions and declarations.

Peter then told me about his day. He slept early, changing the routine he had had for years so he'd always get to spend a few hours with me after my day and before his own work began through the week.

Peter told me he had heard from Patricia earlier and he admitted to telling her all about me. He told me he spilled to his ex-girlfriend Patricia that he had finally found someone he could see a long term with, and apparently she was very happy for us.

"What did you say, exactly?" I asked dying to know.

"I described you to Patricia and-"

"How did you describe me?" I begged turning to face him as his hands slowly moved from my stomach to my sides as I waited.

"I told her you were stubborn, slightly neurotic, beautiful, and brilliant. I said you were a tiny little thing with a big personality. I told her you were nothing I thought to look for but everything I need."

After he spoke I remember being wordless again. His words to Patricia were my exact thoughts just a week prior about Peter. I felt like he had read a journal of mine, or simply read my mind. I felt weird and freaked and slightly unsettled, but I forced it aside. I pushed away the obvious what the hell in the air, and smiled instead.

"Those were all very good things to say to your *ex*-girlfriend," I teased. "Maybe next time though you should make sure she knows I'm way better looking, and skinnier, too. Just so she knows to back off, and so I know I *am* skinnier and way better looking, okay?" I smirked as he laughed at me.

"Will do," he grinned kissing me quickly before stepping out of the tub.

"Do you want to stay in a little longer? I made dinner and it'll be ready in 10 minutes or so."

"You cook, too?" I grinned. "Because I really can't. Soup and sandwiches are kinda my thing."

"Nope. I have 4 meals I can make though, so I try to spread them out through the week. Between the two of us, it looks like we're ordering in most nights."

Laying my head back down against the back of the tub, I moaned, "Sounds good to me," as Peter walked out smiling.

After my soak, Peter and I ate in silence on the couch, watched a little TV, talked about our weekend plans, and snuggled close until he had to leave at 8:00 for work.

Saying goodbye, I knew we both felt it. There was a feeling of sadness and something else, like unhappiness or discomfort, maybe. I couldn't explain the feeling, but it was all around us as we stood in the doorway unable to say goodbye to each other.

Leaning in close, Peter hugged me and whispered, "These are only see you laters, Sophie. They aren't goodbyes, okay?"

"Okay..." I smiled feeling lighter.

*****

And those were our days in cold January. I saw Peter around his shifts- either before or after work, and I loved every minute we were together. He cared for me when I struggled, and he loved me when I was well.

During my period Peter laid with me and held me and though we didn't have sex, we still shared a kind of intimacy with each other, as we lay together in bed talking about everything and nothing.

Peter cooked for me some nights during the week, and I made soup and sandwiches the other nights. Peter was always kind and loving, and he acted as though I was treasured every single day we were together.

During the third week of January, Peter had to go to a recycling conference as the elected representative of his plant, and I dreaded the days without him.

So we spent our first days apart in over a month calling each other nonstop and ridiculously. We even became playful the night before his return, sexting each other throughout the day, while enjoying my first raunchy phone sex in the evenings. I missed him terribly when he was away, but I enjoyed the lightness and the teasing the phone calls provided for us.

When I was suffered the dreaded PMS for which I was apparently known, Peter made me lie on the ground listening to a Chakra therapy CD, until I calmed and felt less irritated. He even gave me a tincture to ingest when I admitted to wanting to kill innocent people in my irritation, which definitely helped. I was calmed and soothed and he was amazing to me, always.

I saw my friends infrequently at best, and I attended less Sunday dinners than my mom liked, but she also understood. I was in love and I wanted to spend as much time with Peter as he wanted to spend with me. We wanted to be together because we *were* together completely.

I gave him every piece of myself whenever we were together and I lived for our moments alone in my home. I never again held back, and I gave him everything I had, from sweet kisses when we met, to little gifts I thought would matter to him.

Unbelievably, in mere weeks, Peter and I created a wonderful life together. We woke with each other when we could, and we loved each other every moment we had together.

Peter was everything to me, and I told him physically all I felt for him every day we spent as a couple.

We were together emotionally and physically always.

With Peter, sex for the first time in my life was amazing, fulfilling, and all about my pleasure.

Peter once told me as he slowly undressed me on our bed, "A man can come from just thinking about getting laid, but the real pleasure, *my* real pleasure comes from yours." And finding myself choking up as he spoke, I nodded and kissed him with everything I had, because Peter was my pleasure, and I thrived with him

We had sex in the shower, sex in our bed, even sex on the kitchen counter. One evening after a wonderful dinner Peter cooked us, we even had naughty sex quite creatively with a pecan pie for dessert. We could be naughty and dirty with each other, but we were always loving.

One night in early February we made love together and it felt like the earth was moving all around us. Everything just shifted around me and I couldn't help but stare in my room, waiting for the building to collapse, like every wall I had ever built had just collapsed within my chest, freeing me to love Peter.

I knew I could breathe with Peter because he taught me how. Peter gave me the ability to breathe in the world, so I could find my place within it.

And I knew in that one moment in time my place was to love him forever.

Work continued for us both, and there were no further incidents of incompetence on my part. I fit in my role as office manager, and I worked very hard within it. I was good, and everyone knew I was good. My bosses complemented me, and my coworkers respected me.

I became Sophie Morley, Office Manager of Halton Facilities, and lover of Peter after hours. I became a woman very happy with her life.

So when Valentine's Day came around, Peter took me to a beautiful hotel an hour away within the wine district to get us out of the routine of my apartment. Peter wanted me to experience him outside my walls, he said, and I was happy to oblige.

We stayed in a quaint little hotel surrounded by vineyards, which was a little odd since neither of us drank, but was lovely regardless. Peter and I held hands and snuggled as we walked, and again, I found myself smiling nonstop like a loser when we were together. I even imagined what we must have looked like to others and though I was slightly embarrassed by my giddiness, I really didn't care.

  Before we left the hotel room for dinner Peter gifted me with a beautiful green chenille robe he said matched my eyes, and then he handed me chocolate body paint to my humor. He laughed at all the chemicals in the chocolate 'paint', and I moaned at the thought of him covered in chocolate after our dinner in an upscale restaurant overlooking the vineyards.

  And when we finally returned to our room after an amazing dinner, I experienced the closest thing to straight up dirty sex with Peter we had ever experienced. We barely made it through the door, before I was lifted and pushed onto the bed, the comforter was stripped, as was I, and chocolate ended up everywhere.

  I was insatiable that night, with a kind of desperation for him physically I had never known before him.

  After covering him in chocolate with the included paintbrush, slowly, and torturously, I proceeded to clean him totally as he writhed beneath me on the bed. I ate him, and devoured him, and took him into my body as deeply as he had ever taken me. I was wild and sexy, and I took Peter with me to my pleasure.

  I was so in love with Peter I became a woman willing to be tested, and tried, and explored. We did things I had never imagined for myself, and I welcomed them with Peter without insecurity or fear.

  I was never insecure again or afraid. Peter gave me the security I needed to just be free with him sexually and emotionally. He taught me to release my reserve with him, and to just live with him in our world of love and passion, and I was greater for it.

  I even opened myself up to people because I became a better Sophie with Peter in my life. I was free from the fear of failure that had consumed me for 24 years. And I was free to just be a 24 year old woman who worked hard, and loved harder. In a little over 2 months together, I was completely changed and not only did I know it, I welcomed it.

  I was in love, totally and completely, and I was truly, undeniably happy in my life with Peter.

When my birthday came Peter gave me tickets to a Matthew Good concert in late April, plus a beautiful framed portrait of myself he had spent weeks on.

He pampered and massaged me that birthday weekend. He cooked and fed me my favorite foods, and he delighted and pleased me sexually. He made me feel like the most treasured, loved woman I had ever known.

Throughout my birthday weekend, I realized Peter was the greatest gift to me I had never known I wanted before he came into my life.

He was everything to me, and we had made our relationship seamless and beautiful over the course of just months.

There were no more struggles or outbursts like we had in the beginning, nor were there ever any moments of anger, fear or disillusionment between us. Peter always maintained a beautiful calm around me, and I learned to breathe with him. I feared nothing and I wanted everything with him.

With Peter I had a wonderful, loving relationship built on trust and mutual caring wrapped in our devotion to each other.

CHAPTER 18

2 weeks after my birthday, Peter finally invited me to meet all his family. I was invited to a party for his aunt and uncle who were celebrating their 35th wedding anniversary in a hall because of the amount of people attending. And Peter desperately wanted me to go with him because it mattered, he said.

They were celebrating because Peter's uncle had been diagnosed with terminal cancer and he wanted to celebrate his marriage to his wife in front of everyone.

Peter was distraught by the potential death, but happy for the show of love his uncle wanted to make. Peter told me he understood the desperation that made his uncle celebrate his anniversary because of the depth of the love he felt for his wife, who still loved him each and every day, of his last days.

Peter's uncle Malcolm was having a huge party in a banquet hall so his wife knew how he had felt about her for the last 35 years they had been together, and presumably for the last year of his life.

When Peter walked to my home at 6:00 I chose to drive because Peter was shaky and sad and visibly off when he arrived. He walked into my place and took me into his arms right against the closet door.

Lifting me, Peter shocked me when he moaned, "Please, Sophie. Please let me be in you. I need to feel your love around me," as I gasped at the sadness in his voice.

Nodding to Peter while kissing his lips, he pulled my nylons and panties away and entered me unlike he had ever done before.

Peter didn't screw against doors, and he rarely screwed me in general. We made love and shared a deep connection with each other. Peter loved the connection with me when we were together, but I could see he wasn't himself that evening, so I gave myself over to whatever it was he needed from me in that moment.

When Peter hid his face in my neck as he moved deep inside me I held him tighter. When he moaned and cried out, I soothed him. When he pulled away from me with a hand on my sternum to hold me up, I met his glazed eyes with a smile. I could feel Peter needed me, so I gave everything I could.

After minutes in his arms, I felt Peter needed to come inside me, so I let him. I knew my cycle, and I knew I was okay. It was not an accident waiting to happen but a gesture of giving. I gave everything to him as he took solace from me in his pain.

And once he was finished taking what he needed, I stopped his sad apologies and kissed him into peace. I left him sitting quietly on the couch as I redressed, and cleaned myself up. I left him to recover while I thought of the gift I had given him when he needed me.

Walking back to my living room as I rejoined Peter he again attempted to apologize for being 'sexually selfish' as he put it, but I took his hand in mine and kissed him better. "I'll make it up to you later, I promise," he moaned somewhat still shaken.

"You always care for me, Peter. So if you needed to screw the sadness out of you, I'm more than willing to help you," I confirmed with a kiss.

And pausing, he nodded before he kissed me deeply trying very hard to shake away all the upset I could feel around him.

Eventually pulling away from me, Peter finally took in my clothing and whistled with a devilish grin. Telling me I looked edible helped. Telling me I was stunning made my heart melt. I knew he knew all of me, so a simple complement about my physical appearance always mattered. Peter never placated, or gave false compliments. He was honest and forthcoming, and just delicious in his suit as I stared back at him with a smile.

"You are absolutely gorgeous in red, Soph. So stay away from my uncle Max, okay? He's a perv and you look too good tonight," he smirked.

"Okay, Peter. No Uncle Max. Anything else I should know?" I laughed.

Grinning, he admitted, "My sisters are going to be all over you, and I can't really stop them. They've been dying to meet you for months, so hopefully in such a large gathering, they'll be well behaved. Then again, they might corner you, so stick with me all night."

"I planned on it," I kissed him again. "You look very handsome in your suit, Peter. Do we really have to go out?" I teased.

"For an hour, at least. Then we can leave, and I'll properly love you later," he said to my surprise, because that was by far the closest we had ever come to the actual words.

We both knew we loved each other desperately, but we had decided early on that the actual expression was too common and too overused for the way we truly felt for each other.

LOST

We knew we loved each other way past the definition of the word. We knew we were something so special the word love couldn't possibly justify our beautiful relationship.

*****

Arriving at the hall by 7:30 I was impressed to see people everywhere, inside dancing and even outside smoking. Drinks were plentiful it seemed, and voices could be heard all around us.
Peter was repeatedly hugged by relatives and friends of the family, and I was introduced to countless people whose names I would never remember.
I met Uncle Max and nearly burst out laughing when he hugged me and Peter damn near growled. Even without the introduction I would have known the creepy perv anywhere. From the once over I received, to the nasty looking, come sit on my lap grin, I could tell he was a player and a pervert. So I quickly extracted myself from his hug, and leaned into Peter as his arm held me tighter to his side.
Walking around tons of people, I finally met Peter's very nice mother who hugged me and welcomed me to the family, followed by Peter's father who was just as warm and friendly, but without the hug.
I met one of his sisters, Carrie, who was very pretty, and the brother-in-law I knew was the disliked one almost immediately, just by the way Peter's demeanor changed as I was introduced to David. And minutes later as Peter and I walked halfway through the crowd of people I finally met the infamous sister Kara.
Kara was attractive, loud, friendly, and she demanded a certain amount of attention in the room just with her presence alone. In other words, I knew not to let her corner me throughout the night.
I also knew she didn't like me when we were introduced, but I couldn't understand why. Kara was perfectly pleasant, but there was an obvious tone I received as we spoke that suggested I was not as welcome as everyone else tried to make me feel. Kara didn't like me, and though I was uncomfortable with that thought, I chose to ignore my surprised insecurity for Peter.

Eventually, after Kara was distracted by another conversation, Peter held my hand harder and walked us over to a table up front where I was greeted by a huge smile when I met the aunt and uncle for whom we were all celebrating.

Uncle Malcolm, I could tell, was a formerly handsome man, already in a wheelchair wilting in front of my eyes. He was lovely as we shook hands, and though I didn't know him at all, I felt the sadness of death all around him. He took my hand and kissed me welcome to his party even as Peter stayed still beside me. I was then introduced to Peter's aunt Karen and I thought I was going to cry right then and there in front of her.

Karen placed her hand on Malcolm's shoulder, introduced herself, and asked if I was enjoying her party. She acted happy, but you could see the strain she felt when her eyes kept darting back to Malcolm. When he squeezed her hand on his shoulder, his hand visibly shook from holding it up, but he continued to hold her for as long as his dying body would allow.

Once the introductions were made, Karen beamed, "I've always wanted a party to say how fabulous I was, and I finally got it," which made me grin.

"Yes you did, Aunt Karen. And you deserve it," Peter finally spoke softly beside me.

Kissing her cheek, Peter seemed to be struggling more with Karen then even with the sight of Malcolm frail in his wheelchair.

"Peter... It's okay," Malcolm said, but even I knew it wasn't. "Go grab a drink for this lovely young lady and take her to the dance floor," Malcolm finished as Peter nodded.

Taking my hand as we walked away, Peter had just one moment of pause when he looked back at his aunt and uncle, but I couldn't tell if it was Karen or Malcolm he looked at. After his brief pause, Peter seemed so sad I wrapped my arm tighter around his waist as we walked to the bar at the end of the hall.

"Are you okay for a minute? I just want to clear my head, but I won't be long. I still want to dance with you," Peter whispered against my hair.

"I'm fine. Go do what you have to do. I'll be here," I soothed with a little kiss as he walked away from me.

Once alone, I grabbed one drink, a tequila sunrise naturally, and I looked around at all the people I didn't know, and thought of why they were there. Not too soon after this party, they would be at a funeral and I found the contrast so sad I wanted to weep for them all.

Looking at everyone I realized how much I had changed since Peter. I realized before him I used to force life to give me more than I needed to prove my own self-worth, but with Peter I enjoyed what I had. I was a different person than I had been before him. I knew I had become a woman who loved completely and lived my life fully. I also knew I didn't want to know or experience the kind of sadness that death and loneliness could bring to me. I wanted to love with Peter in peace.

Eventually, after 15 minutes alone at the bar, I decided to look for Peter. I knew he might need me I wanted to be there for him, like he always was for me.
What I didn't expect to see was him surrounded by his 2 sisters and mother yelling in the hallway toward the washrooms.
Listening to the way he spoke, I was shocked. He was angry and aggressive and so unlike the man I knew, I could do nothing but stand still listening.
"Did you tell her?" Kara yelled.
"Not yet."
"She has to know. You have to tell her. It's wrong and you know it. You *know* this, Peter," Kara continued yelling as his other sister looked at him nodding.
"Peter *please*... You're doing so well, but she needs to know, honey," his mother jumped in.
"You're just trying to ruin this for me. You always ruin everything for me!" Peter yelled right in Kara's face scaring me.
"Oh, *really?*" Kara spat back. "Peter, I've ruined nothing! But you're going to. Tell her the truth. Tell her what you do!"
And as I waited with bated breath, Peter grabbed his hair, and cried out, "I can't. Nothing's happening right now and I don't want this to break-" but then he suddenly looked down the hall at me, and his distress quickly turned to relief. He looked at me like I was a lifeline and he needed me to pull him to safety. He looked at me for that split second like I was everything he had ever needed, so I walked to him.
"Tell me what?" I asked calmly.
"I'll tell you at home. It's nothing," he soothed walking up to me while taking my hand.
"Peter! It's not nothing. It's everything!" Kara screamed as Peter turned back to her.

"Shut your mouth, Kara. You're such a bitch trying to ruin my life and I won't let you! Not again."

"Sophie! Listen to me!" She screamed again, but Peter turned us so quickly, I was whipped around on my heels

"Fuck OFF, Kara. You're not doing this. Let's go, Sophie," he said pulling my arm harder down the hall.

As I scrambled to catch up we didn't say goodbye to anyone, and we didn't pause at the door. Peter grabbed our coats from the coat check station silently, and pushed me outside with my arms holding my coat closed against me from the cold.

When we got to my car, I tried to speak but Peter shook his head no. Shaking, I didn't even know what to do or say. So wordless and stunned I did nothing, even as Peter opened my door and helped me inside.

Running around my car, Peter started it and backed out so quickly, I couldn't even grab my seatbelt fast enough before we were peeling out of the driveway onto a main road. From inside heat and noise, to the chaos of Peter's driving on the slick roads I was stunned silent, until my tears began to fall.

Sudden and without pause, tears poured down my face as I tried to reason what just happened.

Minutes later when Peter tried to take my hand, I pulled away. When he placed his hand on my knee, I moved closer to the door. When he tried to speak, I shook my head no, until he stopped trying.

Peter's driving slowed down and became normal as his breathing became quieter in the silence of my car. Everything seemed to slow down to a manageable pace except for my tears. My tears continued until I was embarrassed each time I had to wipe my face with my hands.

I couldn't even reason what I felt. There were just no words for the confusion breaking my heart. I was lost again, but lost with Peter beside me felt so much worse than lost before him.

"I don't understand what just happened between us," I whispered in the car suddenly.

"Oh, god, Sophie. Nothing happened between us. We're still us. My sister has a way of pushing me too far, and I snapped, but *we're* fine. You and I are good, and nothing's wrong between us," he said. But everything suddenly felt wrong to me.

"What do you have to tell me? If you're married I'm gonna throw up. Then I'm going to kill you," I laughed nearly insane.

"I'm not married. It's nothing like that. Kara is just a nosey bitch and she thinks every part of everyone's life is fair game. But I'll tell you tomorrow if you want."

"I want to know what's going on now, Peter. What the hell was that all about?" I pushed.

"Tomorrow. I promise Sophie, tomorrow I'll tell you," he huffed. "It's nothing, baby, I swear. Tomorrow morning over coffee, I'll tell you everything. Just please let it go for now. I'm sad and desperate, and I just want to be with you," he begged. And like an idiot, I relented slightly.

"Fine. Tomorrow, Peter."

20 minutes later when we were back at my apartment walking from my car, I thought this kind of drama and upset wasn't us. Peter used loving words and declarations to me. He didn't act aggressive and scary, and I knew this wasn't my Peter.

Then again, as I reasoned while I walked, this wasn't a typical night with Peter either. Peter was saying goodbye to an uncle he loved, and he had fought with his family over something I didn't understand. He wasn't himself which made our relationship not itself.

Everything was different because the circumstances were different, so I decided to try harder to let everything go.

CHAPTER 19

When we arrived home, Peter pulled my hand to follow him to my room. He didn't pause, and he didn't ask. He just took me to my room and because I knew he was desperate for my understanding and love I let him lead us.

Pulling me to a stop, Peter lifted his hands to my face as he spoke against my lips. "I am so sorry for my behavior tonight. My sister stresses me out, and I was emotional about my uncle, which is no excuse, but I can promise it won't happen again. Please forgive me," he begged before kissing me into the most beautiful, passionate kiss I had ever experienced with him.

"I wish I could have danced with you tonight. And I wish I'd taken a photo of you. You look so beautiful, I want a photo of you tonight to carry with me always. I absolutely adore you, Sophie," he moaned as I gasped. "I do. You are everything to me in this life, Sophie."

Pulling away from me, Peter leaned me against the wall as he sat on my bed to look at me. Staring at my face, he made his way down my body back to my face again. Breathing deeply, he suddenly looked at me like he was too emotional to speak, so I went to him instead.

Taking his head in my hands, I placed his face against my chest to soothe him. Holding him, I allowed all my strength to help him in his sadness.

"I'm here, Peter. I'm here to hold you when you're hurting, too. Take what you need from me and come back to me," I whispered in the silence of my room.

Moaning, "That was beautiful, baby. Just being with you makes me better. I'm happy with you, and I'm better when I'm with you," he said against my chest as he pulled me tighter to him as he stood.

Taking me into another kiss, Peter unzipped the back of my red power dress and slipped it down my body. Looking at my bra and panties through the nylons I wore, he gently removed them as well. Slipping all my clothing from me, I found myself standing naked before him in the light of my room securely.

Peter knew every mark on my body and every bump I wish I could hide.

He knew my flaws and he loved my imperfections. He was Peter standing with me and I was secure in the knowledge that I was adored.
 "Be with me, Sophie," he begged as I nodded.

  Together, we slowly took each other. Kissing and touching, fondling, and gripping, Peter and I soothed and loved our awful night away.
 He pleasured me with his mouth and fingers, as I took him into my mouth as well. We were nearly delirious with our passion, and time slowly crept away from us. We were insatiable and starved for the connection we shared.
 Peter brought me to my plateau until he pushed me over it seated deep inside me. He was starved for me, and I let him feast. Over and over again he took what he needed, never once leaving me alone in our connection. He whispered words of adoration and affection throughout as he made me ache with my need for his love.

  Sticky and sweaty from our night together I moved Peter to join me in the shower. Standing under the water, after he cleaned my exhausted body he kissed me again in a way that made me whole. Holding my face close to him, I loved openly and honestly with him in our silent moment of complete abandon.
 After our shower, when we stumbled to bed, I was once again wrapped from behind, snuggled tightly by Peter as we spooned before sleep claimed us. But I waited to sleep.
 I waited until I heard his breath even out as his hands stop caressing me. I waited until he was asleep and in peace. I waited so I could say the words to him I always breathed into the silence of night.
 "I love you, Peter…"

  Waking later that night, reaching to touch Peter, I found him watching me from the floor. Leaning against the wall, Peter was staring at me as I slept.
 Smiling as I woke, Peter whispered, "Listen, Sophie," and I did.
 Listening as I shook myself more awake, Peter began gently singing along to Pearl Jam's Black, and I instantly wept. It was so quick and so sudden, I didn't know where the emotion came from, and I didn't know how to contain it, so I just stopped trying.

Weeping on my side as I looked at Peter sitting 2 feet from me on the floor, I was simply overwhelmed by everything between us.

Black was a lifelong favorite song of mine, and to hear my artist lover sing about 'sheets of empty canvas' to me in the night broke my heart.

Quietly, like he knew too much emotion would destroy me, Peter sang Black's final verse with tears in his own eyes, as my hands reached out and grabbed for him. Pulling and nearly falling off the bed myself, Peter stood and climbed back into bed, pulling me to him as he spooned me close.

Silently, we were together until I whispered the only thing I could in the beautiful moment between us, "You're the only sky I'll ever be a star in, Peter."

And during the silence that followed my little confession, I actually felt Peter's body relax against me. Surrounding me in his warmth just before I fell back asleep, I heard him whisper softly in my ear, "I adore you..."

When I woke a few hours later I was alone again. Feeling his absence and panicking from the loss of his warmth surrounding me, I crawled out of my bed to find Peter sitting on the couch in darkness.

Watching him, I was surprised to see Peter distracted, talking to himself, while crying. Watching him for a second, I was afraid as I quickly moved to the back of the couch to wrap my arms around him. I was afraid of his sadness, but as I gripped him from behind he sighed like he was content.

Turning to me while grabbing my hands on his shoulder, he begged, "Please don't ever leave me."

"I won't. Ever," I replied instantly. With a conviction that was absolute, I looked him in the eyes, and told him I would never leave him. I told him what he needed to hear, and I meant it.

After a few silent moments between us, as Peter watched my face he eventually rose from the couch and followed me back to bed. Wrapping me in his arms as he always did he kissed my head, and told me he adored me as I smiled and exhaled the tension of his absence from my bed.

*****

LOST

The following morning Peter seemed much better as he hopped up to make me breakfast. Leaving me in bed to rest, he happily left me once he remembered I hadn't eaten the night before because of our quick departure from the party.

After brushing my teeth, I wore the green robe he bought me for Valentine's Day and I joined him in the kitchen. Watching him cook with coy smiles between us, I couldn't help myself when I walked to him and hugged him tightly from behind. Holding him, I felt so much love between us I couldn't stop myself from kissing his spine.

"Sophie..." he moaned as he shut off the stove, took my hand, and led me back to my bedroom.

And that was the day I made love like they do in the movies.

Peter laid me down sideways across the bed as he stripped me of my robe. Moving slowly, Peter kissed my body from my feet up to my lips, like a slow tease made to torture me. Peter worshipped my entire body with his lips and hands as I waited for his mouth to join my own. And when we finally kissed on the lips there was so much love between us, I experienced a sensation unlike anything I had ever known.

Everything was slow and amazing with almost a dream-like quality between us. When he touched me I felt his touch everywhere inside and outside my body. When we kissed I felt it deep in my stomach. When we moved, I felt like I moved in a trance.

After endless movement and caresses between us I didn't reach and pause at my painful plateau, but I came for the first time in my life with Peter deep inside me. We came together and moved slowly within each other. We experienced a connection so deep, it would always become the moment shared that we tried to reach again. I knew we had reached a point within our relationship that would define our love forever.

We were so beautiful, I said the words I had always wanted to say.

"I love you, Peter. So much I almost hurt inside."

"Oh, Sophie... I love you, too," he moaned before another deep kiss silenced me.

"That was amazing. I've never experienced anything like that it in my life," I grinned after our kiss.

"Me either. I think that's the official make love version of sex," he grinned back as he pulled me tightly into his arms.

"I know. I felt like that, too. It was one of those the earth ended around us but we were oblivious to anything but each other moments. I wonder if we'll ever share that again."

"We will," he smiled with another light kiss to my lips. "Always…"

Breathing Peter deep inside me, we stilled. I laid with him beyond content and so filled with love I couldn't imagine my world without him in it.

Eventually, Peter again stood and promised to finish breakfast, but only if I didn't distract him with my sexy ways. So laughing I agreed, and I even said I'd go for coffee while he finished cooking.

When we left my bed, I took a quick rinse off shower, dressed quickly and headed for the door. Leaving, I yelled goodbye to his head poking out my kitchen door with a smile and I left for our much needed coffee.

I remember walking to the café that morning feeling giddy again and nearly delirious with my happiness. I smiled at everyone, and even found myself giggling for no reason a few times, though I quickly pulled myself together.

Walking home with our coffee and 2 chocolate-filled Danishes, I thought of what Peter had to tell me. I had waited patiently all night, and truthfully, forgot for most of it because of the time we spent together, but walking I suddenly remembered.

Peter had promised to talk to me, and had never broken a promise before, so I was ready to listen. Whatever had happened in his past was his past I had decided and I didn't want anything to touch our future. Of course I wanted to know what was going on, but honestly, I didn't think it would matter to me in the end. Shy of being married or murdering people for a living, I really didn't think anything could change the way I felt for Peter.

Entering my little courtyard, I decided I would listen to him and we'd be okay. We had made love and shared the ultimate connection with each other, and I knew in my heart I could handle anything for Peter.

*****

LOST

Opening my front door, I spotted first one breakfast plate filled on the coffee table, and second, Peter standing against the fireplace mantle.

"Did you finish your breakfast already? Even without a coffee?" I grinned as he turned to me, but then my heart stopped.

Peter turned to me sobbing. He was crying so hard, I thought his uncle must have died in the night, or something equally as shocking. I didn't know, but I had never seen a man display such emotion before. I was actually stunned silent for a second until I processed what I was seeing.

Slowly putting the coffee down on the end table, I whispered, "What's wrong, Peter?" But he didn't seem able to speak.

Walking to me, he gave me a hug and kissed my forehead. Keeping his lips against my skin, Peter cried harder until I wrapped my arms tighter around him.

"What's wrong? Tell me," I begged.

"Being with you scares me, Sophie," he whispered as I flinched.

"What? *Why?*" I croaked through the sudden tightness in my throat.

"The way I feel about you ties me in knots and it makes me afraid of everything. I'm afraid you'll leave me, and I'm afraid you'll be taken away. So I can't really do this anymore. I know you love me and I feel the same, but I have to go now. I know something bad is going to happen to you if I stay."

"No, it isn't!" I yelled trying to pull away, but he held me tighter. "I don't know what you're saying..." I cried.

"I have to go. I'm sorry. I love you, Sophie," he said as he kissed my forehead again and then quickly walked away from me.

Quickly, like almost diving for the door, he walked away as I stood in my total *what the fuck* world.

When he grabbed his coat from the closet by the door he paused for only a second. One second in which I wished I had had the perfect words. I wished I could have said something to make him stay. I wished I could have said *something*. But I was stuck in a spinning, shaking, shocked world of total disbelief.

And I had no words.

As if realizing what was happening, my body jerked forward as I dove for Peter grabbing his back and smashing up against him. Moaning, I didn't have the words. Crying, I couldn't stop what was happening. Begging, I was desperate.

"Oh, *god,* please, Peter? Please don't do this," I cried. "Please don't leave me," I moaned

But he wouldn't even turn to me. Clinging to him I begged, but he stayed silent against the door with me clawing at him to stay.

"I have to go, Sophie. I *have to,*" he said quietly. Then he pulled away to face me, and walked me backward from him. Stopping, he held my upper arms still as he stared into my eyes like he needed to remember that moment forever. He stared at me as I held my breath, silently begging him to stay.

With tears falling from his eyes, dripping down his cheeks slowly, he ended us.

"I have to go, Sophie," he moaned. "I'm so sorry..."

And when I gasped a breath he released my arms to turn and walk away.

Peter opened the door and closed it behind him without even looking back at me once. He didn't look back even for a second. He simply opened the door and closed it behind him as he left me forever.

Watching his back as he closed the door was the last moment I ever saw Peter as I knew him to be.

CHAPTER 20

After he walked out the door everything spun around me into a moving stillness.
There were no sounds, and there was no air. The world vanished behind its brown knotted escape. There was only a closed door and the world outside.
There was no life and there was no death. There was nothing but a silence screaming in its quiet agony.
There was absolutely nothing but the end screaming at me from behind a closed door.

I remember standing behind the couch for what felt like hours. I stood there waiting for him to return. I waited for him to poke his head in the door and smile. I waited for him to return to tell me he was joking- not that it was much of a joke, but I'd take it as an explanation. Honestly, I would take *anything* as explanation for the event that just destroyed me.
I remember standing staring at the door until I actually laughed out loud at its brown knotted smile. I laughed like a crazy person- all manic and hysterical sounding. I laughed because I didn't know what else to do.
But after the laughter faded, as I shook behind my couch staring at the door, I started talking to Peter.
I said everything I had ever wanted to say to him. I told him what he meant to me and what I had wanted to mean to him. I told him about the changes in me, and the growth I had experienced with him by my side. I told him about the Sophie I had become, and how proud I was of her.
I even told Peter about our future.
I told him I was going to marry him and have 2 of his children. I told him about our green-eyed girl and our blue-eyed boy. I told him about our busy lives with our children, and about our quiet nights with them safely asleep.
I told him about the cool, old brick house we would buy in the village and about the colorful paint we decorated our home with. I told him about the herb garden in the back and about the drying closet in the attic. I told him about the pool I wanted, and about the swings our

babies needed.

I then told Peter about the sex we had for the rest of our lives, long after I got fat and carried proudly the stretch marks from our children.
I told Peter about the endless passion we would share until death took us from each other. And then I told him about our funerals and our gravestones, which held hands even in death.
I told Peter everything I had known would be our lives together, until I just couldn't speak anymore.

But when the silence hit, my world felt worse.
Talking seemed to ease some of the fear and pressure from my chest, so the sudden silence brought on the fear and pain that was quickly crushing me.
I was in agony *and* I was numb; I remember that feeling. I remember feeling suffocated by pain, but not actually able to feel it. The pain almost stopped my heart at one point, I remember that, too.
The pain was so great, my chest began throbbing in an unnatural rhythm, while my pulse battered my eardrums and temples. My heart sped up and beat so erratically I tried to find the uneven rhythm, but I couldn't play its beat. Every time I thought I had the rhythm down, there was a missed note, or a sped up beat that threw me off again. I remember not even being able to play my own song as my heart cried in my chest.
But the silence almost killed me, so I talked some more. And if nothing else, I found a kind of insane solace from my unheard words. No one could hear me, but I heard. No one knew I was speaking my life, but I knew.
I was talking to Peter, and the words eased the pain. I talked to Peter behind the brown knotted door until the pain of his absence became bearable, then I finally sat down.
In the stillness of the March evening I sat on my couch and wept.
I cried until I was nothing more than a gasping hiccup of breath. I cried until I was sightless; swollen from the pain of my weeping eyes. I cried until the hours passed and I fell asleep in my pain-filled misery.

When the dreams struck, so vivid and lifelike, I cried out as the orgasm Peter gave me surfaced in my reality. I cried out as I woke to the orgasm brought on by the only true love making I had ever known. I cried out at

the hollow emptiness left from the hollow orgasm of my dreams.
  Waking, I cried again as I stumbled to the shower. Washing, and scrubbing, and crying, I let the water cleanse me as I sat with my thoughts making me insane.

  I cried until I suddenly thought to call Peter and beg him to come back to me. Slipping on the bathroom floor, banging my hip and wrist on the counter, I ran for the phone.
  Dialing, I was insane with the speed and breadth of purpose coursing through me. I just had to say his name. I just had to tell him I needed him. I just had to ask him to come back to me and he's return.
  But he didn't answer. And his answering machine lay dead as the rings drove me to madness.

  After I cried for another hour I knew I was still needed in the world, so I made coffee in my Bodum, dried and styled my hair, and I waited for 8:00am to find me.
  I drove to work dressed and presentable and I began payroll first thing so I knew I hadn't failed at work. I worked hard through my confusion and sadness, and I made it to lunch before walking out the door with nothing said but an *I'm sick* to reception as I walked away from my career.
  Driving home unaware of anything that made sense I found myself stopping for coffee. I actually parked on the side street of the village, stumbled out of my car exhausted and walked into the cafe I loved for my favorite French Vanilla coffee.
  I couldn't understand the comfort I received from the scent of the cafe, or even the peace that threatened to consume me. I didn't understand how a cafe filled with coffee stuff could bring me a sort of peace, but it did. So I ordered my coffee, in house, in their brightly colored ceramic mug and I drank my coffee alone.
  I pulled out my laptop and emailed my boss explaining I was sick and needed the following day off. I emailed Madeline to let her know I wouldn't be in, and then I emailed Peter.
  I wrote to Peter everything I had spoken to the door in his absence.
  For hours I wrote him and told him everything I was, everything I wanted to be, and everything he was to me. I told him everything, and then I 'saved draft'.

I couldn't hit send, but I couldn't hit delete either. I was stuck as I wrote and cried and drank my 4th coffee.

Hours later when I woke up, I was humiliated to have a Barista touching my shoulder as I raised my head. Looking around, there was only one other customer at the counter, and a few employees behind the counter. They were closing, which meant it was 7:00.

"I'm sorry I fell asleep," I whispered as I began collecting my laptop and purse.

"No worries, Sophie. You look exhausted. Rough day at work?" She asked kindly as I nodded my head yes.

"How do you know my name?"

"Um, you always come in here. We all know your name," she answered looking confused.

"Sorry. It's been a long day," I mumbled as I stood up bursting into tears as I walked out the door.

Walking out of the cafe, I began my slippery trek home. Walking one block felt like it took hours. Actually, walking one block *did* take hours. I was unsteady in my heels on the slushy ground, and I was unsteady in my body as I struggled to stay upright.

When I finally opened my main door, I had hoped he would be waiting, but he wasn't. I had hoped I would see my door taped with blue roses, but it wasn't. I had hoped there was a reprieve somewhere from the agony I was in, but there wasn't.

This was my new life I realized, and I needed to live within it.

I slept as much as possible, broken and crying, struggling within erotic dreams and horrible nightmares. But I did sleep, somewhat.

I woke the following morning and proceeded with my day as best as I could. I noticed my hands visibly shaking as I dressed, so I forced myself to eat before I left. I also drank orange juice instead of coffee for the first time in my life.

I eventually left for work, realizing too late to be on time that my car was in the village, so I hurried to it trying to lessen the late I was probably going to experience at work.

Through all the stress of rushing, I arrived to people welcoming me, albeit looking confused because they all thought I would be off sick for the day. People greeted me warmly, but kept away, whether because I looked like shit and they were afraid to catch it, or because I looked like shit and they were afraid to experience it, I didn't know. But I was left

LOST

alone on Tuesday to work quietly in my office, and I did.

Every single time my phone rang early in the day I admit I found myself jumping and hoping. I would pray and beg for him, but Peter never called. So by the afternoon I was numb to the phone's potential to save me from the darkness I was living in, until somehow I made it through the day, leaving at 5:00 because I had left early the day before 'sick'.

Finishing another day, I continued.

By Wednesday morning at 11:00, however, I was finally tracked down by Steven.

Steven finally got to me through my direct line somehow even though I had casually asked Madeline to block all my calls from him. And when she raised her eyebrow at my request, I remember smiling with a sigh and saying, 'family drama' which was apparently enough to make her drop it with a knowing nod.

But Steven reached me Wednesday morning when I picked up without thinking.

"Soph! Where the fuck have you been? I've called you since Friday and nothing! What's going on?"

"Nothing at all," I lied to my brother. Lying, I held my voice calm and I made sure to sound completely together.

"Sophie. Why haven't you called me back? Are you mad at me?" Steven asked with a sadness I knew only my neglect could cause him. There was a sadness in his tone that made me break.

In a near whisper, I answered all I could. "No, Steven. Never. I'm just busy and stuff is going on... That's all, I promise." But even I could hear the distress in my voice.

"Aaaah, Soph? What is it, girlie? Tell me," Steven said with my childhood tease.

But as my throat closed and my heart splintered at the affection only Steven could give me, I begged him desperately. "Not now Steven... *Please*. Later, okay?" I begged as the first sob broke free. "Please, not now. I'm at work and I can't," I cried.

"Okay. I'll meet you at your place right after work. I'll be waiting for you by 5:15 at your door. I'll even bring the Chinese," he soothed, but I couldn't stand it anymore.

"Please don't be nice to me right now because I'll totally lose it. I'll see you after work. I have to go," I cried again as I hung up.

But it was too late to stop the upset. I was crying, and the tears were out of control and soul consuming. I tried for the first minute to stop them, but the pressure became so great in my chest I knew if I didn't let the tears take me I would have some kind of heart pounding attack again, so I gave in.

Sobbing at my desk, I let the agony take me again until I placed my head on my desk and waiting for the gasping hiccups to signal the end of my nightmare, in the short term.

"Let's go to the mall over lunch. You need to buy a hat," I jumped when Madeline suddenly spoke in my closed office.

Looking at her like she was as crazy as I felt, I huffed a laugh. "I need a hat?"

"Yup. I figure you and Peter broke up, but I won't tell anyone, I swear. So we need to go to the mall and find you a cute hat. I did it once and even though I don't have the right face for a hat, I totally felt awesome in the hat after I bought it. So we need to buy you a hat."

Again, just staring at Madeline I couldn't help but wonder who the hell was less sane in that moment. "A hat? Seriously?" I laughed.

"You have the perfect round face for a hat, and with your blonde hair you'll look great in almost any color. So let's go. I promise we'll have fun, and I won't tell anyone. We can even leave separately if you want so no one knows you're with me. But let's go now. Its lunchtime, and you never take a lunch, so let's go buy a hat," she said so forcefully, I stood with another laugh threatening to burst out of my chest.

"Why would I care if people saw us leave together?" I grinned at the conspiracy.

"Because you never socialize with any of us, so it'll look weird if you suddenly do. Plus, I didn't think you would want anyone to know we're talking," Madeline responded honestly but without any malice I could see.

Pausing, I had to know suddenly what people thought of me. "Am I the bitch around here?"

"Not at all. You're the Recluse. Everyone likes you but you never socialize so people just assume you're like a Garbo- I vant to be alone- kind of woman."

"I'm not a Garbo, but I do like my privacy," I defended. "You really want to go to the mall with me?" I whined as I wiped my face a little with a tissue.

LOST

"Yup. Let's go. Okay?" She almost begged, and I just couldn't say no to her kindness. Whether I needed a hat or not, I did need different scenery, and a change from the nightmare I was living in. So grabbing my coat and purse, I left my office with Madeline blocking me a little from the office staff as I walked out with my head lowered, but not too obviously.

When we went to the mall, against all assumptions I had made, Madeline didn't ask one single question about me and Peter. She didn't pry or prompt me to talk. She just talked and pointed out hotties and *ughs* throughout the mall and then she forced me to buy a super cute wool black and red fuzzy toque-like hat with a matching scarf. She was even proud of herself for getting an end of season bargain in the process.

Afterward, when we returned to work, I proudly wore my hat and scarf as I walked back to my office with my head up. My new hat fixed absolutely nothing, but it did temporarily bandage everything that was bleeding inside me.

Dialing Madeline's extension when I sat down, I needed her to know how I felt about her. "Thank you very much Madeline for your kindness today. I really appreciate it," I spoke honestly.

"You're very welcome, Sophie. I'm always here to buy a hat if you need it," she giggled through the phone.

"Okay."

"Okay..." She said as she hung up.

CHAPTER 21

After I finished work, thanked Madeline again with a smile and drove home, I was again exhausted and emotionally numb. I spent my days pushing away any emotion so hard to create a kind of mindless numbness that often I found myself frozen within the numb as I tried to acclimate to my post work surroundings.

But as I walked in my building to Steven leaning against my apartment door, no acclimation was needed. Everything poured out of me on a whoosh.

Charging my brother, I dropped my bag and laptop case for his arms pulling me in tightly. Sobbing in his arms, Steven used his own emergency key to open my door as he pulled me inside.

When I was pulled to my couch I let him. When he shushed me and rubbed my back through my coat, I let him. He was no Peter, but he was the only constant I had ever known.

"I think I'm dying..." I whispered into his chest.

"Oh, Sophie, you're not dying. What happened?"

"Peter left me- like just left. We made love, like really made love- all sweet and beautiful and tender and like in cheesy chick flicks. We made love and we were amazing and an hour later he left me because he was freaked out by his feelings, and he had to go. Seriously. That's what he said," I repeated for the first time with a little anger surfacing.

"What do you mean?"

Pushing away from Steven, I sat up and turned to face him. "What do you mean, what do I mean? Exactly like I said. We were fine. We were so amazing, I knew he was my forever, and I was his. I knew it and I felt it, and everything was fine. Then we had this intense sexual, like passionate connection between us and I guess he freaked out or some bullshit guy thing, and then he walked out. He admitted he loved me, then he said he was afraid something bad would happen to me, then he just left. Like just totally left me standing there in shock. He kissed my forehead and paused for one goddamn second, and then he left me. And I don't get it!" I cried again. Totally snot covered, mascara everywhere crying. I sobbed as Steven stayed quiet beside me.

"When?" He asked quietly.

"Sunday morning. We were amazing and I went to get coffee, and a half hour later he was gone. I don't know what the hell happened. I have NO idea what happened. There was nothing wrong between us. When I went to get coffee he was cooking us breakfast with a smile, and when I returned 15 minutes later he was dumping me. And I just don't get it."

"Have you tried to talk to him?"

"Of course," I answered irritated.

"What did he say?"

"Nothing. He won't answer his cell, and his house phone won't pick up messages. Honestly, I've called him a hundred times since Sunday night. *Hundreds* of times. I call him almost hourly but the same thing happens over and over again, which is nothing. No voice mail and no answering machine, and I don't know what else to do."

Looking at me as I struggled to take off my coat, Steven helped but didn't speak. I think he was trying to help me but no answers were coming to him.

"Um, have you tried going to his house?" He asked as I shook my head no. "Why? Maybe if he sees you he'll talk to you easier. Maybe he just needs to see you again or something. Why don't we drive to his house and I'll stay in the car if you want."

"I can't," I cried.

"Why? I know face to face always pulls my head out of-"

"I don't know where he lives, *okay?*"

"What do you mean? You were together for over 3 months. How don't you-"

"We just never went to his place. He always met me here. He worked and then met me here before or after work. Or like we went away a few times, but we just never made it to his place," I admitted knowing it sounded weird.

"Sophie, that sounds a little strange," Steven said almost as an accusation.

"I know that *now,* but at the time I didn't think anything of it. I just enjoyed being with him so much I didn't care that it was always at my place. It really didn't feel weird at the time," I said with conviction.

"And now?"

Looking at Steven, I knew he knew I knew this, so I just gave in. "Yes, I admit it seems strange now, but he promised he wasn't married or anything when I asked him after the fight with his family. I did ask him Steven," I again defended myself.

"What fight?"

"None of this matters," I growled. "He had a fight with his 2 sisters and his mom the night before he left and they were trying to make him tell me something, but he wouldn't, and then we were together and everything was so amazing, I knew whatever it was wouldn't matter. So I let it go thinking he would tell me over breakfast like he promised, but then he broke up with me-"

"Instead of telling you something?" Steven prompted.

"Yes, but it wasn't like that. I *know* it wasn't. Peter was always so open and honest with me and he adored me, he told me that. He said he adored me and I believe him. But I did ask if he was married or something equally as messed up and he swore he wasn't. He promised he would tell me whatever they were so serious about, but he didn't have time to tell me before we broke up."

"Didn't have time? Or broke up with you so he wouldn't have to tell you?" Steven asked seriously.

"No. I know it wasn't anything like that."

"How do you know?" He pushed.

"Because I knew him, Steven! Shit," I moaned. "Guys like Peter don't have wives and lovers on the side. Plus, when would he have had time? He always spoke to me. *Always*. And if he wasn't working he was with me. We were together every chance we had. Plus, I know him, and I know he wasn't married. He told me about his father cheating once on his mom and how devastated she was and how he became not an asshole because of his sisters and his mother. He's a really good guy and an amazing man, he just-"

"Dumped you right out of the blue with no explanation or reason," Steven said angrily.

"No, he had a reason. He felt too much, and he was scared, and he loves me too much and..." But I ran out of steam. My denials sounded forced even to me. "I can't explain anything properly right now. I just know he was good, and whatever happened was something I must have done or said, or didn't realize was making him want to break up with me," I cried softly.

"Really? *You* did this? Because a second ago you did nothing wrong, but he freaked out and loved YOU too much and he dumped you, but now you did something to provoke it?" Steven questioned angrily.

And crying to my brother I couldn't hide the truth I think I knew. "I must have..." And then there was nothing but silence between us.

   Shaking his head, Steven tried again. "What about his sisters? Maybe call one of them?"
   And again I knew it sounded weird, but, "I don't know how to reach them," I cried.
   "Do you know their last names?" He asked as I shook my head no.
   "His parents?"
   "No... I know their last name is Connor but not where they live. I don't even know if it's here. I think he grew up here but I'm not sure. And Connor is such a common last name I wouldn't be able to even 411 it. Plus, what would I say? Um, could you ask Peter to call me please? I know he broke up with me and I know I'm not in high school anymore, but would you please give him a message and have him call me?" I was starting to get bitchy with Steven, which amazingly felt better than devastated.
   "Look, whether the circumstances around our relationship seem strange or not doesn't change the relationship we had. I'm in love with him, and I know he loves me. We share something very special between us and I don't know how to live without it. I know I'll never find it again, and I don't even want to. I want Peter," I cried out again.
   "Where does he work?" Steven asked without emotion.
   "Um..." Jesus Christ. I remember sounding so stupid suddenly. "In a steel company that recycles steel."
   "A steel company, in a steel town? *Fuck*, Sophie. Did he tell you absolutely anything about himself?" Steven asked while standing over me.
   "Yes... I know everything about him."
   "You know *nothing* about him," he replied angrily.
   "I know *everything* about him! I know who he is and how he loves and who he loved before me and why he loves me the most in his life. I know all I need to know!"
   "Sophie... *Please*. Think for a second. He came across way too strong in the beginning, even a little desperate, then you're madly in love with him within weeks. You've spent only 3 and a half months with the guy, you're left devastated, and you know absolutely nothing about him. He may be a good lay, but-" I died with Steven's words.
   Bursting into tears, I sobbed as the pain lashed at me. I was shaken to

my core with the knowledge that it was more than just sex between us.

   Moaning on the couch, shaking all over, I tried to explain what was real.
  "No one tries as hard as he did to just screw someone," I begged him to understand. "Peter was all about *me*. Never once did he hurt me or take me, or just screw me. It wasn't like that, Steven. I know it wasn't. Peter and I were special- like mom and dad special. And I'm not wrong about that. I'm not." I again wished I could explain us. "You just don't understand the way we were. It wasn't about being a good lay, or just screwing me. It was about our connection, and our emotions, and a tenderness and a love between us that was so rare and unique and special, and just amazing. Peter is everything to me," I cried as I stopped talking.
  I really didn't think Steven was capable of understanding what I was saying. And I would never go into graphic detail with him about our sex-life, but I needed him to understand something very important.
  "Steven, please don't gag and just listen to me. Peter brought me out of my sexual, like, denial or something. He brought me to orgasm because he needed me to have one with him. He tried and learned and did everything right so that he and I could experience that kind of love and intimacy between us. It wasn't about getting laid, I swear. It was so much more. And NOT because I'm a woman and I need to see it that way. But because it *was* that way, because Peter made it that way. I was totally free with him sexually and with a love that was so deep I didn't even know anything like that existed between 2 people. All the speeches mom and dad gave us growing up about intimacy and love and the connection between 2 people was nothing compared to what it actually felt like between us."
  "But you don't know-"
  "I know everything I need to know. He is the absolute love of my life, and I have to have him back. I have to be with him, because I don't think I can live without him," I confessed to a sudden silence in my living room.
  "Sophie, what are you saying?" Steven asked dropping back onto the couch beside me.
  "I'm not saying I'm suicidal or anything like that, but I just know I can't live without him because I won't be living. I'm just going to walk through life without a part of me. Like those identical twins who say they died when their twin died, or like the old couple who dies hours apart because they couldn't live without their partner. I don't know how to do it. And 3 months or 30 years with Peter wouldn't have changed my

answer. I love him, Steven, and I've changed totally in my heart because of him. I just can't do this without him, which is ironic I know. I can't live without him helping me live through living without him. But that's what he means to me," I exhaled my sadness and pain.

"But you have mom and dad, and me and your friends, and your job, and-"

"I know all that. But I hurt too much to be without him. I need you to understand," I begged.

Shaking his head, and exhaling a long breath, Steven tried again.

"I understand that you're suffering your first heartbreak at 25 and you don't know how to deal with it. Most people experience it as a teenager, but you didn't, so now you're fucked up. But that's all this is, Soph. It's a heartbreak. And you will get better and it'll hurt less, I promise. Remember when Melissa and I broke up- well, when she dumped me? I was fucked. I felt like I was gonna throw up, but I got hammered instead with my friends, and eventually I felt better. I still think about her, and I hated hearing she's engaged to some perfect asshole, but I don't feel heartbroken anymore, just sad now. I loved her but she dumped me and it hurt. But I'm fine-"

Looking at Steven my mouth dropped open at the lame comparison he tried to make and I absolutely hated Steven in that moment.

"What you had with Melissa was NOTHING! It was a 6 month nothing. You guys were nothing compared to me and Peter, so don't even try to compare that little bullshit relationship you had to mine! You don't get it and you never will, obviously, so I don't want to talk to you-"

"Because I'm right?"

"No! Because you're an idiot. Get out of my home!"

"Nope!" Steven yelled standing over me again. "I'm not leaving. Be a bitch. Be pissed. I don't really care. You're totally fucked up and you need me, so I'm going to eat my Chinese and let you be a complete bitch to me if you want, but I'm not leaving, so fuck off, Sophie. Seriously." Steven finished his rant by walking to the front door, grabbing the paper bag of food and storming to my kitchen.

Slamming cupboards and ripping the cutlery drawer right off its track as everything spilled to the floor, I could hear Steven swearing up a blue streak. He was pissed and I deserved it. So I cried a little more as I walked to him.

"I'm sorry," I said looking at Steven on the floor. Leaning against the door jamb, I apologized again. "I know you're trying to help, but nothing helps. I just hurt so bad, I don't know how to handle it. I'm okay at work because I have to be strong and professional, but at home or in the car, I'm a mess. I miss him so much, I can't believe it's only been 4 days without him. I can't even imagine 4 weeks, or months, or whatever. I'm just so sad, Steven," I said as he nodded. "This is like an unbearable pain in my chest that makes my heart beat erratically and my head spin with the pain. I don't really know how to get through this, when all I want to do is find him and hit him and love him and beg him to be with me again," I cried to my brother my absolute truth. "I love him so much, I need him with me."

"You just have to get through one day at a time. Honestly, I'm not good with all this emotional shit but-"

"You're doing really well," I smiled.

"Anyway, that's all you can do. Wake up each day until it hurts a little less and then move on eventually. Do what a guy does. Get drunk. Get laid. Buy new shoes like a chick or something."

"I bought a hat today," I laughed.

"O-*kay*... whatever works. But you have to just try to be strong every day until you notice it doesn't hurt as bad anymore, until it actually *doesn't* hurt as bad anymore. You have to, 'cause what else can you do?"

Looking at my brother as he stood desperately in front of me, I was so sad again. I was sad at his wisdom, and sad from missing Peter. I was just so sad, nothing felt right inside me, and everything hurt me.

"I can't believe how much this hurts. This agony is all I'll ever know, and it consumes me," I whispered.

"Ohhh, Soph. It won't always. And I won't say anything bad about him, but I think there's more to Peter than you know, otherwise he wouldn't have been able to leave like he did. That's what I think anyway," he said until he took me into his arms again.

Crying softly, I released all the tension and pain from my body, and let it take me. Pulling away from Steven, he pulled me back to him and whispered, "Just let it get out, girlie," which naturally let it out.

Sobbing, I let it go. As the pain lashed through my chest, and my head pounded from the ferocity of my sobs, I let out the pain with Steven- the only true constant in my life.

"Thank-you," I hiccupped through my tears.

But he didn't reply. Steven walked me to the couch, sat down with me, and snuggled up so I could get it all out.

LOST

    Later Wednesday night after Steven left, I showered and decided to go to bed early. I was exhausted from faking being well at work, and from falling apart at home. I was beyond exhausted from lack of sleep, and from the pain inside me that wouldn't lessen.

    My world was a constant carousel of pain and exhaustion, sadness and shock, and I still couldn't believe Peter had left me. I just couldn't believe it. It was too unbelievable to remember the love and passion we had shared Sunday, compared to the pain and absence of love hours later.

    As I lay thinking in my bed while I slowly began to relax, I realized the love hadn't left me with Peter.

    Peter was my forever, I knew in my soul. I knew that reality was my forever, so my love didn't die, it just changed to a love without a purpose- a love I would always know and always suffer in his absence.

    The love I felt was still there, and probably always would be. The love I had remained, just unrequited and lost.

CHAPTER 22

On Thursday I went back to work, still devastated but determined not to let it show. I walked in, greeted everyone and gave a private smile to Madeline as I tipped my cute hat to her, making her laugh.

My day was an easy one, with no month end rush, or payroll looming over my head. It was easy in that I just had endless paperwork to complete alone in my office without a deadline or fellow employees threatening my sanity.

And Friday passed pretty much the same way, with the exception that Madeline, or Maddie, as she called herself to friends invited me out for drinks, which I gently declined. I let her down easy feigning a family engagement and then I got the hell out of there.

I had forced such a professional, together face all week, by Friday afternoon I was beyond exhausted, slipping into a near psychosis from sleep deprivation and heartache.

Driving home, I remember thinking about my week with an almost proud view of it. I knew I was devastated, but I was impressed with my ability to function when I thought of the depth of the pain eating me alive from the inside out.

And when I finally returned home, after I let the pain and agony take me with a good, long cry, I crawled into bed by 7:30 and I slept. Hard.

Those were my long days and weeks. And that was my time away from Peter. I was robotic and impressive, and I behaved as expected failing no one. I was good, happy on the surface, and professional.

Inside, of course, was different. I was still dying inside. I was absolutely DYING, but I just wouldn't die. Not that one actually dies from a broken heart, but if it was in fact possible, I was ready for it. I didn't want to die, but I was prepared for the inevitability of it happening because my heart simply stopped beating from all the pressure inside and the weight it had to carry alone.

I didn't know how I survived day after day and I really couldn't understand how I functioned, but somehow time passed and I continued to live.

LOST

    The pain was always with me though, sometimes as a dull ache, and sometimes as an acute agony. Sometimes I expected it, and at other times I was blindsided by it. However it came to me didn't really matter though because it was always pain.
    I spent my time alone after work listening to Green Eyes to relive our beautiful life, and I spent my time listening to Black to relive Peter's horrible goodbye.
    I lived in a continuously pain-filled replay, day after day, like my 2 favorite songs.

*****

    4 weeks after Peter left I had only lost a little bit of weight, not even enough to really show, so I looked the same on the outside, with the exception of the dark circles under my eyes. I still had my nails done once a month, and I still put a lighter blonde rinse in my slightly darker winter hair once a month. I dressed the same, and I acted the same, mostly. Well, in front of everyone else I acted the same.
    In reality, I was a bit of a stalker, without the object to stalk. I drove around on weekends looking for Peter. I drove all over my neighborhood and slightly beyond looking for a bright pink car. I went to our cafe in search of him, and I walked the full street of the village from the Chocolatier to Pandora's searching for any glimpse of Peter. But I never found him.

    Finally, on the 4th weekend without him I thought to try Sunshine and Life.
    Hugging Terry briefly after I entered, I casually asked if he had seen Peter. I was casual as I tried to act like I had broken up with him and wanted to make sure Peter was okay, in case Terry knew about our relationship. But when Terry said he hadn't seen Peter in months, I couldn't hide the tears from filling my eyes, or the absolute understanding on Terry's face that it was me who had been dumped.
    Holding in the tears before I left the store, while grabbing my favorite veggie chips, I finally asked Terry why he gave the strange look months before. I finally asked, and he told me the truth as he believed it.

"I think Peter is an undercover Cop, Sophie," he said so seriously I couldn't help my pause, or the laughter that burst from my chest. Laughing loudly in the quiet store, I knew I looked deranged but I just couldn't hold it in.

"A cop?" I laughed. "Yeah... I *really* don't think so. He's wayyyy too in touch with his emotional side to be a cop," I laughed a little more.

But as Terry watched me laughing he said nothing else until just the sound of my laughter seemed so odd in the store, I slowly quieted.

Looking at Terry, I was sure he was joking, but he didn't relent at all with his stoic expression. He stood behind the counter staring at me as I had my strange laughing fit, and then he finally spoke once I stopped.

"Come here," he said moving down the aisle to the back of the store as I followed him almost giggling again.

"I'm serious, Sophie. We've all speculated. We've all talked about it after his infrequent visits to the store before. There is something about the way he disappears, and returns, asking questions about whose been around, or whose been in trouble, or if anything seemed out of the ordinary around the village, etcetera, that made us all question why he asked."

"Please tell me this is a joke," I begged with a grin as I leaned against a shelf.

"I'm not joking. Ask Margaret," Terry continued. "One time Peter came in after no one had seen him in months. We had all left messages for his hand cream which I sell as quickly as he supplies it, but he never called us back. We left messages for 3 months but he never responded, and then one day out of the blue he walked in looking horrible. He was bruised and his hair was long and filthy, and he had this fake tattoo all over his hand, and when Margaret asked if he was okay, he just nodded. But then she asked what happened, and Peter smiled a little and said, 'some bad guys, that's all,' with a grin. And though Margaret tried to press, Peter wouldn't give any more information. But it always felt like there was more to Peter, you know?" Terry asked looking at me expectantly.

"Um... I *really* don't think so. Honestly, I just spent over 3 months with him, and he was never away or banged up, or, like anything like a cop. No offense Terry but I really think you're crazy," I laughed again.

"Look, I know many law enforcement officers, and I've seen police at trials and for pretrial dispositions, and I'm telling you, Peter was like them."

"Like what?" I swear to god, I was holding my breath but in total disbelief.

"Kind of aloof, but warm. Like one easygoing personality for us, and then a very intense personality watchful of everything around him."

"Paranoid?" I tried for a much simpler explanation.

"Not really," Terry paused. "Watchful, I would say. Anyway, it's all just speculation, but my gut tells me I'm right. I really think he's a cop and that's why he disappears, and that's why he returns a few months later, sometimes looking horrible, and sometimes just very worn out. But I don't know for sure, obviously," Terry said while leaning in closer.

Fighting to keep the laughter in, I bit my tongue until it passed. "Do you honestly believe that, or is this a weird joke, Terry? Because honestly, your sense of humor is a little odd," I asked grinning.

Smiling back at me, but shaking his head, Terry answered the question I couldn't believe I was asking.

"I honestly believe that. There's just something about Peter that tells me there's more going on than he admits to, or can tell us. And I think he's a cop," he answered seriously.

"Do you have his address?"

"No. He would only pick up his payments."

"Does he have a SIN number?"

"No. I paid him cash," he answered.

"Do you know where he works?"

"No. Other than what I think he does he's never actually told me where he works."

"Well, he told me. He said he works at a steel company that resells recyclable steel to smaller companies."

"A steel company, huh? Do you disappear for months at a time, and turn up looking, acting, and behaving differently? Do you turn up bruised and tattooed from a steel company?" Terry again pressed.

"No you don't, but I think it's a little too bizarre and unrealistic to think he's an undercover cop. I mean seriously, Terry, who does that? That's a TV show, not reality," I said a little pissed.

Looking at my old boss, I suddenly thought he was a bit of an idiot. Originally I just thought he was a post-trial lawyer, eccentric, reformed hippy guy, but looking at him in that moment, I thought he was more of a Law and Order, CSI, too much TV watching Fucktard, as Steven would say.

Irritated, I decided I was done with Terry and our whole bizarre conversation. Peter had been gone for 4 weeks at that point and I was tired of everyone and everything.

"Well, thanks for the enlightening conversation, Terry. I'll just grab these chips and let you get back to the counter," I attempted to sound final but not too bitchy. "Oh, you never did say why you gave us the weird look when Peter came in on my last day with the book."

"I was worried you'd get hurt if you got involved with him," he said way too seriously.

"And why's that?" I asked with major tone.

"Because I think his job is dangerous, and because I didn't know how long he'd be around until he had to go undercover again," he replied seriously.

Listening to Terry, I had had enough. Laughing again at the undercover comment, I put down the veggie chips, and shook my head at him. Walking back up the aisle to the front of the store as he followed me, I didn't even bother with a polite goodbye or a decent exit. I just laughed at his stupidity, and attempted to leave the store quickly before I said something very insulting.

"Sophie! Ask Margaret. She can give you better examples. Margaret and Peter have had coffee a few times," Terry spoke to my back as I opened the front door to leave.

"No, thanks," I said without turning back to him.

"Sophie! Undercover cops aren't just on TV, you know? How do you think the Police arrest people in gangs? Or other criminals? They actually exist in every city," Terry yelled again.

I was already a foot out the door though as I said a loud, "Okay. Thanks."

Stunned by my shitty morning, I started laughing outside in the cool April air, until I started crying thinking about Peter.

Walking back to my apartment I decided I needed a change. I had spent 4 weeks in a total funk- working all day, crying and obsessing all night. And my weekends were spent with the same crying, hurting, obsessing sadness my nights crushed me with.

I had missed 3 out of 4 Sunday dinners at my parents' since he left, and I had received hundreds of Steven phone calls every single day since Peter left me.

My parents were worried, and Steven was distressed by the weak Sophie I was in his eyes. For the first time in our lives he was the better, more stable twin, which we both hated. Steven was meant to be flighty, and I was meant to be stable. It was how we had worked for 25 years,

LOST

and I needed it back.

I needed to be me again, the pre-Peter me I was happy with. I needed to feel stable, secure, and confident in my world again. I needed to feel like me again. I had to figure out how the hell to get Sophie back.

*****

When Steven showed up at my place Sunday afternoon to take me to my parents' house for dinner, I was pissed. Throwing open the door, I was yelling before I even saw him and I continued yelling well after he was sitting on my couch ignoring me.

Turning on the TV, he flipped to and turned up a basketball game loudly. Ignoring me completely, I was filled with such a sudden rage, I actually kicked his shin, grabbed the remote and chucked it across the room while screaming for him to leave. But the bastard barely even flinched.

"Done?" He asked like a prick and I almost hit him.

I wanted to hit him so badly, just the shock of it stopped me in my tracks. Shaking, I was losing my shit right in front of him and he was watching with a kind of relaxed detachment that drove me over the edge.

"I hate you, you know that? I want to bash your face in so bad, and I swear to god, if you don't get out of my apartment in the next 10 seconds, I'm going to hit you, Steven!"

Looking at me with a goddamn smirk on his face, my hands were shaking with the need to hit him. "I dare you, Soph," he said with a smartass grin.

"I'm going to hit you. I swear to god, Peter-" I gasped. *Peter?* Oh my god! I was totally losing my mind, and I knew it. And judging by the look on Steven's smug face, he knew it too.

"Peter? *Really?* Well, let's find the asshole then so you can hit him and move on, okay? Because I'm sick to death of this shit with you. Mom and dad are beside themselves trying to figure out how to help you, but you're so fucking independent they don't want to piss you off by talking to you about it. And I can't stand to see you look like this anymore.

You're acting like a fucking psycho. Go to work. Cry. Come home. Cry. Go to sleep. Cry. And do it all again the next day. For a fucking month you've been a mess and it's time to stop the shit, Sophie," he said standing in front of me.

"Is it?" I snarled.

"Yeah. It is! This isn't you. You're tougher than this, and you're just wasting away for some fucking asshole who didn't love you enough to stay!" He yelled in my face.

Steven suddenly yelled the words I didn't want to hear and unbelievably I slapped him. A quick slap, right across the face, followed by a gasp from me as I covered my mouth with my hands in shock.

In my wildest dreams, I never thought I'd hit *anyone*, never mind slap my own brother across the face- one of the most demeaning, horrendous things anyone can do to another person.

In the stunned silence that followed the slap I was so sorry and so scared I had caused irreparable damage to us, I grabbed him as tightly as I could, crying 'I'm so sorry,' over and over again as I shook against his chest.

I was beyond a fucking mess and I knew it. Steven was right, but I just couldn't get over it. I just couldn't leave Peter behind.

"I'm so sorry, Peter," gasp again. "Fuck! *Not* Peter. I'm fucking losing it here. I'm so sorry, *Steven*. I'm sorry I slapped you. I didn't mean to. Oh, god, I'm so sorry," I sobbed until he finally raised his arms and hugged me back.

"You can't keep doing this..." he whispered.

"I know, but it's only been four weeks. I'm just not able to move on yet," I cried.

"You don't have to move on yet, but you've got to move forward. You're just stuck in this thing and you're not getting better. You're not even trying to get over him," Steven argued.

Pulling away slightly so I could look at him, I flinched when I saw his face. The red slap was so obvious on his pale winter skin, I wanted to scream.

"I'm trying to get over it, but I don't know what to do. This pain is just as bad as it was the first few days. It's constant and exhausting, and it hurts so bad, I just try to swallow it down all day at work, so when I get home at night I can't hold it in anymore. It's like he just left that day, *every* day. Time hasn't helped at all," I explained.

"So make it help. Change things up. Don't just come home every day and sit here thinking about him. Do anything to distract yourself or just do *something.* I don't know what, but you have to do something. Even Kim called me to talk about you. Kim, who I would bed in a second called me, and all we talked about was you," he smirked.

"What? Why?"

"'Cause she's pretty hot in a dirty sorta way," he laughed as I yelled stop. "She's worried about you, obviously. You're just so different now- almost cold or like emotionless or something. You don't go out and you don't talk to any of us. You just do nothing," he said quietly.

"I go to work every single day. I function enough to not screw up my job," I defended.

"Yeah, but that's it. You're lonely, Sophie. That's what this is. But you don't have to be. You could start going out with me, or your friends, or even mom again. You could leave this place after work and on weekends. You could have a life again," Steven said while pacing in my living room. Stopping to look at me, he was so serious and he looked so sad, I found myself listening to each and every word he said. "You just have to try to move past this," he exhaled.

"Okay... I'll try. But I'm not really into going out with you all yet. I just want to-"

"Wait for Peter to return? Sophie, he's not coming back. At least I don't think he is. So you have to start living again without him," he pleaded.

"Okay, I get it. Next weekend, I'll go out. Maybe we could all get together Saturday night. Um, I'll have everyone here first, and then we'll go out. Okay?"

"That sounds like a plan. I'll call Kim if you want," he again grinned as I shook my head at him.

"She'd never go for you. You're both players, so it would be doomed from the start," I answered seriously.

"Which we would both know, making it just plain old hot sex," he laughed again.

"Gross... Okay, I'll call Kim, Amy and Christina. Why don't you bring a few people with you and we'll have a little party here first then go out? Is that what I should do?" I asked Steven seriously. I didn't know what to do, but I thought that was the kind of start he wanted me to make.

"That sounds good, Soph. You just need to change the scenery a little so you start to feel a little differently I think."

"Okay..." But I was already exhausted from this hour long interaction, and I wanted him to go. I was so tired suddenly, I needed to have a nap.

"Are you coming to mom and dads?"

"Not today. But I will next Sunday, I promise. I'm really tired and I just feel like chilling out tonight. Please?"

"Sure. I'll let them know. Do you want me to stay for a while?"

"No thanks. I want to relax before my work week. I always get stressed out on Mondays," I admitted.

"Okay. I'll call you tomorrow night," he said walking toward my front door.

"You don't have to."

"Yeah, I do," he said again so seriously I felt it in my heart.

"I'm so sorry I hit you, Steven. I didn't mean to, and it will *never* happen again."

"That wasn't my first bitch-slap, girlie. And it probably won't be my last," he grinned as I burst out laughing as he left.

I spent the rest of my Sunday cleaning my apartment, organizing my closet, and putting away everything I had left out for Peter.

The lotion on my bedside table was thrown in a bathroom cupboard, and the jasmine oil and candle were hidden away in a tall closet in the corner of my kitchen. All my Peter things were put away so I didn't stare at them or obsess anymore.

I didn't want to walk into my bedroom and smell the lingering scent of Jasmine, and I didn't want to lay on his pillow smelling him all around me anymore.

It was time to start moving on, and I would. I was Sophie Morley, and men didn't make or define me. I made and defined myself. At least I remembered that about myself.

After my talk with Steven, I went to the Matthew Good concert a few days later with Kim and I had a good time. It was a Wednesday night and though a work night, I chose to live just a little, as best as I was able.

I even had fun with Kim, though I still missed Peter terribly. I had fun, until I returned home to a blue rose taped to my door by Peter with a little note.

LOST

Sophie,
I miss you every single day.
I hope you enjoyed your concert.
Peter
xo

CHAPTER 23

The following Saturday I tarted it up dramatically. 8 people were coming over to my place first, and then we were all going out. I wore a sexy black skirt, a skintight red blouse with ample cleavage showing, and a pair of kickass black over the knee boots I had purchased Thursday after work. I looked just shy of slutty, but I definitely looked hot.

When I applied my makeup heavier than usual, even wearing a dark red lipstick, I knew there would be no mistaking I was single or that I was moving on. I wanted to look single, and quite frankly I *wanted* to move on.

I was tired of feeling sad and lonely. And I was completely finished with waiting for a man who had left me. Steven was right, and though it caused me agony to accept it, it was true nonetheless- Peter didn't love me enough to stay with me. He may have been *my* forever, but obviously I wasn't his.

I knew no matter how long I lived, or what I became, I would love him forever though. I knew without a doubt, Peter would always be the man I loved with everything I had for the rest of my life. I knew he was 'the One', whether I found someone else or remained single for the rest of my life.

I knew I loved him in a way that was truly forever. But I was going to try to move on like everyone wanted me to, and a small party was my first step towards moving on.

Lighting over 30 candles all over my apartment, I made it to the fireplace mantle before I forgot what I was doing. Staring at the male and female candlestick holders I loved thinking only of Peter in that moment nearly brought me to my knees. Crying briefly, I couldn't stop the intensity of pain that ripped through my chest so suddenly I wasn't prepared for it.

I couldn't stop the instant thoughts of Peter from surfacing, but I could try to prevent them. Walking to my hall closet of gifts, I gently placed the candle holders inside my gifts box.

I crouched in the closet, with the lid in my hand and I thought of all the ways I loved him. I thought of Peter until I shook myself out of my

nightmare and whispered a sad goodbye to the candle holders, and really, to the life I had wanted with Peter.
I whispered goodbye finally. And then I forced myself to close the lid, walk back to my bathroom for a mascara check as I pulled myself together before my small party.

20 minutes later Amy and her boyfriend Davis, and Christina and her husband Roger came in and started the party.
Joining me in the kitchen to mix drinks for us all, both woman looked at me strangely until I finally just smiled and said, "I'm okay," to ease the concern. But Amy looked at me like I was full of shit, so I quickly amended. "Okay, I'm not really okay yet, but I'm trying."
"Try hard. This is your first night out with us in forever, so I want you either face down in your own barf by the end of the night, or screaming in bed with a hot stranger. Understood?" Amy said so sternly Christina and I both laughed.
"Yes, mother. Though I don't really recall my mother giving me those 2 ultimatums before," I grinned.
"It gets better, Sophie, I promise," Christina said with a hug and I hoped she was right. I hoped it got better because the alternative absolutely sucked for me.
So trying to enjoy myself, I raised my glass in classic So I Married an Ax-Murderer, Scottish fashion, and yelled, "Let's get PISSED," as they clinked glasses with me to begin our night.

Eventually Kim arrived, quickly followed by Steven and his 2 friends, Trent and Adam, shortly after I began drinking.
When Steven walked in holding up a huge bottle of tequila, all my girlfriends cheered, and Amy said laughing, "I was hoping more for option 2, not the first one," which meant nothing to anyone else, but Christina and I knew she was hoping I'd somehow get laid.
Smirking at Amy, I grabbed the bottle, hugged Steven and walked to the kitchen to pour more drinks.
"Hey girlie... How many so far?"
"This'll be my third, so I'll pace it a little slower. Everyone knows what I lightweight I am," I grinned as Trent walked in with beer for the fridge.
"Hey sexy Sophie. What's going on?" Trent flashed me his sexy as hell smile as Steven groaned and pushed him away from me.

"Dude. Sister."

"Dude. Kim," I reminded him as he smiled.

"Yeah, but not in front of me, okay?"

Undeterred, Trent smiled again and replied, "Got it. Can I entice you straight to the bedroom then so he can't see us?"

"Give me an hour and ask again, okay?" I laughed as Steven made weird la la la sounds to drown us out while he poured us each another tequila sunrise.

Returning to the living room, everyone looked happy and ready to really tie one on. They were all drinking and relaxed, music was playing, and conversations were loud and funny.

When I finished my third drink rather quickly, both Steven and Amy noticed and commented, as I laughed. Begging Steven to make me another because his always tasted better than when I made them, Steven was subjected to a round of mocking for drinking such a girlie drink, until the conversation turned into a discussion of twins and how it was entirely possible that Steven and I liked the same drink not because he was a pansy, but rather because biology demanded it. So we both agreed and bullshitted that it wasn't really our fault that we liked the same tequila, but it was the fault of our 'twin connection' to the humor of our friends.

Minutes later after Steven kindly returned with my fourth drink, I suddenly imploded.

In an instant, I dropped the glass on the hardwood floor as I dove for my CD player. I was dying instantly, and I knew everyone saw it and I knew I was a loser, and I knew I looked like a basket case. I knew everything but I didn't care. I needed to change the CD, which proved quite difficult in my drunken state.

Moaning, I banged the buttons on the multi-CD changer and pushed the volume while yelling at Steven to help me. The problem was it was preprogrammed to hold 8 CD's and to play a set list randomly. The problem was I couldn't stop the set from playing.

"What are you doing?" Steven asked beside me as he stopped the music effortlessly.

"I can't. I don't want to hear it that song. That's his. He sang it to me. Oh god..."

"Stop it, Sophie. Don't do this right now," Steven soothed quietly while shaking me back to my surroundings.

In that instant when I returned to myself I knew I looked like an idiot, and though my back was turned to everyone, I knew they were all silently staring at me. I knew it, so I couldn't really turn around, and I couldn't do anything to get out of the drama I had just caused without them seeing me. I couldn't get out of it without them seeing my heartache and my tears. So I didn't even try to

"Sorry everyone. I just can't hear that song right now. Um, just give me a minute," I begged as I walked out of my living room for the bathroom with my face turned away from them all as I left.

Closing the bathroom door quietly without added drama, I took a deep breath and tried to get my shit together. I tried so hard to breathe until I sat on the closed toilet seat and counted my way back to normal. I counted until Kim poked her head in and I gave a sad smile.

"Total loser, huh?" I huffed.

"Nah... It's all good. I don't think the guys were smart enough to even hear what song it was. They just saw you spill your drink on the floor which was the worse crime for them, I think," she grinned, trying to help my embarrassment. "Why that song?" She asked gently.

"He tried to convince me that I had green eyes, because of the yellow in my blue irises, and he always sang that song to me. In bed, over coffee, anywhere, and all the time. He sang it in the shower so I could hear it after I came home from work, and he sang it to me when we just sat on the couch together quietly. I guess, it's like our song. And the words are so beautiful, and I wish every part of them were true. I wish he couldn't *deny me*... But he did," I said through a gasp of pain.

"You look like shit," Kim suddenly said making me jolt.

"I do? Holy shit, you're terrible at this," I laughed shocked by her. "Like fucking *brutal*."

"I'm just trying to distract you. Is it working?" Kim smiled.

"I guess. Do I really look like shit though?"

"A little bit. The lipstick is way too much, and I've never seen you in such a short skirt. It's practically a belt," she said straight faced until I laughed again.

"So naturally, you want to borrow it, right?"

Laughing, Kim agreed, "Totally."

Looking in the mirror, my face wasn't bad. I didn't have makeup everywhere, and I could be easily fixed. But I was a little insecure about my looks suddenly. Before I could ask though, Kim answered the unspoken question.

"The red lips are too much with your dark eye shadow. You're only supposed to wear heavily either your lips or eyes, but rarely both. But your outfit is awesome. You look good, honestly. I was just teasing you to snap you out of your upset."

"Thank you... I don't know what to do sometimes when I can't stop all the memories and the pain from getting to me,"

"It's fine. But let's get out of here okay? You have lots of drinking to do and I want to get laid tonight. I haven't in like a month and I'm totally desperate. I may even give it to Steven if he begs me later," she laughed.

"And as he said earlier- Dude. Brother."

"Let's go. No one'll stare or poke sticks at you, I promise," Kim said taking my arm and leading me out of the bathroom.

And she was right. Pearl Jam was playing, and Trent was doing a fabulous Eddie Vedder, totally incoherent Yellow Ledbetter impression, so I walked past everyone for my kitchen to make myself a replacement drink.

After my little meltdown the night proceeded and I had a blast when I put thoughts of Peter out of my head for the most part. I sang and danced and drank myself into oblivion. I spilled drinks, and laughed too loud, and fell into a bathroom stall when I finally broke the seal and peed at the bar.

I was an absolute mess but I had fun. Everyone got wasted, so my absolutely trashed barely made their radar, and it allowed me to push boundaries I never would have pushed before.

I was with my friends and my brother and his friends and nothing bad would have happened to me no matter how drunk I ended up, so I said screw it, and I got absolutely polluted until the spins and nausea hit and I cried for Amy to help me to the bathroom as I barfed my guts out.

I barfed forever with Amy and strangers in the bathroom laughing at me. I barfed until I almost passed out, but eventually I forced myself to slowly leave the bathroom, covered in mascara. I even made it outside before another barf hit in the parking lot beside the bar.

I barfed with Amy until Steven, Kim, and Davis joined me in the parking lot laughing at me. I barfed until I begged to die, which made them howl at me, then they somehow got me home.

I didn't know how exactly I ended up home, but thankfully, when I woke, with a hangover to end all hangovers I was in my own bed, whining and crying from the nausea and throbbing head which threatened to give me a stroke.

I woke and damn near crawled to my living room to the scent of bacon and eggs, Kim and Amy talking quietly, Davis in my kitchen, and Steven still asleep on my floor. And it was a bizarre scene to say the least.

We were a fun group, but we were also adults with our own homes, so to see a very high school looking sleepover had taken place was a shock. I felt like an idiot, but I enjoyed the funny scene too.

After the initial teasing and humiliation I suffered, I learned Amy and Davis took the pullout couch, Steven slept hanging off the love seat and Kim slept beside me, far away from my bad breath and potential barf range she said laughing at me.

I learned I was a drunken idiot, and they all thought it was hysterical how many times I begged someone to kill me all night, even after I fell asleep. Kim said I moaned, 'just kill me' a few times while passed out cold, and she admitted she wanted to kill me so I'd shut the hell up and let her sleep in peace.

Everyone spoke quietly as the morning progressed because we each suffered varying degrees of hangovers. We ate when we could and took as many Tylenols as the bottle would allow. And finally by 11:30 they all left me alone to suffer.

Even with the daylong hangover that wouldn't stop, and the dinner at my parents, and the laundry I finished at their house, and the knowing smirks from my brother, I knew I had had fun for the first time in 5 weeks.

After the few setbacks, for the first time the night before, I went out and enjoyed myself, living like a 25 year old who wasn't heartbroken.

I acted normal and I loved it, because being an idiot with friends helped take away some of the pain that I needed to let go of.

After preparing for work, and falling heavily into my bed that Sunday night, I swear I was being watched. I had that feeling of being half asleep- too asleep to move, but somewhat cognizant while sleeping. I felt awake in my sleep, and I felt surrounded by Peter.

Remembering the feeling that night, I may have just missed him so much I imagined him around me. But I swear as I fought to wake up while still deep in sleep, Peter sat on my floor, leaning against the wall watching me sleep like he had so many nights we were together.

CHAPTER 24

Over the next few months my life became one of endless parties and frivolous outings which may have been nothing more than falsely constructed fun, but it was mine.
I became the drunk, ridiculous, flirty woman that used to make me cringe. I became every cliché I had ever hated. I was a drunk; laughing, dancing, flirting, rubbing up against strange men to feel alive and well through all the sexual attention and advances.
I loved having men tell me I was hot as they rubbed up on me, and I loved hearing how they wanted to screw me. I loved it all because it meant someone still wanted me. No matter how gross and drunk they were, I was still wanted by men, which was what I needed to feel after being unwanted by Peter.
No matter how drunk I was I never had sex with them though. I teased the nights away, then always found my escape home alone. I was a dicktease who flirted and kissed, drank and danced, but left alone each time I went out. I was still celibate, but I was a dance floor whore.

For the first few months, Steven and my girlfriends were loving and kind, and they helped me try to get better. They laughed at me as I staggered home or barfed my guts out all night. They made excuses for my drunken behavior, telling people I was simply trying to move on however I could, in whatever way I could. But sadly the attitudes of my friends and brother slowly changed.
Eventually, I became more of a burden than a fun, drunken friend or sister. I was irritating to Kim who was tired of pushing me out of bars when I went a little too far making out with someone all over the dance floor. And I became a nuisance to Steven who would get calls way too frequently from my friends or even from my drunken self to get picked up and brought home.
I began fighting and arguing with everyone, and I was becoming disgusting, even to myself. I knew I was acting like an idiot, but I didn't know how to stop it. I really couldn't control the need to be reckless and drunk, any more than I could stop the feelings that provoked my reckless drunkenness.

LOST

I was struggling. And I felt lost.

*****

Then the third week of June came and I finally had one more concrete moment of Peter. I returned home to a blue rose taped to my door with the message 'Perry's' and that was it. *Perry's.*
Panicking, I looked for Perry's however I could in case Peter wanted me to meet him there. I phone booked, and 411'd, but nothing jumped out at me. There were 2 pizza parlors, a nail salon, and an aquatic store, but nothing that made sense. So I expanded my search to include other towns and cities near me which only increased the number of places that made no sense to me whatsoever.
I couldn't find it, and I didn't know what Peter was trying to tell me with his stupid clue, or hint, or code, or whatever the hell it was. I didn't understand what he meant to tell me, so I became frustrated and eventually moved on from the search for Peter again.

At that point Peter had been gone for 3 months- almost exactly the same amount of time we had been together and I couldn't stand all the pain anymore.
When I thought in terms of 3 months, I knew logically it was a tiny amount of time when compared to a lifetime lived. 3 months was nothing. 3 months was a side note to someone's existence- I *knew* that. But for me 3 months may as well have been my entire 25 years because it felt like that to me.
I felt like my entire life was wrapped in 7 months of actual time distorted into a lifetime of feelings. I had 7 months total of my existence. I felt like I knew nothing but 7 months ever. I didn't remember feeling anything before my 4 months with Peter, and I couldn't process anything but the pain of the 3 months without him.
7 months of my life was the entire sum of my existence, but I continued trying to live.

*****

2 days after Peter's birthday, on Friday July 6th, Madeline and I went to the mall over lunch to find a wedding dress she needed for the next day.

In the mall we walked and talked and we were relatively comfortable with each other. Though it was only our 4th outing together, we were slowly becoming slightly more than co-workers, and I could almost see the potential of a real friendship in our future.

After stopping in the one store Madeline specifically wanted to look in, we decided on food when no dress could be found. But as we entered the food court, I saw Kara. UN-fuckin-believably, I saw Peter's sister, and I almost screamed.

Suddenly dropping my tray of food on the table I told Madeline to wait there. I didn't ask, and I left no question that she was to stay seated by my tone. I needed to speak with Kara, and she *was* going to speak with me.

Walking to her table while she tidied up the mess she and a toddler had made, I called her name. Calling as I approached tables away, I knew I was too loud, and I knew my posture seemed too aggressive, but I also knew it was my only chance for answers so I couldn't let it slip away.

"Kara!" I yelled again as she turned around.

Looking utterly confused by me suddenly standing beside her, she picked up her little boy like I might harm him or something, which was odd. Why she thought I was violent or threatening I had no clue, but I didn't care.

"Sophie?" She asked surprised.

"Yes. Hi. Um, do you know what's going on with Peter? Do you know what happened between us?"

Shaking her head she said no while looking around us like she needed an easy escape.

"Let me just ask this then- Is he married?"

"No," she exhaled.

"Then what's wrong? We were fine, and suddenly he dumped me. We were so happy until that party with your family, then afterward, right out of the blue he broke up with me. Do you know why?"

"No..." She said bouncing the boy against her hip.

"Did you make him break up with me?" I accused.

"Of course not," she sounded completely confused by my accusation.

"Then please... Please tell me what happened," I begged.

"There's nothing to tell. Peter broke up with you. That's all," she said lying. It was so obvious she was lying on the fly I almost told her off.

"Please, Kara. I know you don't know me but I love him and I desperately want him back but I have to know what happened so I can fix it. Please tell me what happened."

"Sophie, please leave him alone. You're the one who has him screwed up," she said as I gasped and cried out but she quickly amended. "Not because of you. Because of him. He can't function with you in his life. He loved you- he was obsessed with you and it was making him make bad decisions. He was screwing up his life and his job to be with you. He was doing everything wrong, and he was going to lose everything he's worked so hard for. He loves you so much he's staying away because he needs to. Please, leave him alone. I love my brother and I like you, but it's not safe for you to be together. For him, please leave him alone," Kara actually begged with tears in her eyes, stunning me from everything she said.

"I really don't understand anything you just said to me. What isn't safe? We were a couple and we loved each other, and we were really happy, and nothing was screwed up between us. *Nothing*. Our lives were normal," I said as she shook her head in disagreement. So I tried one last time. "I still love him so much," I repeated with tears streaming down my face. In the middle of a mall food court with witnesses everywhere, I found myself begging for my life.

"I know you love him, and he loves you. He loves you in a way that made him all twisted up inside because of the things he has to do, and I don't want that for either of you. So please stay away... For him," she begged again. She begged me to stay away from the man I loved for him. For *him*?

"You're not making any sense whatsoever. He dumped me, and I'm the one left crazy and dying inside. I was loved and then I was left!" I yelled too loudly. I was so confused standing there with Kara I just couldn't keep it together.

"I won't do this with you. So leave it alone," she snapped grabbing her purse off the bench seat.

Reaching for her sleeve, I just made contact when her head whipped around to me with so much anger I knew to let go of her jacket quickly.

"Sophie, please. This is between you two, but I'm begging you to leave him alone. I have to go, I'm sorry. Please be safe. For Peter," she said softly, again with tears in her eyes that I didn't understand.

Staring at Kara as she turned to leave with the little boy on her hip, I moaned one final time, "But I love him..." And though she nodded she kept walking away from me as I stood shocked by her, and Peter, and my life, and the pain that wouldn't lessen over time.

Eventually, when a table full of old men started speaking loudly again at the table beside me I shook myself back to my sad reality and I returned to the table to a silently eating Madeline.

I sat down looking at all the food I wouldn't touch as I tried to stop the stream of tears falling down my face.

A minute later Madeline took my hand but otherwise ignored me for her food. Holding her tightly I needed her hand to ground me, and I needed her hand to keep me from floating away. I needed Madeline's support so I could breathe through the reality I was facing.

Later that night when I finally returned home after work, I called everyone I knew to go out, but no one was available. So undeterred, I had one hell of a party by myself.

*****

The following Saturday morning in July, when I was again so hung-over I wanted to cry, I remember Kim and Steven sitting me down together to talk. It was actually funny how far they sat from each other because I was sure they were screwing though neither would admit it to me.

Anyway, they sat me down in my dining room and proceeded to lecture me about my drinking and my behavior over coffee. The 2 biggest sluts I knew were lecturing ME on bad behavior, which naturally made me appalled, then humored, then outright offended, until I lashed out at them.

I told Kim she was a slut who fucked any and every man she could, whereas I had slept with 4 men my whole life- all of which I had had long term relationships with. Then I turned on Steven and let him know he was a notorious pig who fucked and ran every chance he had. I told him it was obvious he didn't give a shit about anyone but himself and he was going to be the old pervy pig woman shook their heads at and laughed at behind his back.

I let Kim know she was a slut no man would ever respect, and I let Steven know he was a fucking pig no woman respected.

I said everything I had ever thought, even briefly, and I made it the sole reality between the 3 of us, even though it was anything but. I just needed to strike back at them, so I did. Horribly.

To Steven's absolute credit he didn't strike back, though clearly because he was more shocked into silence by my anger. He actually bit his tongue while visibly hurt by me. Kim however, not so much.

Kim went for the jugular and slit my throat. Kim destroyed me in a way we would never recover from. If there had been any chance of recovery between us with my endless apologies later for everything I had said to her which though harsh was kind of true nonetheless, we would never recover from everything she said to me.

But it was my fault and I knew it, so I took the full loss of our 11 year friendship as my own doing because I may have taken the gloves off, but she beat the shit out of me with them in self-defense.

Finally, after Kim said every single thing I never wanted to hear, she stood up and slammed out of my apartment. And before I could even breathe through the agony lancing me, Steven stood with only the briefest pause at my door before he too walked out slamming it, leaving me completely alone in a nightmare.

2 hours later, at 1:00 on that awful Saturday afternoon in July, still hung-over but tired of crying and feeling pretty desperate I called Trent, an absolute sure thing for me.

I called Trent because I needed to be with someone who wanted me, and Trent had never been subtle about his want of me. Totally pathetic and desperate, I inhaled deeply and called my sure thing.

"Hello?"
"Hi. It's Sophie."
"Hey babe. What's up?" He asked.
"Do you think I'm stuck-up and prissy?" I asked abruptly.
"Um, no. Why?" He laughed.
"Can you come over?" I asked with absolute desperation in my voice.
"Sure. When?"
"An hour?"
"Okay... Is everyone else coming over?" He asked with an audible grin.
"No," I said leaving the potential of his visit in the air between us.
"Okay. I'll see you in an hour," he said quickly hanging up.

After we hung up I did what any woman would do under the circumstances- I showered, shaved, and put lotion on every inch of my body. I tied my hair up so I didn't have to wash and dry it again, and I wore an adorable little summer dress with a tube-type bodice that ended at my knees.
I spritzed my body with Obsession, and I made sure my makeup was sexy, but natural looking. In other words, I made myself edible, without any confusion about my intentions.

Opening my door to Trent 55 minutes after my call, I was determined. I was beyond determined. I was on a fucking mission. Oh. Ha! I WAS on a *fucking* mission.
When I opened the door to Trent I wanted no misunderstandings so I just pulled him down to my lips and kissed the shit out of him. I kissed him while moving us into my apartment until he pulled away.
"What's going on, Soph?" He asked with concern. But I didn't want concern, I wanted sex, plain and simple. I wanted sex to make me better, so I made my intentions very clear.
"Please don't be a friend right now. Just be a guy who fucks a girl who wants to be fucked. Just fuck me, Trent. Okay?" I begged.
And after the briefest of pauses while Trent looked at me with concern again, probably from just my language alone, he seemed to take the opportunity for what it was, and then he truly fucked me.
With absolutely no finesse or romance, he popped my breasts from the top of my dress, grabbed hold of my nipples, kissed me hard and had a hand in my underwear under my dress within seconds. He fingered me hard and fast, and before I even understood what I was feeling, he had me on my back on the floor, with him putting a condom on as he looked down at my body. He moved my dress up to my hips, ripped my underwear down my legs, and then he pushed inside me.
Quick and nearly brutal, he thrust into me and continued pounding for 5 minutes without a single kiss or loving touch. He didn't even try to speak, or connect with me. He took me to my word and just fucked me like an inflatable, inanimate toy.
Trent pushed my knees up against my chest and thrust into me so hard I was moved across the throw rug in the living room. I was pushed into the bottom of the couch where I was crammed by my neck. And he kept on thrusting even as I lay at an awkward angle, unmoving, and barely breathing, until he came.
Quick and without any thought of me, he came inside the condom

inside me and then he was finished.

He did exactly what I wanted, and I hated myself for it. I wasn't better, and Trent didn't fuck Peter out of my system.

Peter was all around me looking at me with sadness and disgust. Peter was telling me I shouldn't ever be fucked, but that I should be pleasured. Peter was whispering his love and holding me close even as Trent raised up off the floor and walked to my bathroom to clean up.

Peter lowered my dress and fixed the bodice, wrapped me in his arms, and rocked me into the quiet peace I was fighting to maintain. Peter was all around me again, and deep inside me. Trying not to cry, I went a little crazy in Peter's presence.

Holding in the pain of my loss, I greeted Trent as he walked out the bathroom door, thanked him for coming over with a kiss on the cheek, but told him I had to go out. I dismissed him, and sadly he let me dismiss him without a fuss.

In that one moment between us outside the bathroom I knew without a doubt Trent cared for me as little as I cared for him. So we each accepted the thanks and the end, and he walked out with a casual, 'see ya later,' as he zipped his jeans closed and walked out my door as quickly as he had entered.

After closing and locking the door behind him, I remember walking back to my bathroom alone on wobbly legs. Scrubbing, I showered away anything from between my legs, which I knew wasn't arousal, but merely lubrication from the condom, and then I entered my room to change.

I changed into my favorite navy pantsuit, brushed my hair down, fixed my makeup and brushed my teeth. I walked back to my bed with the framed picture Peter painted of me for my birthday shaking in my hands, and I crawled into my bed with Peter.

With Peter back, I cried and smiled, and talked to him about our lives together. I told him everything about our future again. I talked about everything I knew to be true of us, and I told him all I knew and felt about him as I whispered my love to him over and over again.

I told Peter about everything Kim said, and I explained how I knew she was wrong. I knew I loved Peter not because he made me less prissy, and not because he was the first guy I had orgasmed with. I knew she was wrong when she said I was a stuck up bitch who was waiting for Mr.

Perfect, because I thought I was perfect. I knew she was wrong when she said Peter never loved me, but just fucked me good, and I had arrogantly thought he must have felt the same love for me I had felt for him because I was Sophie, and Sophie *always* thought everyone loved her.

I told Peter everything Kim said and he agreed with me that she was totally wrong about us. Peter agreed that he and I were so much more than just fucking, and that we had a love so rare and intense, Kim couldn't possibly understand it because Peter knew what I knew- Our love was beautiful, real, and absolute.

Eventually I even confessed to Peter how badly I had been acting. I told him about the drunk partying, and the flirty teasing. I told him about the sad comfort and reassurance I received when men tried to pick me up, but I also told him I did nothing about it.

I admitted I had kissed a few men at the bars and clubs, but that was all. I admitted to just a few kisses to get me through missing him, but he understood.

Peter smiled sadly, and nodded his head in acceptance. Peter didn't judge me or hate me for the few kissing indiscretions, because I think he knew they meant nothing to me. Peter understood I was just trying to get through the loneliness without him however I could.

After a little silence between us I asked him about everything his sister had said to me. I asked him about his life and job, and I asked him why she said I wasn't safe with him.

I asked what part of his life he was screwing up to be with me, but Peter didn't answer. Peter offered no explanations, but he did hold me tighter to him in his silence. He held me together as I cried to him about my sad life without him.

I cried to Peter and told him I missed him so much I couldn't breathe anymore without him. I cried to Peter and told him he was my forever and I wouldn't live without him anymore.

I cried with Peter wrapped tightly around me, holding me safe as I whispered I loved him forever.

I cried and closed my eyes, safe in his arms, feeling all the love we shared, knowing the life I couldn't live without.

And that was the first time I ever tried to commit suicide.

CHAPTER 25

But of course I didn't succeed that time because my brother found me 2 hours later in my bed.

Steven came back to my place in the early evening to tell me off for all the rotten things I'd said to him and Kim. Steven returned because even though I had been horrible, he still loved me enough to want to tell me off for being such a bitch, hoping to smack some sense into me in the process.

Steven found me, his twin sister, OD'd on her bed dressed in a lovely pantsuit, wrapped around the framed picture the love of her life had painted for her when he still adored her months earlier.

When I regained consciousness after having my stomach pumped, and meds pumped into me intravenously for the potential kidney and liver damage, I was finally well enough to talk, which I was good at.

I managed to convince a doctor and nurse that the pills were accidental because I was having major back pain earlier, and the more pills I took for the pain the less coherent I was remembering how many I had actually taken. It was horribly accidental I convinced them, and by 11:00 that night I was told I could leave the following morning.

I was warned about taking pain killers with alcohol, and I was warned about the dangers of self-medicating back injuries with over the counter meds which I had also lied about. I had never had a car accident, and I didn't suffer any long term back pain from the made up car accident. But the story worked.

After thanking them for their concern, and speaking to a nurse about alternative medicines and therapies for back pain, which I found truly ironic, I was left to sleep in my hospital bed alone.

I was finally left alone, in a kind of funny no harm/no foul world where I was still the mature, professional, Sophie Morley who would never be as stupid as some woman who takes painkillers with alcohol to ease the pain in her chest.

The following morning however, I was greeted by my worst nightmare.

My parents were waiting with Amy and Kim for the 7:30 visiting hours to begin.

I was greeted first by my red-faced, weepy eyed mother and my stoic, but sad looking dad, followed by a pale Kim and a crying Amy. I was greeted by them all as they entered my room quietly.

Watching them enter, I wasn't ready for the potential shitstorm I had created though, so I calmly asked them all to leave me alone, except for my mom. I asked them all to leave me, and after another tragic pause among them, Kim stepped forward until I shook my head no at her, and Amy immediately left my room crying harder.

They left eventually without words, and I was faced with just my mom, who I knew I could convince to make the others leave me alone. So as soon as the door closed behind them, I tried.

"Mom, I swear to god this was an accident. I hurt my back the night before, and I was in tons of pain and I took too many pills stupidly. It was just an accident, and I promise I'm fine," I said firmly.

"Sophie... I really don't believe you, and nobody else does either. You may have convinced the doctors you're fine, but I think you and I both know you're lying," she replied just as firmly. Looking at my mom's expression I knew in that moment I should have picked my dad to convince, but I tried again anyway.

"It wasn't on purpose. I was just in pain after I fell and I guess I had enough alcohol in my system from the night before to cause a bad reaction. But it wasn't on purpose."

My mother stood beside me at that point staring at me undeterred as she questioned, "Why, baby? What was so bad that you had to do this?"

"I didn't. I wouldn't. And I need you to believe me!" I cried.

"Well, I don't. And if I didn't think you'd hate me forever, I'd push for the 48 hour mandatory psych hold. But I won't. Instead, you're coming home with us, and I'm going to talk to you until you work this shit out. You're a mess, Sophie, and I love you too much to care if you're pissed at me for trying to help you. I'm going to help you, because I love you. And your dad is absolutely beside himself over this desperately wanting to help you, too."

"But I didn't do anything! It was an accident!" I yelled frustrated.

"Don't you get it? No matter how old you get, you're still our daughter, and whatever hurts you absolutely *kills* us. So stop lying to me, and stop lying to yourself. You're the only one screwed up here. I'm your mother, and I can fight you any day of the week. And I'll always win. So give it

up, Sophie," my mom said without emotion.
"There's nothing to give up. It was an accident," I mumbled lamely.
But it was clear she was winning and I was losing this battle of wills. Watching my mom walk to the door and call my dad in, I realized I was totally screwed.

Grasping at anything, I tried to figure something out quickly as my dad walked back into my room, but I had nothing.
"Sophie's coming home with us for a few days, and we're going to help her deal with everything that's hurting her. We're going to help her until she can help herself. Okay?" She asked my dad who had not spoken but just stood still watching my face as my tears slowly fell.
"Of course..." He whispered in a choked voice which forced the first sob from my chest.
"Daddy, this was just a stupid accident, I swear. I took too many pain killers with some alcohol in my system, but I'm fine. It was just an accident," I tried again, but my dad just nodded at me.
"Are you ready?" My mom asked again without emotion.
"I just want to go home," I whined.
Glaring at me, my mom said again, "You're coming home with us or I'll go talk to the doctor you spoke to last night. I'll tell him what I really think happened, and we'll see what your options are then. Would you like that?" My mother asked like a total bitch, and I knew I wouldn't win again, so I gave up.
Nodding my surrender, I was helped from the bed as we left my room with a nurse pushing me in a wheelchair to my parent's car.
Moving down the hallway, I noticed the absence of Amy and Kim, and naturally I wondered where my brother was. But I didn't ask, and I didn't really want to know.
I assumed Steven was super pissed at me still for all the horrible things I had said, and I couldn't stand the thought of Steven my constant being mad at me on top of everything else I was feeling.
So leaving, I didn't speak, and neither did my parents the entire drive to their home. We were silent, and in the silence I realized I would probably never speak of my pain for the rest of my life.
I didn't need to talk about it because I knew it all and so did Peter.

When we arrived at my parents' I asked if I could go lie down. I asked simply with every intention of avoiding their immediate attention. I asked because just the thought of my parents thinking I had lost it, or that I was weak in some way made me want to scream. I asked so I could avoid the unavoidable.

I was a 25 year old, professional woman who was stuck in her parents' home like a goddamn grounded teenager. And to be honest, the longer I was with them, the angrier I became.

I hated the fact that my mother blackmailed me, and I hated the fact that she was being such a hardass to me. Actually, if I was being *really* honest, I hated everything about everything and everyone at that time.

I was so tired of everything, I just wanted to go home to my bed.

*****

When I woke up a few hours later, my mom was sitting in my room on the window seat.

"I'm sorry..." I whispered. "I didn't really mean to, I was just confused and so sad I didn't want to feel the sad anymore. But I wasn't really trying to do anything wrong," I spoke quietly. "I just needed a break from all the pressure and pain..." I cried.

"What pressure?"

"Everything. I just feel like I have to be so good all the time or people won't like me, and I couldn't really handle all the pressure anymore."

"Who's putting pressure on you?" My mom asked leaning forward.

"Everyone..."

"Like who?" She persisted.

"Everyone. All of you," I said quietly with a bit of fear.

Looking at my mom quickly, I waited for a bad reaction, but again she stayed completely calm. "Really? How so?" She asked.

"I don't know. I'm Sophie, I guess. I've always been good at everything, and I've never failed before and I try to be so good all the time that sometimes it feels like it's a lot of pressure or something," I mumbled.

"That sounds like *you* putting pressure on yourself. I don't recall a time ever your dad and I asked for perfection, or for you to not fail. I don't recall ever expecting anything more than you just trying. Am I wrong?"

"You didn't *say* it, but I've always been the good twin. The one who did everything right, and you guys liked me that way because you didn't stress out about me," I admitted to my mother, who surprised me again with her reaction.

"Sophie... You couldn't be more wrong if you tried," she said exhaling deeply. "*You* were the one we stressed about. It was you that we worried about constantly. Steven is just Steven. He was a good kid who made mistakes, learned from them and moved on. But you weren't like that. You were so uptight and almost obsessive about things. You studied and stressed over having everything perfect all the time and you freaked out if you were slightly less than the best-"

"No, I didn't," I said defensively.

"Yes, you did. God, I used to try to make you have fun. I'd dance around the kitchen and try to make you be silly with me, but you never did. Steven would jump in and spin me around, and you'd just watch us. Yes, you laughed, but you never joined in and just had fun. God, you talked about your forever plans since you were a little girl. You always had a plan. And if you didn't have a plan you were unsettled," she said moving to sit on the end of my bed. "You were an adult by 6 years old, and *that* stressed me and your dad out," she exhaled.

"No I wasn't. I was normal-"

"Of course you were normal. I'm not saying anything bad to you, I'm just trying to make you see you've always been so driven and intense you used to make yourself sick before exams, or before interviews, or before anything at all that you could possibly fail at."

"No I didn't," I argued again. "I was never that way. I was fun and I-"

"You were fun within very strict guidelines," my mother smiled. "Sophie, you never just let loose, and you've never just been a person who reacts naturally to the world around her. You study everything and behave accordingly. You have called yourself 'stable, professional, Sophie' since you were 12," she quoted as I flinched. "But you didn't have to be, and we didn't want you to be. Your dad and I just wanted you to be happy, and we thought being so rigid was what made you happy, so we didn't try to change you after you were a teenager," she paused looking at me. "But I don't think you've ever been happy," she exhaled slowly.

"Yes I have! I've always been happy," I defended.

"No. I think you've been content. I don't know if you know what true happiness is. I don't think-"

"I was truly happy with Peter," I suddenly cried. "I was. He made me feel things and say things, and be different. He let me just be myself, PMS included," I huffed a laugh. "Peter made me happy, and he was my forever, but I wasn't his, and I don't know how to move on," I choked. "I just don't know how to move past the only person, beside you guys that I've ever loved like that. He was just everything I ever wanted but in a way I didn't know I wanted it," I said as I forced down the pain in my chest.

Whispering, I admitted to my mom my absolute reality. "I didn't even know men like him existed, and then I found him and he loved me and I was so happy. He was everything," I suddenly sobbed.

"Sophie, he wasn't," she shook her head. "He may have been everything you ever wanted, but he wasn't everything. He's gone, and you need to be happy without him, because even if you two meet again or even love again you'll have nothing to give him or yourself. You're too wrapped up in just being happy with him beside you, that eventually you'll run out of your own happiness to give. Do you know what I mean?"

Shaking my head, I moaned, "No..."

"Okay. Just listen for a second. I love cooking for example. I don't do it because I have to, I do it because I actually love cooking. And every time I'm excited about some new recipe I've made, your dad is happy for me. He tries everything I make as excited as I am to have him try it. And though there have been a few gross concoctions," she said smiling, "Your dad still eats it and tells me it was good, even though we're both gagging it down. See, he's happy that I was happy cooking, so the food somehow doesn't taste quite as bad or something. It's hard to explain, but I'm happy when he's happy and excited about something, and vice versa. If we had nothing of ourselves individually, we'd be bored by now. Can you imagine what it would be like if I lived only for your dad now that you kids are gone? Can you imagine what it would feel like for him to know he left for work, came home, and I was just sitting there waiting for him to make my evening happy? Like if I had nothing of my own and I needed him to make me happy as well as himself? He would be exhausted, and I would seem boring and uninspired, and that would make *us* boring and uninspired. But we're not like that. We do our own things, so when we do spend time together, we're happy to spend the time together. We're not dependent on each other for happiness. We *add* to each other's happiness," she finally stopped as I listened carefully.

"I worked..." I said pitifully.

"Yes, you did. But what else did you do with Peter- *besides* Peter?" She said laughing as I blushed. "Sophie, you stopped socializing, and you didn't even come here for Sunday dinners. Steven missed you but you were so wrapped up in Peter you saw nobody else *but* Peter."

"But at the beginning-"

"I know. At the beginning of a relationship everyone becomes a little obsessed. Trust me, I remember I couldn't keep my hands off your dad, and he couldn't get enough of me. But we also had lives apart from each other. We were still 2 people who loved, but we were 2 separate people. And I don't think you did that," she pushed.

"I was. I did. I just liked being with him," I argued.

"I know. Why wouldn't you? From what I understand from Kim, Peter rocked your world sexually," she grinned. "But I also saw you completely disappear around New Years' and that was the last we knew of what was going on until March. You didn't talk to anyone and you basically ignored us, or always had an excuse to hang up quickly. We don't even really know anything about your new career because everything was totally eclipsed by your relationship with Peter."

"I was just busy, that's all."

"With Peter."

"No with everything," I argued.

"That revolved around Peter," she pushed back.

"No..." But again I always lost when my mom called me out.

"So now you have to make some serious changes. It's time. I know you're hurting, I get that. Honestly, I understand how much this breakup has hurt you, but it's time to stop wallowing."

"I'm not *wallowing*," I said totally offended.

"You are. But not in a whiny, I want sympathy sort of way. You're wallowing in the upset because you don't know how to move past it. And getting hammered every weekend, acting like a tart to get attention isn't the way," she said knowingly. Looking at her, I was suddenly very embarrassed to be called a drunken tart by my mother.

So I tried to explain. "I just needed to know men still wanted me," I admitted pitifully. Crying softly, I hated having to admit to something so weak and ridiculous, but it was true.

"Oh, Sophie... You shouldn't need drunken idiots wanting you, to feel wanted. You *are* wanted. You're beautiful and intelligent but you can't see what's right in front of you. You have a whole life just waiting for you. You're only 25, so you have time for love still, and you have lots of time to move past this breakup and the pain you're suffering. But you have to decide to move past it instead of just waiting for it to pass, because it isn't going to. You're going to feel this for as long as you fight letting it go."

"I tried to let him go," I whispered softly, but I knew I was lying. I didn't let him go because I couldn't let him go. I still loved him and I wouldn't let him go no matter how much I pretended to move on. So I asked the question I couldn't believe I had to ask.

"What do I do? I honestly don't know. I have no idea what to do to move on like everyone keeps saying to. Even his sister Kara told me to move on. She accused me of not being good for Peter- of screwing up his life and his job, which makes no sense by the way. But she just kept saying to let him go and I wish I could because I hate feeling like this, but I hate thinking of not being with him more..." I finished my confession with a gasp of pain.

"How about you just start by just taking care of you right now. Focus on your job and your friends and yourself. Make *you* a priority. Eat better, drink less, or not at all I'd recommend, and just make this time about you living day to day well, until it hurts a little less. Maybe when you focus on yourself and your own real needs a little, you won't feel only the absence of Peter in your life. Could you try that?" My mom asked taking my hand. And after she spoke it just seemed so simple suddenly, I nodded.

"Just try Sophie, and if it doesn't get any better in, say, a month, then we'll talk and try to figure something else out. Maybe you need some medication for depression, or maybe you need to talk to someone about your issues. Whatever it takes to make you feel even a little better is a good step. Can you try?"

"Yes..."

"And I'm here, always. I've always been here for you, and I'll always be here for you when you need me. I'm your mom, Soph. And I'd do just about anything to make you better," she finally spoke with emotion.

"I know you are. I just didn't know what to do anymore. I fought with Steven and Kim, and I saw Peter's sister Kara on Friday and I did something really stupid with Steven's friend Trent," I said as she raised an eyebrow in question. "Yeah, I was really stupid and it was awful, but I thought if I had sex with someone else I might not miss Peter as much, but it was horrible with Trent and it did the opposite. I was way worse. I felt slutty and gross and used, even though it was me using him, but it was awful, and not something that would've ever happened between me and Peter. So it was just the worst 24 hours since Peter left me, and I didn't know what to do... I'm sorry."

"Do you still feel like hurting yourself?"

"No. And I never really did. I wasn't trying to hurt myself, I just wanted to sleep away the pain and confusion. That's all I was trying to do, I think."

"Do you still feel confused?"

"No, just sad still. And I'm pretty tired," I admitted.

"Okay," she exhaled. "You sleep for a while longer and I'll come get you for dinner. You're staying here and you're not going into work tomorrow so-"

"No!" I panicked. "I have to go to work. I swear it's good for me. I'm distracted at work, and I feel better when I'm working because I'm not thinking about everything else. I have to go to work," I begged.

"I really think you should take a few days-"

"Mom, listen to me. I know what you're trying to do, and you've been awesome with me. You've been great, but I know I'm right about this. I have to go to work tomorrow, otherwise I get all screwed up thinking about everything else. Work is a good thing for me. Please?"

"You're sure?"

"Completely."

"Okay. Sleep now, we'll eat in 2 hours, and we'll talk about work later," she said pulling me into a hug. "I love you so much, Sophie. You have been one of the three greatest joys of my life, and I can't imagine a world without you in it," my mom finally choked up.

"Ohhh... Please don't. If you start crying I'm screwed. Okay?" I asked hugging her tighter.

"I love you, Sophie," she said rising from my bed with a sad smile.

"I love you, too. Um, I should probably call Steven to apologize for our fight," I groaned.

"Not now. Just have a rest until dinner and talk to him later. Talk to him when you're stronger, okay?"

"Good idea. I think Steven's going to kill me for all the horrible things I said yesterday."

"He might surprise you," she whispered as she walked to my door.

"Sleep, Sophie," she smiled before leaving me alone.

Once she walked out my door I immediately slept. Even though I had tons of things going through my head, and I was overwhelmed and emotional, it felt like the second my mother closed my door, I was sound asleep until she woke me for dinner 2 hours later.

Before I went downstairs to eat I did work up the balls to call my brother though. Holding my breath, I was scared shitless, but I called him anyway because I owed him that much for all the horrible things I said to him. I desperately needed to call him to apologize for being a class-A bitch, but he didn't answer to my relief.

When I eventually joined my parents at the dining room table I remember feeling very small. I felt young and though I was physically smaller than my parents, I hadn't actually felt small in years. But sitting down, I remember the strange feeling of youth wrapping all around me as they smiled and started reaching for all the food.

Looking around the table, I started to laugh cry when I took it all in. My mother had cooked 4 of my favorite foods all together though they didn't match at all.

"And chocolate pie for dessert," my dad grinned as I looked at him.

"Thank you..." I whispered trying to casually wipe my face with my napkin before I reached for a huge helping of all my favorite foods.

"Where's Steven? He never gives up the chance to eat mom's cooking," I asked my dad with a grin, but instead of answering he looked at my mom for help. Turning to my mom I could see she too was struggling to answer.

"What's wrong? Did something happen to him?" I asked too loudly for our quiet dinner table.

"No, Sophie. Relax. He's just having a bit of a hard time dealing with yesterday," she soothed.

"I'm going to apologize for everything I said to him. I already tried but he wasn't answering. I'll call again right after dinner."

"Um... Why don't you give him a day or two?" My dad suggested.

Shaking my head, "I can't wait. I was so bitchy. And though he should be used to that by now, I really want to apologize," I laughed to dead silence. "What? I know I was mean, but I was just going through a bad time, and he and Kim caught me off guard so I lashed out a little. But I'll apologize and we'll be fine."

Exhaling, my dad actually sat up a little straighter before he spoke.

"No offense honey, but you can be a little dense sometimes," he said as I flinched. My dad had never spoken to me like that in my life. "Steven's a guy, so he really couldn't care less about you being bitchy to him. But he's messed up right know, so it's probably not a good time to call him yet. He actually can't talk to you right now," my dad said angrily.

Turning to my mom, I asked why. Looking at my mom for answers, she also dramatically exhaled and put her fork down on her plate with a clang before speaking.

"Your dad is right. You *are* dense sometimes," she said with a huffed laugh. "Sophie, Steven found you unconscious on your bed yesterday after taking pills. He found his sister- his *twin* sister- unconscious on her bed hours after you had a fight. He doesn't give a shit what you fought about, but he can't stop thinking about what would've happened if he hadn't gone back to your apartment to yell at you-"

"I didn't realize-"

"*What?!* What didn't you realize? That that might've fucked up your brother? Would it have fucked you up?!" She suddenly yelled at me, as my dad leaned forward to take her hand.

Exhaling before she spoke again, I held my breath in shock. My mom never swore like that, and she never spoke to me like she hated me. Staring at her, I could actually see she waited for a second to calm down, as I waited stunned by the sudden anger directed at me.

"Your dad was with him earlier when you were sleeping the first time, and I was on the phone with him the entire time you just slept. Steven is a total mess, Sophie," she exhaled. "He can't stop thinking and talking about seeing you lying there in a suit with a framed picture of yourself in your arms. He can't stop thinking about you like that, and I don't think he will for a very long time. So I suggest you don't call him until he's better. Steven, your *brother* who found you yesterday unconscious is a mess. Your brother who thought he found you dead first, then unbelievably alive but unconscious second. Your brother who thought he lost the closest person he has in the world," she moaned before stopping for a second. "Do you get it now? It's not about a goddamn fight you had, it's about what you did and what he found!" My mother yelled once more as she pushed her chair back loudly from the table and left the room just as quickly.

She left with me just staring shocked at her exit. She left me shaking and scared of everything again.

When my dad suddenly took my hand I jumped in my chair. Turning to him he had tears in his eyes, but otherwise smiled a little at me.

"*See?* Dense," he grinned sadly. "Your mom's just tired and scared and struggling with what you did and with wanting to help you but wanting to help Steven through this nightmare, too. You didn't just hurt yourself, Sophie. You hurt us all and you almost destroyed your brother," he whispered to really make it sink in.

"I'm so sorry... I need to talk to Steven," I said even as my dad shook his head no again.

"He doesn't want to talk to you right now. He's hurt and angry and really just mad at everything. Give him a few days to cool off, okay? Trust me, in a few days the worst of this will blow over and then you two can talk. Please?" He begged me until I nodded.

"Okay. I'm just going to go to my room to think."

"Not until dessert," he insisted.

"I'm not really hungry," I tried.

"Your mom will kill me if I have the chocolate pie without you. And I need it," he said so seriously, I actually laughed a little as I stood.

Walking to the kitchen, I grabbed the delicious chocolate pie from the fridge with 2 forks, and slumped back into my chair beside my dad.

Handing him a fork we didn't even pause, we just dug into the graham crust and both moaned at how good it was. Digging in deeper, I was repulsed that I could eat so much pie, but with my dad keeping up forkfuls, it almost became a game to see who would give up first. It was a funny, necessary, game of distraction from our shitty little emotional world until he dug into the last bite of the pie we had just finished together and smiled a big, gross, chocolate teeth victory smile at me.

He smiled, and I laughed as I sat back in my chair with a groan. I laughed but I needed to finish my round of apologies.

"I'm sorry I hurt you. I wasn't thinking clearly yesterday."

"I know baby. Go to bed if you want. I'll tidy up here and we'll talk tomorrow, okay?"

Agreeing, I stood and leaned into him to kiss the top of his head as I wrapped my arms around his shoulders and whispered, "I love you." Nodding as he held my hands against his chest, my dad whispered it back to my relief.

Later, I talked to my mom again before bed and told her I absolutely needed to go to work, until she finally relented. I thanked her for helping me, for our awesome talk, for my delicious dinner, and I told her about the pie my dad and I wolfed down, to her humor.

My mom insisted on my sleeping there again the following night. And though I tried to give her the 'I'll be okay' speech, she wouldn't listen.

She demanded I go back to their house the following night so we could talk about my day, my job, and what I was feeling. She was adamant, so again, I gave in.

My mom was so kind to me I ended up lying on her bed beside her apologizing again for being so dense about everything, especially about Steven. I apologized for accusing her of putting pressure on me when in reality she had been right- it was always me. And finally, I apologized for scaring her.
I apologized for everything I could think of until she hugged me and told me to stop. She hugged me tightly in her bed, then told me to stop worrying, stop thinking, and to go to sleep. She told me she loved me very much and that together she and I would get me past this setback.
She told me she loved me as I closed her door for the night, which was the end of my weekend from hell.

*****

Thankfully, Steven did talk to me by the following Thursday when he called me and said he was coming over.
Thursday night, 5 days after the last time he saw me, Steven came over and ripped the shit out of me for my stupidity, for scaring him, and for breaking his heart. Steven explained what seeing me like that had felt like for him. Then he turned the awful scenario on me until I agreed I wouldn't have survived something horrible happening to him. He made me see what he saw, and then he cried.
Steven cried and I died a little inside from his pain. But he stopped crying soon enough, told me he loved me and left me alone in my apartment with the promise to see me the following night for Chinese, which we did.
Friday night Steven and I talked all evening after work about everything leading up to the previous weekends' mistake, even the Trent thing and Steven's need to pound the shit out of Trent, which I admitted horribly embarrassed to my brother was totally my fault.
I begged him to let it go, promised I would never sleep with another of his friends, and we eventually calmed enough to watch a little TV before he left.

Kim and I had it out BIGTIME the following Saturday, and I immediately let her off the hook for the pills thing when she asked if it was because of how mean she had been to me that I made my mistake. Exhaling through the tension between us, I told her the truth of that shitty weekend, with our fight only being a small part of the tragic whole, and she and I eventually hugged it out.

I apologized for everything I said, admitting though she may be a little slutty I never thought of her as the horrible woman I described. I admitted to Kim everything I said was all I could think of to hurt her with because there wasn't much else to work with, which made her laugh at me and my confession.

Amazingly, Kim and I slowly mended our 11 year friendship over a long Saturday afternoon, drinking coffee in my apartment, until we eventually moved on and put all the nasty behind us.

*****

After that weekend, when everything calmed down a little and I eventually took the time to think about me and my relationship with Peter I realized one important thing regarding our breakup- Peter was still stringing me along with his little gestures, and notes. Peter kept giving me hope that he would return to me because he remained tied to me by the notes he left me.

Almost once a month there was a random note from Peter, until after my weekend from hell I received a little note that changed everything. Opening the note taped to my door, I was stunned as I read his words to me. I read only three sentences, but they were enough to make me continue past all the hurt and sadness.

Sophie,
Just live, baby.
And be safe.
I love you,
Peter xo

Peter wanted me to live, and I would.

... and LOST

Sarah Ann Walker

CHAPTER 26

If I learned anything from my weekend from hell it was that I was loved, and I had taken many people for granted, misjudging and underestimating my importance to them. I realized I had misjudged everything about my life after my breakup with Peter because I couldn't see past it.
So I changed again. I had another personality change- my third in only 7 months, but I was trying every day to find the place I was most comfortable. I was trying to find the place I belonged, because as sad as it was to admit to myself, I knew I didn't really belong with Peter anymore.
I made a decision to move on, and I slowly did. I focused on work, and I focused on my family and friends. I stopped being a drunken tart, and I started taking a pottery class on Saturday mornings, and a Yoga class on Tuesday and Wednesday evenings.
I moved slowly, but admittedly, I hurt a little less. Each day that passed became one day with a slight lessening of the pain inside me. The love never left me, but the pain slowly faded to just an ache in my chest that I was so familiar with it barely registered over time. The ache was a constant throb in my heart, but it was no longer an acute agony for me.
I could actually feel I was starting to move past the life I thought I would have with the man I would love forever, until sadly, I accepted our end.

Slowly, I was no longer quite as robotic, but I was still just a little lifeless as I made my way through the months since my bad weekend.
I was doing well at work, and I had pieces of pottery all over my home, at my parents' house, and tragically covering every single surface at Steven's place. I was becoming the pottery queen of the village in only 4 months. It was even a joke between me and my instructors that I created and finished a piece every single time I walked into the studio compared to the others who could spent multiple classes or even weeks getting just one piece right.
I didn't care about my successful creations though, I just had to sell them or give them away quickly because I ran out of room everywhere else. I didn't care where they ended up, I just needed to keep working

on my crafts to kill my time alone.

I rented space at the studio so I could work on my stuff anytime I wanted, which quickly became every Friday night after work, and all day Saturday. I became obsessed with pottery and I was really good at it, too. My mom even joked that I had finally found a beautiful outlet for being so intense, methodical, and driven.

After a few months, one of my friends at the pottery studio even found me a small used kiln to purchase which kindly my parents allowed me to put in their basement after they promised to show me their electric bills before it arrived and then after. I made them promise to let me pay the difference because pottery was *my* new little obsession, and reluctantly they agreed.

Over a few months, I slowly became content again with my simple life.

I worked all week and I made everything I could with clay. I perfected beautiful bowls and I experimented with glazing techniques quite successfully. I made cute sets of 4 colored mugs with little spoons inverted into the handles to sell at the cafe in the village, and my beautiful bowls were sold at Pandora's, in the Pottery studio, and at a store near my parents' house.

My set of 4 brightly colored mugs with spoons sold every single weekend, and I was behind a set always, which was kind of stressful, but awesome at the same time.

I loved that my stuff was so well received, and by November, the cafe actually placed an official order for 10 sets, which I couldn't possibly have ready before their Christmas rush, but I tried hard to fill the order.

I worked 2 full Saturday and Sunday weekends straight in the studio and I ended up at my parents almost every night after work firing and glazing the mugs for 3 weeks straight which I *knew* was killing their electricity, but they didn't seem to mind. My mom even offered to help remove the molds and finished mugs after each firing, and she set the kiln an hour before I showed up for more firing so it was ready when I got there.

My mom took no credit when I offered it, but she quickly became my pottery savior. She was the absolute backbone of my little pottery adventure, and I thanked her profusely.

In November, after accepting the contract from Java Bean I had to make forty mugs in one month, which doesn't sound so bad, but in reality was difficult because of waiting times for the clay to harden, and because I was a little obsessed with absolute perfection.

Once, I even lost a set of 4 mugs because I tried to fire them early knowing they still held too much moisture, but wanting to hurry. And when I opened the kiln to 3 cracked mugs, warped and destroyed, I was pissed at myself for my impatience.

The fourth mug survived though, albeit misshapen and lonely, but I loved it. That single mug became my favorite, and I used it always. One single surviving mug became the tragic symbol of my life.

I too was alone, less than perfect, but still functioning and good enough to be loved.

I was a mug, which was just about the funniest, saddest thing my mom had ever heard. But as we both laughed at my declaration, she told me it was her favorite mug, as well.

So on December 1st, 8 and a half months after Peter left me, I walked into the cafe with Steven and my parents carrying boxes of my mugs. I had succeeded in making 9 sets, 36 mugs, and 2 Christmassy colored bowls, and the manager was excited.

Actually, she was so excited she snatched up 3 sets immediately as her own, and 2 employees grabbed a set each, which suddenly brought me to only 4 sets to sell, which seemed sad somehow after all my hard work. Yet as my dad pointed out it didn't matter who bought them as long as they were being bought, and word of mouth from two coffee baristas in the village could only help me, I smiled at his logic and moved on.

Therefore, even though I only had 4 sets and 2 bowls to sell in the cafe, on my very own little shelf with my name on a cute little plaque, 'Sophie Morley- Handmade designs by local artist' which sounded way cooler than I felt, I still made a little money, but more importantly, I could breathe because the contract was finished.

But 2 days later I received a phone call from the cafe that changed my life again.

Reaching for my cell in the pottery studio Friday night, I was told by the manager Cori everything had sold that day. I was told my bowls and the 4 sets of mugs were purchased and then I was asked if it was possible to make any more quickly before Christmas, which honestly stressed me right out again. I was shocked and excited that everything went so well though, until she told me it was one man who had bought everything I made. And I knew.

Swallowing my mouth full of bile, I asked the unbelievable. "Who was he?"

"I don't know. Some military guy. He said he just returned and he had to have all your pottery. He was a little intense, but I guess that's normal for them," she laughed.

Cori hadn't been around the café back then so she didn't know about me and Peter, but I knew. Snapping out of my shock, I asked all I could as I tried to just breathe. "Did he leave his name?"

"No, why? He paid in cash and left with a box of your mugs and one bowl. He bought everything that was left because I'd already sold a set of mugs and one bowl earlier," she answered calm to my anything but.

"What did he look like?" I choked.

"I don't know... Long hair, muscly, a banged up eye and cheek. I don't know. Why? Do you have a stalker?" She laughed.

"What color hair?"

"Brown, I think."

"Eyes?" I begged.

"I couldn't tell. I don't remember. Why?" She asked again instead of talking.

"I'm just curious. Did he say anything about me?"

"Not at all. Why? What's going on, Sophie?"

I was totally losing my mind with Cori's lack of information, so I tried harder to keep it together.

"How do you know he was a military guy or something?!" I asked way too loudly on the phone.

"Um, his clothes were like cargo pants and a black shirt and he said something about stopping in for a coffee after duty. I don't remember exactly, but it just made sense or something from his look," she said sounding irritated with me.

"With long hair?" I asked desperately.

Huffing, Cori replied quickly. "Look, Sophie, I don't know anything else, okay? Some guy came in and bought the last 3 sets of your mugs and the last bowl. He had longish hair and was dressed in black cargo pants and a black shirt. I think he even had boots on. He mentioned being off duty, and that's it. I just wanted to let you know all your stuff sold, and I wanted to ask if you could make anything else quickly, like in the next 2 weeks. Even if they aren't mugs, I'll take bowls, or anything else you've made. That's all I was calling for," she said totally exasperated with me.

"I'm sorry... I've just been looking for someone and I wanted to know if the guy was him. Anyway, I have some stuff I can bring over Sunday morning, and I may have a few mugs ready as well. Thanks for calling and for all the opportunity, Cori. I really appreciate it," I tried to soothe the irritation between us.

"No problem. When do you think you'll be in Sunday? I'm working until 2:00, and I'd like to see and price what you bring in."

"I'll be there before 2:00. Thanks, Cori," I said as we hung up.

And then I panicked. Totally, absolutely panicked. I knew it was Peter- I *knew* it.

Breathing a *holy shit* to no one in particular in the studio, I just couldn't believe what I totally believed. Peter was back, or alive, or well enough to buy my stuff. Peter was still around, and I was spinning.

But there was nothing I could do at 8:00 Friday night, other than drive around the village looking for him. And there was no one I could tell he was around because everyone thought I was all better. Spinning, I knew I had to think of a way to see if the mystery man I knew was Peter was Peter.

The following day I went back to the pottery studio as early as it opened. Grabbing and firing every single decent piece I had ever made in their huge kiln made me feel productive, though I was loopy for sure having only slept for a few minutes here or there while I obsessed about how I would find Peter.

Once everything was in the kiln, and there was nothing more to do but wait, I left the studio on a mission. I had to find Peter, and the best I could come up with was Sunshine and Life again.

So I drove quickly from the studio home to drop off my car, then ran to the health food store where everything began for me.

Walking in the store I was greeted by Margaret, thank god. Margaret was there and not the knowing eyes of Terry. Margaret who had spoken to Peter and knew a little more about all this military or cop crap.

So reeling in my excitement and delirium I walked up to her with a big smile. Reaching, I even gave her a hug when she said hi back in the empty store which had just opened.

"Hey Margaret... How are you?" I feigned interest.

"Good. Are you ready for the holidays?" She asked pleasantly.

"Not completely. I still have a few gifts to buy, and no idea what to get."

"What have you been up to?"

I remember all the pleasantries between us were absolutely killing me. I wanted to ask her everything so badly, but I didn't even know how to start without sounding rude or desperate.

"Not much. Um... Margaret? Can I ask you a few questions about-"

"Peter?" She cut me off.

"Yes..." I gulped my nervousness.

Smiling at me, Margaret admitted, "Terry told me about your little confrontation a few months ago, and since you haven't been back til now, I thought you probably wanted to know something. So shoot," she said almost bracing herself against the counter, even as I found myself leaning into it.

"Ah... Well, what do you know about Peter? I don't know if you know but Peter and I dated earlier this year, and then we ended a little abruptly and I've been left with some questions about his-"

"Job?" She cut me off again as I nodded. "Okay, well I don't know anything for sure, but I think he's either a police officer or maybe military of some sort. Peter never actually admitted anything to me, and the few times we'd spoken he was pretty evasive but I picked up on a few things."

"Like?" I asked dying. I was frigging shaking with the need to know.

"Okay. Peter mentioned once just getting home from work, but then said after 'duty' he needed to stop to get a coffee, which was weird because no one says duty after steel-mill shift work. And then he was gone for a while once and mentioned just returning back to the 'real world', which was why he didn't reply to our messages. And when he brought me a coffee once and I told him about being mugged downtown with my husband he acted all weird- like sat up straighter and started asking questions like a police officer would. You know, approximate height and weight, but then he said, 'Where there any identifying marks, tattoos, or disfigurations' which sounded way to official to me," she said pausing for effect.

"What else? All you've said was words, but nothing really concrete," I prompted impatiently.

"Okay. Physically, I've seen Peter disappear, reappear and act totally exhausted when he returned, almost like weary or something. I've seen him super slim and sickly, and bulked right up with muscles. I've seen him with long hair looking rough and beaten, and then I've seen him a few days later clean shaven and dressed normally. I've seen him physically beat up with tattoos all over his arms, hands and neck, and then a few days later with nothing at all, almost like he was acting a part or something..."

Shaking her head sadly she continued after a few seconds. "Even his demeanor and behavior was all wrong when he was in character, but then when he would pop back in a few days later, he was just Peter again. A nice, handsome man who made the best hand lotions, soaps and tinctures from his very own herb garden, I'm told."

"But why wouldn't he just tell you he was a police officer? I mean, he doesn't have to say anything too in depth if it's a secret. But why not just admit to someone that he's a cop?"

"Because he can't?" She asked. "I don't know. But I'm telling you Sophie, my gut is saying he is way more than he appears. He's just too different sometimes to not be up to something. Oh! And this one time specifically when he was beaten up, I asked what happened and he only smiled and said 'we got the bad guys,' but nothing more even after I tried to push."

"'We got the bad guys' or just 'bad guys' like Terry said?"

"No, I remember clearly, 'we got the bad guys,'" Margaret confirmed as I exhaled deeply.

"Why do you think he disappears for months at a time?" I asked.

"Because of his real job, I think. I don't know, Sophie. But I swear he's doing something like that. He is just too hyper-vigilant or something. He talks about wanting to protect people, and wanting everything to be safe. He was just so sweet whenever he stopped in, that I felt almost sad for him when he would return looking terrible and exhausted. He made me feel very badly for him when he was in character or whatever it was he was doing," she said sadly.

Looking at Margaret, I'll admit it, I was annoyed by her concern. I don't think I was jealous, but I hated that she might have known the man I loved better than I did. So trying to reign in my annoyance I asked, "How often did you guys talk?"

"Whenever he was in the store, which was maybe once or twice a week for a few months at a time since Terry opened the store 4 years ago. Then he would disappear for a while, until he came back again. But he was just so secretive. He never talked about his past or his family, or anything else. Peter never said anything specific which seemed so odd that it made me wonder if he *couldn't* tell me anything. I don't know..."

"But you think you know. You're totally sure he's something like the police, or military, or something like that, right?" I begged trying to understand.

"Yes... I'm sure," she nodded again. And though a couple had walked into the store, neither Margaret nor I acknowledged them in the slightest.

"And you think he's something undercover?" I asked still horribly skeptical.

"Absolutely. His evasiveness seemed designed to let him disappear and reappear after a while. Like he needed to go undercover for a few months until it was maybe over, or until they had enough information or something, and then he could return. He was evasive but so warm and kind it seemed to almost tear him up to not be able to talk about anything personal. But he wanted to, I'm sure of it. He has too kind a soul to not want to connect with people," she said so honestly I was jolted into a nostalgic realm of pain.

To connect.

Me and Peter connecting.

Peter wanting to connect with me.

Every time he said the word connect, he seemed so desperate for me to share myself with him. He always seemed so in need of a connection with me.

Suddenly finding myself trying not to cry, I thanked Margaret. I thanked her as she looked between me and the 2 customers down the aisle. She looked like she didn't want to stop talking to me but felt she should at least acknowledge the others in the store.

"Margaret? When did you see Peter last?" I asked holding my breath.

"Sadly, the third week of March, before the paintings arrived at Perry's."

"What paintings? What's Perry's?" I begged nearly breathless.

"The little art gallery past Medina's Chocolatier," but I was at a loss. I never had to pass Medina's chocolatier so I didn't know there was a little art gallery beyond it.

"Does he still have paintings there?"

"I think so. You should go see his work. They're beautiful," she smiled kindly. "If I see Peter should I tell him you were asking about him?"

"Yes... I want him to know," I admitted sadly.

"Okay. If I think of anything else do you want me to let you know?"

"God, yes. Thank you, Margaret. And please tell Terry I'm sorry I was such a bitch the last time I saw him. I just didn't really believe anything he told me."

"And now?" She asked calmly.

Looking back at Margaret's kind face, I confessed. "I'm not going to lie- everything you just told me seems so farfetched and kind of insane, but you seem so sincere, and little things you said I remember Peter saying, so it's a little easier to believe, though it's still really crazy to me. Did that make sense?" I laughed.

"Yup. My husband thought I was crazy too, but then he met Peter here once and he said immediately Peter was 'on the job'," she quoted. "He said as soon as he met Peter he knew he was on the job because of his mannerisms and the way he answered questions. So there you go. I might sound crazy but I'm not wrong, I don't think," she smiled.

"Thank you again. I'll go see Perry's art gallery and maybe they can tell me something about him," I said leaving quickly with a wave and filled with purpose.

"Good luck!" Margaret yelled walking to the back of the store.

Once outside I was again surrounded by *what the hell?* Everything Margaret said sounded almost plausible, and yet my logical brain wanted to dismiss everything she told me because it just seemed too unbelievable and made for TV or something.

But I remembered a few things as I bundled up tighter outside. I remembered weird moments of Peter looking around suddenly, or taking my hand and suddenly leading me a different way when we walked. I remembered a few times he would act a little paranoid and we would have to leave a restaurant or store while he looked around intensely.

I remember the time in Murphy's when Peter jumped up almost abruptly and said he had to leave while he looked around strangely. He was being weird, and I felt the weirdness all around me, but we were so new then I didn't know what was wrong, or why he acted so paranoid when he left the pub quickly.

But maybe...

Walking down the street my head nearly exploded with the conflict between *as if* versus *maybe?*

CHAPTER 27

   When I finally walked to Perry's Art Gallery from Sunshine and Life I was freezing. It was mild for December but there was still a definite bite in the air, and because I hadn't dressed for walking outside for 2 and a half blocks, my hands and face were numb by the time I arrived. But as I entered the little gallery I was quickly filled with warmth.
   The gallery was so colorful and just warm. There was warmth everywhere. The music was soft instrumental, and the art was so lovely I stood still to take it all in.
   Immediately, I could tell it wasn't a place of abstract artistic craziness, or paintings that screamed what the hell am I looking at? It was a place of beautiful paintings of people within scenes with people, surrounded by people seemingly sectioned off by each artist.
   Looking, I knew what I was afraid to see. But without any arrogance, I was sure I would see a portrait or painting of myself inside.
   When a gorgeous man sitting at a little corner desk came and greeted me, I almost begged, *Am I in here?* But amazingly, I kept it together.
   "Hi," he smiled. And he really was gorgeous, and even straight I think. "Is this your first time here?"
   "Yes. I live not too far away in the village, and I was told to come in. It's beautiful," I spoke honestly. "But I've never made it past the delicious Chocolatier," I grinned.
   As he laughed, he nodded. "We hear that a lot on this end of the block. Don't feel bad," he grinned. "Why don't you have a look around, and let me know if you have any questions. Everything in here is by a local artist," he said smiling again, as he slowly walked away and sat back at his little desk, semi-hidden in the corner. So I looked.
   I tried to make it seem like I was interested in the art because I didn't want to just run through looking for myself. I even faked an interest in at least one piece of almost each artist's section of wall. But I was dying inside and I needed to know.
   Eventually, in the middle of the gallery I gasped when I finally found myself. On a wall, halfway through the little gallery, behind a panel that separated the room into 2, I was up on the wall, and I was stunned.

There was no mistaking me. There could be no mistake to anyone who knew me or had ever met me that it was absolutely me on the wall.

I was painted 4 times in vivid color, dressed as I always did, looking like I remember I looked when I was with Peter. There were 4 beautiful paintings of me in various displays of happiness with Peter.

I was smiling outside surrounded by snow in one, and in the next I was sitting on my couch smiling straight at anyone looking at the painting. In the third painting I was striking a pose at my bedroom door in a sexy little negligee, beaming at the watcher. And in the final painting I was sleeping and snuggled up in my sheets but looking content as I slept.

I looked beautiful in every painting, truly. I may have been attractive, but Peter's ability to make me look beautiful was amazing. I couldn't stop staring at all the color and the life in my eyes and through my smiles as he saw and painted me.

Trying to take it all in, I realized the 4 paintings were mounted as corners with a charcoal sketch sitting sadly in the middle, which seemed awful somehow in comparison to all the color of the paintings.

Looking at the center piece I saw it was a dark, charcoal drawing of devastation. It was a tragic portrait of me that Peter had captured. It must have been the very look I had when I stood by the door, almost leaning against the back of my couch when he broke up with me.

Looking even at my clothing, I realized it *was* that exact Sunday morning in March. I was wearing tights and a long brown sweater and I still had my brown riding boots on after getting our coffee that morning. My hair was down, and slightly disheveled from the cold March morning blowing through me.

Looking closely, the sketch actually showed every emotion I had felt that day. And sadly, I looked like a woman who had just been destroyed as she walked into a nightmare.

Staring for however long, I let the first sob take me until the tears caused me to sit on the floor underneath the sketch of myself as I cried.

And as time passed while I sat in my heartbreak, I heard myself moan just once, "Peter..."

Eventually, the gorgeous guy asked, "Can I get you anything?" But I shook my head no while he looked at me until recognition clearly dawned on his face. He didn't whip his head back and forth between me and the wall, he just looked once at me and back to the paintings, and he so clearly knew I was her on the wall, he seemed to shake his head at the pain he was experiencing.

"I see you're familiar with Mr. Connor's work," he gently prodded.

"A little," I moaned. "He painted a few portraits of me, and sketched me a few times. But I didn't know about this," I cried.

After a few minutes of silence, gorgeous guy introduced himself as Michael and asked if I'd like a chair to sit on, which I did. And once he placed a chair beside me, I sat down, perfectly situated in front of myself as I stared, and remembered, and felt everything of my life with Peter.

At one point, a couple walked through the gallery and past me, but thankfully, they didn't acknowledge me or otherwise hover around. I didn't know if it was because I was clearly dying in front of them, or because gallery etiquette meant you didn't hover around someone else's devastation. But for whatever reason, they were there and then gone as I sat staring at the beautiful paintings.

Staring, there was no mistaking the brilliance or the light that came from each one. Even the sleeping painting captured me in total bliss as I slept. I looked like a woman totally in love, sleeping with almost a private little smile in my slumber. I looked so happy in the painting, I could actually feel the happiness all around me in my current sad reality.

Looking at myself sleeping, I wondered about the watcher. I wondered how many times Peter must have watched me, and what he was thinking about me when he did. I thought of our last night, and Eddie Vedder's voice faded away as I remembered Peter gently singing Black to me as I wept in the tender moment between us.

Exhaling my misery, I looked next at the beautiful bedroom doorway painting which was just that, *beautiful*. I looked so lovely standing there gazing at the person I was going to be with. I looked like I was happily entering my room for the best sex of my life. I looked sexy, but so in love the painting took all the potential smut and sleaziness out of the pose and clothing. I didn't look slutty or trampy, even though the negligee was slightly transparent.

You could definitely see the slight coloring of my nipples through the pink negligee but it looked beautiful, not slutty. It didn't matter that you saw the slight dusting of my nipples, because you were drawn almost immediately to my little smile and bright eyes. I looked like a woman so in love, everything else faded but that minute before I walked to the love of my life waiting for me in my bedroom.

The couch and outdoor painting were also just a lovely representation of nothing specific but everything loving in that moment. I was sitting on the couch staring at Peter, and I loved him. And in the outdoor painting I was standing with the backdrop of white snow highlighting my green coat and eyes as I smiled at the person I loved in front of me. I was loved and adored and my smile told our story beautifully.

But naturally, I was drawn back to the charcoal drawing in the middle. Looking at the drawing, I finally noticed the only words to be found anywhere, because the exhibit itself wasn't titled, and Peter's name wasn't listed below.

The only words to be found were at the bottom of the charcoal drawing. In a desperate looking script, almost like the word appeared before the sketch itself, it read... LOST.

That's all there was- One word to sum up everything I was in that exact moment of time and everything I became afterward.

I was *lost*.

Sitting there, I realized I could almost make a play on the word itself. Thinking about the word I realized I was lost, yes, but I had also lost. I lost Peter. I lost my lover. I lost the life I wanted. I lost everything I had ever wanted when he walked out the door. I had lost.

And I *was* lost.

So I cried again. I cried a harder, soul-consuming cry of agony and defeat. I cried like a total loser right in front of my paintings in the middle of a quaint little gallery at the end of the village on a brisk day in December. I cried almost one year after the first date I ever had with Peter.

Crying, I suddenly realized nothing seemed more cruel to me than knowing Peter understood completely who I was and what I had felt that day, but he left anyway. He captured me as I was with him, yet he still ended us.

And that became the greatest cruelty of our life and ending together.

Peter knew and saw but he still left me alone. Peter knew but he still left me alone and lost.

*****

After forever I noticed Michael checked up on me from time to time. But other than a quick look which I ignored, he never spoke to me again or made me feel embarrassed for my breakdown in his gallery.

Michael brought me a bottle of water which I accepted with a nearly inaudible thanks, and then I was left alone with myself, then and now.

Eventually, after what felt like hours in the gallery I knew I had to leave. I knew I had to function again. I knew I had to move on again but I felt trapped in the gallery. I didn't want to leave and I didn't want to say goodbye. I just didn't know how to leave Peter in the gallery without me.

So I called my mom and asked her to please meet me, which amazingly she said she would without question or even pause. My mom said she was coming for me, but she could be up to a half hour away, giving me another half hour to sink deeper into my despair.

However long later though, I heard a soft whisper of my name as I turned to my mom walking toward me. Walking to me with kind eyes, I finally released everything I had felt for the hours I sat staring at my previous life.

"*See*. This is what we were together..."

"Oh, baby. I see it," she said kneeling on the floor, wrapping her arms around my shoulders as I buried my face in her neck and sobbed all over my mom.

"I'm fucked up again," I choked.

"It's okay to be," she whispered in my ear.

"Can you see it? I wasn't delusional or wrong or dramatic, or even an idiot. It was real because he saw it too."

"I see it, Sophie. Can I take a better look?" She asked as I released her so she could really look.

Still kneeling beside me, she kept one arm around my waist but she seemed to only see what was in front of her. She stared at the paintings of me while I cried silently beside her. I didn't want to interrupt her by crying loudly, so I held in the sobs that wanted to destroy me. And I kept my hands in my lap so I wouldn't rip the paintings from the wall and run.

With tears slowly falling from her eyes, I knew my mom finally understood.

"These are so beautiful. I can't believe how he painted so much life and love in your eyes."

"He could because that's what I was. I was alive and I loved him," I whispered sadly.

"I can see that. Oh, god... Sophie. This hurts *me* to look at, so I can't even imagine what you're feeling. This is the most amazing and tragic thing I've ever seen in my life," my mother cried softly. "The middle drawing-"

"Was the last day," I cried to my mom's obvious understanding. "That's what I was wearing and that's what I must've looked like when he walked out of my apartment for the very last time. That was me that day, and I feel..." But there were no words.

Looking at the woman's face in the charcoal drawing who stared back at me was beyond tragic. She looked terrible and so destroyed you could actually feel her pain.

"That's how I still feel even though I've physically moved on. Inside I still feel like that all the time," I wept.

"What do you want to do? What can I do to help you, Sophie? Tell me what I can do." My mom begged me.

"I don't know..."

"Okay. Just give me a minute," she said rising, as I nodded while I stared at the lost woman on the wall.

After a few minutes I heard raised voices, but I still couldn't get off the damn chair. Sitting there staring at myself, I wanted to know what my mom was yelling about, but I just couldn't move.

"Sophie!" I jumped. "Show him some ID," my mom barked walking back to me from behind the partition.

"What?"

"I tried to buy the paintings, or take them, or friggin' steal them from the wall, but I can't. But he said there's a note for a Sophie Morley with the paintings," she said loudly as I gasped and stood so quickly the chair toppled behind me.

"What note? What?"

"Sophie. Open your purse and take out your Driver's License," she annunciated slowly for me.

Scrambling for my little purse beside my coat on the floor, which incidentally I had no memory of removing, I grabbed my wallet with shaking hands, as my mom took it from me.

Opening my wallet, she ripped through the credit cards and bank cards, until she pulled out my driver's license and practically assaulted Michael with it.

"Here! Jesus, it's not like you couldn't tell it was her on the fucking wall," my mom snapped scaring even me a little.
 But totally professional, Michael held his own against the crazy bitch and her psychotic daughter in front of him.
 "Look, I didn't doubt for a moment she was the muse of the paintings. I just needed proof of her name before I gave her the letter. Mr. Connor insisted on it," he said with gentle patience.
 "Fine. I understand. But she's Sophie Morley, you have your proof, now give her the letter please," my mom demanded, even as I still stood dumbfounded watching the exchange between them.
 "There's something else," Michael said as he handed me the envelope with a slight humor that seemed completely misplaced under the circumstances.
 "What?!" My mom demanded as sensed her impending explosion.
 "I'm to sell all these paintings to Sophie Morley for 5 dollars..."
 "*What?!*"
 But as my mom asked the obvious question, I burst out laughing, and crying, and laughing at the absurdity of this situation.
 Looking at me, my mom recovered quickly. "I don't understand," she said exasperated.
 "I do! It was always 5 dollars between us. If I was bitchy I owed him 5 dollars. When he was an asshole, he owed me 5 dollars. Whoever got out of bed and went for the coffee run owed the other 5 dollars. Oh, god... It's always been 5 dollars between us," I laughed and cried at once.
 Watching me and my mom, Michael handed back my ID at that point with a letter from his pocket, and asked if I could wait until the next night to take the paintings. He told me he needed them for a little exhibit he was having that night, and the following morning, but otherwise for 5 dollars they were mine. He almost begged me to leave them in the gallery, and after his kindness I just couldn't refuse him, no matter how badly I wanted to take them with me right then and there.
 "But they're of her..." My mom protested until I stopped her.
 "It's okay. I know they're here now and I'll have them tomorrow night. What time can I pick them up?" I asked obsessively rubbing the letter in my hand.
 "We close up by 5:00 on Sundays, so maybe quarter after. I'll make sure they're taken down and packaged for you as soon as we close. Is that okay? You can pay me then if you'd like?"
 But again my mom was losing her patience. "Oh, for Christ's sake. Hand him a five, Sophie," she barked as I quickly found a five dollar bill in my

wallet and handed it over.

I wasn't ready to be finished just yet though. There were so many things I needed to know.

"Um... How long have these been here?"

"Since the first week of June, I believe."

Nodding, I went for broke. "Do you know where Peter lives or how to contact him?"

Pausing like everyone else, Michael shook his head no but asked, "Don't you?"

"No. Did he leave an address to mail his payments or anything?"

"No. These weren't for sale. Ever. Peter agreed to display them, but they were under no circumstances to be sold. Well, except to you," he smiled.

"Do you know anything about him? Has he been in recently? Does he come in often? Do you ever see him around?" The desperation in my voice was becoming more and more obvious.

"I'm sorry, I don't. Mr. Connor seems someone reclusive and-"

"No *shit!*" I jumped in by mistake as my mom laughed at me. "Sorry..."

"Anyway," Michael continued. "He's been in only a few times since he dropped them off and though I've told him about the interest from a few Buyers and I've given him business cards from a few people who would like him to paint for them, he had no interest. Mr. Connor only asked if a Sophie Morley- *you*- came by and received his letter. Then he'd leave again," Michael answered somewhat sadly.

"How did he look?" I begged.

"Look?"

"You know what I mean. How did he look? Was he well or like weird or anything?"

"I really couldn't say. I don't know him at all, so I don't know what his well looks like. Plus, let's face it, I work with artists all day and some are crazy, some are eccentric, and some are completely normal. I've learned to not expect or notice anything about the artists who come and go."

"If I give you a something tomorrow when I pick up the paintings, would you please give it to him? Please?" I begged desperately again, though I truly didn't know what the something would be.

"Of course I will," Michael said as he squeezed my hand in a kind little gesture of reassurance.

"Thank you so much Michael. You have no idea what today is like for me," I said sadly.

"I probably don't. But I like seeing a happy ending of sorts," he grinned even as my heart broke again.

I knew he thought this was a happy ending *of sorts,* but it still felt like a tragedy to me. I was still no closer to Peter than I had been for the last 8 1/2 months of my life.

"Let's go, Sophie," my mom said tugging me into her arms as she tried to turn me from the room.

"Thank you, Michael," I whispered again as my mom pulled me out of our area. Holding up my coat she helped me put it on, and as we reached the door and I paused for a second, she continued to pull me through the front doors.

"Where are all the people?" I asked suddenly.

"They're closed between 2 and 4 every Saturday."

"Oh! What time is it?" I asked confused again.

Looking at her watch as we stood outside I learned from my mom it was close to 3:30. Shocked, I did the math in my head and almost laughed again.

"How long have you been here?"

"About an hour. Why?"

"Because I sat and stared at myself for over 3 hours," I laughed.

"Wow. Narcissistic much?" My mom said so deadpan, we both burst out laughing. "Where's your car, baby?"

"At home."

"I'm parked just a little down the street, so I'll take you home. Do you want to come home with me, or to your place? And it's okay to come home with me. After the day you've had, I would love to be there for you," she smiled on the street still holding my arm in her own.

"Sorry. Being stubborn as usual I just want to go home. In a weird way I'm sad, obviously, but I feel a little good, too. I know I'll probably lose it sooner or later, but something feels good about all this, so I think I'll be fine tonight. Oh *shit*!" I suddenly remembered. "I was supposed to bring a bunch of pottery to the cafe tomorrow, and I totally forgot to get my stuff from the studio. *Shit,*" I moaned again frustrated.

"Well, let's go. I'll help you carry it all in. Let me just call your dad," she said pulling out her phone as we walked toward her car.

As we walked, I still held the letter in my hand, trying desperately not to crumple it, but wanting to hold it tightly at the same time.

Actually, I was pretty impressed with my mom not ripping it out of my hands to read, or even asking about it. It must've been killing her not to know what it said, like it was me, but amazingly, she left it for me to deal with as we each sat in her car while she finished up talking briefly to my dad.

2 hours later, my mom and I both carried a heavy box filled with pottery into my quiet apartment. Entering while juggling the box to turn on the light I was immediately obsessed with the walls of my home. Looking around, I nearly threw the box of breakables on the couch while I spun around and tried to figure it all out.
My mom looked around too, and seemed to know where my head was at. She knew everything I was thinking, I could tell.
"Are you sure it's a good idea to keep them in your home where you'll see them all the time and be reminded of..." But she didn't finish.
"I have to," I said absolutely sure.
"Okay. May I make a suggestion then?"
"Of course."
"Put them in your bedroom," she said so seriously I was surprised.
"But I'll think of him every night."
"You do anyway," which was true. "Here's what I'm thinking. They are so personal you probably don't want anyone who comes over to see that side of you, or your relationship with Peter. Plus, if they're in your bedroom, you can feel closer to him while you sleep, which I know has been one of your biggest battles since this all happened to you. And for those of us who love you, it'll be very hard to see you like that, both the beautiful paintings and the tragic drawing. I know it makes me want to cry, your dad *will* cry," she said with a grin. "And your brother will be angry at your devastation. So hanging in your bedroom seems like the logical choice. Plus, you never have men over, so you don't have to worry about potential lovers seeing that side of you until you're ready," she faded out.
Listening to my mom, everything she said was exactly right. So naturally, I cried a little as I walked to her to give her the biggest hug I could.
"Thank you so much for coming to me so quickly today. I know I couldn't have survived today without you. You were amazing, and actually a little scary to Michael," I whispered as she laughed.
"Mama-Bear Syndrome. You'll understand one day."

"Let's hope," I replied sadly. "Anyway, thank you so much for being there for me."

"You never have to thank me for being there for you. It's my job and even if it wasn't I would be anyway. I love you so much, Sophie," she whispered back squeezing me tighter. "So what do you want to do now?"

"Absolutely nothing. I still don't even want to read the letter yet, but when I do I'll tell you what it says, I promise. I'm just so tired, all I want to do is lie down, watch shitty TV and go to sleep early. And you have to get home to dad who is probably pacing right now waiting for you to give him the scoop you wouldn't give on the phone in front of me," I grinned.

"Yup, he is. Are you sure?"

"Yes. Go home, and thank you so much for today."

"Can I call you later?"

"Sure."

"Okay. I'll call around 9:00 to see how you're doing. And we'll go with you tomorrow to pick up the paintings, okay?"

"Thank you."

"Good night, Sophie," she said walking to my front door. Looking back one last time, she leaned in and kissed me on the cheek with a gentle smile that made my eyes fill, but shook her head no to my tears and walked out my door.

Closing the door behind her, I realized once again my mom saved me, cared for me, and then left me to do the rest on my own, like she knew I needed to.

CHAPTER 28

    I can't even explain the compulsion that made me hold the letter in my hand but not read it. I can't explain why after my mom left I had a shower, cooked some soup, and sat on my couch eating, but didn't read the letter.
    I think I was afraid Peter would say something mean, or maybe I was terrified he would tell me our relationship meant nothing to him. I think I was desperate to still believe I had meant to him what he had meant to me.
    I was afraid of the letter because his absence left an opening to rekindle our love due to my lack of closure. But the letter had the potential to give the closure I didn't want to have which scared me from not reading it. So I waited.
    I waited until I couldn't stand the wait any longer. Jumping up, I ran to my kitchen to grab his Jasmine candle from the cupboard, and I ran to my bathroom drawer for his jasmine massage oil, then I ran for my bed with my heart pounding.
    I grabbed my phone on the way to my bed and made a desperate call to my mom.
    "What's wrong?" She asked immediately.
    "Nothing. Look, it's almost 9:00 and I didn't want you to call me and interrupt. I'm going to read his letter now, and I don't want you to call me, okay?"
    "Sure... But-"
    "I'm okay, I promise. I just don't know what it says, so I don't want you to call me before I'm ready. Please don't call?"
    "But how will I know if you're okay?" She asked sadly.
    "I'll be okay. I'm much stronger now, and even if he breaks my heart again it can't feel much worse than it did before, so please don't call. I'll call after, I promise."
    "Okay, Sophie. Let me know. Call me anytime tonight. I don't care how late."
    "Thanks. I have to go," I said desperately as I hung up to her mumbling something I couldn't hear.

Preparing for the letter, I lit his candle and rubbed a little jasmine oil on my chest and neck before washing my hands of the oil. I could smell and feel Peter all around me, and I remembered everything between us in that moment as I sat on my bed cross-legged.

I breathed him in as I opened the letter to Sophie Morley, recognizing his handwriting instantly with a sad smile.

Sophie,

I love you so much I don't have any words greater than you are adored by me. You are adored like you've always wanted to be, and I wish I could express it better than that. You are adored and loved by me, now and forever.

I'm sorry I hurt you, and I'm so sorry I left you. I wish I could explain my actions, but I can't. There are things you don't know and things you'll probably never know about me, but I wish I could tell you so you understood- it was never about me not loving you when I left. You are, and will always be the greatest love I'll ever experience for the rest of my life. You are the only person I have ever connected with so intimately and so deeply, you often nearly shook me from my purpose.

But I can't be with you because I made promises before you. I have things I have to do, which you would understand if I could tell you, but I can't. All I will say is this- and I hope you keep this with you always; you were sacrificed for the greater good. Being with you has been the greatest gift of my life, and leaving you has been the greatest sacrifice.

Please don't look for me because you can't find me. I don't exist, and I can't be with you. You are too important to me to ever risk your safety. And I need to know you are safe for the rest of your life, even if that safety is without me.

I love you so much, there simply are no words.

Peter xo

After I exhaled the tension in my body, I read and reread Peter's letter. With an absolute belief in his love, I read his letter until it became a beautiful chant in my heart.

I *was* loved and adored. *I knew it!*

I knew I couldn't have felt what I felt alone. I knew it wasn't possible for one person to feel the depth of love I felt without the other person feeling the same love. It simply wasn't possible.

Peter loved me as I loved him, totally and completely. But for whatever reason he couldn't tell me, we couldn't be together.

After reading his words, the relief I felt was overwhelming. Reading I was loved and treasured was everything. The absence of him still ripped me apart, but there was a definite comfort in knowing the truth.

I was loved and adored by the man I loved and adored.

With a smile and a few tears, I calmed my stomach of its knots, and I curled into my bed holding his letter tightly. The absence of him still hurt, almost unbearably so, but knowing there was a reason for his absence was the closure I had needed since the moment he left me.

And once I accepted his absence for reasons that were valid but unknown, sleep came much easier to me for the first time since he left me.

*****

Later that night I had the most amazing dream.

Peter and I were together again. We made love and we connected so deeply, I felt him in my soul. We were together again, and I was happy once more. I had experienced our greatest pleasure and I had taken him into me as part of my own life.

I experienced his mouth on mine and his mouth and tongue devouring me. I felt his body move inside me and I felt my release in his embrace.

Peter was everything to me and I was adored by him.

Each touch was amazing, and beautiful, and fulfilling. We made love for hours and we experienced pleasure so completely, we seemed to breathe each other's breath as we moved within each other. We once again shared the intimate connection we had always known together.

I was alive again, and I was sexually and emotionally whole. I was alive in his arms where I would stay forever.

After we made love, Peter and I showered and dressed each other. We held each other and walked together for coffee. We entered our cafe with private smiles and loving embraces. And it was obvious to everyone in the cafe that we were in love with each other by the return grins and smiles we received from strangers.

Then our day changed.

When Peter and I left with our coffees, still holding hands, I was suddenly thrown to the ground against the brick wall of the cafe as I screamed through a sound like no other I had ever heard as I turned back to see a falling Peter. Holding his chest, he fell beside me as a man stood suddenly in front of him.

Screaming, I reached for Peter desperately. Reaching, I had just grabbed Peter's hand as his eyes held mine for a brief second before slowly closing. Then I screamed.

With renewed purpose, I found the strength past the death of my heart to reach and hold Peter. I held him until I was overcome with the grief that was destroying me. I held him until gasping and shaking, I begged him to stay with me. Over and over I begged him to stay. Pleading, I offered him everything I had if he would stay with me for just one more moment.

But I knew he was lost and I died with him on the sidewalk.

When I woke up crying and moaning, and shaking, I couldn't shake the unreality of my world. I felt his pain, and I felt his death so clearly, it was an agony ripping through my chest.

Scrambling for the phone, I called my mom hysterically, until moving, I could hear her dressing as she tried to soothe me calm.

Then I was talking to my dad who also tried but there was no comfort or understanding to give. I knew my reality, and I was nearly psychotic with the death facing me.

Peter was lost. I knew it in my soul.

Suddenly, nauseous, I dropped the phone my dad stayed on and I ran for the bathroom. Throwing up, I was stricken with such grief, it was like an ice pick puncturing my heart over and over again. I couldn't stop crying, and I couldn't stop vomiting.

I was nothing in that moment but death and decay on the bathroom floor until the exhaustion hit me, and then I was nothing more.

When my mom woke me on the floor, I cried out as she held me.

Pulling me into her arms, she gave me all the strength she could. She tried to shake me coherent, and she tried to lift me back to reality, but I was gone.

Trying to explain, I mumbled, "Peter is dead," until pausing with me in her arms, my mother stopped trying to bring me back.

"What do you mean, baby?"

"I mean I felt it tonight. I know he's dead. I felt him die..." I cried harder.

"What do you mean, Sophie? How do you know?" My mother sounded confused.

"I dreamed about him dying. It was a dream, but it wasn't. It was real. I know it was."

"You had a dream?" She asked me again sounding more confused.

"Yes. I know it was a dream, but it wasn't. I'm telling you, Peter died tonight. I felt him die," I moaned.

"In a dream?"

"*Yes!* I know it sounds fucked up, but I'm telling you mom he died tonight. I felt it and I can't explain it, and I know it sounds weird, but I know he died. I *know* it..." I faded out because even in my despair I could see the absurdity of my statement. "I just know..." I cried.

"Come out here with me, Sophie. Let's go talk in the living room," she soothed trying to lift me off the floor. But I couldn't let her distract me until she understood.

"I'm not crazy, mom. I'm really not. I actually know how crazy this sounds, but I'm telling you it's the truth. I know it's not possible, but somehow I felt him die tonight. I wasn't there, but I kind of was and I looked at him and he looked at me for one second before he closed his eyes and died. I was there, even though I know that's not possible," I tried to explain.

"Sophie, I need you to come talk to me. Now, Sophie."

Giving in like I always did with my mom, I let her help me off the floor until I pulled away and mumbled I needed to use the washroom. Looking at me, my mom relented slightly, but as she left the bathroom she did push the door wide open like she didn't trust me to have any privacy.

Minutes later when I walked into my living room my mom and brother were sitting on my couch. I didn't know he was there, and I didn't even know what to say to him.

"When did you get here?" I asked passing behind him on the couch.

"A few minutes ago. What's going on, Soph? Mom told me about earlier with the paintings, but what happened tonight?"

"I read his letter and it was beautiful," I moaned. "He really does love me as much as I love him."

"What did it say?" My mom asked taking my hand.

"Everything I've ever wanted to hear from Peter. He didn't leave me on purpose. He left me because he had to. He said loving me was the greatest gift he'd ever known and leaving me was the greatest sacrifice. He told me he didn't want to but had to, and I believe him. You can read it if you want," I said standing to get the letter from my room.

Walking, I was half numb and still shaking from the horrible dream earlier as I handed the letter over to my expectant mother, and my curious brother.

Waiting as they read my beautiful letter side by side, I stood watching them understand my newest reality.

Exhaling herself, my mom looked up at me and smiled. "It's beautiful, Sophie. I'm glad he could at least explain that he couldn't explain why he left you. How do you feel about it?"

"Relieved. I still miss him and love him, but at least I understand there's more going on than him just not wanting me, or not loving me like I loved him. It feels better somehow, but I still want him so much I feel horrible, too," I added as she nodded her understanding.

Steven didn't say a word to me about the letter. He just watched our exchange like he either had nothing to add, or maybe couldn't think of the right thing to add. But at least he stayed with me and listened to me.

"What happened earlier?" Steven asked pulling me down onto the couch between them.

"Um..." Suddenly, the reality of what I was going to say struck me as ridiculous. I felt like an idiot for believing what I believed, but I did still believe it. "I had a wonderful, loving dream about me and Peter, and then it changed into a nightmare and he was killed in front of me. I know it sounds crazy, but I really feel like he died tonight. I just feel it everywhere inside me," I cried softly.

"Can we google him?" Steven asked, and I was stunned. Considering all the stalking, watching and waiting I'd participated in the last 8 months of my life, I couldn't believe I didn't just google him to see if...

Jumping, I ran for my laptop in my dining room, until I returned seconds later and crashed down between my mom and brother on the couch.

"I don't think... Would it be in the news yet? I'm... But it happened tonight-"

"Just start with his name," Steven pushed, so I did.

Googling, all I had was Peter Connor- 32 years old. I typed his name, his birthdate, our city, his parents, everything I could think of until the information was too hard to distinguish.

Every once in a while, my mom or brother would point to a site with specific Peter Connor looking news but just as often we'd find an article about a Connors living in Petersburg, or a Peter living in Connorsville, Indiana, etc. There were so many things to look at and read, but nothing seemed current, or relevant. Nothing seemed anything like Peter Connor, a 32 year old something, from somewhere, doing who knows what that we could find that sounded like my Peter.

We read about a football captain named Peter Connor who scored the winning touchdown in Grade 12 at a local high school, but we couldn't see his face through the helmet to be sure. We read about a Peter Connor 23 who was in a bad car accident. We read about a Peter Connor arrested for burglary one town over, and even about a Peter Connor who died 5 years earlier from leukemia. It was endless, and sadly, completely pointless.

We tried military records, and even the local police. We tried to find his name mentioned on the police force or in the service somewhere, but we came up empty, which almost seemed stranger when we thought about it.

Everybody is on google at some point. Steven was mentioned because of a baseball tournament he was in, and my dad was mentioned because of the company he works for; there was even a photograph of my dad in the article. My mom wasn't mentioned anywhere which made her fake pout, but I was mentioned twice because of a college paper I won an award for, and even for my pottery which was an entry only three days old.

Everyone has something on google, but there was nothing about my Peter that we could find. However, as I sat there feeling totally frustrated and defeated Steven finally drew my attention to the obvious.

"There was no mention of a Peter Connor being shot or dying, Soph. There is no mention of anyone being killed last night or even recently. So maybe your dream was just a dream," he said bumping my shoulder with his own.

"I know. But I'm sure something's wrong. Maybe he wasn't shot. Maybe he died doing something else," I cried. "I swear, I *feel* something bad happened," but I too was fading out of my conviction.

It was 5:30 in the morning, and my mom and brother had come running for me in the middle of the night because I was mental. They had come again to my rescue like I was beginning to expect from them.

For all the independence and solitude I had had self-imposed growing up, I suddenly realized the comfort and love I had missed out on by being my formerly completely independent self.

"Thank you so much for coming over. I'm really sorry this seems so stupid now. But when I woke up I was just so sure he was dead. I was sure the horrible feeling inside me was him dying."

"And now?" My mom asked gently.

"Now I feel a little stupid, and very confused. I can't explain it. I know logically I had a bad dream, but the emotional part of me says it was for a reason. But I'm okay now. You can go home. Actually, please go home. Dad's probably still waiting to find out what his psycho daughter is up to, and I still need you to go with me tonight to get the paintings," I said leaning into my mom on the couch.

"We'll be here at 4:45 to pick you up."

"And I'm coming, too," Steven piped up.

"Ahhhh... I don't think you want to see one of the paintings. It's a little sexy," I laughed embarrassed.

"I doubt it," Steven teased. "They're of you," he said laughing as my mom swatted the back of his head making Steven and I burst out laughing.

For such a strange night, that swatting of Steven's head was so nostalgic and funny to me after all the years my mom did that when we were teenagers, I suddenly felt a little warmth creep under my skin for the first time since Friday night.

"I'm so sorry for freaking everyone out again," I said embarrassed.

"It's okay, Sophie. This has been one hell of a weekend for you so don't worry about it. I'll curl up to your dad and sleep till noon, which I suggest you do as well. We'll see you at 4:45, okay?" Nodding, I walked both my mom and brother to my door.

Once they left, I was alone again with Peter all around me as I walked back to my bed. Crawling in, I snuggled up to his pillow and whispered a lonely goodnight to him again, like I did every night since he left me.

CHAPTER 29

    After I woke up at 10:00, I obsessively googled Peter until 12:30, when it was absolutely time to quit. It was so hard for me to let Peter go, but by 1:30 I eventually struggled to my car with my 3 boxes of pottery.
    Walking in at 1:55, Cori met me near the door and took one of the large boxes from my hands immediately. Helping me to my designated shelf, I told Cori I had one more box in the car, which she was happy to hear as I walked back outside.
    Grabbing the final box from my car, I looked across my front seat to see Peter leaning against a street sign. Unbelievably, Peter was standing across the street watching me.
    Peter!
    Screaming his name, I smashed my head on the roof of my car as I jumped back out and tried to run for him. Screaming, my door was left wide open, my purse was on the seat, and I was delirious trying to cross the street. But he was gone.
    Standing on the side of the road, where the cars passed me slowly and infrequently, I scanned everything I could. I looked from left to right, and even up in case he was somehow in the little building across the street. I looked everywhere, shaking and out of breath, as my heart pounded and my mind raced, but he just wasn't there.
    Crying out my frustration and sadness, I turned on my heels, walked back to my car, grabbed my purse, and the last box of pottery. Slamming my door with so much force it sounded like a bullet ricocheting down the sidewalk, was a little too ironic for me in that moment.
    But after the near miss with Peter, I collected myself as best as I could and I entered Java Bean Cafe as calmly as possible. I pulled myself together enough to pretend to be calm, cool, professional Sophie Morley, when inside I was so hurt and angry I wanted to hit someone. Specifically Peter.

    Once Cori and I had placed and priced all my pottery, we made a little handwritten receipt that we each signed. I would always just break even with my pottery, which really, was only supposed to be a little adventure designed to help me move past Peter- The asshole.

I knew as I left the café I really was deranged at that point. I was angry and frustrated, and quite frankly, if I ever saw Peter again I'd probably punch him in the face before I kissed him to death.

When I sat back in my car to return home I tried to remember what he had looked like in the street, finding it almost strange that I spotted him immediately. Peter didn't look like himself at all, though I recognized him instantly. Bundled up against the cold in the green bomber jacket I knew, it looked like Peter was much heavier, with a lot of facial hair he never had with me. But even with the physical changes, I was sure it was him watching me from the sidewalk across from Java Bean.

I was sure he was there which meant he was alive, and everything I had thought I knew to be true the night before was completely wrong. He didn't die beside me- he was alive and well, just not beside me anymore.

Peter was alive and I felt more stupid than ever after the night I put my parents, brother, and even myself through.

Evidently, I had been wrong about my dream though I would have sworn on my life that Peter was hurt just an hour before. I was sure he was gone, and this new reality hurt me as well. I was happy he was alive, obviously, but I was pissed again that he was alive without me.

And so I continued- around and around again.

By 5:10, my parents and I arrived at Perry's, as Michael and another man opened the locked door for us. Smiling widely, the other man introduced himself as Perry of Perry's while shaking my hand, followed by my parents who introduced themselves as well.

"You're quite the little story for us around here, Sophie," Perry smiled.

"Am I? Well, that wasn't my intention," I said a little uncomfortably.

"There are a few pieces over the years I have thought of and studied nearly religiously, and the darker charcoal drawing of you was one of them. I had hoped I would meet Peter's muse one day, and here you are," he again said brightly, which only added to my discomfort until my mom suddenly jumped in.

"Yes, here she is. Peter's muse. Do you mind if we get the paintings now? We have plans this evening and we'd really like to be on our way," she said in a tone which ended any further conversation.

"Of course. I believe you've paid the required 5 dollars-"

"Yes..."

"And the letter?"
"I have."
"So we'll just finish packing up the paintings for you," Perry said walking away from us in the entranceway.
When Perry left us Michael leaned forward a little and whispered, "Sorry. Perry's a bit intense, and this whole thing bothers him for some reason, but I don't think it's because of the money. He just seems a little intense about Mr. Connor, I think."
"Why? Does he know him?" I begged.
"I don't think so. Well, no more than the rest of us do. I think he was pissed that the paintings are leaving, and because he couldn't convince Mr. Connor to paint any more for the gallery this afternoon. Actually, he vehemently refused saying he only painted for you, and Perry felt a little slighted I think," Michael admitted to me and my listening parents.
"You saw him today?" I gasped.
"Briefly."
"And? How was he? Did he look weird?" I asked stupidly as we walked closer to the wall of me.
"Weird? Not really. He was very quiet though and very shaken that you finally found them, I think. I guess he's been waiting for months for you to find them, so he was almost freaked out or something now that you have. But that's just my guess. He didn't talk about you at all, no matter how much Perry tried to engage him in conversation over you."
"Thank god... I don't like to really talk about myself, and these paintings are kind of personal," I said pitifully.
"Of course they are. I'll try to get you out of here with as little Perry as possible, okay?" Michael smiled, and I swear I loved him a little in that moment for his kindness.
"Thank you..."

45 minutes later with my mom running interference every attempt Perry made to engage me in personal conversation, we were heading to the front door with my dad carrying the final drawing, when Perry tried one last time.
Pausing before speaking to me, it was obvious he didn't like me, but for reasons I simply couldn't understand. I had never met the man, nor was I any trouble. I was just a woman picking up paintings she had bought, albeit for only 5 dollars, but still. There was NO reason for me to be

disliked by Perry, which I clearly was.

"Ms. Morley... I do hope you appreciate the beauty of these paintings and I hope you appreciate the significance of the artist who painted them," he asked as I stood shocked by the tone he gave me.

Recovering quickly from his tone though, I whispered, "I do."

"So you understand that it's not every day a woman is the subject of such a beautiful series of paintings from a very talented artist such as Mr. Connor," he again almost sneered at me.

Annoyed, and suddenly feeling strong against his misplaced aggression, I answered as best as I could before my mom ripped him apart, like I could almost bet she was gearing up to do.

"I am well aware of how beautiful these portraits are, and I'm also aware of Peter's talent. And seeing as I'm the subject of these paintings, it would seem obvious that I understand the significance behind them. More so than you ever could," I snapped.

"But Peter is-"

"None of your business, in regards to me. This is my life captured in multiple paintings, so unless you want to tell me where Peter lives, or how I can get in touch with him, we have nothing else to say. I'm sorry I only had to pay you 5 dollars for them, but that's what you and he decided. Not me!"

Looking totally insulted, Perry continued to my growing frustration. "It's not about the money. It's about the pain Peter must be feeling about-"

"*ME!* This is between Peter and *me*. And I'm really sorry you got in the middle of it. I don't know what you know about Peter, but we're in love, and these are apparently the only way he can show me his love, so please stop being a dickhead to me. You know nothing about me, and I doubt you know anything about Peter. Do you?!"

"Not really... He just comes in sporadically and leaves quietly. I know nothing about him which adds to the mystery of you both, I guess," Perry finally added a little embarrassed, I think.

"Well, there's no mystery other than Peter himself. We love each other and he painted me as I loved him. End of story. But if you do ever find out anything more about Peter, I'd really appreciate you letting me know. Michael has my phone number," I finished with my own sneer, as my mom pulled my arm with a smirk on her face.

Walking to the front door with my mom, my dad smiled at me and said quietly, "You get that scary from your mom," as I laughed a little huff of frustration while walking out the door.

LOST

After we arrived home my parents stayed quiet. They again let me lead the tone of our night based on my mood, and I was horribly sad again. After the false bravado I held yelling at Perry had worn off, I fell into a sad exhaustion as I unlocked my door and walked inside with the drawing, while my mom and dad carried 2 paintings each.

I was home with my paintings and I wanted to be alone. So begging, I finally told my parents where I was at.

"Thank you for everything this weekend. Thank you for coming to me last night," I said hugging my mom after she had propped my paintings against the living room wall. "And thank you for coming with me tonight. I don't think I would have been half as brave with Perry if I hadn't known you were standing there reading to jump in," I grinned. "But I really want to be alone now." And when she looked like she might protest I finished quickly. "I'm okay, I promise. I'm not super depressed, or even super sad. I'm more numb actually, but I'll be okay. This weekend has been very hard, so I want to just make a sandwich and eventually go to bed early. I have payroll tomorrow, which always stresses me out, and I need some sleep."

"Why don't we just grab a quick bite, and then we'll leave you alone? It's only 6:30," my mom pushed, but I shook my head no.

"Do you want me to help you hang these, Soph?" My dad asked quietly.

"No... I'm not sure when I can hang them, but I don't think it's tonight. If I need help tomorrow though would you come after work?"

"Sure, honey," my dad nodded.

"Thanks," I replied happily, with an obvious falseness we could all read on my face.

I truly appreciated my parents, but all I wanted was to be alone. I wanted to try to understand the beautiful woman Peter painted as she used to be.

Walking to my door my mom asked, "Are you sure you-"

"I'm absolutely sure. I'm okay, I promise."

"Will you call me if you need to? You can, Sophie. You can call me any time tonight. Even at 3:00 in the morning if you need to," she grinned.

"I will, thanks. But please go home now, no offense," I grinned back as she hugged me and left me alone finally.

And once they left, I was truly alone. I was alone in a way I hadn't felt in months, and I was alone in a way that hurt.

Peter was everywhere and nowhere at once. He was holding my hand, and pushing me further away. He was breathing me in and blowing me away. He was everywhere and nowhere all around me.
So I did what was natural. I took the drawing, and crawled on my bed with Peter's letter, which I read over and over again until I finally passed out cold.

*****

I continued the 'I'm okay' facade for my friends and family all through the holidays.
I still missed Peter like hell, and the near misses were killing me, but eventually our story slowly warped in my mind as a different story for us entirely. A revised story was born that I actually started to believe.
Peter didn't dump me- he left me. He had somewhere to go, like abroad for work, or away for school, or on sabbatical elsewhere. He didn't leave *me,* he just left. I may have been totally delusional, but I felt better with my delusions. So I accepted the delusions and I made my way through the holidays like I was better.

2 weeks later, I opened and placed my paintings against the wall in my bedroom, and though I didn't remember exactly the feeling I had at the time, it didn't matter anymore. The paintings themselves were so expressive, I felt what the beautiful green-eyed blonde felt at the time, and I smiled for her.
Afterward, I walked to my living room and placed the sad, tragic ending, LOST on my fireplace mantle in the center and I walked back to my bedroom to the happy paintings, which made me feel loved again.

And on New Years' Eve, I said my goodbye, *finally.* I told Peter I wasn't going to live for him anymore, because I decided to live in the new year Peter-free and happy.
I had one drink at home by myself, toasting in the New Year, of course thinking of Peter. But instead of missing him, I wished him well, and I prayed he was safe in whatever life he was living.
I said goodbye to the love of my life, and I crawled into bed alone.

CHAPTER 30

Sleeping with Peter was always beautiful.

Making love with Peter was always an amazing experience filled with love, and pleasure, and a connection so deep between us, we were each other within the space between us.

Peter and I learned how to move, what to do, and how to feel. We learned each other until there was no longer thought, but mere reaction. We learned each other so intimately, a gentle smile alone could announce all the expectation, love, and want between us. And as I moved with him again, it was no different no matter how much time had passed between us.

Moving against him, I knew how to arch, and how to breathe to experience the connection between us. I knew how high I had to reach, and I knew how painful the reach would become until my ultimate release. I knew how to push past the building intensity to reach the height of our love and pleasure together, and I was almost there.

Pushing a little further and breathing a little deeper, I writhed and moaned until the building intensity crested, and I lost myself to the release.

Breathless, I came on a rush as my body arched and my mind caved to the pleasure. Releasing with a fractured scream, I was boneless and replete. But the intensity continued.

Struggling to keep Peter away like he knew I always needed, he continued inside me. Begging, I tried to breathe and speak but I wasn't able. I was struggling for breath as the weight of Peter began to slowly suffocate me.

Gasping, I tried to move my head but the weight continued to hold me down. Shaking and crying out, I tried to move my hands, only to realize I was pushed flat into a pillow by my head. Trapped, my arms were held tightly, one behind and one beneath me.

I was drowning among the cotton and down and I couldn't get out. Panicking, I fought as best as I could, but the force against me was too strong. I was held down on my stomach with an arm lifting me under my waist, as my body throbbed and screamed with each thrust I endured.

I was suffocating and unable to move the weight that crushed me, but I was aware. Finally.

"Please..." I begged but my words were muffled. "Help!" I cried as I struggled for breath. But nothing changed. The thrusting continued and the pain intensified.

My world began spinning as I gasped less and less air in my lungs. My face was pushed nearly through the pillow into the mattress and I couldn't move from the weight holding me down. I couldn't move away from the pain, and I couldn't move away from the reality that was crashing down all around me.

This wasn't my Peter... and I had come for another man.

Gagging, I cried out in repulsion as he continued. Begging silently, I stopped all fight and waited for him to finish me.

I had been alone in my beautiful dream, but I was not alone in my nightmare. This was not Peter, and there was no Peter to save me. In that quick horrible moment of understanding I thought to myself, *I didn't stay safe like Peter asked me to.*

I had failed Peter and I had failed myself. I had failed, so I let go and waited for the end.

When I woke up again I was on my back no longer struggling. I woke up slowly and tried to see his eyes, but I couldn't. I was held down and I was hurt. I could feel the ache all over me and inside me. I was throbbing everywhere and there was nothing I could do. I had become nothing more than pain as I woke, and I knew there was nothing left for me in that moment except closing my eyes and waiting for my death to take me.

In that moment of nightmare panic I remember thinking for one split second *I hope this doesn't hurt* as I closed my eyes and waited for the pain. But it did hurt.

I felt a lightning strike of pain rip through me, but luckily my mind stopped a second later. My mind didn't register what was happening after that one moment of searing pain. I didn't know what was happening to me, and I didn't care. I was ready to stop.

So I let go completely as I imagined Peter holding me tightly in his arms easing me through the pain.

*****

When I gasped awake I realized I wasn't alone still. There was a man near me and another man across the room. I wasn't alone and I screamed with everything I had to try to get away from them.

Moving, and shaking, and fighting everything I could, I screamed and fought nothing at all. Neither man moved, but they did speak.

They spoke to me words I knew but couldn't understand. They spoke to me until my mom held me in her arms, and then I let go again.

Crying out, I was scared and disgusted and hallow. I stared hard at the two men, wrapped in my mother's arms, almost daring them to try to hurt me. I stared and cried. I was nothing but pain wrapped in a nightmare of misery.

"Where's Peter?" I cried out.

"Here's not here, Baby. What do you mean? Was he there?!" My mother gasped and cried.

"He wasn't there! Oh, *god*. It wasn't Peter. It wasn't Peter and I thought it was, and I came! I came mommy, and I thought it was Peter! Oh, god... Help me...I had an orgasm and it wasn't him!" I screamed as she hugged me tighter.

"*Sophie*. Stop! Listen to me-"

"I came. I thought it was him and I thought we were together and I thought-" but I gagged. "I thought it was him inside me but it wasn't. And I came. I was- I came with him because I thought it was Peter with me," I moaned as I gagged again and cried.

Shaking and crying, I couldn't believe my reality in that moment. Looking around, the 2 men still didn't move. No one moved but me as I struggled to breathe.

Begging my mom to understand, I whispered, "I didn't mean to. I thought it was Peter..."

"Ms. Morley, do you consent to a rape kit?"

I remember that sudden shock of reality so clearly when the man spoke. I remember the word rape, and I remember the truth of that moment. I had been raped, but I had enjoyed it.

The man against the wall spoke as he scribbled notes down. He spoke like he read the question he posed to me from his notebook. He spoke like it was the most obvious question in the world. He spoke like I was the most insignificant person in the world.

He asked me a question I was completely incapable of answering because I didn't understand a single word he said to me beyond the word *rape*.

"Ms. Morley, I'm Doctor Newman, and we'd like to help you. Can you answer a few questions?" He asked even as I was shaking my head no.

"Sophie... please. Dr. Newman wants to help you but he has to do an exam so they can catch the person who hurt you," my mom coaxed gently.

But I wasn't stupid. I knew what the exam would be like. I knew he would see my shame, so I answered as best as I could.

"I enjoyed it," I spoke clearly, even as my mom flinched beside me. "I'm a slut. I'm sorry," I almost cried but kept it together.

"Sophie- you're confused, honey. You didn't know what was happening. Do you remember anything about-"

"I remember *everything* about it," I choked.

"Ms. Morley, could you please answer a few questions," the wall guy asked before finally introducing himself. "I'm Officer Sam Dolby and I'm the responding officer. I'd like to ask you a few questions while the memories are still fresh. Could you please answer a few questions?" He asked finally looking at me like I was actually a person. He looked at me like I was significant and I finally felt like a person again, so I nodded.

"Did you know your attacker?"

"No."

"Are you sure? Sometimes women may know their attacker but not realize it until much later. Would you like a minute to think about it?"

"No. I didn't know him and I didn't see him, I don't think. Do you know Peter Connor?" I asked suddenly. I was suddenly given the potential to get answers from a cop and I jumped at the chance.

"I don't believe so. Was he your attacker?"

Yelling, I couldn't hold in the revulsion. "No! Absolutely not! Peter would never do that to me, and it wasn't him."

"But you did believe he was there?"

"Yes. But not really. I was confused and I had a dream, and I thought Peter was with me until after..." I faded out.

Everything was spinning again, and I hurt everywhere. Looking down at myself, I saw I was in a hospital gown and I saw my shoulder and arm wrapped up. I saw what I looked like and I saw a little blood at the top of my gown.

"What happened to me?"

"You were attacked, Sophie," my mom said gently.

"I know. But I mean what *happened*. What's all this?"

"Your shoulder was dislocated, but you suffered no series damage. We were able to clean the facial wounds and stitch you closed around your temple," Dr. Newman said beside my bed.

"My shoulder was dislocated?" I asked kind of laughing a little.

"Sophie..." my mom warned with a gentle tone.

"I'm sorry. But why dislocate my shoulder? Isn't that weird?" Though the question itself was weird and my calmness was weird, the whole thing seemed so weird to me, I couldn't help but ask anyway.

"We believe you either moved at the last second, or the Perp heard your neighbor banging on your door and pulled your arm too hard from behind," the officer said.

The Perp? I remember how funny that sounded. The Perp- like on CSI again. I was surrounded by TV watching Fucktards everywhere, which made me laugh.

Maybe my laughter seemed ridiculous, or stupid, or silly, but it made me feel better. The fact that I could look at these people and laugh at their stupidity made me feel better. I *was* better because I was still smart and together, while they were idiots who watched too much TV.

"Ms. Morley. I still have some questions for you. I'd like to get an accurate description of the Perp," he said again as I laughed harder, but he continued anyway. "I also need an accurate timeline of the events you remember."

"What's to remember? I was sleeping with Peter-*in my head*- having an amazing sexual experience, I thought. Then I was awake with someone else inside me, fucking the shit out of me from behind while I tried to breathe through the suffocation of having my face held down and forced into a pillow," I said slightly bitchy as my mom actually released a sob beside me. "Sorry, mom. What else do you want? I was a pig who got off because I thought Peter was there, but he wasn't Peter."

"Sophie, you did nothing wrong. You have to-"

"Why didn't you do a rape kit earlier?" I cut off my mother.

"Because you were coherent off and on and if the patient is coherent for minutes at a time, we must get consent first, especially when the patient is combative, which you were initially," the doctor answered.

"I don't remember being coherent *or* combative. When was I awake?"

"You were always awake, just confused, baby," my mom explained.

As Officer Dolby walked to my bedside, he finished off the story. "Your neighbor was talking to you through your front door, and I was the responding officer who talked you into opening the door for us. Do you remember talking to me until you unlocked your front door?"

"No..."

"The ambulance joined us shortly thereafter and we took you to the hospital immediately. You were completely coherent and even helped sit on the gurney yourself." Finishing the story, Dolby said, "Your apartment is presently a crime scene."

"Why didn't you take my statement then if I was awake?"

"I did. And now that you're no longer in shock, I'm taking it again to get a more accurate record of the events that took place," he said patiently.

"Did you get him?" But I think I already knew the answer I just didn't remember it.

"No," he shook his head as he asked again, "Would you consent to a rape kit?"

"Okay. But I only want the doctor in here. No one else," I said looking directly at my mom. If I was going to suffer another humiliation then I wanted no more witnesses. "Will you catch him if I do the kit?"

"There's a good chance. Most rapists don't strike only once, and usually they strike someone they know. So between the DNA evidence, and the subsequent investigation, we usually find the connection to the victim, and inevitably, the attacker," Officer Dolby answered my question seeming so insensitive and emotionless, it's like he read that answer directly from his notebook again.

And the more I looked at him, I realized I didn't like him. He was too unfeeling and he seemed to lack the sensitivity or something for being the officer in charge of a rape investigation.

"Do you know Peter Connor?"

"You've asked me that already, and I said I wasn't aware."

"Okay. But you wouldn't tell me the truth anyway, would you?" I sighed my frustration.

"Why wouldn't I tell you?"

"Yes, why wouldn't you?" I smirked at him because I knew.

"Sophie, you have to stop honey. You're hurt and tired and you've been through so much tonight, you-"

"Yes, I have mom. *I've* been through so much. So why don't you stop trying to calm me and let me deal with this however I can. Sound good?" I asked like a total bitch, but luckily, my mom just nodded at me silently.

"Ms. Morley, can you tell me what happened tonight?"

Again, as my backbone straightened and I felt more like myself, I sounded bitchy, but calm. "I can tell you everything, and I will. But I would like to get this exam over with first, and then I'll tell you anything you want to know. Is that good enough?"

"Certainly. I'll just wait outside for Dr. Newman to finish up," he agreed as he walked to the door.

When my mom didn't move, I again asked her to leave. I asked her to leave me alone and I actually saw the pain and distress flash across her face before she stood and left me with an 'I'll be back as soon as you're done.'

But I didn't care. I felt irritated and angry, and sad, and disgusted. I was a whore and I couldn't believe I had sunk so low. I couldn't believe I was so desperate to be with Peter that I didn't even realize another man was fucking me from behind. I actually got off to someone hurting me because I wanted it to be Peter so badly.

Sitting on the raised bed of my hospital room I was so sad thinking of my level of desperation and depravity, I finally started truly sobbing over the events of the night.

Crying as the doctor moved around the room until he left for a minute to return with a nurse, I cried the whole time. I saw him prepare instruments, and I watched him wheel a metal cart near me. I saw him scrub and glove his hands, and I heard the nurse speaking to me as she handed me tissues, but I didn't understand anything in that moment other than my desperation.

And I was lost.

"I'm going to remove the sheet, and lift your gown, Ms. Morley," the doctor said gently. "If you feel any discomfort at all, please tell me. I need to know about pain, and I need to catalogue anything you can tell me, okay?"

"Ms. Morley, you just look at me, and everything will be over quickly, okay?" The nurse said beside me so I nodded at her.

I waited while the doctor pulled me gently lower to the end of the bed to lift my legs and placed them in the stirrups, and I remember singing in that moment inside my head to drown out the pain of my nightmare. *It's just a Pap. It's just a Pap. I do this once a year. It's just a Pap. It's just a Pap. It'll be over soon. La la-la la-la-laaaa.*

"Ms. Morley, you have-"

"Oh god... Sophie, *please*."

"Sophie, are you in any discomfort right now?"

"Yes..." I moaned.

"Can you explain where?"

"Everywhere. Inside and outside. Everything hurts right now. Please hurry," I said as I heard my foot start shaking in the stirrup as my anxiety climbed.

"Sophie... Breathe deeply. You're struggling against me, and I want to be quick for you," he said again gently, as the nurse took my hand and squeezed it.

So I closed my eyes as the tears slowly spilled from my eyelids onto the pillow, and I tried to relax everything inside me.

I tried to let go of the tension holding me still with my legs pulled tightly closed. I tried to forget a man was looking at me and seeing what was done to me, and I tried to forget a man had taken me earlier and saw everything he did to me while he did it.

"Sophie... Almost done. Are you aware of any anal penetration?"

"Um... No. I don't know. But I'd feel it right? Everything hurts, but not there, and I've never done that, so I'd feel it, right?" I begged through my near hysteria.

"I'm going to take an anal swab anyway, just to be sure, but I don't think your anus has been compromised," he said so seriously, I actually found it a little funny.

"A compromised anus? That sounds like a porn movie," I giggled to my horror.

I was totally losing it then. I knew it, and Dr. Newman, and nurse whatever knew it. I was laughing at stupidity when I should have been crying in horror. Dr. Newman continued on though like I wasn't being ridiculous.

"Sophie... You have a small vaginal tear, which I'm going to leave alone because stitches are often worse for potential infection in that sensitive area. You also have much internal swelling, which though uncomfortable should lessen in a day or two. And as I said, I don't believe you were abused anally, but we'll know for sure after the swab," he said clinically.

"Okay... Thank you."

"I'm going to take a few photographs of you now quickly. And after I scrape under your fingernails I'll be giving you antibiotics to fight infection, plus the morning after pill to prevent a pregnancy. I'll follow up with a prescription to fight any potential STD's until your blood work and the test results come back, which should be in a day or two, at the latest. The hospital rushes test results after a sexual assault so the victim doesn't have the added stress and worry of STD's as well," he said finally sitting further away from my nasty vagina.

"Oh, that's good. I'll probably have a lot more to think about anyway," I laughed again.

"We have a rape counsellor on sight, waiting to speak with you after the Detective does, and I'd like to administer more pain medication once you're through speaking with Officer Dolby," he said after raising the table end and lowering my legs gently while covering me up again with the sheet.

"I don't want to talk to him."

"Sophie," the nurse soothed. "You have to talk to the Detective to catch the person who hurt you. You should try hard to remember any detail you can, so it'll be easier to find the assailant."

"I don't want to talk to *him*. I don't like him," I cried.

"We can get another Detective if you'd be more comfortable. A female?"

And nodding my head, I whispered, "Yes, please..."

After Dr. Newman took some photos of my body and face, he gave me some medication- the morning after pill I think. He then recommended I speak with the Detectives quickly, so he could give me the pain meds I needed. He didn't like the fact that I wasn't as numb as I should be for the shoulder adjustment but he knew I couldn't be mentally impaired in any way while making an official statement, at least that's what he said.

Eventually, a female Detective joined me in my room alone, after I insisted my mom stay in the hallway. I loved my mom, and she was a comfort to me totally, but I honestly couldn't handle telling the police what had happened with her looking at me. I just couldn't do it to either of us.

Detective Dent was much better than Dolby. She was straight forward and professional, but she seemed to have some emotion as well. She nodded when I cried, and she was patient with me when I paused. She listened and took notes, but she seemed to still be emotionally in the room with me, as I told her the truth.

"I didn't know I wasn't dreaming at first, and I had an orgasm from whatever he was doing to me, but then I woke up more and I was being held down against my back with my face pushed hard into my pillow, nearly suffocating me, and then I couldn't really breathe and I think I passed out because I woke up on my back just before... he finished."

"Did you see his face?"

"Never."

"Did he speak to you ever?"

"I don't think so..." But then I remembered. Jumping in my bed, and moaning in pain from my shoulder down, I remembered. "I heard him say a name! I don't know what he said exactly though. I don't know because everything is blurry, but I think I heard him say Perry. Oh my god, I think he said something about Perry."

"Who's Perry?" She asked still writing quickly but looking up at me.

"He owns the art gallery in the village. I met him last month. He had my paintings and I bought them, and he was a total asshole to me, but I don't think it was him, 'cause the guy was big enough to weigh down my whole body *and* still push my head down, but Perry is all wimpy and skinny, and he seemed gay, too, so he wouldn't do this," I almost laughed.

"Okay. You heard something 'Perry'. Can you think of anything else?"

"No..."

"Now, what about Peter Connor? You've mentioned him a few times, and-"

"It was NOT Peter. Peter is my ex-boyfriend, and I think he's a cop, or in the military, and I would know Peter anywhere, especially if we were together. It wasn't him, but I thought it was when I was sleeping, and that's why..." I choked.

"You had an orgasm," she said matter-of-factly.

"Yes..." I moaned. "I'm such a slut," I shook as I cried in both pain and embarrassment.

"Sophie... You're not a slut. And you are not the first victim who had an orgasm while being raped. Yes, it's rare because the act is typically very violent, but from what you've described, your assailant began while you were sleeping, and you didn't realize what was happening, but once you did, it was no longer an act of pleasure for you but of force, right?"

"But who does that? What kind of woman gets off with a rapist?"

"A woman who was confused by the circumstances she suddenly found herself in, in her own room, while sleeping, unaware of the reality of her situation."

"I guess... But I feel like a pig. I got off and I enjoyed it."

"Until you didn't..."

"Right," I nodded. "Until I knew something was wrong. Then I tried to fight him, but he was too strong for me."

"That's right. You fought him as best as you could until he hit you a few times and fled the scene."

"Yes, that's what I did. I fought him once I knew it wasn't Peter. I didn't like it and he was hurting me, and I tried to breathe, and I tried to fight it. Thank you. You're good at this, Detective Dent," I gave a little smile.

"I'm not good, I'm being honest. You did nothing wrong, Sophie. And you need to remember that as you recover. This was a violent act done *to* you, not done with you. Do you see the difference?"

Nodding slightly, I did see the difference. Staring at her I still felt dirty, but suddenly a little less so.

"Do you know Peter Connor?" I asked desperately.

"No. Does he work out of this city?"

"I think so."

"Would you like me to try to find him? Do you want me to have him get in touch with you?"

"Yes, please," I begged. I wanted Peter to help me so badly, it was like another pain in my body.

"How did he get in?" I suddenly thought to ask.

"We don't know for sure, but we believe through the kitchen window, because there was no other point of entry. When Officer Dolby arrived you were behind your locked door, and we found a small blood sample on the kitchen floor, but otherwise, there was no other entry. And considering how far your bedroom is from the kitchen, I doubt you would have heard him entering the kitchen even if you had been awake."

"Oh... What do I do?" I asked scared.

"I would recommend a security alarm because you're on the ground floor of a building with lots of coverage and places to hide. Almost every window in your apartment has the ability to hide an intruder, plus the courtyard offers zero protection on your bedroom/bathroom side. I, myself could see right into your bathroom from the tiny gaps in your blinds," she said as I gasped.

"I didn't know that. I never knew that. I thought the blinds were perfect when closed. I thought I was covered. Oh god, people could see me use the bathroom, or even naked in the shower? I didn't know."

"No one knows until it's pointed out. Please, I'm just trying to help you, not scare you."

"I know, but..." I was still shaken.

There was nothing safe anymore. I had been beaten up and raped in my own home. People could watch me pee, and I hated that someone may have watched me naked in my bathroom. Everything just sucked so badly, I started to really cry.

"We're through for today, Sophie. I'm going to give you my card, and I want you to call me with any information you remember, no matter how small. Call me anytime, and I'll talk to you right after the test results and DNA samples come through, okay?"

"Okay..."

"I'll send Dr. Newman back in with your meds now. Take care, Sophie. I'll talk to you soon," Detective Dent said walking to the door.

"Thank you..." I whispered as she nodded and left the room.

After she left, I was alone for 5 minutes. I was completely alone with a body that ached and throbbed everywhere. Amazingly, even my feet hurt, which I couldn't understand. For whatever reason, there was nothing that didn't hurt on me, and my shoulder was absolutely on fire. I needed pills so bad, I almost hit the emergency call button myself before Dr. Newman had time to arrive.

Panicking still, I sighed an audible sound of relief when Dr. Newman finally returned.

"I hurt everywhere, Dr. Newman. Can I please have pain killers now? Please?"

"Would you like to speak with the rape counsellor first?"

"Not now. Please, I just want to sleep and take some pills to help the pain everywhere."

"Of course, Sophie. Just give me a second and Rebecca will come back to administer them. Within minutes you should be sound asleep and pain free. But I'll be back throughout the day to check on you, and to make sure your shoulder was set properly, okay?"

Nodding again, I was in pain and tired. I didn't care what Dr. Newman said to me or if he came back, I just wanted to sleep my nightmare away.

I wanted Peter to help me with some of his scents, and herbal concoctions, and with his chakra therapy, or breathing exercises. I wanted Peter to fix everything.

I wanted Peter with me, period.

CHAPTER 31

The following afternoon I was released from the hospital when my shoulder had been x-rayed again and the doctors were pleased with the set of the dislocation. My body still ached and burned everywhere, but I think it was more psychological than physical at that point. My vagina was healing I was told after another horrible internal exam, and though peeing still burned, I otherwise tried to ignore my body. Actually, I tried to ignore everything.

I spoke to the rape counsellor twice, but I hated how she kept talking about the events, and how I could move past them, and what I should do to move on. I hated talking to her because she seems like a total know it all, and she was just annoying with her soft, calm voice, and her constant nods of understanding, no matter what I said.

I couldn't talk to my mom about anything either, though she tried. She tried a few times to engage me gently, but I closed down still horribly embarrassed by everything that had happened when I became aware in the hospital room.

The fact that I originally yelled to my mom, 'I came! I orgasmed! I enjoyed it!' was too much for me to handle. My mom was super cool, and I wasn't a verbal prude by any means, but screaming 'I came!' to my mom was beyond embarrassing and not something I wanted to further discuss.

I wasn't able to see my dad or brother either, because they were men and I didn't want them thinking of me ever having sex, never mind being raped. I didn't want my brother getting visuals he'd have to bleach from his brain, and I didn't want my dad thinking of his daughter getting off and then fighting her rapist.

Pulling it together, I decided it didn't happen, and I wasn't going to discuss it anymore because it simply didn't happen. Therefore, I wouldn't talk about what didn't happen anymore. And that's what I did. I stopped talking about it.

When I was going to be released and I informed my mom I wanted to go home, she finally raised her voice at me instead of being the quiet, calm woman I didn't recognize as she fought my decision hard. She demanded I come home with her and she explained how I might feel in my apartment and how the memories might be too much. She even told me of the shock I may go through when I entered my home again. She was very logical, albeit loud, but I didn't give in.

  I fought back, until I was so damn tired, I eventually cried out in frustration until she gave in, but not before she told me she was staying with me for a few days. She told me so sadly and lovingly that she was staying with me in my apartment, I just couldn't refuse her.

  And that was it. The moment we left the hospital together I decided it was the end of the rape, as far as I was concerned.

*****

  Walking back into my place I was surprised it looked spotless, which meant either my mom or my brother cleaned it up while I was in the hospital. I didn't know who, but either way it was another nightmare for me. I pictured the blood and stuff on my sheets, and I imagined the blood which must have collected at my front door when the police were talking me into opening it for them.

  I tried to imagine what everyone saw, but I didn't want to, so I ignored it. The only thing I did do, was walk to my kitchen to see a perfect pane of glass where he may have entered. I couldn't see the blood sample on the floor that was mentioned, and I wouldn't have known anyone entered that night through the window if I didn't know it had actually happened.

  After the kitchen, I walked to my bathroom to look at the covered window and blind, realizing I maybe should have known I could be seen. So testing it, I shut off the light, and I did see sunlight through the little tiny holes where the strings attached to the end of each slat, but the holes seemed so insignificant to me, I couldn't believe someone would even put forth the effort to stand there, potentially getting caught by anyone passing for the main door, just for a tiny glimpse through an even tinier hole to see me using the washroom or naked in and out of the shower.

  After seeing the tiny bits of sunlight, I walked to the hall closet and pulled down 3 towels one-handed. Calling my mom to help she joined me in covering up the window completely with the towels. She helped me cover it and then I walked back to my hall closet and pulled out more.

Walking to the kitchen window, I asked her to help me cover it as well. Then the dining room window was covered, followed by the living room next.

Once I ran out of towels, I grabbed sheets and little throw blankets which my mom helped me cover the 2 living room windows with without protest or even speaking. She covered them as I gave them to her one-handed and determined, until there was only my bedroom window left, which I couldn't enter.

My mom seemed to understand my silence though as I stood still outside the room, so she grabbed the last of my throw blankets, and even a dark sheet and went into my bedroom to cover the window as I moved to sit in the suffocating darkness of my living room alone and unable to speak.

When my mom finally joined me on the couch, she asked if she could turn on a light and I nodded yes. The darkness certainly wasn't helping my mindset, so hopefully some light would.

"What are you thinking about?" She whispered.

"I don't know..." I answered honestly. "I'm scared, but I'm not. I'm tired, but kind of jacked up on adrenaline or something. I feel sad and not like myself at all, and I have that weird stoned feeling from the meds, but I'm still really aware of everything, too."

"What can I do to help?" She asked taking my good hand.

"Order Chinese?" I huffed a laugh as she grinned beside me.

Laughing at my stupidity, she said, "I can't wait for the day you finally lose your awesome metabolism and get fat."

"What?" I laughed.

"I used to be tiny too, you know. You've seen the pictures," she sighed and I had seen them. I had the same smallish body of my mom when she was younger. "But then I had kids, hit thirty, and voila, I got a huge ass and a belly that won't go away," she said pushing her stomach in with her hand.

"So you want me to get fat?" I again laughed.

"Kind of," she grinned. "Just so I won't feel so irritated when I see you eat half a chocolate pie with your dad but still fit into those tiny jeans of yours."

"That's mean…" I giggled.

"I know," she laughed again. "But I guess after shitty hospital food you're entitled to some edible food. Where's the menu?"

"In the second drawer beside the stove," I grinned as she rose for my kitchen.

After we ordered, while we waited for the food to arrive, neither of us spoke. We literally sat in silence in my dimly lit living room because I didn't know what to say, and clearly, neither did she. We didn't speak, but she did sit right next to me holding my good hand in her own while we waited. However, when the food arrived we abandoned the silence to eat like total pigs.

I ate nonstop and without pause. Long after my mother groaned and pushed her plate to the coffee table, I was still happily eating my 2nd huge plateful of Chinese.

"Maybe I should get fat, then I won't worry about…" But I suddenly stopped my words.

I knew how horrible and sad they sounded. And I hated how pathetic and desperate I sounded. I knew I was being irrational and unrealistic, but I couldn't help thinking of the ways I could prevent ever being hurt again.

"Sophie, you didn't do this. And you can't think that way. You just can't. Being small or big doesn't change anything. What happened to you is horrible, but you didn't do it to yourself because you're small. It was a-"

"It's okay. I don't really want to talk about it, okay? I was just kidding about getting fat," I exhaled with a fake smile. "I'm going to lie down for a while. Feel free to leave or put the TV on, or whatever. My shoulder hurts and I can't take another painkiller for a few hours, so I just want to sleep for a bit," I said attempting to remove the couch cushions on my end of the couch.

"Are you sleeping here?" My mom whispered.

"Do you mind?"

"Not at all. Let me help you," she said standing.

So together we unfolded and opened up my sofa bed. My mom took from me the remaining sheets I had in my hand from the closet, and she helped me make the bed. My mom grabbed the extra pillows in the closet and after putting on fresh pillow cases, she quietly asked if I wanted my comforter from my bedroom. Gasping I shook my head no. I never wanted to touch those sheets or blankets again.

"Would you like me to get you something to sleep in?"

"Please..." I moaned because just the thought of walking into my bedroom made me want to throw up.

So I excused myself for the bathroom, though it was only 5:00 in the evening, and I waited for her to hand me a shirt to sleep in with my tights.

Amazingly, I managed, albeit painfully, to remove my sling and arm from my baggy sweater, and I almost succeeded in putting on the long shirt. Almost. But my shoulder was too sore, and I couldn't quite get my arm back in the sleeve without help.

"Mom? I'm sorry, but I'm stuck," I laughed from the bathroom door, with half my boob hanging out, and my arm killing me as it hung trapped in the sleeve opening.

So jumping up to help, my mom slowly, painfully pulled my arm through the sleeve, ignoring my boob completely.

"Is that all?" She asked.

"For now... Thanks," I said closing the door again, but I knew what I had to do.

I had been cleaned at the hospital. I had been cleaned with a sponge bath, and even a half shower that a nurse helped me with before I left, but I needed to wash myself again with my own soap. I *had* to.

So tucking my t-shirt under the collar, it was up and around my chest, as I pulled down my leggings and underwear.

Pulling them off, I started the shower. Pulling them off, I ripped down my underwear and pantyliner, gagged once, and threw them in the garbage can in the corner.

I didn't know why I gagged, but I swear I smelled sex on me. Logically, I knew I was wrong and I couldn't possibly smell like sex, because the morning after pill actually made me bleed a little off and on, but I just couldn't get past thinking I smelled like dirty sex.

Looking at my tub as the water warmed, I knew my hair was filthy, but there was nothing I could do about it in that moment. I needed help holding my shoulder out of the water because of the weird bandaging which seemed totally impossible to stay dry when washing hair, but I could wash my body without help.

Stepping over the tub wall, I sat on the edge with the handheld and I cleaned myself one-handed. Moving the spray around, I used soap all over my lower body and I washed myself as cleanly as possible. I even stood and washed myself from behind as best as I could. The soap stung the vaginal tear, but I didn't care. I was washing away everything that could be left on my body from that horrible night. I was making myself clean again, because I *was* going to be clean again, I decided.

  An hour later when my mom knocked on the bathroom door, I finally jolted and recognized my surroundings. Calling out, 'one minute', I finally turned off the water and my tears.
  Grabbing a pair of neatly folded pajama bottoms from the wicker shelf, I dressed again cleanly. I even looked in the mirror for the first time as I brushed my teeth and saw the damage to my face; damage which though painful didn't look half as bad as I had thought it would.
  My hair covered the stitched cut on my temple, and the black eye wasn't as dark as they looked in the movies. My black eye looked more like I hadn't slept in a week or two, more like dark coloring all around my eye, which somehow I thought I could easily cover with make-up.
  But I really didn't care about how I looked, I was just glad to be clean. I felt clean, and I smelled clean, so I decided nothing bad happened to me.

  When I left the bathroom finally, I laid on the sofa bed with my mom watching TV beside me and I slept a dreamless, medicated sleep of exhaustion. I slept knowing unconsciously my mom was beside me, and I slept knowing I wasn't in my bedroom of shame.

*****

  The following days with my mom were easy, and sometimes even a little fun. My mom and I watched way too much TV, ate endless amounts of crap food, drove to the grocery store for more crap food, and took little walks around the neighborhood together.
  We drove to Home Outfitters and I bought black-out curtains for every window in my apartment, and a new comforter with matching sheets. We even stopped at the cafe once, but I wasn't in the mood to speak, so she ran interference as I left and waited outside for my French Vanilla with chocolate shot.
  We just did nothing and everything until it became almost boring. And then I begged her to leave Saturday evening the following morning.
  I explained I was going to work Monday morning and I wanted to settle

into my own routine again. I promised I was okay, even after she protested, but she gave in like I knew she would even though she didn't think I was well enough to go to work, or to be alone. I knew she thought I was a step away from losing it, but she was wrong.

I had decided the previous Monday night hadn't happened, and I was actually starting to feel like it didn't really happen. When I ignored the various aches and pains, and the residual bruising around my temple, eye, and cheekbone, I felt like I looked like a normal woman.

So on Sunday morning before she left, I put on a flimsy nightgown and my mom stood in the bathroom beside the tub helping me shower and wash my hair.

She actually washed my long hair because I couldn't move my shoulder properly, and she was soaked by the time we were done. But other than making a few jokes, she didn't seem to care. She helped me slip the nightgown off, wrapped in a towel without any of my body being seen naked, and then she dried my hair for me.

My mom was so kind to me I choked up once when she was drying the back of my hair and told me to tilt my head forward. She was so kind, I cried a little, and whispered a very meaningful 'thank you' when the dryer finally stopped.

Before my mother left Sunday morning she told me she'd come back anytime in the night if I needed her, and then she let me know what I might expect at work, which honestly I hadn't thought much about, but clearly should've.

I didn't realize I had made the papers as an unnamed 'sexual assault' victim, and I didn't know my parents had told the head of HR about the attack. I hadn't really known what they said, but somehow I thought it was something like, 'Sophie's sick', or 'Sophie fell and screwed up her shoulder', or even 'Sophie needs the week off for personal reasons.' Never in my worst nightmare would I have thought my coworkers had been told the truth.

Crying from her betrayal, my mom didn't let me close down completely without hearing how she *had* been evasive about my absence until a Madeline and a Deborah had contacted Steven as my next of kin with questions regarding what had happened and when I would be returning. And so my mother told them the truth, but with a promise of absolute confidentiality. A confidentiality she actually had faith in, that clearly I had none. And as she spoke calmly, I realized my job at Halton Facilities was probably over, because I knew if Madeline knew, everyone knew.

After she explained what happened I put on my game face, thanked my mom for everything, pretended I understood why she betrayed me, and gently forced her to leave my home.
We hugged, and again she offered me endless words of love and affection, with the opening for her to return just a phone call away, until finally, she left me alone.

After she left me I walked around my place, unsettled, and insecure, until I eventually passed the day away with mindless TV and an attempt to read Beautiful Losers which I had once loved.
But I was horribly unsettled.

When I finally brushed my teeth at 9:00 and tried to go to sleep, I realized I was scared. The door behind me held the potential for being attacked unaware, and I realized I couldn't lie there with the doorway and door behind my head. I found it weird that my sofa layout hadn't bothered me at all when my mom was there, but suddenly, I was scared to death of being unable to see my attacker walk into my home again. So I quickly rearranged the furniture.
One-handed and in agony, I slowly pulled the couch over and over until it was sideways in almost the middle of the room, until the area rug was bunched up because I wasn't strong enough to move it under the couch, or even out of the way, but I didn't care what it looked like. I just needed to know I would be able to lie on my side facing the door so I could see the attacker walk back into my apartment to kill me while I slept.

CHAPTER 32

On Monday morning I started my life again, but the following day and week was a total nightmare for me.

I was welcomed back to work with fake smiles and knowing glances. *Everyone* knew what had happened it was obvious, and though they tried hard not to look like it, I could see the questions of morbid curiosity, sometimes repulsion, or even flat out pity on their faces. I could see it all, though I stayed in my office for most of each day.

Monday I completed payroll and stayed fairly quiet, though Madeline did enter my office at lunch to see if I needed anything, and again when I was leaving at 4:30 to kindly help me into my winter coat.

She helped me without even acknowledging what she was doing, and I thanked her for her kindness. I thanked her even though I was unsure if it was her who had told the entire office about what had happened to me. But then I realized it didn't really matter if it was her, because chances were pretty good everyone would have found out eventually.

Throughout my return to work, Steven left me messages each morning before I arrived at work to let me know he loved me and was thinking about me. Something about my best friend being my brother, and a man, and my twin made it impossible for me to talk to him still, but I loved my little messages in the morning which told me he was there for me whenever I needed him. He always said he loved me before he hung up, and he always made me feel good and loved by his words and voice.

So I made it through the week, slowly, and with as little interaction with my coworkers as possible. I even managed to keep Deborah away from me though that was a little more difficult, because she had the HR department and my job security to back her up. But after a few quick words, nodding about counseling, and being offered a leave of absence which I refused, Deborah left my office after my constant assurances of 'I'm fine.'

I spoke to my mom each night and gave her the lowdown of my day, but otherwise kept it together. We did have a tense moment on Wednesday night when she approached the subject of therapy to help me deal with everything that happened to me, but I vehemently refused explaining I needed to handle things on my own, and if that meant therapy down the road, then I'd get it.

Eventually, my mom backed off but she did beg me to let her come to my pottery studio Saturday morning because she missed me. She actually said that, and I cried before thanking her for being so awesome again, and I told her I'd love to see her at the studio Saturday morning, followed by lunch with me, my treat.

I decided I couldn't go back to the studio on Friday nights, because nights were still a little scary for me, but I would go back the following morning in the daylight to meet my mom.

I had taken the sling off Thursday, and though my shoulder still hurt like a bitch, it was tolerable for most of the day. So I left work Friday at 4:30 with nothing planned but McDonalds for dinner, and more useless TV to keep me company through the long night alone.

But I was attacked in my courtyard instead.

Dropping my food, I was quickly grabbed from behind and lifted right off the ground with my mouth covered. I was grabbed, and I'd love to say I fought, but I didn't. I simply froze, and allowed the man to lift me and cover my face without a single movement or even a sound from me.

I wasn't capable of fighting from the sheer shock and memory of what I'd already endured, and there was just no fight left in me anyway. There was nothing, but the little moan that escaped my chest when realization dawned that I was going to be hurt again. So I closed my eyes and waited for the pain.

"Sophie, stop! Sophie, it's me," he said as I felt my brain leave me.

I knew I was being tricked again, and I knew I was dead. There was no way to fight the inevitable, so I let it take me.

"Sophie, please. It's me, baby," he said again as he shook me hard in his arms. Squeezing my chest, he continued. "I have to get you inside. Please baby, I have to talk to you," he growled in my ear.

Finally releasing me gently and standing me back on the ground, I was turned against the wall before the main door to look at him.

Shocked still, I could only whisper, "Peter...?"

"Sophie, you know it's me. Come on, baby," he said shaking me again.

"Oh *god*... Where have you been?" I cried.

Shaking and crying out I stood deathly still staring at his face. Shocked, I took him in as I tried to get my brain to work properly, but I couldn't reason reality from fantasy. I knew Peter was standing in front of me, but I couldn't understand it. I was so confused, I could only lean forward and smell him, which was when I finally woke up. Peter looked like shit, but he smelled the same.

"Sophie, we have to get inside," he said nearly pushing me toward the front door. I let him push the door open as I walked under his arm, and I let him pull me to my door as he took my purse from me and found my keys to unlock my door.

I let Peter lead because I was too afraid to ruin anything. I didn't want him to leave, but I didn't know how to make him stay.

When we entered my apartment, Peter leaned me against the door and quickly locked it. Looking around, he made a *shhhh* motion with his finger against his lips as he motioned for me to stay where I was, until he suddenly left me as I desperately reached for him.

Quickly, he went to my kitchen then he walked out to the dining room. Looking around my living room, he seemed content that no one was there. He walked back to me and opened the closet beside me and pushed my coats and jackets around. After closing the closet, he walked to the hall closet, then the bathroom as I heard the shower curtain quickly thrown open. Just waiting and watching, I still couldn't believe he was there in my home.

When Peter walked to my bedroom I almost yelled no, but stopped myself. My bedroom door had been closed since the first night my mom and I returned from the hospital, and other than opening it quickly to get my work clothes in daylight, it was always shut behind me.

After Peter was in my room, doing whatever, looking for whoever, he returned to me calmly. He returned to me, staring hard at my face, but I just couldn't speak.

Staring at a silent Peter who looked so sad, I waited until he whispered, "Sophie... Please don't be afraid of me."

"I'm not afraid of you. I'm just afraid," I answered truthfully as he nodded.

"Can I hug you?" He asked quietly.

"Yes..." I nearly begged just as quietly as I felt the first tear fall down my cheek when he held me.

Peter took me in his arms like he always had, and I felt my heart shatter in my chest. It didn't feel good, and I wasn't filled with warmth. The pain in my chest was every agony and devastation I had felt for the past 10 months of my life without him. I was broken, and I felt lost.

"Why are you here?" I choked.

"I just found out what happened, and I had to come to you. I'm so sorry, Sophie. I'm so sorry you were hurt, baby. I wish I could've stopped it, and I wish I could've helped you. I'm sick over what happened to you, and I came as soon as I heard. But I can't stay," he said pulling away from me slightly to look at my face.

"*Why?*" I cried.

"Sophie, I'm working a job right now, and I can't just leave. I'm in too deep, but I had to come to you. I had to see you. So I found a way to get out tonight, but I can't stay. I'm so sorry," he begged me to understand.

And I did understand, kind of. "So you are a cop?"

After I asked, Peter stared at me like he wouldn't answer, but eventually he nodded like he couldn't say it out loud or something. He acted first surprised that I knew, then resigned to the fact that I did know.

"A message came to me yesterday about you and what happened, so I got out as quickly as I could. But I can't stay, baby," he pleaded which almost annoyed me.

"So you've said. Multiple times. Why did you even bother coming at all if you can't stay? I'm fine without you here. I'm good without you. You should probably just go if you shouldn't be here," I said coldly.

"Please come sit with me," he said trying to take my hand.

"Why?"

"I need to talk to you and I want to hold you. And I need to know you're okay."

"I'm fine, Peter."

"You're not fine, Sophie. You've been through so much, I need-"

"WHERE THE *FUCK* HAVE YOU BEEN?!" I suddenly screamed as Peter jumped and quickly covered my mouth with his hand.

Staring at me, Peter looked almost afraid and angry at once. His head whipped around my apartment and he opened my door slightly to look down the hallway to the main door. After looking at nothing he closed the door and relocked it but still kept his fucking hand against my mouth. So I bit him.

I was losing my shit, and I didn't care. I hated him.

Keeping his hand against my mouth, he glared at me in a way I had never seen before. He was pissed and I couldn't care less.

"Where the fuck have you been?" I snarled again once he removed his hand from my mouth and wrapped it around my arm.

"I can't tell you, but you have to be quiet. You have to keep your voice lowered in case I was followed. You have to speak quietly, Sophie, so no one can hear us. Do you understand? Otherwise, I have to go."

"Go, then! I don't give a shit. Get the fuck out of here!" I snapped because my heart hurt and my head was pounding. My shoulder was aching and I absolutely hated Peter Connor in that moment as he stared at me silently.

"I'm not leaving yet. Come here. Let's go sit on the couch and talk."

But there was no couch. There was a perfectly made sofa bed, and there was a love seat. There was nowhere to talk unless we sat close to each other on the love set. And I didn't want to sit close to Peter.

Looking at my furniture, I was suddenly struck with the absurdity of my situation. For nearly 10 months I had begged and pleaded for him to return. I had cried thousands of times and thought of nothing but Peter back in my life. I had thought he would return one day and I would know why he left. I thought we would fall into each other's arms and everything would be as it once was. I had truly believed that, and I had wanted that from the moment he left me. But suddenly I found myself with Peter and I felt like I hated him.

Every anger for every single thing I had felt and endured for the last 10 months had crested into a totally irrational hatred for Peter.

"I hate you..." I moaned still standing against my front door.

"Well, I *love* you," he said fiercely.

"Fuck *you!*" I exploded.

"Sophie, please don't do this. I only have a little bit of time and I need to talk to you. Please? Come sit and talk to me. I miss you so much," he said choking up.

Looking at Peter's desperation, I instantly thawed. As quickly as the anger and hatred came to me, it left when I watched him beg me.

So I pulled off my boots and I walked to the love seat to talk. Sitting down, I tugged at the sleeve of my coat and winced when my shoulder ached, but Peter quickly jumped in to help.

"What's wrong? What happened to your arm?" He asked with the old Peter concern I remembered.

"I had my shoulder dislocated," I answered without emotion.

"Dislocated?" He flinched. "When? Oh god, I didn't know."

"It doesn't matter. It's better now, and it only hurts when I do certain things, but its fine."

"I didn't know, Sophie. I just found out today about what happened last

Monday to you. But I didn't receive any specific details when the message was given to me."

"It's fine. I don't want to talk about it."

"I think we should talk about it. I want to help you with-"

"You can't help me. And I don't want to talk about it," I said looking away.

But he didn't stop. Taking my face in his hand he tried to turn me to him as I fought him.

I didn't want to look at him, and I didn't want to talk about what happened. I wanted to know where he'd been, and why he left me, and how he could stay away. I wanted answers to all the basic questions I had. I did NOT want to talk about what happened to me.

"Sophie, look at me," he said as I shook my head no. "Look. At. Me. I want you to look at me and tell me what's going on with you. I want to know how you're feeling and how I can help."

Exhaling, I spoke the truth. "You can't help me, and I don't want you here anymore. You killed me when you left, and you keep killing me. Everything that has happened has been because of you. Well, not everything I guess, but a lot of it. And I'm tired of always loving you when you don't love me back."

"I DO love you. I left you the letter and the paintings, and I tried to tell you, but my hands were tied. They still are."

"How? Please explain it to me," I begged finally turning to look at him.

Looking, I finally saw him as he sat beside me, and he was gross. Peter smelled clean, but he looked dirty. It's almost like he purposely dirtied his clothes before putting them on. He looked unwashed but he smelled clean, which was a total contrast I could actually see.

Peter's hair was too long, and his nasty beard was raggedy and ugly on his smooth face. Everything just looked so wrong about him I couldn't quite figure it out. I wanted to know why he looked like he did, with the fake tattoos down his neck and the ugly clothes. I wanted to know why he looked terrible but still smelled clean like the Peter I remembered.

"What's happening?" I asked quietly.

CHAPTER 33

"I can't tell you anything... But I can show you how I feel," he said leaning forward to kiss me instead of talking.

Peter kissed me and after my initial gasp I was instantly thrown back into the passionate relationship we had had. Peter kissed me like I remembered, and I let him. He took my lips in that slow methodical way he had of exploring my mouth as his hand held my face close to him. Peter kissed me and I forgot all the anger and the confusion surrounding his sudden return.

Kissing me, Peter slipped out of his filthy jacket, and as I pulled away to look, I saw his clothes underneath were clean and normal looking. He wasn't filthy underneath at all, it was just the surface that was gross.

"Why?" I begged, but he shook his head no again.

"Sophie... There's so much I have to tell you, and I will as soon as I can. I'm not asking you to wait for me though, I'm just asking you to be patient for the answers I can't tell you right now. I'll find you later when I can, and I promise to tell you everything. It's just not safe right now, and there's too much to lose if I start talking now."

"You don't want me to wait? What if I move on and find someone else? What then?"

Calmly, like he knew it was too hard to imagine me moving on, Peter said, "Then I'll still find you and tell you all the answers you want, but I'll walk away afterward. I'm not looking for you to wait for me, I just need you to wait for the answers. That's all, I promise."

"And if I find someone else to be with? Someone to love?" I asked with dread in my heart.

"Then I'll tell you the answers only, and I'll wish you well, always. I want you to be happy, Sophie. I always did. I always tried to make you happy when we were together."

"I was happy..." I moaned.

"Then I did okay. I loved you as best as I could for as long as I had."

"But you left me," I cried.

"Not by choice. *Never* by choice. I didn't want to leave you ever, but I

had to," he seemed to beg me to understand.
 Frustrated, I just couldn't let it go. "You keep saying you didn't have a choice, but it doesn't fix anything."
 "It's all I've got. So it has to be enough for now," he said sadly.
 Breathing him while thinking of everything Peter, I looked at his sad face and realized it was enough. For now.

"What happened to you last Monday?" He asked so calmly, I answered the question calmly. There was always something about Peter that just calmed me and made me open up to him. Even after all the time apart, it was still the same between us.
 "I was raped in my bedroom," I confessed as he looked away for a second and visibly shook beside me.
 After I spoke softly the silence dragged for only a few seconds until Peter looked back at me sadly and took my hand in his own.
 "Do they have any leads, or a suspect?" He asked in a different tone than I was used to.
 "Not yet. There was no DNA evidence in me which hurt the investigation, but was better for me because obviously he used a condom," I said as he nodded. "They did get some skin cells from under my one hand though, but a blood sample from the floor was mine."
 "Did he hurt you badly, Sophie?" Peter asked shaking.
 Stunned, I snapped at his stupid question. "Of course, Peter. How couldn't it hurt?"
 "I mean emotionally. Are you still struggling?"
 "*Jesus, Peter...* Of course I am. Of course I'm *emotionally* messed up. I'm sleeping in the living room because I'm afraid of my bedroom, and I'm scared of the front door being behind me even though he probably came through the kitchen window. I haven't seen my brother since it happened because I don't want him picturing me being raped, and I hate my job now because everyone looks at me all weird. My mom's still great but she keeps pushing me to go to therapy which I don't want to go to, and I wanted you to help me but you weren't there!" I yelled.
 "I'm so sorry I wasn't there to protect you," he cried.
 "It doesn't matter."
 "It *does* matter."
 "It really doesn't. It's over now," I exhaled.
 "Is it? Then why are you sleeping in the living room?"
 "Because my bedroom is contaminated now. It's not the same anymore," I said but didn't explain why.

I couldn't possibly say it didn't have him in there anymore, and I couldn't possibly explain the shrine to all things Peter that had kept me living through his absence. I didn't want him to know I still loved him, and I didn't want him to know my bedroom was dirty now that he had been raped out of it.

"Come with me," he said standing, but I knew what he was doing. I knew it, and I couldn't possibly do what he wanted me to do.
"I'm not going in there."
"Yes, you are. With me. I'm going to show you your room isn't contaminated," he pushed trying to make me rise by pulling my hand. But I shook my head no again. "Well, I'm going in, and I'll wait for you to join me. I'll show you its okay," he said leaving me.
After I watched him leave, I waited for what felt like hours, but was probably no more than minutes. Then I did what I'm sure he expected- I walked to the hallway and leaned against the doorframe of my room. I waited and watched Peter watching me while sitting on my bed.
"It's inside the covers," I whispered.
"No, it isn't," he replied standing and pulling down the new comforter and sheets to slide in. "It's not contaminated. Everything is clean and healthy in here. Your bed isn't contaminated, Sophie. Nothing is."
"I am," I choked.
"You're not."
"I am. I had an orgasm, Peter," I cried out embarrassed.
"That doesn't matter."
"Yes, it does. I got off until he started hurting me. I got off Peter, and I'm filthy now," I whispered desperately through my humiliation.
"Come here, Sophie. Come sit beside me," he begged with his hand extended beckoning me to him, until I did. Unbelievably, I walked toward him and sat on the edge of my bed.
Still crying, I wiped my face and nose on my sleeve, as I sat rigid beside Peter- the man who made me come.
"I thought it was you..." I confessed.
"Who raped you?!" He asked stunned.
"No. I knew then. But at first I thought I was having a dream of you making me... And then I got off thinking you were doing it, but then I knew it wasn't you, and I tried to fight, but he was too strong, and everything just got worse. And then he tried to kill me, or just hurt me,

or whatever he was trying to do, and I can't get past the fact that I enjoyed it at first."

"But you didn't enjoy it with him, you enjoyed it with me. That's the difference, Sophie. If you thought it was me, I would hope you enjoyed it. I would've wanted you to. I always tried to connect with you in a way that we were intimate, *together*. But you were confused, and then you weren't. You did nothing wrong, Sophie."

"That's what everyone says, but it feels wrong because it wasn't you that made me orgasm," I cried out shaking.

"But you thought it was me. And that's all you should think about. You believed it was me, which is a good thing, and then you knew it wasn't me and you tried to stop him doing the bad thing. Tell yourself that over and over again until you finally believe it," he moaned as he stared hard at my eyes. Sitting still, living only to breathe, Peter watched me as he had a hundred times before.

"I can't believe you're here," I suddenly whispered through my tight throat.

"I came as soon as I heard."

"I still love you, Peter, which makes me hate you."

"Sadly, I actually understand what you mean. I know how hard it was for you to let go to love me, but I never took it for granted, and I never loved you any less than you loved me. I still love you, and I will never hate you, Sophie. I adore you too much to ever hate you," he said again sadly.

"Peter... I don't know what to do anymore," I whispered.

"Just live, Sophie," he said taking my hand. "Move past this horrible thing that happened to you and live. Find someone who makes you happy, and-"

"*You* made me happy," I choked.

Looking away I stared at my paintings still leaning against the wall on the floor and I couldn't believe the pain I felt. Everything hurt again. It's like he was breaking up with me all over again.

Crying out, I leaned forward and wrapped my arms around my stomach as I sobbed. Nothing was right and everything felt unfair. Love shouldn't always hurt this much I thought over and over again.

"Sophie," he moaned lifting me off the bed and pulling me into his lap. Holding me, I cried all over his shoulder as my own shoulder ached, reminding me of all the pain around me. But I held onto Peter for an eternity as I cried out every single hurt I had felt since the moment I met him. Crying, I released all the pain I held, and washed it away with my tears.

"When do you have to go?" I whispered in his ear.

"Soon..." he whispered back which was all I needed to hear.

Turning my face I kissed Peter for the last time. I knew it was the last time for us and I wanted it to mean something. Even covered in tears, I held his face to mine and I kissed him goodbye.

We would never be together after that moment I knew, so I kissed him goodbye forever.

When Peter pulled away to lift my sweater, I let him. When he paused and kissed around and on my facial bruising, I wept a little more. He touched me and kissed me like he always had, beautifully and with a connection I would never again know for the rest of my life.

When his hands touched the top of my chest and bra, I whispered, "Take it off," and he did. Slipping my bra from my body, his hands gently held me as he stared at my eyes before kissing me again.

And that was the beginning of our end.

I pulled his shirt from his body, and kissed him harder. I wanted him. I wanted all of him to clean me and cleanse my room. I wanted him to give me the last memories of love I would ever know, so I took them.

Moving onto my bed, I laid down and unzipped my dress pants. I tried to pull them from my body, but Peter knelt on the bed and pulled them from me, kneeling between my opened legs, pausing at my panties. Bending low, he rested his face between my thighs and exhaled all the tension between us.

Then he paused again unsure and shaking. "Sophie...?"

"I need this..." I cried. "You're the only one who can fix everything inside me, Peter. You are what I need," I whispered desperately as he choked up and nodded his surrender.

Peter then took me gently with his mouth and fingers. He took me slowly, building me up to the plateau I hated and had learned to fight past. He touched me and kissed me and worshipped my body. He pushed me, until begging, he finally entered me slowly.

Covering my body with his own, with bent elbows at my sides he held my face with his hands as he kissed me and slowly moved within me. He kissed me and allowed me to fall back down a little, only to be pushed

back up by his gentle touches and his slow movement.
  Peter loved me like he always had, and I was okay.

"I will never know anything greater than you wrapped around me, loving me whole, Sophie. I have never and will never love anyone else like I love you. And I need you to know that for the rest of your life," Peter cried against my lips as he moved slowly within me.
  During, I never once thought of the attack, and I never once had a moment of hesitation or confusion. I knew without a doubt I was with Peter and every hurt and past trauma faded away when we were together.

When I suddenly flashed back to that horrible night though, I asked a question I never thought would come from my mouth. "Would you finish me from behind so you're the only memory," and choking, I finished desperately. "The last person I remember like that?"
  Though visibly shaken, Peter nodded like he understood what I needed from him, and gave to me what I needed as he always had.
  Moving out of me, Peter gently turned me onto my stomach and settled back behind me. Kissing my spine, Peter reminded me he was there as he gently lifted my hips, and slowly, without pain or fear entered me again.
  Moving so slowly, Peter was all I knew. He was everything I felt, and everything inside me. I was with Peter and I tried to release the last of the nightmare I had lived.
  Reaching around, Peter began touching me with his fingers as I pushed back to my building arousal. He pushed me until I stopped thinking and only loved against him for the release I needed.
  He touched me and made love to me, and stayed with me.
  As time passed, Peter asked quietly against my shoulder, "Give me a number," and I actually laughed.
  "9. I'm like a 9," I said grinning into my pillow, as he touched me harder and moved faster.
  Moaning and moving, I found myself almost there. I was where I needed to be, and where I wanted to be. I was almost there, but I just needed a little bit more. I needed just a little-
  "Oh! Ummmm... Peter," I gasped on a broken exhale as I released.
  Peter then turned me back around, and spread my legs wide as he entered me again slowly through my tension.
  Staring at me with his classic Peter connective intensity, he looked at

me with all the love and the adoration I had come to know only with him. He watched me, and then he kissed me. He loved within me and kissed me until pulling away he let me watch his own release.
But there were no agonized faces, nor animalistic grunts from Peter. He simply closed his eyes for a split second and then opened them as he leaned down and kissed me the last kiss I would ever know.

And as it began for us, I released all the tension and burst into tears again from the intensity of everything between us.
I cried as I always had with Peter after so deep a connection, and I said goodbye to my forever.
I cried as he turned us and wrapped his arms around me for the last time. Peter spooned me safe for the last time in my life, I knew.

Minutes later I actually asked him to leave. I said the words I never thought I could possibly say, and I felt everything I knew would be my forever from that moment on.
"Please go now. You're going to leave anyway, so go now when I feel like this, so this is the last memory I have of you."
"I can stay for a little longer," he begged. But I knew it wouldn't matter.
"Please, Peter."
"I'm coming back. I'll be back to love you and adore you forever," he whispered kissing the back of my head.
"Okay..." But I knew he wouldn't.
The very atmosphere around us told me I would never see Peter again. Whether killed on the job, or simply too much time passing to still hold on, I didn't know. I didn't know what the end of us would be officially, but I knew in that one moment, I was witnessing our end.

Eventually, Peter dressed to leave my room for the very last time. He dressed and knelt on the floor, holding my face in his hands as he kissed me goodbye with tears in his eyes.
"There was no one before you, and there will never be anyone *but* you, Sophie," he whispered as he stood to leave.
Leaving me again, Peter kissed me like the forever he was, and then he left me as the forever he would always be.

*****

The following morning after endless tears and a heartache that went beyond pain, I finally attempted to rise from my bed. I had a date with my mom at the pottery studio, and I had a date with the rest of my life.
My forever was gone, and I decided I would try to finally let him go.

Showering quickly and massaging my aching shoulder I honestly felt lighter than I had in 10 months, and maybe even the years before it.
My body was sore, but the good kind of sore. The vaginal tear had healed enough that Peter hadn't hurt me, and my muscles were aching from our movements, not from the previous pain I had endured.
I actually felt good as I dressed for my date with my mom.

When I arrived, my mom was waiting, and I knew she knew instantly. Without asking anything specific, she looked at me with a grin and said, "You look very happy this morning, Sophie."
Smiling, I said more than I ever could with words and explanations because I didn't think she could ever understand what my night with Peter had meant to me.
She wouldn't know he had helped heal me, and she wouldn't understand sex with Peter helped wash away the rape. She couldn't possibly understand my room was no longer contaminated and neither was I.
So I nodded and smiled and asked what pottery she'd like to make.

And I just lived, like Peter told me to do.

LOST

CHAPTER 34

2 weeks after my night with Peter I attempted to quit my job at Halton Facilities. I tried to resign because I just couldn't do it anymore. There was nothing holding me to the job because I had lost the happiness and excitement I once had for my career. I also knew I needed a change.

I was no longer stable, mature, professional Sophie Morley, and I didn't want to be anymore. I decided I needed to change everything about my life and I needed to find some happiness within it.

So I tried to quit on a Friday afternoon, but Deborah refused my resignation. Actually, she vehemently refused, which was pretty funny considering I could just walk out the door.

After she refused, she surprised me though by saying she was filing the paperwork for a leave of absence. She had all the paperwork ready, and upper management had already signed it. She said she was just waiting for me to make a move before she approached me with the offer.

Deborah handed me the contract from a folder and as I looked over it, I was still determined to leave regardless. But honestly, I was shocked by the terms of the leave. She had made everything so easy I couldn't believe what I was reading. I was unable to even comprehend what I was looking at, until she explained it all to me.

"You're an amazing employee who has been through a lot this past month, so I drafted a proposal for you to look over. Basically, you stay as an employee, on leave for exactly 6 months from the day you sign this, and we agree to continue paying 60% of your salary while on leave. You must sign a non-compete, only valid for the 6 months you're on leave, but otherwise, you're free to do whatever you want. Take a vacation, relax at home, get a part time job out of the industry," she smirked. "But come back when the 6 months is over, or come see me if you decide you really are resigning. Either way, you have 6 months with partial pay to figure out what you want to do."

Looking at Deborah and the kindness she was offering I choked up a little as I asked, "Why?"

"Like I said, we don't want to lose you, and I think you just need a little time. I understand you've had a lot going on personally, and though you were ridiculously professional at work, I could see you were personally struggling. So before you came in to quit, which we didn't want, I set up this proposition for you."

"But I could just take a leave anyway, and file-"

"With the government, yes. However, you would make just slightly less than 40% of your current income. So, by doing this, I had hoped with the larger income we were willing to pay you for 6 months, you would feel obligated to return," she grinned again. "Look, I don't know all the details of what's going on with you, but I know you were recently sexually assaulted, according to the little bit of information your mother gave me, and I know this must be a very hard time for you. So I was trying to make it a little easier for you to get help, get better, and then come back to us here. And again, we don't want to lose you. So take the paperwork, read over it this weekend and let me know what you decide on Monday."

"This is so generous," I said still a little stunned by the offer. "But who will do my job?"

"We'll have it covered. Don't worry about it. Worry about you," she said kindly.

"Okay. Thank you. I'll sign it right now. I don't need to read over it. Thank you so much, Deborah. I did just need a little time to figure everything out. Thank you," I said again already flipping through the pages to the little colored stickers where I had to initial and sign.

And that was it. After a hug, and a few more soothing words from Deborah, plus the offer to call her anytime, I walked out of Halton Facilities an hour late Friday night, but free.

I was free from the stress and pressure of my job while I tried to get my life back together.

My birthday was just over a week away and all I could think about was turning 26. That was my first goal with my new freedom- my birthday. I *needed* to be 26, because 25 had been awful for me.

And financially, I was okay. 60% of my income would make everything tight, but I also had a tiny amount of savings, so if I did find a part time job to make up the difference, I could actually make it work. I could take my little breather while I pulled myself back together. I needed the little break Deborah offered, which was better than I would have had if I'd actually quit, which I had intended.

*****

During the 2 weeks after Peter's visit, I had been struggling worse than ever, but I pretended harder than ever to look okay. No one knew he had come to me, and no one knew I had let him go. And as each day passed, *I* couldn't even believe I had let him go.

There was a part of me, albeit very small that tried to take comfort in the fact that he was a police officer doing something more than I knew or understood to help the greater good. That little part of me struggled every single day, fighting the depression and the sadness that threatened to strangle me in my bed, but I tried so hard to make it enough to continue.

I fought every single day getting out of bed, and accepting the fact that the man I loved *couldn't* be with as opposed to didn't want to be with me. But it was hard. Knowing he was more than just a man who broke my heart helped. *Slightly.*

Every single day I had a pep talk with myself, and tried to reason every other person on the planet had suffered a break up. Everyone else knew it hurt, suffered the initial pain, but then got over it. Everyone knew what I was going through, and they all survived. I knew that logically, but the reality felt anything but.

No one could possibly understand the depth of my pain because I simply couldn't express it. I was weak and broken, and I hated myself and my feelings, and my insane inability to move on.

I was stuck in my tragic world of missing him, wanting him, and looking for him everywhere. Peter coming to me and making love to me may have emotionally helped me move back into my bedroom, and maybe even helped me move past the rape quicker. But his visit prompted a whole new devastation over his absence again.

But I tried to live, like he told me to.

3 weeks after I left Halton Facilities I did get a part time job, working in Pandora's, which I loved. Pandora's was cool as hell and close to my apartment, and really, just an opened door away from seeing Peter again, should he enter it.

Peter was everywhere all the time still, and I missed him with everything I was. But at least he was helping do something greater than I understood, which was the mantra I held each and every day of my life.

I still held onto the knowledge that Peter was doing something good, something worthwhile, even as I slowly wasted away looking for him.

Driving down streets I looked, and in every window of every store in the village I looked for him. I looked everywhere, and I looked always.

But I never found him, until I did.

CHAPTER 35

"Sophie? I'd like you to tell me why you're here?"

"I am. Please... Just listen. I'm almost there. We're almost done," I say bursting into tears.

"Why are you crying, Sophie?" He asks me gently.

Exhaling my sadness as I look at him, I try to understand why I'm here, but all I can think about is the last year and a half of my life. I think about the little pieces of happiness I've felt- the happiness that I held onto, as the only thing that got me through all the pain I've lived. I remember the 3 months of happiness I had, but all I feel is the pain of its loss.

"I'm lost..." I whisper suddenly.

"How are you lost? What are you feeling?"

And looking at him I take a deep breath before speaking my absolute. "I still love him," I say simply. And that is all I feel. What else can I possibly say?

"Tell me about your rapist?" He asks suddenly. So I tell him.

*****

I received another call from Detective Dent on March 4th telling me they had a suspect in custody. She told me she was sure they had the right man, but obviously there was more investigating, and more forensics needed before they formally charged him. She did tell me quite adamantly though that she was sure she had him.

Dent told me they picked him up outside Perry's gallery, based on a tip from Michael Sharpe who she had spoken to after the attack. She had spoken to both Michael and Perry after the attack, and though both had alibis, and were never suspects in my rape, she did want me to know that she believed Perry's gallery was involved. So she waited for a break in the case.

Apparently, Michael called her to tell her about a man who was in the gallery often. He told her of the man who was very unassuming, but who for a few weeks had been asking many questions about Peter Connor, his paintings, and about Sophie Morley. He asked if I had been around again, and he asked if more paintings of me would come in and where he could buy them. He asked too much about Sophie Morley, and Michael became very suspicious because no one knew who I was in relation to Peter's paintings.

Dent received a description of the man, and asked Michael and Perry to try to detain the man for as long as possible should he return. She asked them to call her immediately if he returned so she could ask the unknown man some questions.

I was told the man entered the gallery again and Perry maintained a long conversation with him about me, to my horror, until Michael could reach the Police. The man was subsequently taken into custody for questioning by Detective Dent and her partner Detective Dolby.

I also found out 4 hours after the first phone call, that the man named Frederick McGregor confessed to everything and didn't seem to even care that he was being charged with rape and sexual battery.

Sadly, I was told by Detective Dent he had no remorse, nor did he even request a lawyer's presence. Frederick McGregor was my rapist, confessing to everything that occurred, even giving additional information the Detectives withheld from him, which obviously I was curious about, but didn't ask.

I was called later again and told a formal statement from me was required again because I didn't recognize the man's name, and I was also asked to look at his photos to see if I recognized him physically at all.

I was promised when I arrived at the police station there was absolutely NO chance of seeing the man because he had already been moved. I was also told I would be safe, and I could have someone accompany me to the police station for further questioning while I looked over the mug shots. I was told to try to remember anything I could on the way to the station to help ensure a conviction.

So late in the evening on March 4th, my mom and I went to the police station again. We went quietly, and with little said between us as she drove. My mom was stoic and strong as usual, waiting for my mood to set the tone once again. But I had no mood.

I was scared and numb at the same time. I was glad the nightmare of who did it, and why did he do it was going to be over, but I didn't really feel much of anything at all.

Once inside, everything moved quickly and smoothly. I looked first at the photos and knew I had never seen the man before in my life. I answered all the questions asked, and was even recorded given my sworn statement as to the fact that I didn't know Frederick McGregor at all.

There were a few questions about Perry's and the paintings, and if I had told anyone about my association with the paintings, but I hadn't, so I answered truthfully. I explained that I had only told my immediate family, and didn't know anyone else who knew about them or even about me for that matter, other than Margaret at the health food store.

Eventually, Peter was brought up and I was asked if I knew his location, which I didn't. Strangely, I was asked if I had seen Peter Connor since the assault, so I lied and said I hadn't.

I'm not sure why I felt like I needed to lie, but if Dent was asking, it meant she wasn't the one who had reached Peter to tell him what had happened in the first place. I didn't know why, but I felt like I needed to protect Peter from being found during whatever job he was on.

But I answered everything else asked of me honestly and calmly while my mom waited in the hall. And then I asked my questions.

After Detective Dent stopped recording, I asked why he did it. I asked such a simple word with all the potential in the world. Why? That's all I needed to know- *Why?*

Looking at me with compassion, I knew she couldn't tell me anything specific because of the investigation and subsequent charges, as had been explained to me earlier, but she did anyway.

Exhaling deeply, while repeating the obvious, 'this is confidential- NOT to be repeated', Detective Dent leaned back in her chair further from me and the table, and said the only words that mattered.

"All he said as an explanation was 'Peter Connor loves her, so I had to take her.'" And I nearly threw up after she spoke. "That's what he said no matter how hard Dolby and I pushed for more information. He admitted to everything regarding the entry of your apartment, to loving the paintings, to sexually assaulting you," she said as I sat in a stunned silence. "Are you okay," she suddenly asked reaching for my hand, but I could only nod. "We're through here. You'll be contacted soon, but probably not to testify because he's confessed."

On a gasp, I begged, "What else did he say?"

"Are you sure?"

"Yes..." I shook my head to clear it. "Please tell me what he said, I need to know."

"Well, he said he didn't mean to hurt you," she said gently as I cried out. "He said *you* hurt your own arm because you were fighting him. He also said the only reason he physically assaulted you was because you refused to open your eyes. He said you kept saying Peter over and over again, so that's why he punched you in the face until the neighbor started banging on your door."

"What else?" I begged again when Dent paused.

"There's nothing more, Sophie. I'm sorry. We tried to get more from him, but he stopped talking. He didn't give any more explanation than that, except for his full confession to the actual assault. But before he was led out to booking, he did ask if you were okay, and then he asked if you still had the paintings?"

"Why?" I choked. "What the hell do the paintings have to do with anything? I don't understand," I moaned.

"I don't know, but we're trying to find Mr. Connor to bring him in for questioning. We need to know if he knows Mr. McGregor, and if so, how."

"Peter doesn't know him. Well, maybe he does. I don't know. But Peter didn't know how he hurt me."

"How do you know?" Dent asked me suspiciously. And in that moment I realized I had screwed up.

"Um, I just do. Peter wouldn't know someone like that guy," I gave as a lame excuse, but I could tell Dent knew I was lying. I could see the calculated look she gave just before she asked again if I had seen Peter Connor since the assault. But again I lied.

"Are you protecting Mr. Connor, Sophie?" Dent asked professionally, almost like she didn't like me anymore. But I didn't care. If Peter was in trouble, or these were the kind of cops Peter was up against, I knew he needed my help. I knew he needed me to protect him while he was doing whatever he was doing.

"No," I breathed with as much conviction as possible in my voice. "I haven't seen Peter, and I don't know where he is. I haven't seen Peter since he broke up with me almost a year ago. Can I go now?" I asked accidentally, knowing my mistake as soon as I asked it.

If I wasn't hiding anything, I wouldn't have wanted to get the hell out of there so quickly. If I wasn't lying, I would've sat calmly and waited for Detective Dent to finish up with me. If I was being honest with her, I wouldn't have looked guilty as hell while I tried to get out of there as quickly as I could.

She let me go anyway though. Knowing I was lying, and knowing I was full of shit, Detective Dent let me walk out of the door, to my waiting mother in the hallway. She let me go to face the endless questions I would obsess over alone.

When my mother and I returned to my apartment I was exhausted.
"What can I do to help?" She asked.
"Honestly, nothing. Thank you for taking me and for coming over, but it's late and I'm exhausted, and I want to go to sleep. Do you mind leaving? I promise to call in the morning."
"You're so strong, Sophie. You always act so together and tough all the time, but just remember, you don't have to if you don't want to. I'm here if you want to just freak out a little, okay?"
"I will," I smiled and that was all we said as she walked out my door for home.

Once she left, I was again alone with my paintings and my drawing, and a world filled with question after question regarding the elusive Peter Connor.

I was left with a world full of pain and sadness and confusion and paranoia.

I was sure McGregor had something to do with Peter's life or his job or the undercover investigation, or whatever the hell he was doing, but I had no way of knowing, or of finding Peter to tell him.

I was exactly back to where I had started. I loved a man I couldn't find, and I begged for a man who wouldn't come.

"But what about your rapist? What came of him?" He again asks me gently.

"He's going to be convicted, which apparently he wants. The DNA collected from my nails matched his, and he has fought nothing while he waits for his trial. He refused a trial by jury, and though he has representation, he doesn't want it. He has told anyone who will listen that he raped me, and he doesn't seem sorry in the least. He apparently has a history of mental illness and he lives in a halfway house not too far from where I live in the village. But that's all I know."

"And how does that make you feel?

"The same. Nothing. I feel nothing about anything anymore."

"Can you elaborate? What don't you feel?"

"Can I finish my story first?"

"Of course."

Knowing the end, I take a big breath and finish.

CHAPTER 36

4 days ago, 2 months after Peter left me again, I saw him.

I saw him and suffered the worst of karmic cruelty.
The very day I knew I couldn't keep living without him, I found him lifeless in the street.

Leaving Pandora's, I decided to walk home, keeping my car in the little back lot overnight. It was warm for April, and it was a clear Wednesday evening and I decided to walk for no other reason than the Fates had finally stepped in. The Fates decided enough was enough, and they stepped in to give me back Peter.
Walking home, I passed Murphy's and thought about a plate of their awesome cheese fries, but knowing I hadn't eaten in a few days meant serious gut rot if I did, so I passed Murphy's and...
The déjà vu was so intense I stopped dead in my tracks.

I remembered him. I saw him once when I first moved in almost 2 years earlier. I saw him, and I knew.
Leaning against the wall was the creepy, dirty homeless man I remembered from my first walk through the village. The homeless man who was moaning against the wall. The man who was so out of place in the village I merely passed by quickly. But there he was again, the homeless man I knew.
Staring, I could only breathe. There was no movement nor thought. There was nothing in that single moment but horror.
Gasping, I finally opened my mouth and whispered, "Peter?" But the man didn't look up or acknowledge me in any way. There was nothing to him that I could see.
Finding the strength to finally move my legs took me to him. Moving, my knees allowed me to collapse in front of him on the sidewalk. Moving, I joined him in hell.
"Peter?" I whispered as he looked in my direction.
With a blank stare and the darkest eyes I'd ever seen, Peter looked right

through me as if I was nothing more than air. He looked through me, past the street and buildings, into another world entirely. He looked beyond me, and my heart broke a thousand times over.

"Peter, what's wrong? Oh, god, Peter... What happened to you?" I cried as I tried to touch his hand. But jerking, Peter pushed further into the wall, and looked around frantically.

He looked like he was waiting to be hurt. He looked like he was looking for something. He looked like he was looking for someone. And then it hit me.

Whispering, I leaned in closer and asked the only question I could think of. "Are you working undercover right now?" And he nodded. The slightest of movements, almost unseen by anyone else but me in front of his face, he nodded. "Should I leave?" I asked quietly.

Looking around again, Peter seemed to fully understand where he was, and what was happening. He seemed to shake himself back to the world around us.

"Baby... Take me home," he wept suddenly, killing me when I heard his voice.

Looking at Peter, I was so confused and scared my heart pounded in my chest as tears filled my eyes. He looked so distressed I couldn't breathe. He looked so sad, but if he was working...

"I don't know where to take you," I whispered again on the sidewalk as he slowly pushed into me while I helped him slowly stand.

Collapsing on my shoulders, I struggled to hold his weight. I struggled, but I would struggle forever to help him. The strength needed to hold him up against my little frame came to me as the desperation to help him filled my body with the power needed to carry him away.

"Please, help me," he moaned as I tightened my grip around his waist and chest. "They're coming back for me so we have to hurry," he continued whispering as we walked forward down the street.

Passing Pandora's, we turned right on Elm Street and continued at our slow, sloppy-looking pace. We struggled and staggered, looking horribly drunk I'm sure, but I didn't care. I just held Peter up with as much strength as I had while we walked further down Elm.

We walked in silence as Peter moaned and I grunted from his weight on my shoulders. We walked in silence blocks and blocks down Elm, stopping occasionally for Peter to look around. We stopped when Peter felt the need to bend and fake tying his shoe as a car passed, and we stopped when Peter turned us into hedges along Elm so we could hide as a car passed.

Eventually, we turned down another street further from where we began. We continued walking endless blocks until Peter finally turned us down an old alley between Ash and Cedar Street.

We walked silently until he pushed through an old chain gate beside a garage numbered 26 that backed onto the alley around us.

Looking around to see every angle he could in the near darkness, Peter hunched down again and fought all his clothes to pull a key from inside a deep low pocket in one of the jackets he wore. Wiping the sweat from his head, he blew out his hair from his face, turned back to me and took my hand as he made a sprint for the side of the huge garage in silence.

Without being told, I knew Peter needed me to move quietly, and I knew I had to calm my pounding heart, and the breath rushing from my lungs. I knew I needed to be silent as Peter and I tiptoed around the large garage behind a huge backyard, backing onto an alley on Cedar.

Struggling with the lock, Peter finally released a latch, and unlocked a door hidden on the side of the garage between the neighbor's fence and the building itself. With only a foot in between, I waited, holding my breath as Peter finally pushed open the side garage door and pulled me inside to a dead stop in total darkness. Pitch black was all I could decipher in that moment with Peter.

"Don't move and stay right against this wall, Sophie. I need to check out the loft," Peter said as I nodded to no one.

I heard Peter move at that point. I heard almost silence, but for a creaky floor, or a quietly moved object, presumably furniture as he left me in my darkness and confusion.

I heard Peter walk near, and then away again. I heard his breathing and I heard what I though was the soft rustle of fabric, or clothing. I didn't know what I heard exactly but my senses were definitely heightened by my lack of sight, while I tried to figure out what to do.

Inhaling deeply, I smelled a mixture of scents, some known and some unknown. Dust tickled my nose, and the smell of paint reminded me of my dad's old shed. The garage smelled clean *and* dirty, like it had been cleaned but then time had dirtied or dusted it up again.

Moving my hands behind my back I felt the cool walls, and I was actually surprised they felt like cool drywall when outside the large garage had been made by cinder blocks. I stood silently while Peter walked above and around me, I could hear.

"Stay against me," Peter suddenly said in my ear as I gasped. I hadn't even heard him or felt his presence walking to me. I didn't realize he was against me until he was. Scared, I reached out my hands and held a piece of his jacket while my heart pounded from the quick fear.

Holding my coat against his back, as I wrapped my arms awkwardly around his stomach, Peter and I walked slowly and quietly steps away from the door we entered. I walked awkwardly behind him, with my feet almost marching on the outside of his so I could stay pressed against him until he whispered, 'stairs', and then I felt his body shift higher, as my toes hit the bottom step in darkness.

Climbing behind him, I focused only on my footing. I didn't know if there was a railing, and I couldn't see even Peter in front of me. My eyes hadn't adjusted and there was still nothing but pitch black around me, but eventually he stopped.

Turning me to lean against a wall again, I was so disoriented I felt almost nauseous. I had never moved up and around in so much darkness before in my life, and I felt sickened by it.

Actually, as I leaned against a wall, I realized I couldn't remember a time in my life where I was in only black without even the slightest of moonlit light, or the faded light from a clock or even a button on the TV lit up. And then my confused thoughts wondered if anyone with sight had ever truly stood in darkness before. Crazily, I thought of people who suffered blindness, and I felt a whole new respect and sympathy for them when I realized darkness really was an affliction to suffer in a world of light.

Quite suddenly the atmosphere changed around me though. Almost unperceptively, the world around me offered the slightest of light as Peter stood before me with a tiny battery operated tealight lit in the palm of his hand casting a slight orange-yellow glow to light him from the darkness.

"Where are we?" I whispered, nearly unheard.

"Come here," he said tugging me over to the opposite side of the room without answering me. Tugging me, I tried to see, but with the small light in front of him, the view behind and around me was quickly swallowed up by the darkness again. I couldn't see beyond a foot around me. I couldn't see the shape of the room, or even the stairs we had just climbed. All I saw was the dark shape of Peter in front of me.

Groaning, Peter sat hard on a bed, pulling me down beside him. I couldn't see much of anything specific, just a kind of chaotic mess around us. There was stuff everywhere piled on or near more piles of stuff. Every surface, from the floor to the bed we sat on was just stuff that made no sense.

Looking around me, only maybe 2 feet beyond the light I was surprised by the chaos I saw. The place where we sat was disgusting, and I was shocked Peter would know the place or even stay there. Peter was like me, and he had always cleaned and tidied up after us in my home. He understood my need for order and cleanliness, so to see the madness around us was a little shocking. There was nothing there that reminded me of the Peter I knew in my home.

"You're staying here?" I whispered surprised.

"Not really," he said turning to me.

"Can we turn on a light?"

"No. Every window is covered and the foundation cracks have been sealed, but I still can't risk any light being seen outside. I don't know who saw me, and I don't know if we were followed."

Gasping, I was totally afraid in that moment. All the confusion of our walk, and the stillness of the dark faded as I felt the first real, true, feelings of fear for my safety.

"Who would've saw us, Peter? Who are you hiding from?" I asked still whispering but with definite panic in my voice.

"I think we're okay, baby. I was careful, and I'm sure we weren't followed," he said taking my hand. "But I don't want to turn any lights on, just in case. I can't risk you being here," he again said as he raised my hand to his lips and kissed it. "We're okay for now..." he breathed like he was trying to convince me of something I didn't understand.

Looking around, as best as I could see with only the tiny light guiding my vision, I asked again, "What is this place? I mean I know you don't live here because there wasn't a greenhouse in the yard, but I don't understand what this is."

"Ummm..." Peter looked at me a little suspiciously or something. There was a look, like he wasn't sure if I could be trusted, or like he didn't want to trust me. I didn't know what the look was exactly, but I did know I felt hurt and offended by it.

"Peter. I would never betray you. Ever. So why are you looking at me—"

"I'm not. It's not you, Sophie. I know I can trust you. I was thinking more about your safety and whether I should tell you what's going on, and what I'm doing." He exhaled while shaking his head slightly. "This is my little safe house. No one knows about it and I only come here when I need to lay low quickly. I never bring anyone here," he mumbled.

Peter looked almost frustrated, which was also offensive since it was him who asked me for help. It was him who needed me to help him walk for the miles and blocks we covered.

"What's wrong with you?"

"Nothing," he barked at me.

"I mean with your walking. You needed my help, and you were struggling when I found you."

"Oh. Sorry. My leg is a little banged up, so putting weight on it is excruciating," he moaned again into the silence around us.

"Can I help you? Can I see it?"

"I probably should clean it out. Stay here, Sophie. Right here. I'm going to go to the bathroom for a minute," Peter said rising.

As he left me alone, I thought where could I possibly go? He was walking away with the only light in the room, and I was bathed in darkness within seconds. I wouldn't even know how to leave other than crawling my way the direction we came from the stairs. And then nothing. I knew I couldn't leave that place even if I tried.

Waiting, I sat in total darkness listening to Peter however far from me. I heard the sound of water and a slight movement beyond me, but otherwise even outside noise was silent. We weren't in a place near any main roads, but even at the back of the property against an alley, somehow I still expected to hear some sound. I expected something, but all I heard was darkness.

I remember thinking, this was not how I ever envisioned seeing Peter again. This was not-

"I can smell you," Peter suddenly whispered jolting me from my thoughts. "I miss you every single day, and I want you every minute of every day. I miss you so much, Sophie," Peter cried.

"Where are you?" I asked desperately.

"Find me," he begged.

Rising from the bed, I immediately walked to where his voice had come from. Walking slowly and nervously, I stepped into piles and knocked over stuff with my shin. I walked to where I thought he was, until he pulled me to him on a gasp. And then he kissed me.

Kissing me, Peter moaned into my mouth, and pushed me backward again. He pushed me backward, even as I stumbled and recovered against his lips and arms holding me to him. He kissed me through the darkness as he pushed me back to the bed, and then he landed on me.

Crushing me beneath him, he took my lips harder. Tugging at my jacket, and scratching my skin with his nails, he tore my clothing from me

between desperate kisses. He pulled at me until I was scared *and* aroused.

"I need you, Sophie. I need you to remind me about the good, so I know I can keep doing this. I need to love you again," he cried until I realized in the sudden stillness, he *was* actually crying.

Peter was crying on top of me, trying to remove my clothing so he could be with me like he needed, and that was when I realized he was already naked.

Knowing another absolute, I kissed him softly, and said, "Let me help you," as he moaned when I tugged at my own clothing to remove it. Twisting under him, he sat up on his knees while I tossed my jacket, and removed my sweater and bra. Waiting in the darkness above me, Peter finally went for my jean zipper and tugged it, pulling my jeans with him, and then he paused.

Inhaling my scent deeply, I moaned at the intimacy I once knew.

Peter then took me like he was dying without me, and I let him. After Peter removed my underwear and inhaled my scent deeply, he moved over me and thrust into me deeply. He didn't prepare me, or wait like he always had before. Peter took what he needed and I gave it without speaking and without question to heal him.

"Sophie, you feel the same. I remember every single day how you felt around me, and you feel exactly the same. Oh, *god*...I can't keep doing this. It's just so hard to stay away from you all the time."

"Then don't," I begged.

Pausing for a moment, Peter held my face for a lifetime and breathed the words I hated. "I'm so sorry. But I have to."

With my soul screaming and my heart ripped from my cheat, I nodded my understanding. But I didn't understand. I didn't understand anything, and I didn't want to. I just couldn't accept us like this, versus the Peter and Sophie who had to be apart.

I didn't accept it, and I'd never understand it.

Crying silently, the tears spilled from my eyes, but I was able to hold in the sounds of my sadness. The tears poured down my temples onto the bed and my heart ached from the pain of his absence from my life.

Peter was lost and I could feel the distance so heavily between us, I could barely contain my shaking body.

I knew the heartbreak I was suffering in that moment was less still than the heartbreak without him, so I gave in and opened my body for his use.

I didn't speak and I didn't react to Peter inside me. I remembered the only other time Peter screwed me, the time against my door when he was destroyed by his grief for his dying uncle. I remember when he took me so suddenly, I gave freely because I knew he needed me. I knew then that I was the physical solace he needed from the emotional pain he was suffering. I knew, so I smiled and let him take his comfort from me.

I also knew this time was no different. There would be apologies, and promises for more later. There would be words of love and declarations of adoration between us. So I gave freely what he needed to take from me, because Peter wasn't suffering inside me, but he did suffer.

Whatever he was involved with had changed him and I was the only thing he could take into him to ease his burden. I was all he needed, and so I gave it to him again.

Once I understood what he was doing, I cried out in his reality, and wrapped my legs tightly around his back. I held onto his shoulders with my arms, and I pulled him heavier to me. I opened up my body and I let him take me as he needed, until minutes later he was done.

CHAPTER 37

With a deep groan, Peter came in me and dropped heavily on my body. He dropped on me as my breath left my lungs. He dropped on me and the desperation I felt was so consuming, I finally released the sobs from my chest.

A few minutes after he was complete, Peter pushed some stuff onto the floor with his arm, then collapsed next to me. Pulling me to him, he spooned me as he always did. Peter held me exactly the same as he used to in the night. That moment in his arms was exactly the same as countless we had shared before he left me, so I pretended *we* were the same together as we were before he left me.

I pretended Peter was the same, and slowly everything felt better inside me. My heart hurt less and my body shook less. I didn't quite feel the same sense of dread I had when I found Peter, and I could actually breathe a little easier in his arms.

Waiting for something, Peter finally spoke in our darkness. "I just need to rest for a few minutes with you in my arms, Sophie. I need to. I have to hold you again while I rest before I go back out there. I'm afraid this is our only chance. Okay?"

And choking, I asked all I could. "Why is this our last chance Peter? Please tell me."

"I think my partner betrayed me, and I think I'm in a lot of danger. I know others are after me, so I have to hide out for a few hours and gather my strength."

"But why are people after you? Why are you scared? Please tell me what's going on. Please, Peter. I've waited for so long to understand, and I'm dying without you, and it's killing me to not know what's happening. Please..." I begged, because that's all I could do.

"It's safer if I don't tell you details. But I will say I've been working a job for almost 10 months, and we're almost finished, and we've almost got everyone we were looking for, but something changed tonight. I was roughed up in an alley too close to my home, and I think it was a message. I think I'm in trouble this time, and when I saw you I just couldn't stop myself from seeing you one more time. I needed to be with you just one more time, in case-"

Shaking, I cried, "Oh, god... I don't know what any of this means. The last time because you're leaving me again? Or the last time because you're going to," but then I paused. Could I really ask what I was thinking? Could I actually say those words to the man I loved more than my own life? Could I really be thinking about his end in a way that was so shocking and unimaginable to me? Could I ask it?

"Sophie, I adore every single piece of you. I always have, and I always will. I'm sorry I was unkind to you when I left, and I'm sorry I hurt you 10 minutes ago. I knew what I was doing, but I didn't care because I just needed to feel you and touch you and be inside you again. I needed to feel you around me. But I'm sorry that that's the last memory you'll have of me. I'm really very sorry for that."

"It's okay..." I smiled into the darkness. And it was okay. Peter took me without me, but he was sorry, so everything dark inside me faded away with his apology.

"It's really not okay- I know that. And if we had more time, I would make love to you like you deserve and I would love you like you should be loved. But we don't have time, so all I can do is tell you that you are absolutely everything to me. You are the strongest, most beautiful person I have ever known, and in case I don't have the chance to say it again- I love you," he whispered as I cried softly.

I knew what he was doing. I knew he was saying goodbye again, because I knew he was leaving me again. My brain spun with the realization that Peter was in trouble and he might not make it out safely. I realized as crazy as that simple reality was, it was just that- Peter's reality. He was involved deeply in something I couldn't understand, and would probably never really know. So I needed him to know everything I could when I had the chance.

"You need to listen to me Peter," I said turning and climbing over his naked chest. "I need you to come back, and I need you to finish whatever this job is. I need you to be safe, and I want you to know I *will* wait," but when he tried to interrupt me I continued over him. "I'm going to wait, because I know we have something once in a lifetime. I know it, and so do you. So when I leave tonight or tomorrow morning, or whenever I have to go, know I'll be waiting for you."

"But I don't know when I'll be free to see you-"

"It doesn't matter. You are my forever. And just knowing that will give me the strength I need to wait for you. But you have to promise to come back. You have to promise you'll stay safe and finish this job. You have to promise me you'll come back, just like I'll promise to wait. Can you do that? Can you promise me you'll come back to me?" I begged Peter with everything I had. As my tears fell on his chest, and my body warmed with purpose, I begged him.

He couldn't see my face, but he could hear my voice. And I was never so sure of anything in my life. I would wait forever for him. I would wait forever for my forever with Peter.

When I was suddenly pulled down to his face he kissed me hard. He didn't kiss me like his usual sensual kiss of devotion, he kissed me like a pact, and like a promise. He kissed me like the forever he wanted to be.

"I'll come back, Sophie. I promise. I have to get in touch with my handler, then I'll know if my partner betrayed me."

"What's a handler?" I asked again confused by Peter's reality.

"Nothing. He's nothing you ever need to know about. Just know I'll be back to love you again. And you're right, I am your forever, Soph. I always was. I just couldn't stay when I wanted to, but I promise I'll be back," he said again in a near whisper against my lips.

After his words, I exhaled and dropped lower onto Peter, snuggling under his neck to just breathe him in.

A random thought struck me though and I suddenly giggled, totally disrupting our beautiful moment of promises and confessions. I giggled, even as Peter pinched my butt and asked, "What?"

"Um... I was just thinking about all the people I called *too much CSI watching TV Fucktards,* and I feel the need to apologize to everyone. I was pretty shocked by the people who thought you were an undercover cop. I *am* pretty shocked that people are actually undercover cops. It's just so weird, but kind of cool, I guess. I definitely owe Margaret and Terry some apologies," I giggled again. "But I guess I can't because that would be confirming it, right?"

"Um, right. Quite frankly, I may have to look into another line of work if I can't even hide my undercover status from 2 hippies in a health food store," Peter laughed under me.

And smiling against his chest, I whispered, "Please do..." as Peter hugged me a little tighter to his chest.

"I love you, Sophie Morley."

"I love you, too, Peter *Connor*?"

"Yes," he laughed. "I really am Peter Connor, just not quite the Peter you knew. But everything between us was real, and everything I was with you was really me, I promise."

"Okay. Should we go? Do you need to leave? I don't want to keep you from doing something, or interfere in whatever you're doing."

"I'm okay for an hour or so. But I want to get dressed before we lie with each other a little longer. I want to hold you right now because I'm not sure when I'll be back to get you. I'm not sure when I'll be in the clear."

So I nodded against him and embraced his hug as the only thing he could give me until he was free to give me everything.

After Peter and I made our oath to be together once again, we dressed quickly, looking everywhere for our discarded clothes. And once dressed, we snuggled in a beautiful silence wrapped around each other, until the whole world exploded around us in a barrage of light.

Literally.

CHAPTER 38

Gasping at the sudden light around us, I was tossed backward by Peter as I slammed into the wall. Screaming, I hit the wall until it knocked me silent. Scrambling against the wall as Peter pushed harder into me, I was absolutely blinded by light and panic.

I had never known such an intensity of fear in my life as I did in that moment. I was sure we had been found and I was sure we were dead.

Grabbing my leg and arm, Peter tossed me off the bed until scrambling to stand, he dragged my knees across the floor to a door in the corner. Dragging me, I cried out when he pulled my hair and arm, as I crawled as quickly as I could to the door. I scrambled, but ultimately I was dragged by Peter to the door and pushed inside.

Gasping for breath, I was still struggling just to understand the events of only one minute before. I couldn't understand how we went from laying together peacefully on a bed to me thrown and tossed about, injured and scared beyond anything I could even comprehend.

When Peter suddenly pulled me up into his arms and closed the door behind us, I knew I was looking at Peter at his worst. He was breathing hard and his eyes were darting all over the tiny washroom we ended up in. There was only a little light that escaped the doorway into the room, but it was enough to see his face. His hands shook as he held me and he didn't make eye contact with me even once. Peter was a mess and as the seconds slowly passed, he finally looked at me, and I could see he was someone else.

Peter was the ghostly version of himself from just hours before sitting on the sidewalk, swearing, and shaking, with eyes that no longer looked even blue. His pupils were so blown they swallowed up all the blue I had once loved.

"Don't say a word, Sophie," he whispered in my ear as he held a hand over my mouth. So nodding, I tried to show him I could be silent. "You distracted me," he said angrily as I shook in his grip. "All my weapons are downstairs. I fucking left them downstairs because I needed to be with you. Fuck! Okay... Don't fucking move, Sophie," he growled as he released the hand from my mouth, and loosened the tight hold he had around my chest.

Dropping me to the floor silently, Peter looked around frantically and I didn't dare speak. I was so scared, I suddenly understood the feeling of lightheadedness associated with true, blind panic in that moment. My mind was so wrapped up in what was going to happen, my body reacted on its own to what was actually happening.

"We're fucked, Sophie," he said softly as he kissed my forehead.

And I remember in that moment thinking about the word fuck and how Peter had said it more in the last 45 seconds of our life together than he had for the months we were actually together. I know it was illogical, but that's where my brain went in my confused desperation until he spoke again.

"I'm not going to make it out of here," he said simply as I gasped. "Oh, Sophie, I'm not. I'm so sorry, baby. But it doesn't matter. I want you to be safe. This is *my* job, so I'm ready to be taken, but I can't have you hurt. Never again. I want-"

Begging, I whispered, "Peter, please? We'll be fine. We just have-"

"Listen. To. Me. I'm going downstairs to see who entered. And then I'm going to cause a distraction. I'm going to fight for as long and as hard as I can, and then I'm going to yell your name so-"

"You can't-" but he spoke right over me again.

"I'm going to yell your name and I want you to run past me. Run as hard as you can. Run through the alley down to Cedar and flag anyone at all. Flag anything and get the fuck out of here. Can you do that?"

"No... I can't just run while you-"

"Are you ready to die for me? Are you, Sophie? Can you honestly say you're prepared to take a bullet in the head for me? Because that's what's-" But then we both froze.

A sound came right outside the little bathroom door, and my gasp was so loud, Peter jumped as he glared at me and covered my mouth quickly. Holding me to him, Peter stared me silent again, as he slowly removed his hand.

Mouthing, "I'm sorry, Sophie," my heart shattered in my chest. With another gasp I couldn't help, and a sob that tore from my chest, I was killing us quicker than I intended, but there was no helping it. I was destroyed in that moment with Peter.

Looking at Peter anxiously waiting with a hand on the bathroom door for whoever was coming, I was so numb to our end I felt lost.

Thinking quickly about my escape, I realized I didn't really want to. I knew it was insanity, but I didn't want to leave him alone to fight. My fight or flight had kicked in, and for the very first time in my life, I didn't want to flee. I wasn't going to leave the man who loved me alone, and I wasn't going to choose my needs over his.

For the very first time in my life, I was going to fight for the love I wanted instead of abandoning it.

So taking Peter's hand again, while listening to the sounds beyond our corner washroom, I whispered, "I love you," as I nodded at the door.

"Sophie. They might be cops sent by my partner. You can't, baby."

But I just nodded harder toward the door, and whispered again, "I love you," as Peter paused to stare at me before slowly nodding his head. Peter nodded and somehow I knew he had just agreed to our death sentences. He agreed to the end of us, and in a weird way I was resigned to our end.

I had one fleeting thought of my mom which quickly morphed into thinking of my beloved brother Steven, but somehow I hoped they would understand. I wasn't committing suicide, though agreeing to fight by Peter's side was an act of suicide nonetheless.

I was going to fight I decided, but I was suddenly out of time.

With a dramatic push, everything exploded around us again.

Peter was fighting before I even knew what was happening, and I was jumping through the doorway at one of the men before I could even reason our surroundings.

Fighting every fear I had, I tried to land a punch but was knocked right on my ass within seconds. Landing hard, the breath left my chest as I gasped, and my head spun with the pain of the assault. But I could hear Peter still.

Hearing Peter fight and yell and swear gave me a little strength. Trying to see what was happening, I managed to flip over to my stomach as I forced my legs beneath me to stand. Crouching on the floor, I had one more burst of energy to run or fight, so screaming I tried to engage in the fight for Peter and my life.

Like a warrior cry, I screamed into the brightness of the loft, even as a gunshot rang out around me, which signaled the end of us.

The gunshot effectively stopped my fight and Peter's agonized yell announced my end.

Dropping onto my butt, I lowered my head, placed my hands on the floor beside me, and I waited for the bullet in the head Peter had described.

Waiting, I never made eye contact and I didn't acknowledge my end in the slightest. Peter was dead, and I was next. I knew I was next, and other than maybe being raped again beforehand, I could think of nothing worse than knowing I was sitting feet from my dead forever.

But nothing happened.

I heard talking and noises, and more noises and more talking but I understood nothing. I felt like those sad victims who know they're about to be executed, but they sit up on their knees with their hands raised behind their heads waiting, because they know nothing is going to change the outcome. They just kneel knowing they're about to be killed and with a last moment of pride and defiance, they lower their head, whisper a quick prayer, and wait for the bullet to claim them.

I could think of nothing but Peter, and I could hear nothing but Peter's last agonized scream before he died. Over and over, I heard his last scream and then the deafening silence that surrounded us. I heard his scream and his silence as I waited.

But the bullet never came.

Eventually, sounds and voices permeated my brain, until I was roughly picked up and pushed against a wall. Moving as I was pushed, I didn't fight, or even try. There was nothing left to do.

When I was moved to the stairs, I finally lifted my head and was stunned still. Even as the arms holding my hands behind my back shoved me a little harder, I simply couldn't move. I was just too stunned to move.

Looking down the opened staircase of the loft I took in the scene before me. Looking, I tried to understand what I was seeing. Looking, I tried to grasp reality from delusion, but I was too lost to see it. I was surrounded by me, and I was shocked into a living nightmare.

Looking, every single inch of wall space were paintings of me, sketches, drawings, or my name splattered with paint. There were hundreds of me everywhere you looked. I was living in a freak show funhouse of myself, gasping and turning, as the arms behind me held me from falling down the stairs.

"Oh my god..." I moaned as I shook my head to clear it. I shook my head but nothing cleared. I was overwhelmed by the view in front of me. I was overwhelmed as I looked at everything Sophie Morley all around me.

From the colorful mess on the walls, to my name spelled with paint on the carpets, every surface was a mosaic of Sophie Morley. Even the wall beside the very stairs I stood still on had my name written upon its ascent in dark purple paint.

"What is this...?" I begged, but no one answered me as the world started spinning around me.

My chest began beating very hard and fast in my chest as my breathing turned ragged and labored. I could feel the irregular beats in my chest squeezing tighter and tighter until gasping, I moaned, "I can't breathe," to no one and everyone around me.

Suddenly leaning forward, I was sat hard and fast on the step I was stuck on as my hands were loosened. I was still held with a hard hand on my shoulder, but I felt nothing greater than the shaking my whole body suffered.

Words were spoken, and directions were given. But I heard and saw nothing.

When a man was suddenly kneeling in front of me, removing bloody gloves, my devastation was complete.

Gasping quickly, my body arched backward, smashing into someone else as I tried to reach for my own chest. Gasping for breath as each silent sob assaulted me, I could do nothing. There was nothing left in me. I was going to die I knew, and it was painful and terrifying. It was not a quick peaceful death in the night, and it was not an easy end with the man I loved.

It was hard and painful and so shocking in its intensity, I begged anyone to kill me. I begged them all to kill me. I begged the man before me and the man behind me. I begged as I tried to reach for my own chest. I begged to die as my eyes closed to my inevitable death.

The breaths in my body came too infrequently for any strength left and the pain was too unbearable to continue. I couldn't continue, so I closed my eyes and begged them all to kill me.

I didn't pass out for long though- just long enough to be moved down the stairs by someone until I opened my eyes again to me everywhere, which was so disorienting, I felt all the anxiety rise again inside me. And it was weird and nauseating, and simply overwhelming to see so much me all around me.

But I managed to ask anyone and no one specific, "Did they get Peter?"

"Who?" A woman asked but I couldn't answer. I didn't know if she meant who-Peter? Or who were they? I didn't know what I could say, and I didn't know what to do. I didn't even know if these were the very bad people who killed Peter.

And then it hit me. Peter was dead.

Crying out, I screamed his name as I gasped with the pain. I was lost in it. I was nothing more than a pain so intense, I couldn't see or feel or hear beyond it. The pain struck hard and fast and ripped the life from my soul.

Peter was dead.

And I was lost.

CHAPTER 39

I can't even describe the series of events that took place after Peter was killed.

I remember being in shock and screaming and crying forever until my fate was simply taken from my own hands. I was manhandled and fought, and taken, and eventually even sedated.

I was wrapped in my misery, fading in and out of life unsure of my own existence and unaware of my physical mortality. I was neither living nor dead. I was in a deranged purgatory with people all around me.

But I was no longer aware of anyone or anything other than my loss. My love was lost, never to be mine.

Eventually some speech permeated my fog when I found myself in a hospital once again. I was in another hospital, months after my rape and I was starting to listen to all the people.

I was waking from my sleeping fog and starting to try to hear the people around me. Finally one person stepped completely through the fog and I recognized her immediately.

Detective Dent walked to me and actually leaned down with a hip against my bed and slowly spoke my name. Reintroducing herself strangely, like I could possibly forget her, she spoke until certain words and broken sentences started to make a little sense.

Dent spoke to me until I finally decided to trust her. She spoke to me until the pain of my loss was just that- pain. It was no longer an acute agony distorting my reality.

Leaning forward in my bed, motioning with my head for her to come closer, Dent leaned in to me even as I felt the eyes around us watching, and then I whispered my reality to her.

"Peter was killed by police officers I think. He said his partner betrayed him, and he had to reach someone who handled him or something, and I was so scared, but Peter said he loved me forever, and then he fought them and was shot. And I'm not sure why I was left alive, and I don't know who to trust, and," I gulped hard, "I think I'm going to be killed, too. But I didn't see anyone or anything so I don't need to be killed," I begged with my eyes. "Do you think you could try to find out who his

boss is so you can tell him about Peter's partner?"
 And as I placed every hope I held left in her hands, Dent pulled away from me and gave such a twisted fake trying to be reassuring nod, I knew I had screwed up. I could see it all over her face. I could see she was involved, and I knew I was dead. The little smile she wore on her face filled me with the dread of my inevitability. She was in on it all, and I had fucked up.
 Knowing my reality I stopped talking, until frustrated by my lack of answers to all subsequent questions, Dent and the 2 other police officers finally left me alone in my room to mourn.

 I was then spoken to by a doctor and told I was free to leave as soon as the Police released me. My knees were cut and scrapped and I had a bruise on my cheek, but otherwise, because the obvious anxiety attack was over he said, the doctor felt no need to keep me.
 I was free to leave, and so I left. And it was exactly that easy.
 In a strange, calm world, unlike the TV shows I hated, I was not chased, and I wasn't forced to hide out and wait, watching around corners for the people to come get me. There was NO drama anywhere. I simply walked out of my semi-curtained room, opposite to a nurses' station, then down the hall to a group of hallways clearly laid out with diagrams and pictures to show me to the multiple exits, parking lots, and the city transit system entrance.
 I chose an exit that wasn't on a main street, but more the side street of basically a hospital block, and then I walked out the door. And once outside there was nothing to see and no one to hurt me. There was however a cab dropping off a horribly limping man.
 So walking over as casually as I could, quickly, but without looking rushed, I hopped in the backseat, closed the door behind me and told him my address while I thought of a plan.
 I thought about a plan until I really had no plan at all. The best I could come up with was grab clothes quickly, and take another cab across town until I could get some money from a bank machine while cabbing it somewhere else- probably to my brother's place to wait for him to help me get away from everything and everyone.
 So on autopilot, I waited for the cab to drop me off, scrounged up enough loose money from my pockets to pay him, and thought about my lost purse at Peter's safe-house. I simply blocked out the pain of Peter from my mind while I thought of my temporary escape.
 Running around my apartment frantically, I let the adrenaline sweep me

away. I allowed my body to push me forward through the fear and the haze of what I was doing and where I was going.

In my room, I grabbed clothes and tugged the suitcase from under my bed as quickly as possible. Filling it with everything I could, I needed to hurry.

Before I ran for my toiletries, I grabbed and stuffed the emergency Visa from my top drawer and the little bit of cash I always kept in the drawer in case I felt like Chinese delivery into a purse from my closet.

I rushed and hurried, and dumped all my makeup and hair crap in a little carry-on case, and then I emptied my medicine cabinet and left tugging the suitcase with the purse and carry-on over my shoulder.

I was ready, and I don't think I was more than 15 minutes in my apartment before the first knock sounded.

With a panic that crushed my chest, I heard the knock and gasped in the hallway unsure of what to do, or even how to move. I was struck stupid as the shaking took over my whole body.

"Sophie! Soph, it's me! Open up, girlie!" And as his voice swept over me, I almost threw up from the quick shift from panic to relief.

Ripping the door open, I screamed, "Steven!" as I grabbed him and pulled him awkwardly into my home. Falling into the wall with Steven, my body was acting strangely. It was like my body was drunk but my mind was clear.

"What the fuck, Soph?" Steven pushed at me as he tried to straighten against the wall.

"I can't tell you everything, but we have to go. Like *now*. I'm in a lot of trouble, and I think it's dangerous here. We have to go. Grab my suitcase," I yelled turning for my dropped purse and carry-on, but he didn't move.

To my unbelievable shock, Steven stood still against the wall and shook his head no. He even lifted his arm to block the door as I tried to push past him. Steven then gave me the look I knew from my brother that demanded more information.

"We have to go. Peter's dead," I said with a weird moan. "And I was there, and they'll probably come back for me, and I can't stay here anymore. Look, I think his partner betrayed him, and I think some police are in on it. I think the cops last night were sent to kill us, but somehow more showed up, so they couldn't hurt me." Frantically, I said as much as I could to get his attention in as little time as I had to explain.

"Listen to me Steven, we have to go, or I have to. Can I please use your car? Mine's at Pandora's and I need to get out of here. I have to. But I'll call you soon. Please?" I begged, but he just wouldn't move.

"Mom and dad were at the hospital waiting to see you when the doctors were finished. We've all been everywhere tonight trying to find you. The police are looking for you, and mom is going to hurt someone soon if she doesn't find you. So can you please just slow the fuck down for a second and explain what's going on. We're getting all these half-assed reports, and phone calls, and nothing makes any sense to us. So tell me, Soph, so I know how to help you," Steven said with his arm still blocking my escape.

Exhaling all my tension for a second, I tried to explain quickly again.

"Peter was in trouble with whatever case he was working on, and they got to him. Now I think they'll probably come for me, so I have to go. It's as simple as that. Oh! And I'm sure Detective Dent is in on it. She looked guilty as hell when I tried to confide in her, or like she knew I knew too much or something. So I think she's a dirty cop and I need to get away from-" but then I heard people suddenly outside my door, so I dove down the hall to my kitchen even as Steven chased behind me.

Smashing into the counter I grabbed a huge knife from the butcher's block and turned just in time to NOT stab my brother, but not in time to stop people from entering my apartment as they called my name.

I knew I was out of time, so grabbing Steven as hard as I could I spun him in a millisecond and placed the knife right across his throat, as I begged him to understand.

In a whisper against his ear, I shook on my tiptoes, and breathed the truth for my twin. "This isn't real. I would never hurt you, but I have to pretend to so I can get out of here. That's all this is, I promise," I said in less than a whisper as his head nodded only slightly in understanding against me. And I knew he understood because he stopped moving, and the tension and fight quickly left his body.

He was so much taller than me, I had to look around his shoulder to see past my kitchen doorway, but it was enough. The knife to his throat stopped Dent from moving any closer. It didn't stop my mom however from shoving past Dent as she stepped a foot into my kitchen.

Suddenly looking at my mom, I tried to plead with my eyes that she'd play along. I tried to give her a look that told her to keep up the charade so I could leave quickly. I wanted to beg my mom to hit Dent so I could get away, but I couldn't risk asking her in case Dent hurt my mom instead.

"Sophie, you need to sit with us for a minute. You need to come to the living room and talk to us," my mom tried to soothe, but I shook my head no.

"Sophie, Officer Lockley would like to talk to you for a minute," Dent tried, but I didn't know who the hell that was, so I had no interest.

"Officer Lockley knows Peter and wants to talk to you," Dent again tried, but she wasn't getting me so easily.

"I need to leave. I'm taking Steven with me to the door, and then I'm leaving," I pushed as Steven walked a step forward without me even trying to make him move.

As we moved my mom and Dent backed up into my dining room, and Steven and I walked a little forward, kind of sideways, trying to make it out of my kitchen. We shuffled slowly while I watched Dent's face and body the whole time to see if she'd try to hurt me. We shuffled against each other and I was suddenly struck with the realization that Steven was completely relaxed, but *my* body was shaking uncontrollably.

While we walked, Steven placed his left hand against the outside of my left thigh and squeezed it to give me strength. It's like he knew my body and mind were fading, so he held the outside of my thigh to give me a little more support as we moved past our mom and Dent, past the dining room, and into the open hallway for the front door.

But it all ended as quickly as it began.

I was grabbed hard around my waist by someone hiding against the front door, and my wrist was nearly broken as I cried out in pain and smashed my head back against a chest. I was lifted like I always hated, and I was pulled away from my brother as I desperately reached for him. I was pulled away from my brother as I screamed his name and tried to fight the arms around me, but it was too late.

Quickly I was spun as my cheek landed hard against the wall near the door. I was smashed against the wall as the breath left my lungs in a whoosh, and my brain stopped for a second in pain. I was stuck with a huge body behind me crushing me to the wall. So I stopped fighting everything.

Trying to gasp air back into my lungs, I dropped my arms from the arms around my waist, and I bowed my head a little against the wall. I stopped because I had again lost.

"Sophie? Do you remember me?" He asked and I didn't know what to do. I was still pressed hard against the wall, with my mom crying near me and my brother panting close to me, I could hear.

I was still pushed against the wall until I was quickly turned to a face I vaguely recognized but couldn't remember. I knew him but I didn't know how I knew him.

"I'm David Lockley. Do you remember me, Sophie?" But I shook my head no. "You met me at a party for the Connor family last March. I'm Carrie's husband, David. Do you remember when we met?" Looking at him, I suddenly recognized him as the brother-in-law Peter didn't like.

So gasping once more, I croaked all I could. "Yes, I remember you. Did you shoot Peter?" I asked with venom dripping from my mouth.

After an initial moment of shock, he seemed to answer as best as he could though. "No. I would never hurt Peter. I've known him for years, and we've been family for 8 years," he said looking truthful. But it didn't matter because I couldn't trust anyone anymore.

"Do you know who killed him?" I asked as he flinched.

David looked at me for a moment, like he was in pain himself. And shaking his head, he actually whispered, "Peter isn't dead, Sophie. He was wounded in the leg, but he's very much alive. He's in Mercy right now recovering from the gunshot wound," he said as I stared numbly at him.

Stunned is an understatement, and shock held nothing to how I actually felt. I was beyond confused and shaken so heavily, my body simple closed in on itself.

"I don't understand," I managed to whisper before landing on my knees as David grabbed me under my arms and my mom dove for me. My brother grabbed me from David, and like a goddamn doll I was lifted right over the back of my couch to fall in a heap upon it.

Gasping, I shook my head as a strange moan rumbled from my chest.

"I don't understand," I choked out before a wave of nausea threatened to take me. "I heard him stop," I gagged.

I remember the feeling I had of being completely sure of myself, but desperate to believe in that one moment what David was saying. I was so conflicted, I didn't even know how to function.

But before I could even think what to do, Steven was beside me taking my hand and David was kneeling in front of me on the carpet.

Closing my eyes, I could only breathe. There was so much chaos in my head, and so many emotions battling my chest, I could do nothing but breathe as I fought the nausea and the collapse that threatened to take me.

"Sophie. What did Peter tell you was happening? Do you know what he was doing?" David asked gently, as Steven rested his arm behind my back for support.

"Um..." But I didn't know what to say. I knew he was working a job, but I didn't know who I could trust.

Suddenly panicking, I whipped my head to my left, and saw Dent still standing right behind my mom. Afraid Dent might hurt her, I again tried to tell my mom with my eyes to come closer. I tried, but she didn't understand my look.

"What is it, baby?" My mom asked quietly.

"Can you come here? Please?" I begged as she jolted and moved toward me immediately. Dent then stood only 4 feet from us, but it was enough to give me a little relief.

So turning back to David I took a chance. Whispering, I asked, "Can we talk privately? Without her?" I nodded slightly to Dent. "I need to talk to you alone," I begged with my eyes.

I didn't know if he understood or not, but he did seem to understand my intent not to speak in front of Dent, so exhaling, he asked her to please wait outside.

I don't know what she asked him. And I don't know what she said because I was just so afraid of everything in that moment I tuned everything out but my own breathing.

I still didn't know if I could trust David, but knowing he at least knew Peter helped a little. So when he leaned back toward me, and I felt Steven's hand against my back urge me a little I finally just spoke.

"I don't know exactly what Peter was doing, but I think he was set up," I confessed with a big exhale. "I might even be in trouble if whoever he was investigating thinks I saw something or know something. I don't know what's happening, but last night was insane."

Nodding, David asked what I knew he would ask. "Did Peter tell you what he was doing?"

"No. I don't know anything. I just saw him yesterday when he was trying to get away from them, and he was limping, and he needed my help getting away from them, so I helped him. But he didn't tell me anything except he was roughed up too close to home, and he thinks his partner set him up. That's all I know. And then we were at his safe house and we were alone and we-" but I blushed before I told anymore. "Anyway, then Peter and I were attacked and I thought he was dead because no one told me he wasn't dead, so I didn't know. Is he really alive?" I whispered.

"Yes, Peter's fine, I promise. What else did he tell you? I need to know to help him," he seemed to beg me. And looking at his eyes finally, I noticed David seemed legitimately upset by this whole situation.

"Are you going to help him?" I cried softly.

Sitting there I was suddenly just exhausted. I was shaken, and I had experienced too much shit for too long to maintain my strength.

"I'm so tired from all this fear, and I need to know he's going to be helped. He said he needed to reach the man who handled him. Do you know who that is?"

"His *handler*?" David asked with surprise as I nodded. "What else did Peter tell you?"

"Are you going to help him?" Then it hit me that I was trusting a man Peter didn't like, so I asked the obvious question. "Why doesn't Peter like you?"

Again, David looked a little surprised, but I swear I saw hurt or upset wash across his face as well while I waited for his answer.

"Peter does like me. He's my brother-in-law and my friend. We've been friends for longer than Carrie and I have been together, and I've always been close to Peter. He just has a hard time separating the past from the present sometimes, and it comes across like he doesn't like me. That's all there is between Peter and I- a past," he said so sadly, I had to ask.

"What about his past? What's between you?"

"I'll tell you everything if you want, but I need to know what else happened yesterday so I can help Peter. Please, Sophie? You were the only one there yesterday and I need all the details so I can help him," he pressed me again, but there was nothing else I could give.

"I told you everything. I found Peter on the sidewalk looking hurt and messed up, and he asked me for help, and he told me he was being sought after, and I helped him walk forever until we ended up in his safe-house and-"

"His safe-house?" David asked me again surprised.

"Yes, where we were found. Peter said it's his emergency safe-house and no one knows about it but his partner, and then people were there which confirmed his partner must have betrayed him, but that's all I know. I was in the hospital for shock after Peter was shot, and then I left to come here. I'm trying to get away before I get hurt, too. Um, will you help me?" I suddenly begged.

"Sophie, what else do you know about what Peter was doing?"

LOST

"Nothing! That's it. Everyone knows he's an undercover cop, but not what he's actually doing. I know nothing," I insisted, almost begging him to believe me.

"What else has Peter told you about his past?"

"Nothing," I moaned embarrassed. "I know about his ex-finance who's married, and about his schooling, and about his job at the 'steel company'," I said using quotes. "I know he's a very talented artist but he's hidden and working and basically he has a double life which drove us apart for whatever reason. I guess because of my safety or something Peter couldn't be with me when he was on a case because of the danger involved. But that's it. Until yesterday, I had only seen him twice since he left me. Once in the street for a split second in December, and once in February for a few hours at my place," I remembered with a little cry.

I remember my mother squeezing my hand at that point like she must have always known Peter had come to see me after I was raped. She had to have known because I *recovered* too quickly for a rape victim. But I didn't recover, I just healed a little faster because of Peter's visit. I healed a little after Peter's visit because all the bad was loved out of my apartment by him.

When David suddenly exhaled, I watched him closely. Turning, he stood from his knees and grabbed a chair from my dining room like he needed the moment to compose himself. He walked slowly and shook his head more than once while he walked back and placed the chair in front of me. Shaking his head again, David slumped down into the chair and exhaled again loudly in the silence of my living room.

Waiting, I felt my brothers arm tense up behind me, and I felt the sweat between my mom's hand and my own.

I was nervous as hell at what David was going to say about Peter, but I needed to know so I could maybe help him with his investigation. I needed to help Peter however I could so he would be free from the case that had caused him to look terrible, get shot, and seem defeated.

Peter seemed almost resigned to the fact that the case was going to kill him, and I couldn't stand to see him hurt.

"I'll do anything to help him with this case, David. Just tell me what I need to do to help him finish up so he can be safe again," I whispered another absolute to everyone in the room.

Nodding, David took another moment that dragged out forever as my body was losing the fight against the shakes and the exhaustion that was quickly devouring me.

CHAPTER 40

David waited after my question, looking like he wasn't sure how much information about Peter's case he should tell me, until he finally did speak.

"Sophie... Peter isn't a cop. He's a paranoid schizophrenic," he said and paused. Almost like he understood I didn't know what the hell he was saying, he paused as I stared at him.

"Do you understand me?" He asked but continued past my pause. "Peter is a paranoid schizophrenic and he's having an acute episode right now. He's been missing off and on for a few months from his residence, and he no longer has a grip on reality. Right now, he's lost," David said while visibly choking up.

I knew I heard him, but I didn't hear him at all. Nothing he said made any sense, and everything he said was bullshit. For a moment I just stared at the stranger in front of me and I wanted to both laugh at him and punch him in the face.

I was stunned beyond words. But my mom wasn't. In classic Mama-Bear fashion, my mom voiced exactly what I was thinking.

"What the *fuck* are you talking about?!" My mom yelled as I jumped from the sudden chaos of sound, and then laughed at the absurdity of our situation.

"Peter has been a diagnosed paranoid schizophrenic since he was 23 years old. After a terrible car accident which either triggered the onset of the schizophrenia, or was the pre courser, we don't know. But after the accident while he was trying to recover, he was just never the same. Sophie, I know this is a lot to take in but I'm telling you the truth. Peter is-"

"You're *lying*," I growled low in my throat.

"I'm not lying. Carrie and Kara can be here in minutes if you want, and they'll tell you anything you want to know. They've been caring for Peter for almost 9 years, and they know everything about schizophrenia you could ever want to know. I just have to call-"

"You're a fucking liar!" I screamed. Catching my breath, I was stunned. I was whatever is *beyond* stunned. I was so far gone, there simply were no words to describe me in that moment.

"Peter has very good lucid times, for many months at a time. He seems normal and almost healthy, but then he stops taking his meds, and he gets really sick again. He can't function or control his impulses, or even really stop his behavior. Peter has been living in a halfway house for the better part of the last 4 years and overall he's doing really well. But then he has these episodes and he can't get better until he is physically forced to. He is usually hospitalized for a few weeks until the schizophrenia is medically controlled again and then he is placed back in the residence until another uncontrollable episode occurs," David continued speaking quickly. Almost like if he was quick I wouldn't stop him or laugh at him or even just lose my mind with all this crazy that was choking me from the inside out.

"Peter stopped taking his medication again last year just before he broke up with you and Kara and Carrie knew he was getting bad again."

"Was that the fight at the party?"

"Yes. They knew he was losing it again because he was starting to mumble and talk to himself again, and Kara visited him the day before at his residence to talk about their uncle and she knew he was getting sick again. Not that he isn't always sick, but when he's lucid, sometimes it's almost easy to forget he's actually a ticking time bomb waiting for the next episode to make him really sick again. But Kara knew and was trying to get him help, and trying to keep you away from it all, and trying to keep you both safe but he-"

"Peter never would've hurt me," I moaned as I felt the first tears slide down my cheeks. I felt them and that's when I realized I was starting to believe David a little. I was starting to believe his unbelievable story because I was no longer ready to rip his face off. Instead, I was crying from the warped reality I was slowly facing.

"You don't know that. Peter isn't himself when-"

"I DO know that. He never once hurt me," I said but then jolted in my own skin. Remembering the time he lost it when I took too long getting coffee, I knew I was afraid of him physically that day. I knew the way he tossed me around he could hurt me, but then he never acted like that again, so I let it go until I forgot about it totally.

"What are you thinking about? Did Peter ever hurt you?" David asked.

"No..."

"Sophie, you're moaning and staring off like something happened," my mom pushed.

"It's nothing. Um..." Turning back to David I was trying so hard to except what I was hearing, but I was losing the battle between listening and shutting down.

"Ask me anything, Sophie. Peter's in a lot of trouble, legally, though I think most of the guys involved in yesterday's altercation will go lightly on him, I know charges are still going to be pressed, and I know Peter will have to spend some time in a facility. But I'll try-"

"How did he know so much police stuff. Like how did he actually hide he was sick but convince me and other people he was a cop. Isn't that weird? How couldn't I know?" I asked the question I was dying to understand.

How could I not know the man I absolutely loved beyond all reason was mentally ill? How could I essentially live with a man for 3 months but not see he was sick? How could he hide it so well from me?

I then wondered if he did hide it well from me at all. Maybe I just loved him so much I didn't want to see anything wrong with him. Or maybe I couldn't believe he wasn't what I wanted because he was everything I wanted so much.

Maybe I was the delusional, schizophrenic one I though which made me laugh. Just a little laugh, nothing insane or scary. Just a laugh of complete confusion.

"Sophie," my mom said gently like she was trying to pull me back again.

"Um, I'm a cop, and Peter was going to be a cop too before he got sick, and he's obsessed with cop shows and documentaries, and-"

That was it. Bursting out into a real, loud, horrifying laugh, I couldn't stop myself.

"Oh my *god!* He's a too much TV watching Fucktard!" I yelled as my previously silent brother burst out laughing with me. To my mom and David's horror, Steven and I laughed like crazy people in front of two people who thought we were crazy.

Laughing, of course, slowly turned into sobbing. Like every movie scene I've ever witnessed, my laughter faded to a snotty-nosed, throat drying sobbing that consumed me.

Crying, I let everything David said take me away from the life I had wanted with Peter.

Crying for the thousandth time since the day I met him, I was finally truly tired of my life and Peter's involvement in it.

After giving me the time and space needed to come back down, David continued sitting in the chair and my mom stayed silent beside me. Steven was no longer laughing, and the return of silence cleared out my mind a little.

"Does everyone know? Like all his friends? Because I know they don't know at Sunshine and Life, so..." But I lost my question. What I really wanted to have was confirmation that I wasn't some psycho, delusional loser who wanted to be adored so badly, I couldn't see any issues in front of my own face.

"Peter has no friends, Sophie. Well, other than Kara, Kara's husband Dylan, Carrie, and I."

"Yes, he does. He has Cam who he plays in a band with and his wife Emily, and even his ex-girlfriend Patricia and her husband, and I think he mentioned a Dave... Oh! Is that you?"

But David stayed silent. Staring at his face, I actually saw a look of sadness wash over him, and I couldn't believe what I was seeing. It was the kind of tangible sadness on his face that I knew intimately.

"Yes, I'm Dave," he choked. With tears filling his eyes, David continued. "Patricia Cooper, Cam Donaldson and Emily Tyler died in a car accident that Peter and I survived when we were 23. It was awful, and I was the least hurt, followed by Peter because we were in the front seats, but Emily, Cam and Peter's fiancé Patricia were all in the back-" I gasped out loud as he finished. "But they were killed nearly instantly when we were crushed by a truck that hit us from behind."

Crying out I tried to understand. "But he said-"

"Peter always has a story about how he and Patricia broke up. It's like he imagines a different ending for them than the sad reality of it. And of course he suffered survivor's guilt, like I did, but then he changed and the schizophrenia became apparent, and Peter says whatever he wants about their deaths, because nobody wants to remember how they really died..." He said again with so much sadness I suddenly felt like I needed to comfort him a little.

"Peter was devastated over the accident while he recovered from his injuries. He got a tattoo for Patricia, and seemed so depressed afterward and nobody could help him, but it was most likely the onset of the schizophrenia making him seem so out or it, or depressed, or just awful after the accident."

"The tattoo on his arm... P.C."

"Patricia Cooper."

"I thought... Oh, it wasn't his initials like I thought," I moaned to another long, sad silence.

"What about his pink car?" Steven asked unemotionally, like he was trying to change the subject for us.

"That's Kara's, obviously," he grinned. Though I had only met her twice, somehow even I understood the grin. Kara seems like she'd have a hot pink car. "Peter steals it sometimes. Did he when you were together?" He asked as I nodded.

"But he has a house...?"

"Actually, he *had* a house. He bought it only a few months before the accident when we were 23, and he was so proud of himself. So after he was diagnosed, Kara lived in the house with him for a few years while he was in and out of the hospital, but then she met Dylan, and they wanted to get married. So Kara begged Peter to understand that she wanted to buy a different house with Dylan, and Peter was lucid enough at the time to understand, but he was very sad about selling it. He's never really been able to let that house go. We've even had to put a restraining order in effect, so Peter wouldn't go there all the time, but we know he still goes way too frequently for the current owner," David said with a little frustration.

"Um, how could he spend so much time with me? We were together nearly every day for over for 3 months." That question stumped me totally.

"Well, when Peter's schizophrenia is controlled they loosen the reins a little at his residence. Plus, he always visits Carrie and me, and Kara, and even his parents for overnights, so his curfew is rarely monitored. And he's been sick for a long time, so unless the staff psychiatrist deems him unwell, or slipping back into an episode, Peter is free to come and go as he pleases before the 10:00 curfew."

"But every day?" I asked still surprised by the lack of security or something for a paranoid schizophrenic.

"No, not every day, but it is a semi-voluntary residence, where patients sign up for the rules and medical evaluations, and inevitable treatment they may need when their sickness is acute, only when they're lucid. So basically, when Peter is aware of what's going on, and taking his medication as prescribed, he's given the freedom to come and go. But because he signed all the forms required for his psych evaluations 3 times a week, he is also offered a relative safety net in case he suffers another acute episode."

"But we went away twice for the weekend when we were together."

"He probably lied and said he was going to Kara's or his parents for the weekend, so he was granted a 3 day pass. Schizophrenia isn't treated like it used to be, Sophie. Schizophrenics aren't subjected to hospital stays, or even to being committed against their will. The Psychiatric community has changed their views on schizophrenia and actually treat it as more of an affliction, with outside services and family intervention to allow the Schizophrenic to have as normal a life as possible."

"But when he would go to work he-"

"He landscapes for Kara's husband, but he stopped for a while to spend his days with you I assume. And then he really became sick last year and-"

"I don't understand. He can go out whenever he wants and it's just, I don't know..."

"It works, Sophie. Well, until the last year and a half it worked. Peter would even stay with us or at Kara's when he was well for a while, and then he'd go back himself when the *voices* started talking again as he put it. But he was really sick last year, then got better, then really sick again this February, and that's basically the last any of us really saw of him. But we looked everywhere. Trust me."

"For almost 2 months? But you're a cop," I said stupidly.

Nodding yes, David exhaled hard again while staring at me. "I *am* a cop, so it was very hard for me not being able to find him. My captain knows all about Peter, and even my buddies on the force know him, so believe me, everyone I know was looking, but we just couldn't find him. It's like he vanished until he triggered the alarm in my garage. He simply vanished after he heard about you in February," he said then stopped abruptly.

Actually everything stopped with his words. My mom's hand stopped soothing mine, and I think Steven just stopped breathing altogether.

The room was silent and so still, I waited for anything to release me from the stillness I was drowning in.

"You *told* him I was raped?" I croaked.

"No," he said shaking his head again. "But I did tell his staff psychiatrist when I found out, and we assume Peter read over his own file one afternoon when he was alone for his evaluation. I guess he played it cool throughout the exam, but bolted from the residency immediately afterward. And I'm assuming that's when you saw him in February?" He asked to my silent tears as I nodded.

"Why didn't you tell anyone about Peter? I don't understand why Dent and Dolby were looking for Peter but you didn't tell them who he was. Or did you? Did they always know who Peter was?"

"No. Your assault was obviously posted on the bulletin board at our precinct and I recognized your picture. But I didn't tell Dolby I knew who you were and I didn't tell Peter what happened to you. I didn't even tell Carrie. I thought it was safer for Peter *and* you to stay quiet, and I only told his resident Psychiatrist, so he was prepared in case Peter ever found out, which he did. And again, I assume that's when he went to see you in February?"

"Yes, he came to me to help me get better," I cried again.

At that point I was truly, and completely done. I didn't have any tears left, and I wasn't capable of thinking or feeling any more. The last 2 days had stretched out to years for me, and I was so done, I needed to sleep. I needed to sleep for a week before I could even attempt to deal with every emotion I had crushing my chest and blowing my mind.

I needed to sleep until I could function and only then could I deal with Peter.

"There's one more thing, Sophie," David said quietly, and as I blew out a hard breath I remember thinking, *of course there is.* 'Cause this shit couldn't possibly be over for me.

"The man who raped you was also a resident at Gravenhearst with Peter," and as I screamed a little in shock and frustration, my mother stood quickly, grabbing me up in her arms.

"Enough! Just leave her alone for now, okay? She doesn't need to hear any more of all this shit, and neither do I! Just let her deal with one bombshell at a time, okay?!" My mom yelled at David while I shook in her arms.

"I wanted her to know so she wasn't surprised later. I thought it best to tell her everything now, so she could deal with it all at once," David said sounded honestly saddened by the circumstances. "Sophie, this is the last thing, I promise. Detective Dent knew about Peter from me, but not that he was *your* Peter. And when she told me about Gravenhearst when they picked up McGregor, I knew what was going on. I knew he knew Peter so after Dent and I talked a little, she asked McGregor a few more questions, and he confessed to everything. He took a key of yours from Peter, and he hurt you because he's insane and he thought he wanted what Peter loved so much. He wasn't trying-"

"ENOUGH! Holy *shit*! Enough. Give her a fucking break," my mom yelled again.

Moaning, I was done. "He didn't use the window, then? He used Peter's key." Shaking uncontrollably, I so was devastated, I said all I could. "Thank you for telling me everything. But I really have to sleep now. I have to or I'm going to die I think."

"Soph," Steven moaned.

"No, Steven. I'm done. I have to sleep. Thank you David, and maybe I'll see you some other time, but-"

"Sophie, you have to give an official report of everything that happened yesterday, and I can't be there. Detective Dent isn't assigned to this case, but she's offered to be with you because we thought you might be more comfortable with her, since you-"

"Okay. That sounds good. Please? Please let me go now," I begged even as my mom hugged me tighter.

"I'm so sorry, Sophie. Kara and Carrie and all of us are just so sorry any of this happened to you."

"I'm not," I said as my mom stiffened against me. "Sorry, mom. But I'm still not. I love him even though everything is totally fucked up," I cried as I pulled away from her.

Without even looking back, I walked to my bedroom and just collapsed on my bed. I didn't cry and I didn't look at my paintings. For the first time since I had found them months prior, I didn't look at my beautiful paintings before I fell asleep. I couldn't. I had no strength to even keep my eyes open for one fleeting second.

I was so lost in my confusion and despair, my body simply shut down on me.

CHAPTER 41

The following morning, after she slept on my couch, my mom woke me and told me we had to go to the police station to make a report.

With little drama and with questions answered as calmly and accurately as possible, I put in my time, explaining the events as I knew them 'for the record'.

When I had finished my statement and answered all questions, I learned that the police had decided they weren't going to lay charges against me for my involvement in the altercation with Peter. I also learned they had every right to do so.

I remember hearing from the Interviewing Officer I *wasn't* going to be charged, and I was so confused I asked, "Why would I be charged? What did *I* do?"

"Ms. Morley, you assaulted a police officer, resisted arrest and-"

"But I thought they were going to kill us! I thought Peter and I were going to be killed, and he was going to die, and-" but I choked up before finishing, while the Officer waited a moment in silence for me to get it together again.

"Ms. Morley, that is exactly why you are *not* being charged. Officer Lockley and Officer Dent have both given a sworn statement as to your involvement with Peter Connor. And they have each sworn that your involvement in the altercation was accidental, and manipulated in such a way as to make you believe you were in fact defending yourself. Also, we've learned that though the Officers involved did announce their presence, you were under the assumption that the police themselves were there to cause you bodily harm, therefore, you again believed you were only defending yourself. Am I correct?"

"Yes..." I admitted. "I think I only hit one guy, once. But I don't really remember resisting arrest though. What about what I did to my brother?"

"What did you do to your brother?" He asked somewhat kindly.

Thankfully though, I was coherent enough to shut my mouth. If the police didn't know about that, I sure as hell wasn't going to tell them.

"Ms. Morley, go home. As far as the Police are concerned your involvement is over. You were a victim of Mr. Connor's delusions, and we don't want to further victimize you by pressing charges, or by keeping you involved with the investigation any longer than is absolutely necessary. We have your statement, collaborated by the Officers involved, and even by Mr. Connor himself, so you're free to leave. Ms. Morley, this is over for you now. Go home," he again said almost kindly.

Nodding, I smiled at him, stood up with a little thank you and made my way out the door.

I was *not* free, and this would never be over for me, but at least I wouldn't have a criminal record I thought while giggling a little as I left.

After the interview, my mom and I were ready to leave, but I had one final request of David who was waiting in the hallway for me to finish. I didn't know why he was waiting for me but I took the opportunity offered and ran with it.

Looking at David, I begged him to take me to Peter. I begged him even as my mom protested beside me, and David told me it was impossible under the circumstances. David explained immediate family could only see him under police supervision, and in one final push of insanity, I argued I *was* family.

In the hallway of the police station in front of my worried and exhausted mother, and to a man I barely knew but felt kind of friends with, I begged him to let me see the man I loved.

Actually, I think I said, "Please let me see Peter because he was supposed to be my forever, and I have to see him so I can finally say goodbye," which was a little dramatic and over the top, but it really was the truth as I felt it.

I needed to see Peter one last time before I could let him go, and David reluctantly agreed to take me to him.

Entering the hospital escorted by Carrie's husband David and my mom, was weird, but I felt nothing. I was like the walking dead going to face Peter.

I didn't know how I even felt anymore. I didn't know what I felt or even what I really was anymore. I didn't feel like the old Sophie Morley or one of her many incarnations of the last 16 months, nor did I feel like the

LOST

Sophie of even 12 hours before.
 I was weightless and powerless and confused, and just lost.
 The absolute shift to my reality caused an emotional imbalance and a feeling of hopelessness deep inside me. I felt scared and desperate, and just hollow inside.

 When we arrived at the door to Peter's room, I think I begged to see him alone. I seem to recall being told it wasn't protocol, and I think my mom jumped in again with something like, "Is *any* of this protocol?"
 I think I remember even laughing for a split second at my Mom's Mama-Bear Syndrome which effectively shut up the police and scared them into bypassing the protocol they chose to ignore.
 I was told about keeping my physical distance, and not interfering in his care at all. I was told I would be removed immediately if I aided Peter at all with escape or with his binds. I was also told someone would be checking up on us regularly so not to 'get any ideas'.
 Then it was time.
 Holding my breath, my mom put a comforting hand on my back, pushed open the door for me and then held back in the hallway as I stepped a foot forward.

*****

 I walked forward slowly while taking in my surroundings quickly. And everything was just so sad.
 The room was quiet but for the machinery beeping, and everything was pushed against the walls. There was nothing of significance available to the one thing I was immediately drawn to.
 Peter.
 On a typical hospital bed of white, with his head turned to the opposite side of the room, he faced away from me as I took him in.
 Lying lifeless and alone, Peter looked like an angel in his bed of white.
 He was still and silent, and he seemed to glow in the otherwise fairly empty room.
 He seemed to glow, like he always had for me. Beautiful and charismatic and enchanting with an otherworldly calm about him.

And I was totally broken staring at him.

I couldn't move and I couldn't advance. I was stuck in the love I had for the beautiful angel on the bed of white.

"Sophie... You came," he whispered as I cried out. Crying, my heart was ripped from my chest by the sad sound of his little voice.

"Hi Peter..."

"Can you move closer? I can't hurt to you. I'm tied down," he said so sadly, I felt a moment of outrage turned quickly to anxiety for him. I thought about what it must feel like to be tied down, and I imagined what he felt like to be forced to be still.

"Sophie?"

Shaking my head, I tried to calm myself before I spoke. I knew he would know I was devastated by my voice, so I tried to cover up my sadness.

"I'm here, Peter. And I know you wouldn't hurt me. Um, how are you?" I asked like everyone asks when struggling with something greater than they have the ability to understand. It's like in asking, we hope they don't actually tell us the whole truth, but just enough to give us an idea, while giving them the feeling of being cared for because we asked.

"Nothing between us was ever not real, baby," Peter whispered.

He whispered and he answered the unspoken question I was dying to ask as a shiver passed through my whole body. He answered like he always knew I would wonder and question his love. He answered like it was important for me to know, and it was.

"When I was healthy you were everything to me. And even when I wasn't okay, you were still everything, but it was just so hard," he continued to whisper with tears in his voice. "I always wanted to be okay with you, and I tried so hard, Sophie..."

And that was it. Crossing the room I needed him to see me and know.

Moving to the other side of the bed, I was stunned to see him looking like he looked when he was with me. The nasty beard was shaved off, and he looked clean. He looked just like the man I loved, but I could see he wasn't really. There was still a strangeness to his darkened blue eyes, and he looked too pale and too tired to be my old Peter. Then again, as I looked at him and tried to find all the words I needed to say, I realized he *had* been shot only 2 nights before, so he probably would look different even if the truth wasn't known.

Seeing a chair a few feet away, I picked it up and moved as close to Peter as I could. I wanted to touch him and I needed to comfort him, but I didn't know how he would react to touch.

Moving his eyes to my face, Peter moaned. As tears slid from his eyes, he seemed to struggle with getting comfortable in his bed, while struggling to still look at my face.

"You're so beautiful, baby. You look like an angel sitting there," and I laughed a sad laugh of knowing as I interrupted him.

"I was just thinking the same thing about you. When I walked in the room and saw you lying there in the white sheets, I thought you looked like an angel to me."

"I'm sorry for all this. I tried so hard, Sophie," he whispered again.

"I know. It's okay, Peter."

"It's not okay. I know I hurt you and I'm trying to understand what I did and what happened and Carrie told me a little about what happened at the loft and I'm so sorry. But now that I'm on the meds I'm a little bit clearer about everything. I'm still not good with the details when I'm out of it, but I understand a little more now. It's just so hard," he choked.

Reaching for him, I tried to take the hand I saw strapped down against the rail. I tried to take his hand, but when he inhaled sharply I was afraid, so I stopped my movement as quickly as I reached for him.

"No! Please hold my hand. I didn't think you'd want-"

"I always want to hold you," I whispered, silencing us both as he cried harder. "Tell me what's going on. I know the reason now, but what actually happened to you?" I pleaded.

"Um... When I'm on the medication I'm pretty lucid for long periods of time. I function pretty well, and I can keep myself together really well, but then I guess I think I'm okay, or all better and I stop taking the medicine and then I turn back to sick so quickly, I don't know it really happens until someone steps in again and forces me back on the meds. It's a strange back and forth, sick and not sick way I live that gives me a false sense of security until I go off the medication and get *really* sick. But," he stopped suddenly.

Prompting him to continue, I sat closer and brushed a hand across his cheek, as his eyes closed and his body shuddered at the contact between us.

"I loved you- *love* you so much, and I was doing really well. I was on the medication almost the whole time, but then I started getting the feeling like I was all better again- better because of you, so I went off it, and that's when I started getting bad again. Near the end, I was struggling all the time, but hiding it from you because I wanted you to just love me-"

"I did love you," I confessed.

"I know, but you loved the lucid, not sick me, and I was always afraid of being the other me, until I screwed up and stopped the meds making me not me anymore. But then I get confused and think I can do it on my own, which I can't and I get worse and worse. The voices get so loud in my head, and I try so hard to block them out with other things, like different herbs and sedatives, and the last time I used you to help them go away. It was like I could wrap you in my head and say your name over and over again until your name became a chant or something that helped to dull the other voices but then they never really go away and then they get louder and I get so tired, and then I can't really stop the sickness from getting me fully. Then I'm not me anymore. And then I'm not me anymore, at all. It's just like I'm not me anymore," he said rambling while looking like he was struggling again as the tears began pouring down his temple and across the bridge of his nose with his head tilted toward me.

Wiping away his tears, I tried to comfort him with a weird soothing, like cooing sound, as my thumbs brushed the tears from his face.

"You sound so lucid right now," I whispered in the room as he nodded.

"I know and that's the problem. I *am* lucid right now and I will be as long as I stay medicated, but I never stay medicated, so I get sick again."

"But what if I force you to take the medication every day?" I suddenly thought out loud.

"It doesn't work that way. I take it for a while until I feel totally rational again and then I stop it so-"

"But what if I force you to take it every day?"

"I always find a way to trick people into thinking I'm taking it," he shook his head in disgust.

"But if I made you do it in front of me? Maybe you wouldn't try to trick me?" I begged holding my breath.

"I trick Kara and she's been dealing with me for 9 years like-"

"But I'm not Kara. I'm special to you. I could make you take the meds because you love me and then you would stay lucid and-"

"Sophie, there is nothing I want more in my life. I want to live with you and love you forever, but it doesn't work. I always-"

Interrupting again, I just couldn't contain my desperation. "But you're not in love with Kara. She's your sister but you *love* me. You adore me. You would want to be healthy with me-"

"I *did* want to be healthy with you and I tried so hard, but look at us. David told me I fought police and was shot and you could've been too if they hadn't known my history. They knew what they were going to deal with, they knew David and Carrie and they couldn't stop me even though they knew what they were doing. They never would've shot me, and there were other officers coming for me, but I went for the gun and wrestled to get it and I was shot in the leg because that was all he could do. Officer Tesone has even been in to see me and apologized for shooting me. *He* apologized to me, even though I think everyone else knows there was no telling what I would've done to him if I had gotten his gun in my hands when I was like that."

"You wouldn't have hurt him," I exhaled.

"I *would* have, Sophie. I was paranoid and delusional and I thought someone was going to hurt you, so I would have stopped anyone who got in my way while I thought I was protecting you," he said almost angrily, until I understood what he was saying.

"So you're dangerous?"

"When I'm not on the medication, yeah. I'm too strong and it's hard to handle me but I don't mean-"

"To do it. I know you don't, Peter."

"I live in a halfway house where they monitor everything I do. That's where the herb garden and greenhouse is. I used to live in Carrie's loft but I fucked up and got really bad and they had to move me into a halfway house for my own protection and even for theirs. I even lived with Kara for a few years, but when she had babies it wasn't really safe for me to be around all the time, which I understood logically because I was on the meds. But it still hurt to know Kara needed me to leave for the safety of her family. Then I went off the medication again and I was so sad thinking my family didn't want me I actually broke into her house while they were sleeping and I took my nephew outside to the backyard just to hold him because I loved him," he suddenly choked.

Crying again, Peter turned his eyes from my face and moved like he was trying to wipe his own face, but his restrained hands prevented it. Frustrated, he growled but with an audible sadness, not an anger I could see.

"What happened?" I whispered.

"Nothing, thank god. Kara was able to talk me into giving her back Bradley and I cried in her backyard until an ambulance took me away to the hospital again. But that's what it's always like for me," he moaned. "I think I'm okay until I'm not okay and then I don't know I'm not okay until

I'm medicated and temporarily fixed. And that's what happened with you," he smiled back at me sadly.

"What do you mean?"

"You made me so happy," he continued as I choked on the sob in my chest. "And then I felt happy, which made me think I was happy and all better, and then I went off the meds and I didn't realize I wasn't better anymore."

"But I didn't see it," I said shaking my head.

"Because I hid it."

"Okay, but you'd think I'd notice the man I slept with and spent every evening with acting sick," I said gently. I didn't want to say fucked up, or psycho, or anything else that would hurt him, but I just couldn't wrap my head around how I wouldn't know he was mentally unstable.

"Um, you became the thing of my obsession. It's like, when you were at work I was fucked up, but I waited and then when we were together, I was better because you were with me. But then when you were sleeping or something I'd get paranoid and panicky at night, so I'd go to the living room to fight it, and then I'd get a handle on it and go back to you in bed. So I freaked out if we weren't together, but I was better when we were. That's why you didn't see it. But Carrie and Kara knew."

"How? We were never around them. I just met them the night before our breakup," I asked confused.

"Everyone knew, Sophie. The doctors at the place I live. My shrink. My family. Everyone knew I was starting to get sick again. They could see it and they know me-"

"*I* know you."

"You do, and you don't."

"I know you, Peter. I know everything I need to know when we're together," I cried. "And we can fight this. I'll help you. I'll make you take your meds, and I'll make you stay healthy with me. Now that I know what's wrong, I'll read about it and I'll do everything right so you can stay okay," I pleaded desperately again. I knew what I was taking on, and I knew what I wanted to do. "You can live with me and I'll take care of you. I'll keep you healthy, Peter. I can do it, and I'll be the best person to do it, too, because you love me and I love you and I'll make you better, I promise. I'll-"

"I'm going to be in the hospital for months, Sophie. I might seem okay right now, but that's just the initial push of the Risperdal. After a few days, when my system becomes used to it again, I need more and I become agitated and then combative and then finally the dose is

LOST

corrected until I stay somewhat lucid. But it always changes and I can't control-"

"I'll control it. When do you get out of the hospital?"

"I don't know. I'll be moved to Mountview when my leg is better, and then it could be months until I'm safe enough and lucid enough to function again at the halfway house, *if* I'm even allowed back. I don't know what charges they're going to press against me, and I don't know if I'll be in a mandatory hold until I'm charged or convicted. I don't know how long I'll be away this time. I was gone for a long time before you found me, and Kara and everyone were looking for me, but I managed to get away until I went to the loft with you."

"You can stay with me when you get out and-"

"Forever? I can stay with you *forever*, Sophie?" He asked skeptically.

"Yes..." I said so sure of my answer I smiled for the first time in days. I smiled because I was starting to feel hope in my heart, and reason in my mind. Everything was becoming clearer for me. I knew what I wanted and I knew what I had to do.

"I can't live without you, Sophie," Peter said sadly, and I agreed.

"You don't have to. I'll take care of you," I cried leaning my face against his cheek. "I'll take care of you until you're better and then we'll take care of each other again when you're well. I love you so much, I'll fight for you," I said sobbing.

Absolutely sobbing, I knew another absolute- I was lost without Peter and I wouldn't live without him ever again.

"I don't know when I'll be free to leave the hospital. Will you wait for me? Will you visit me? I can't stand not seeing you. I need you with me all the time to make me better, Soph. I need you with me or I'll die. I'll stop trying and fighting. I'll stop everything if I can't be with you," he pleaded.

"I'll figure it out and I'll be back. I'll see you every day until we can be together forever," I tried to calm and reassure him, because I would.

Crawling onto the bed over the rails, I rested my smaller body on his stronger one and straddled his hips as I laid chest to chest with Peter to reassure us both. Snuggling in deep, it didn't matter that his arms were held against the rails, or that he could only nuzzle into my neck. It didn't matter that he couldn't hold me because I was strong enough to hold him this time.

"I'm strong enough to hold you up when you need to be held, Peter," I

whispered his words into the beautiful silence around us, as we each wept softly wrapped in our absolute.
  We couldn't live without each other, and I decided for us we never would again.

  A few minutes later the door was opened widely and I was quickly reprimanded for lying on Peter. All throughout our conversation I knew a head would poke in the door to make sure we were fine, but I ignored it. Peter and I spoke past the person checking up on us, but that last time, there was no more time.
  I was quickly asked to get off Peter as a doctor and a police officer walked into the room, so I did. Kissing his lips quickly, I struggled to get back over the bars as my feet hit the ground, but I was okay.
  I had a purpose and a love so deep inside me, I knew what I had to do, and I knew this little separation wouldn't distract me from my purpose.
  Leaning into Peter as his eyes spilled tears once again, I smiled. Smiling at his beautiful face, I whispered the truth to him.
  "I love you, Peter. And I'll be back very soon."
  After I spoke he watched me with understanding, nodded and gave a sad little smile back to me. And that was the end of our visit
  I touched his cold cheek quickly with my hand, and I walked from his room to my waiting mom and to Peter's brother-in-law David as I begged my mom to drive me home.
  I walked to my mom, who incidentally looked beyond exhausted and really, just so sad I needed to comfort her as best as I could.
  "I said goodbye," I lied. "Let's go home, okay?" I asked as she nodded when I took her hand in my own to leave my love in the hospital.
  "Will you come back home with me? Can we drive to my house?" My mom asked and I nodded.
  "Sure," I said a little too brightly, until I quickly changed my voice to one she would expect. "I need to be at your house tonight. I need you around me," I lied to my mom again. Well, not lied, so much as manipulated the truth. I did need her, but not like she expected.
  I knew it was all going to be okay for me and Peter once I was safely in my old bed in the comfort of my parents' home with their watchful eyes all around me.
  They would be watching, and I could breathe easily with the knowledge and purpose inside me.

CHAPTER 42

"Sophie. Why are you here?" He asks again sounding not quite frustrated with me, but more anxious to hear the end, which was obviously coming.

"Just a little bit more. I'm almost done," I said with a smirk, because I was already done, but he didn't need to know that.

"Sophie, we really need to address what you've done and what you want to accomplish by-"

"We are. Just listen, please?" And as he nods, I continue.

When we arrived at my parents' house, I spoke to my parents and to the police again. David Lockley and Detective Dent followed us to my parents' house after my hospital visit, and I had to finish up the last part of my statement with them.

I even spoke to Mrs. Connor on the phone briefly. I spoke to her and I spent 10 minutes listening to her apologize on Peter's behalf and from her whole family for the events I was involved in. She even apologized because they couldn't find me earlier to explain. She was very nice, and apologetic, and I responded to her kindly.

I learned Peter had not only hidden himself from me, but he'd hidden me from his family as well and that's why I wasn't told what I was facing with Peter in my life. Apparently, like with me, Peter's family was never told my last name, so even David, a police officer, couldn't find me until he saw my picture after the rape and knew who I was.

After the call, and my final statement, Carrie's husband David left both as a sort of friend, and as a cop.

After the police left Steven tried to talk to me, but I begged him to leave me alone. With a smile and a big hug, I begged my brother to just let me rest for a while upstairs, while I tried to figure out everything in my head. I begged Steven to please give me a little space, and sadly after a moment of confusion and desperation he agreed.

Hugging me tightly to him, Steven whispered his words of love, as only my brother could, choking me up, and making me hurt for him, but there was nothing I could do to help him.

I needed to rest.

After I made my way upstairs, I quickly showered away my 2 day nightmare and redressed in clean clothes I kept in my old room before I finally laid down.

Dumping my purse on my bed, I found all my old pain killers and I once again gave into the pain I felt trapped in, but with a purpose.

Unlike the first time when I was confused and sad and couldn't function any longer, in that moment I had reason and purpose backing my decision.

I knew what I was doing, and I knew what I had to do. I also knew I would be found in time by my family.

So I did it. Again.

That was the second time I tried to kill myself for Peter.

*****

"Sophie. Why are you here?" He asks me again.

"I told you. I'm here because I love him."

"I understand that, but that doesn't answer my question."

"You know Dr. Harris if someone told me I would end up like this, even the day before I met Peter I would have laughed at them. I'm not this woman, and I never was before. I used to be strong, independent, and self-sufficient. I was proud of my accomplishments because they were mine. I worked hard for what I wanted, and I was proud of what I had."

"I believe you."

"There was never a day in my life before Peter when I hurt people, or took advantage, or was an embarrassment to others. I was a good, strong woman who had her head firmly planted on her shoulders with a path I followed to fulfill my forever plans."

"And?"

"And I was never sad or lonely or depressed, or weak. But now that's all I am," I exhaled.

"I understand what you're saying, but we need to get to the reason behind all this. I know you saw Peter. But why are you *here*?"

Swallowing the sob threatening to spill forth, I whisper, "So we can be together again."

"But it doesn't work that way, Sophie. Peter isn't here. He isn't even in this building. You trying to kill yourself doesn't bring you any closer to Peter," he says with pity.

"But it might. I might be able to get closer to him," I moan.

"Sophie, you will never get to Peter this way," he again says firmly.

"We'll see..." I smile knowing exactly what I was doing for me and Peter.

"Sophie. Peter left you a letter this morning in his room. He left you a letter to read because he killed himself this morning after he was taken for an x-ray," he says so seriously I actually believe him.

"Ohhh..." I whisper on a long exhale.

And that is the last sound of sadness I utter for a lifetime.

Pausing in the silence of my hospital room, Dr. Harris doesn't even seem to breathe as I slowly process what he said to me. But I too can't breathe, and I can't think.

I can't understand anything beyond Peter is dead again. For the second time in 3 days my forever is dead.

I don't know what to do, and I don't know what to say. I can't even ask how he did it. There is just no question or answer that makes any sense to me anymore.

I can't explain the pain that is gutting me. And I can't explain anything I'm feeling or thinking or dreaming or accepting.

All I know is my forever is really gone.

And we have lost.

Sarah Ann Walker

Dear Sophie,

I'm so sorry, but I'm tired of always struggling with this sickness, and I almost forgot I was sick when we were together. But then everything happened again, and I knew I was sick and you weren't safe and I almost hurt you and I don't want to risk you ever again.

So I'm ending my sickness now with the greatest happiness I've ever known and with the greatest love I've ever had in my life.

Loving and adoring you is the happiest I've ever been.

And with me ending it now, like this, when you were willing to do anything to help me and to love me, you get to always be MY forever.

I love you so much Sophie, there simply are no more words.

Peter

xo

Our End
04/22

EPILOGUE

After endless medications for depression and countless therapy sessions, I finally let go of Peter enough to have a life of my own.

I eventually rebuilt my life slowly the only way I knew how. I studied and learned about my temporary mental health issues, and I obsessively studied everything I could find on Paranoid Schizophrenia. I wanted to know what it was like, and I wanted to understand how Peter had felt. I needed to understand why he left me as abruptly as he did.

But when no true explanation came to me no matter how much I studied what Peter must have gone through, I finally let go of him.

I let him go, and I finally rebuilt my life with the help of my parents and brother, and with Kim, Amy and Christina pushing me forward day after day.

I didn't make it to Peter's funeral because I was trapped in the hospital, nearly catatonic with my sadness. But I don't know if I could've gone had it been an option anyway because I was destroyed. Afterward, when I heard a framed drawing of me was placed on his coffin when it was lowered into the ground, I was relieved I could still hold him in his darkness.

I also never asked how he actually accomplished it. I didn't want to know the way he died in case it was ugly or painful. I didn't ask David, or my parents, or even my brother, because I just couldn't know.

Instead, I made up a story of Peter dreaming of our life together, falling asleep happily but never waking again.

I made up the story of Peter loving me in the exact moment of his death, so I would remain his forever, forever.

Today, I work in a little store in the village, my own store actually. I work surrounded by all the things I love, in the village I love, with all the memories I love. I sell everything I love from herbal tinctures, to candle holders, to my own pottery. I sell everything I love in my bizarre little eclectic store in the village.

I'm married too.
I met and married a kind, patient man 3 years after Peter left me, and my husband lets me be me without questions about or consequences for my past. He loves me enough to just let me be the Sophie I'm most comfortable with, and he loves me even when I can't tell him why I'm sad.

My family is still wonderful and supportive, as well. My parents are terrific, and Steven is actually getting married in a few months. Steven stopped the love em' and leave em' for his own version of forever with Kim and I'm truly happy for them.

I can honestly say I'm happy overall with how my life turned out. I'm happy with my husband and the love and support he gives me. And I'm happy with the thought of any future children we may have and the love and support I know I'll give them.
I'm 31 years old, and I'm finally happy.

But not a single day goes by that I don't still look for Peter on every street corner in the village. No matter how much I have healed and changed, I look for him, and still love him like the forever he will always be.
Peter may be lost to me, but I take what little comfort I can in knowing he adored me in the end. And though he is lost, and I live with a sadness that will always remain deep inside me, I'm okay now.
I'm okay because I know I will always remain *his* forever.

ABOUT THE AUTHOR

Sarah Walker lives in Canada with her American husband and their son.

In her real life, Sarah is a devoted mother and wife, and an absolute junkie for coffee and high heels.

Sarah can be found on Facebook
www.facebook.com/SarahAnnWalkerIAmHer

Amazon
http://www.amazon.com/author/walkersarahann
http://amzn.com/e/B00AW22K56

Goodreads
https://www.goodreads.com/Sarah-Walker

Twitter
@sarahannwalker0

Made in the USA
Charleston, SC
19 October 2014